STEPHEN LEATHER

FIRST RESPONSE

HODDER

First published in Great Britain in 2016 by Hodder & Stoughton
An Hachette UK company

First published in paperback 2016

1

Copyright © Stephen Leather 2016

The right of Stephen Leather to be identified as the Author of the Work has been
asserted by him in accordance with the Copyright, Designs and Patents Act 1988.

A CIP catalogue record for this title is available from the British Library

A format paperback ISBN 978 1 473 60461 2
B format paperback ISBN 978 1 473 60457 5
Ebook ISBN 978 1 473 60456 8

Typeset in Plantin by Palimpsest Book Production Limited,
Falkirk, Stirlingshire

Printed and bound by Clays Ltd, St Ives plc

Hodder & Stoughton policy is to use papers that are natural, renewable
and recyclable products and made from wood grown in sustainable forests.
The logging and manufacturing processes are expected to conform to the
environmental regulations of the country of origin.

Hodder & Stoughton Ltd
Carmelite House
50 Victoria Embankment
London EC4Y 0DZ

www.hodder.co.uk

cleanskin *n.*

1. an unbranded animal;
2. a terrorist with no obvious links to terrorist groups, and who therefore does not appear on any watch lists.

Sarah Khan sat down in the last free seat in the carriage and took a deep breath. She looked at her watch. She had plenty of time before her interview. She never enjoyed interviews, probably because she didn't like being judged. They would look at her and ask probing questions and on the basis of that would decide whether or not she was suitable to work for them. If she said the wrong thing, if she made a joke that was taken the wrong way, her CPS career would be dead before it had even started.

Sarah knew she had a tendency to be flippant when she was nervous. It was a defence mechanism, an attempt to defuse a moment of tension. She was going to have to be careful, but not too careful because her interviewers might mistake hesitance for duplicity. She knew that she had to smile, but not smile too much. She had to maintain eye contact but not stare. She closed her eyes and tried to think calm thoughts.

She had spent the last week running through every possible question she might be asked. Why the CPS? Why not join one of the big law firms? Why criminal and not corporate? How would she cope with the long hours, the stress, the responsibility? She had all her answers prepared. She wanted to make a difference. She wanted to make her city a safer place to live. She wanted to protect its citizens. She wanted to be a superhero. She smiled to herself and opened her eyes. Maybe that was going too far. But she had never spent all those hours studying law to spend her time in a corporate environment helping to make rich people richer.

She sighed and looked around her, wondering how many of the people sitting in the carriage she might come across when the CPS hired her. How many were planning criminal acts? How many had already committed offences and had yet to face justice? The businessman with his metal briefcase perched on his lap: had he defrauded his employer? The teenage girl in an army-surplus jacket with the sleeves rolled up: had she killed her cheating boyfriend and buried him underneath the patio at the back of her house? The young Asian man standing by the door with a backpack slung over one shoulder: was he carrying cannabis in his bag? Or cocaine? On the way to a drugs deal?

She realised he was staring at her and looked away, feeling guilty and wondering if he'd read her mind. She gave it a few seconds, then looked back. He was still staring at her with his deep-set eyes. They reminded her of a bird of prey she'd once seen on a school trip. A peregrine falcon. She'd been only eight years old but she'd never forgotten the way the bird had seemed to stare at her with cold, unfeeling eyes, as if it had not the slightest interest in her. She smiled at him, but that seemed only to intensify his stare.

The train picked up speed. Sarah looked away from the man with the baleful stare and tried to concentrate on the interview ahead of her. She had to show all the qualities they would be looking for. Intelligence. Diligence. Honesty. And a desire to work long hours for a lot less money than she would earn in the private sector.

She found herself staring at the man again. He wasn't looking at her any more: now he was staring at a woman with a young daughter. The girl was three or four years old, holding a small Paddington Bear. She smiled at Sarah and Sarah smiled back.

The man straightened and raised his right arm. He was holding something in his hand, something metallic. He took a deep breath, threw back his head and screamed at the top of his voice, '*Allahu Akbar!*'

There was a blinding flash, then everything went dark.

*   *   *

BRIXTON (10 a.m.)

Father Morrison was getting towards the end of the mass and had to consciously focus to stop his mind wandering. How many masses had he taken during his thirty-seven years as a priest? Thirteen thousand? Fourteen thousand? Was it any wonder that he had a tendency to switch onto autopilot and say the words without connecting with their meaning? He forced himself to concentrate, knowing that his congregation deserved his full attention.

There were two dozen worshippers, and Father Morrison knew them all by name. It was mid-week, when only the most devout of his parishioners came to mass. Sunday was a different matter. There were four Sunday masses at the Corpus Christi Church in Brixton Hill. Sunday was an easy day to go to church, but mid-week required more of an effort. Most of the men and women in the pews were old, and Father Morrison couldn't help but think that in some cases it was loneliness rather than devotion that had brought them to the church. But there were some eager young faces, mainly recent immigrants from West Africa, who seemed to be hanging on every word of his homily.

The door to the church opened with a groan, and Father Morrison frowned as a latecomer stepped inside. He was an Asian, bearded with a hooked nose, and even from where he stood at the altar Father Morrison could see that he was in some distress. He was sweating and his eyes were darting from side to side. He was wearing a long coat buttoned up to the neck and he shuffled from side to side as if he wasn't sure what to do next. Father Morrison continued to talk, but his attention was focused on the newcomer. The man turned and pushed the door closed, then reached up and slid the bolt across.

Father Morrison wasn't sure what to do. He didn't want to interrupt the mass but there was no doubt that the man was behaving strangely. People with mental-health issues weren't an unusual sight in Brixton, and the area had more than its fair share of dirty and unkempt citizens wandering around, muttering to themselves. Beggars weren't unusual either, and many would drop by the church. Father Morrison never gave them money but he kept a cupboard full of biscuits and snacks that he would offer, along with a blessing. But the Asian man didn't look as if he wanted a handout. He turned and started walking purposefully towards the altar. He was in his late forties, with skin the colour and texture of old leather.

One by one the heads of the parishioners turned to check out the new arrival but he ignored them as he strode down the nave, his boots squeaking on the stone flags. Father Morrison moved towards him, holding his hands out at his sides. 'Can I help you?' he asked. 'We're in the middle of mass. Please, take a seat.'

The man's lips tightened as he continued to walk towards the priest. He held out his hand and Father Morrison extended his own as a reflex. The man took the priest's hand, gripping it tightly, his nails digging into the flesh. The priest gasped and tried to pull free but the Asian was too strong. Then the man's left hand lashed out and something fastened around the priest's wrist. He released his grip and stepped back. Father Morrison stared in amazement at the steel handcuff locked around his wrist. As the man stepped away, the priest realised there was a matching handcuff on the man's left wrist and they were joined by just over two feet of steel chain.

'What are you doing?' asked Father Morrison. 'What's this about?'

The man didn't reply, just walked back to the door, yanking the chain so that the priest was forced to follow him. The man unbuttoned his coat with his right hand, then reached into his pocket. As he and the priest reached the door he turned and held up his hands. His coat fell open, revealing a jacket containing more than a dozen pockets, each filled with a block of grey material. Red and black wires ran from block to block, and as the priest stared in horror, he saw that the man had some sort of trigger in his right hand, held in place by a strip of black Velcro.

'*Allahu Akbar!*' shouted the man at the top of his voice. 'Everybody must do exactly as I say if they don't want to die!'

WANDSWORTH (10.20 a.m.)

'Do you have this in a ten?' asked the girl, holding up a black and white dress. She was in her twenties, with dyed blonde hair pulled back in a tight bun that only served to emphasise the crop of old acne scars across both cheeks. She had a twin buggy with identical toddlers, who were eating Mars bars and smearing chocolate over their little fat faces.

Zoe flashed the girl her most professional smile. If she was a size ten, then Zoe was a Dutchman, a flying one at that. Zoe was an eight and the girl with chocolate-smeared twins was at least twice her size. 'I can have a look in the back,' she said. 'What size is that one?'

The girl squinted at the label. 'Fourteen.'

'Why don't you try that on and see how you go?'

The girl's eyes hardened. 'Are you taking the piss?' she said. 'You saying I'm fat?'

'Of course not. I just mean that you'd get a better idea of what it looks like if you try it on first. They can be a little tight. That's all.' She widened her smile and nodded enthusiastically, always the professional. In fact, she thought the girl was more than fat: she was bordering on clinically obese. To be honest, a high percentage of the customers who came into the shop could do with losing a few pounds. There were four other women browsing and Zoe doubted that any of them would be able to fit into a size ten. She worked hard to keep her figure – she was careful with what she ate and three times a week she worked out at the Virgin Active gym upstairs in the Southside shopping centre.

She liked working in Southside. When it had opened in 1971, more than twenty years before Zoe was born, it had been the largest indoor shopping centre in Europe. There were plenty of larger ones now, but it was still among the biggest in London, with more than half a million square feet of retail space taking up much of Wandsworth town centre. Zoe lived half a mile away and ever since she had left school she'd worked at the centre. The boutique was her fifth sales job in the complex and she was starting to think about moving again. She'd already dropped her CV into Gap, Next and River Island.

The woman was still trying to decide whether or not Zoe had insulted her. Another customer walked in and Zoe used his arrival as an excuse to turn away from the overweight mother. It was a man, an Asian, and he looked lost. He was tall and thin and wearing a raincoat. He looked around as if expecting to see someone. 'Can I help you?' asked Zoe.

The man flinched as if he had been struck.

'Are you okay?' asked Zoe. The man's forehead was bathed in sweat and he was breathing quickly, as if he'd just been running.

The man nodded and forced a smile. He was in his

twenties, with glossy black hair, a close-cropped beard and dark brown eyes that reminded Zoe of a puppy she'd had when she was a kid. It had disappeared when she was ten. Her mother said it had run away but Zoe had always suspected it had been run over and her mother hadn't wanted to tell her.

The man walked towards her and she realised something was wrong. She took a step backwards and banged into a rack of jeans. She yelped in surprise and tried to slip to the side but he was already in front of her, blocking her way. His hand clamped around her wrist and she felt something click, then cold metal. She looked down. He'd hand-cuffed her.

He grinned in triumph and stepped back, unbuttoning his coat. Zoe's blood ran cold as she saw what was beneath it. She'd seen enough photographs of bombers to recognise a suicide vest when she saw one – blocks of explosives, detonators and wires all bundled onto a canvas waistcoat. And in the man's right hand, a trigger that he held high in the air above his head.

'*Allahu Akbar!*' the man screamed. 'Stay where you are or everybody will die!'

BRIXTON (10.25 a.m.)

Father Morrison smiled at the man in the suicide vest, the same sort of smile he used at funerals when consoling the recently bereaved and assuring them that their loved one was in a better place, basking in God's glory. 'What is your name, sir?' he asked.

'Why do you care?' snapped the man.

'We are both human beings in a stressful situation,' said the priest. He raised his right hand and jiggled the chain that connected them to emphasise his point. 'Surely I should know the name of the man I've been chained to.'

'You talk too much.'

'That's my job,' said the priest. 'Anyway, I'm Father Morrison, but you can call me Sean. Or Father Sean.'

'I don't have to call you anything.' The man turned to face the parishioners, who had followed his instructions and sat together in the front two rows of pews, close to the altar. 'How many of you have phones? If you have a phone, hold it up in the air.'

Several held up their phones immediately. The rest fumbled in their pockets and bags and after a minute or so most of them had their hands in the air.

'Now, listen to me and listen carefully,' said the man. 'You are to use your phones to text your friends, and to post on Facebook and Twitter and anywhere else you want. You are to tell the world that you are now prisoners of ISIS, the Islamic State of Iraq and Syria. You are to explain that ISIS demands the release of its six warriors who are being held in Belmarsh Prison. You are to say that if the six warriors are not released, you will be executed.'

A middle-aged woman in the front pew began to weep and her husband put a protective arm around her.

'When the prisoners are released we'll all be going home.

Just spread the word and tell as many people as you can. Nobody has to die here today.'

Some of the parishioners began to tap away on their phones.

'Is that true, what you just said?' whispered Father Morrison.

'*Inshallah*,' said the man, quietly. 'If Allah wills.'

FULHAM (10.45 a.m.)

Eddie Cotterill sighed as he pushed open the door to the Fulham Road post office and saw there were at least a dozen people queuing, with only one member of staff on duty. He did a quick calculation in his head – twelve people, two minutes a pop, he was going to be there for a good twenty-five minutes. And half the queue were elderly, which meant they'd be moving slowly, and a scruffy student type was holding five boxes, which Eddie figured would each have to be weighed and probably need Customs forms. He looked at his watch. Ten forty-five, and he had to be in the office at eleven because a client wanted to view a two-bedroom flat that had just come on the market. Eddie prided himself on always being punctual, so his godson's birthday card would just have to wait.

He turned to go out but his way was blocked by a bearded Asian man wearing a long coat. Eddie held the door open for him. 'After you, mate,' he said.

The Asian didn't seem to hear him, just pushed his way past. He smelt rancid, as if he hadn't bathed for several days. 'You're welcome,' muttered Eddie, though, having lived in London for most of his twenty-eight years, he was well used to rudeness in all its forms.

He kept hold of the door as the man joined the end of the queue. There was something wrong about him and it wasn't just the smell. He was nervous, and seemed to have a twitch that made him flick his head to the left every few seconds. He had dark circles around his eyes as if he hadn't slept for days. Eddie frowned but decided he had better things to do than worry about an Asian guy with mental-health issues. He was about to let go of the door when the man shouted, '*Allahu Akbar!*' and grabbed at the arm of the woman in front of him. He fastened something metallic to the woman's wrist, then stepped back, raising one hand in the air. 'Stay where you are or you'll all die!' the man shouted.

Eddie was already running down the street, the birthday card fluttering to the pavement.

BRIXTON (10.47 a.m.)

'Trojan Four Five One, attend Corpus Christi church in Brixton Hill. Reports of a suicide bomber.'

'Say again, Control,' said Baz Waterford, leaning forward to get his ear closer to the speaker. He was in the passenger seat of a high-powered BMW X5.

'We're getting nine-nine-nine calls from people saying that parishioners at the Corpus Christi church are being held hostage by a suicide bomber.'

Waterford looked at Bill Collins, who was driving the

armed-response vehicle with the casual professionalism that came from more than a decade in the job.

'On our way, Control,' said Waterford. He looked at Collins. 'Blues and twos?'

Collins grinned. 'Probably a hoax,' he said. 'But if it isn't, sirens will only spook him. Anyway, we're five minutes away at most and the traffic's light.' He pressed down the accelerator and the car leaped forward.

'A suicide bomber in a church sounds a bit unlikely,' said Mickey Davies, from the back seat. He was a relative newcomer to the ARV team, but had already proved himself calm under pressure. All his shooting to date had been on the range but he was a first-class shot. Unlike Waterford, who was greying, and Collins, whose hair was receding by the day, Davies had a head of jet-black locks that he held in place with a smattering of gel.

'You never know,' said Waterford.

Collins got to the church in a little over four minutes. He brought the car to a halt close to the railings at the entrance. Immediately Davies began unpacking the three SIG Sauer 516 assault rifles. The SIG 516, with its telescoping stock and thirty-round magazine, had replaced the Heckler & Koch G36 as the Met's assault rifle of choice.

Davies handed out the weapons and all three officers checked they were locked and loaded.

'Right, in we go,' said Waterford, looking up at the redbrick building with its tall spire and vaulted stained-glass windows overlooking the street. 'Softly softly, a quick recce and that's all. If we see anything like a suicide bomber we fall back and set up a primary and secondary perimeter.'

Waterford led the way through a gate in the railings and

up the path to the entrance. Davies and Collins were either side but further back. All clicked their safeties off with the thumbs of their left hands but kept their trigger fingers outside the trigger guard.

The door to the church was closed. Waterford reached out slowly for the handle. It turned but the door wouldn't budge. He looked at Collins. 'Do they lock churches?'

'It's Brixton, they lock everything,' said Collins. 'But there should be a mass about this time of the day.'

Waterford pushed harder but the door wouldn't budge. He put his ear to it but the wood was thick and he doubted he'd hear anything even if there was a choir in full song on the other side.

'There'll be a back entrance,' said Collins, heading to the rear of the church, which butted onto a Catholic school. Waterford and Davies followed him, cradling their SIGs.

There was another, smaller, door at the back that led to what appeared to be an office. There were a couple of computers, a printer and shelves full of filing cabinets. One door led to a toilet and another opened into a corridor that went into the church. Waterford took the lead, with Davies and Collins spaced out behind him.

There was another door at the end of the corridor. Waterford turned the handle slowly, then pulled it towards him. He nodded at his companions, then opened the door fully. They stepped into the rear of the church. Ahead of them was the altar, and beyond that the pews. The parishioners were packed into the front two rows and most of them seemed to have their heads down as if they were praying. As Waterford moved towards them, he realised they were all holding phones. He stopped and raised his hand. Davies and Collins froze behind him.

Waterford frowned. There was no priest at the altar, and the only sound was the faint clicks as the parishioners tapped on their phones. He took a tentative step forward and froze again as he spotted the priest further back in the pews. A middle-aged Asian man was sitting next to him, his beard flecked with grey. The priest saw Waterford and stiffened. The Asian noticed the reaction and leaped to his feet. His coat fell open and Waterford saw a canvas vest with wires connecting various pockets. There was something black in the man's right hand and the left was connected to a steel chain that snaked towards the priest.

'It's a suicide vest!' hissed Davies, stating the obvious.

'Get out!' screamed the Asian man. 'Get out or we'll all die.'

Waterford couldn't tell if he was angry or scared. 'No problem,' said Waterford. 'We're leaving. Just stay calm. We'll get someone to come and talk to you.' He took a quick look over his shoulder. 'Back away, lads,' he said. 'We need to de-escalate this now.'

'The ISIS prisoners must be released or we will all die here!' shouted the man.

'I understand,' said Waterford. 'Just stay calm. We're leaving.'

He stepped back and gently closed the door.

'Did you see that?' said Davies. 'That's a bloody suicide vest he's got on.'

Waterford ushered them down the corridor and back into the office. 'Mickey, you need to evacuate the school now,' he said. 'Talk to the head teacher, get everyone out and away from the church. I'll call it in and get you back-up.'

As Davies headed towards the school, Waterford took a deep breath as he called up the mental checklist of everything that needed to be done now that he had confirmed there was a suicide bomber on the premises. He reached up to activate the microphone by his neck. 'Control, this is Trojan Four Five One, receiving?'

SCOTLAND YARD, VICTORIA EMBANKMENT (10.50 a.m.)

Superintendent Mo Kamran sighed as he looked at his email inbox. It was the first chance he'd had to check his email that morning and already more than a hundred messages were waiting for his attention. Some were spam, offering him cheap Viagra or a mail-order bride from Russia, but most were nonsense generated by jobsworths in the Met with nothing better to do. While the number of constables walking the beat or manning the capital's stations had been consistently reduced over the past decades, the ranks of office workers in health and safety, racial awareness, equality and human resources had swelled to the point where the majority of Met staff had never even seen a criminal up close. The rot had set in at about the time that the Metropolitan Police had started to refer to itself as a service, rather than a force, and the public as customers, rather than villains and victims. Kamran had been a police officer for twenty years and a superintendent for two. As part of the promotion he had been moved away from what he saw as real policing – latterly on the Gangs and Organised Crime Unit – to an office job that he frankly hated. He was running Emergency Preparedness within the Special Crime and Operations branch, and most of his time was spent dealing with the London Emergency Services Liaison Panel. LESLP met every three months and consisted of representatives from the Met, the London Fire Brigade, the City of London Police, the British Transport Police, the London Ambulance Service, the Coastguard, the Port of London Authority and representatives from the city's local authorities.

The main thrust of the LESLP's work was to prepare for major emergencies, anything from a terrorist incident to a meteorite strike, and to make sure that when something major did happen, all the different agencies knew what they had to do. Kamran's two years on the LESLP had been the worst of his professional life. The police representatives were easy enough to deal with, as were the Fire Brigade and the Ambulance Service, who were in the same boat as the police, being asked to do more on operational budgets that were constantly being slashed. But the bureaucrats working for the local authorities were a nightmare. They were all primarily concerned with protecting their own little empires and tended to nitpick and argue over every tiny detail. What made it worse was that the local authority representatives tended to be paid a lot more than the emergency service members, and drove better cars.

Kamran had asked for a transfer several times but had always been knocked back. He was doing a valuable job, he was told, and the earliest he would be moved would be following the completion of a new version of the LESLP manual, which detailed who should do what in the event of pretty much every conceivable disaster that might befall London. He sipped his coffee and started to go through the emails. Even the most tedious and pedantic required at least an acknowledgement that he had received it and understood the contents. At least half came from the local authority bureaucrats, who seemed to think that the longer the email, the more they were justifying their six-figure salaries.

He was halfway through the seventh email when his intercom buzzed. 'It's the deputy commissioner,' said his secretary. 'Urgent.' She put the call through before he could reply.

The deputy commissioner got straight to the point. It was clear from his voice that he was under pressure. 'Mo, we've a major terrorist incident on the go and I need you as Gold Commander for the time being. From the look of it, it's an Operation Plato. Drop everything and get to GT Ops. I'll call you back on your mobile and brief you en route.'

'On my way, sir,' said Kamran. The line went dead. Kamran's heart was pounding. Operation Plato was one of the worst scenarios they trained for: a multi-seated terrorist attack on the city. GT Ops was the call sign for the Lambeth Central Communications Command Centre. There were three command centres in London, in Bow, Lambeth and Hendon. Between them, they handled the city's daily six thousand emergency and fifteen thousand non-emergency calls. They were also used to provide specialist communications for major incidents, with experts from the police, Fire Brigade, Ambulance and any other of the emergency services that might be needed. Kamran grabbed his jacket and briefcase and rushed to the door. His secretary was standing at her desk, looking worried. He flashed her a confident smile. 'Have my car downstairs, Amy, I'm going to GT Ops. Take messages for me and I'll check in with you when I get the time. Clear my diary for the day and tell the Rotary Club that I won't be able to do that talk this evening.'

Kamran's mobile phone buzzed as he headed for the stairs. Reception was patchy at best in the lifts so he took the stairs down to the ground floor. 'We have three suicide bombers in the city,' said the deputy commissioner. 'Brixton, Wandsworth and Fulham. The attacks appear to be co-ordinated and we fear there could be more coming. I've arranged for MI5 and the SAS to be represented at GT Ops but, as Gold Commander, it's your show, Mo.'

'Thank you, sir,' said Kamran, though he knew his show could well turn out to be a poisoned chalice.

'We have armed-response vehicles at all three locations and hostage negotiation teams on the way. We don't know what their demands are yet but there's no need to tell you this is going to be a tough one.'

'I hear you, sir.'

'We'll try to get a more senior officer over later this morning but at the moment you're the most qualified. Good luck.'

Kamran put his phone away as he hurried down the stairs. He was going to need more than luck, he was sure of that. He pushed open the door that led to the reception area and walked outside. His car was already waiting for him, engine running.

KENSINGTON (11.10 a.m.)

There were times when Sally Jones would quite happily have given Max Dunbar a smack across the face. He truly was a nasty piece of work, mean-spirited with a foul temper and a tendency to bite. The snag was that Max was four years old and Sally was a twenty-seven-year-old childcare professional, paid to take care of him and another dozen children of the rich and well connected. There was a waiting list to join the Little Kensington Nursery and it was able to pick and choose who it accepted. Sally just wished the owners had been a little more selective when it came to Max. His parents were go-getters in the City, the father a merchant banker, the mother in PR, but the high six-figure salaries meant they had little time for child-rearing and Max was an only child so had few, if any, social skills.

Max had been biting for the past month, and they weren't playful nips, either. He thought it was funny to fasten his teeth onto a girl's arm and bite until he drew blood. Sally figured he'd either grow up to be a vampire or a serial killer. He had taken a particular liking to a sweet little girl called Henrietta, who wouldn't say boo to a goose. He had already tried to bite her twice that morning and Sally was at her wits' end. If Henrietta ended up with a bite mark, Sally would get the blame and she really didn't need the grief. There were sixteen children in the class and two teachers. Sally and Laura had split the class into two and unfortunately she'd been stuck with Max. Punishing the child was out of the question, but there was no way of reasoning with him. His parents never said no to him, and at home he spent most of the time with his two Scandinavian au pairs, who catered to his every whim.

'Right, let's have story time,' she said, clapping her hands. 'Max, why don't you choose the book?' She pointed at the bookcase and nodded encouragingly. 'Something with ponies, perhaps?' Hopefully if she got him to participate, he'd forget about sinking his teeth into Henrietta's arm.

The door to the classroom opened and Sally frowned as she saw a tall, thin black man walk in. His head was shaved and he had sunken cheeks, one of which had a curved scar across it. Sally knew immediately he wasn't a parent. London might have been one of the most ethnically mixed cities in the world, but the nursery wasn't and the man certainly wasn't related to the Chan boy or the Indian twins, who were the only non-white children on the premises. Sally's first thought was that he was a beggar. His long coat looked cheap and he didn't appear to have washed in a while. But it was his eyes that worried her most – they were wide and staring, almost fearful.

'Can I help you?' she asked. She looked at Laura, but Laura was busy organising a painting exercise and hadn't noticed him.

The man tried to smile but it was more like the grimace of an animal in pain. 'I am sorry, madam,' he mumbled. He wiped his face with the palm of his hand and Sally realised he was sweating. Maybe he was sick. He certainly appeared disoriented.

'I think you might be in the wrong place,' she said, pointing at the door. 'This is a nursery school.'

'I am sorry,' he said again, but louder this time. He took two steps towards her and grabbed her hand. She yelped. Before she could say anything he had clamped something metallic around her wrist. She stared at it in horror, trying to comprehend why he had handcuffed himself to her.

He stepped back and several feet of chain rattled from the pocket of his coat. He undid the buttons with shaking hands and Sally's eyes widened with fear as she saw what lay beneath it.

'*Allahu Akbar,*' he mumbled. He closed his eyes, his lower lip trembling. 'Do exactly as I say, or everyone will die.' He nodded at Laura. 'You, lock the door. And then get up against that wall with the children.'

LAMBETH CENTRAL COMMUNICATIONS COMMAND CENTRE (11.15 a.m.)

The Lambeth Central Communications Command Centre was at 109 Lambeth Road, and the three numbers were posted in huge white letters to the left of the four-storey building, a stone's throw from the south bank of the River Thames. Kamran had to show his warrant card to get in, even though he was expected. He took the stairs down to the special operations room, which occupied the entire basement of the building. Sergeant Joe Lumley was waiting for him at the door, holding a mug of coffee. Kamran grinned as he took it. 'You read my mind,' he said. 'And keep them coming.'

Kamran hadn't specifically asked for Lumley so was pleasantly surprised to see that the sergeant had been assigned. He was a twenty-year veteran of the Met, a former Special Patrol Group officer, who was totally calm under pressure, the perfect number two on a day when the shit seemed to have well and truly hit the fan. 'There's an inspector manning the fort but I thought I should give you a heads-up before you go in,' said Lumley.

'Good idea,' said Kamran. 'They're saying Operation Plato, is that right?'

'Three hostage situations in play and an AVR had sight of a suicide vest. They're releasing their demands through social media at the moment but we haven't made contact with any of the terrorists yet.'

'What time did this kick off?'

'There were tweets and Facebook postings about the first incident from five past ten onwards,' said Lumley. 'The second incident was at Wandsworth and social media there kicked off at ten twenty-five. Now we have another in Fulham. I've put myself next to you in the Gold Command suite, and because of the nature of the threat I've put the MI5 rep there too.'

'Five are here already?'

Lumley nodded. 'Yes, she's in your suite until you decide where to put her. And there's an SAS captain just arrived. He doesn't seem to require a workstation so at the moment he's just floating around.'

'Fire Brigade, Ambulance?'

'Already here.'

'And who's the TFC?' The tactical firearms commander was an inspector who was responsible for the sixteen armed-response vehicles stationed around the capital.

'Marty Windle.'

Kamran nodded his approval. Inspector Windle was a safe pair of hands. 'Okay, into the lion's den,' he said.

Lumley pulled open the door and Kamran stepped into the special operations room. It was half the size of a football field, with no windows, just banks of fluorescent lights overhead. It was filled with dozens of pod-like workstations, several of which were already occupied by shirt-sleeved police officers, their triple screens filled with data and CCTV feeds. To his left were two suites, one for himself as Gold Commander and next to it the Silver Command suite where the various commanding officers could hold their own briefings.

At the far end of the room there were four pods, each made up of three desks in a triangle, all with the same high-backed black ergonomic chairs. To the left was the Diplomatic Protection Group pod and next to it the pod used by SCO19, the armed police. The DPG were armed and SCO19 could draw on their resources as needed. Marty Windle was at one of the desks and waved an acknowledgement to Kamran. Kamran waved back. The pod in the middle of the group was manned by the Pan London support staff, who handled outgoing calls to the various units around the capital. At the far right were the pods of the London Ambulance Service and the Fire Brigade. Spaced across the room there were white supporting pillars a metre or so in diameter, and a dozen or so whiteboards on stands for when a scribbled note was more efficient than the keyboard.

Closer to the door a pod of supervisors looked after the support staff and next to them the General Policing Command pod was generally staffed by a chief inspector and an inspector. Dozens of other pods could be staffed by whatever resources the Gold Commander considered necessary, usually one police sergeant and two constables or civilians. 'According to the deputy commissioner, I'm the interim Gold Commander,' said Kamran. 'Let's make sure everything is up and running by the time my replacement gets here.'

Kamran strode over to the Gold Command suite, where a woman in her late twenties was waiting at a desk. She stood up and smiled. She was short, just over five feet tall, with blonde hair and a sprinkling of freckles across a snub nose. She held out her hand confidently, even though she had to tilt her head back to look him in the eyes. 'Lynne Waterman,' she said. 'Here to help in any way I can.'

'Pleasure to meet you,' said Kamran, putting his brief-case and coffee mug on his workstation, then shaking her hand. It felt tiny and he took care not to squeeze too hard. He doubted that she had given her real name; MI5 officers almost never did. 'Have you been in a special operations room before?'

'First time,' she said. 'Though I know how it works, obviously.'

'Sergeant Lumley can get you settled at the workstation next to mine,' he said. 'I think I'm going to be needing a lot of intel from you.'

Lumley took the MI5 officer to the neighbouring work-station as Kamran removed his jacket and slung it over the back of his chair. An inspector in shirt sleeves came over.

'Superintendent Kamran, Inspector Adams. I've been holding the fort until you got here.'

They shook hands. 'We haven't met before?' Adams was in his thirties, slightly overweight with receding hair and square-lensed glasses with thick black frames.

'I was with the Fraud Squad, transferred to the command two weeks ago,' he said. 'Trial by fire, from the look of it.'

'First name?'

'Ian.'

'Right, Ian, bring me up to speed,' said Kamran, sitting down and picking up his mug.

The inspector nodded. 'There are three suicide bombers, all of them holding hostages. One in Brixton, one in Wandsworth, one in Fulham. We have three ARVs at the Brixton location, including a supervisor vehicle. There's another supervisor vehicle at Wandsworth with another ARV. There's one ARV at the Fulham location with Trojan One en route.'

Trojan One was the inspector's vehicle, the most senior officer on the ARVs. The supervisor vehicles had sergeants on board. Trojan Ones were also known as kit cars as they carried extra weapons, ammunition and various items of equipment to help them gain entry to buildings.

'As this is being treated as a terrorist incident radios have to be in TXI mode, right?' Transmission inhibit mode meant that personal and vehicle radios were prevented from searching for transmitter sites as that could accidentally detonate a device. Personal radios were not to be used at all within fifteen metres of a device, and for vehicle-based radios that was increased to fifty metres.

'That's in hand, sir.'

'Negotiators?'

'All en route,' said the inspector.

'So no one is talking to them?' asked Kamran.

'No, but social media is going into meltdown,' said Adams. 'Facebook, Twitter, Tumblr, the works. The bombers are allowing their hostages to use their phones.'

'Wonderful,' said Kamran. 'How are we monitoring that?'

'At the moment we're all looking at the various feeds.'

'Right, I need one person collating everything. Anything important copied immediately to Sergeant Lumley. How are we doing with CCTV feeds?'

There were close to half a million CCTV cameras in London and the centre had access to all those controlled by the government and the local authorities.

'We have coverage of all three locations but, to be honest, you can get better pictures on television. All the news sources are there, Sky, the BBC, ITV, the works. The TV cameras started arriving within minutes of the hostages tweeting.'

'What about helicopters?' The Metropolitan Police's Air Support Unit had three Eurocopter EC145 helicopters equipped with night-vision and infrared cameras, which could be used as aerial observation and communication platforms.

The inspector smiled awkwardly. 'Ah, didn't think of that.'

'Let's get as many up as we can,' said Kamran. 'Now, what are their demands?'

'The tweets and Facebook postings all say the same,' said the inspector. 'There are six former ISIS fighters being held in Belmarsh Prison. All six are to be released and taken to Biggin Hill airport where they want to fly out on a twin-engined jet.'

'Well I wish them good luck with that,' said Kamran.

'What do we know about the explosives they have?'

'We're analysing CCTV footage at the moment but in the pictures we've seen they're wearing coats.'

'We need an explosives expert here,' said Kamran.

'I've already put a call out to the Bomb Squad. They're sending someone over from Euston,' said Adams. The Metropolitan Police was unique in that it had its own bomb-disposal team on staff. Other forces around the country called on the expertise of the army, in particular the 11EOD Regiment of the Royal Logistic Corps. They formed part of the Terrorism Command – SO15 – and were based at the old Traffic Police garage at Drummond Crescent, not far from Euston station.

'Good,' said Kamran. 'Now, we're going to need to ID the hostage-takers as soon as possible. We need CCTV and photographers at the various locations. As soon as we get a clear shot, pass it to Joe and he'll run facial recognition.' He looked at Sergeant Lumley. 'Liaise with Five, obviously.'

'Will do, sir,' said Lumley.

'And let's get the details of the six ISIS prisoners they're referring to.'

A young female officer stood up from her terminal and waved at the inspector. 'There's another one, sir!' she shouted. 'Kensington. A childcare centre!'

MARBLE ARCH (11.40 a.m.)

'Do you want a muffin?' Hassan asked his father, even though he already knew the answer. Imad El-Sayed always had a chocolate muffin with his morning cappuccino. It was as much a part of the man's daily ritual as the five times a day that he prayed to Allah.

El-Sayed frowned as if it were the first time he had ever been asked the question, then nodded. 'A chocolate muffin would be good,' he said. He manoeuvred his vast bulk over to a table by the window as Hassan joined the queue to order their coffees. El-Sayed was a big man, with folds of fat around his neck and a massive stomach that protruded over his belt. He had gold chains on his wrists and an even thicker one around his neck. His watch was a gold Rolex, studded with diamonds. El-Sayed was a rich man who liked to flaunt his wealth. Several Arabs at neighbouring tables nodded a greeting as he sat down, and he acknowledged them with a tight smile.

The coffee shop was busy but not yet crowded. The morning rush had passed and there was usually a lull until noon. Hassan and his father were regulars there as it was a short walk from the bureau de change El-Sayed owned. The staff of three dealt with currency conversions for tourists on the street, while offices behind handled larger transactions. It was a good business, which paid for a large house in Hampstead, a Bentley for El-Sayed and a Maserati for Hassan.

El-Sayed settled into his chair and linked his fingers over his belly. He closed his eyes and listened to the babble of conversations around him, mostly in Arabic, spoken with a multitude of accents – Kuwaiti, Lebanese, Egyptian, African . . . Not for nothing was Edgware Road between Marble Arch and Paddington Green known as Little Arabia. The street was lined with Arabic banks and shops, Lebanese restaurants and halal groceries. It felt like home and in many ways it was because, other than biannual trips back to his native Lebanon, he had lived in London for the past twenty-five years and all his family were now British citizens.

'Father?' said Hassan.

El-Sayed opened his eyes. His son had placed his coffee and the muffin in front of him. He smiled and thanked him. A television on one wall showed the Arabic version of Al Jazeera news. There was a picture of a church and a reporter was describing what had happened. A suicide bomber was locked up with a priest and worshippers in a Catholic church in Brixton. The bomber was demanding that six ISIS terrorists were released from Belmarsh Prison.

The channel switched to a studio discussion where another reporter was talking to two terrorism experts, a Westerner in a suit, the other a Saudi in a long-sleeved, ankle-length robe similar to the one that El-Sayed had on. El-Sayed listened intently. There were four suicide bombers in various parts of the city and they were all demanding that the ISIS prisoners be freed. 'Did you see this?' he asked his son.

Hassan put down his coffee. 'It has only just happened,' he said. 'Everyone's talking about it on Twitter.'

'Twitter?' repeated El-Sayed. He snorted. 'You spend far too much time playing with your phone.'

'It's not playing, Father,' said Hassan. 'The news was on Twitter long before it was on TV. The brothers are allowing their hostages to spread the message.'

'Do they really believe that this will work, that the government will release the ISIS fighters?'

Hassan grinned. 'Wouldn't it be something if they did?' he said. He sipped his coffee again. 'You had no idea that something like this was going to happen?'

El-Sayed shook his head. 'None at all.'

'There are four of them. It must have taken a lot of organising.'

El-Sayed nodded thoughtfully. 'No question,' he said. 'But why bombs? Why not just kidnap hostages and threaten to behead them, as they do in Syria? Or shoot them as they did in Paris?'

'Because this is bigger, Father,' said Hassan. 'Can you imagine how effective it will be if they show how easily they can strike, even in London?'

'You sound as if you would prefer the bombs to go off, my son.'

'And why not? We need to bring the fight here, don't we? This is where we need to make changes.'

'Things will change here,' said El-Sayed. 'They are changing already.'

'But not fast enough, Father.'

The door to the coffee shop opened and an Asian man in a buttoned-up coat walked in and looked around. Instead of joining the queue for coffee he stared for a few seconds at the television screen, which was now showing a shot of the Southside shopping centre in Wandsworth where armed police were standing outside the main entrance, guns at the ready, as uniformed officers helped with the evacuation.

The man looked around the coffee shop again, then headed towards where Hassan and his father were sitting. He stopped and looked down at the space next to Hassan. Hassan shook his head. 'Please, we are sitting here,' he said.

The man smiled and held out his hand, as if he wanted to shake, then lunged forward and grabbed Hassan. Almost immediately he fastened a steel handcuff around the young man's wrist.

Hassan stood up, trying to push him away, and a look of terror flashed across his face. 'I'm wearing a bomb!' the man shouted. 'Be careful!'

Hassan struggled to understand what the man had said, but everything became clear as the man unbuttoned his coat to reveal a vest covered with packages and wires. 'Nobody move or we will all go to Heaven together!' the man shouted at the top of his voice. '*Allahu Akbar!*'

LAMBETH CENTRAL COMMUNICATIONS COMMAND CENTRE (11.45 a.m.)

Kamran walked across the special operations room to the SCO19 pod. Marty Windle had a headset on and was talking in a low voice as he stared at a CCTV monitor on his centre screen showing a view of the Kensington child-care centre. A police car had stopped outside, its lights flashing, and two uniformed constables were standing at the door and peering inside.

Windle finished his conversation and took off his headset. 'There's an ARV en route, ETA six minutes. It's definitely a bomber?'

'Two of the teachers are tweeting,' said Kamran. 'Same as at the other locations. If the six ISIS fighters aren't released from Belmarsh by six p.m., everybody dies.'

'Bastards,' said Windle. 'It's kids in there.'

'Since when have they cared about kids, or women?' said Kamran. 'They see all Westerners as valid targets. Now, how are you doing resources-wise?'

'We're running low on ARVs,' said Windle. 'We've got all three kit cars tied up already. I've put a call out to get any off-duty SFOs to come in, but that'll take time.'

The two constables who had been checking the nursery walked back to their car. 'That's a good picture. Where's it coming from?' asked Kamran.

'Local authority,' said Windle. 'The parents were causing problems when they were parking so the council set it up to fine them. It's not quite a live feed, there's a delay of about two seconds, but that's good enough.'

'Can we access the stored video?'

'I don't see why not.'

'I'll get Joe on the case, see if he can get us a shot of the bomber arriving.'

'What's happening on the negotiation front?' asked Windle.

'Nothing so far,' said Kamran. 'To be honest, it's all happened so quickly we don't have any negotiating teams in situ yet. All their demands are coming through social media.'

'And what do you think?' asked Windle. 'They can't release the ISIS prisoners, can they?'

'I don't see how they can, but that decision is going to be taken at a much higher pay grade than mine,' said Kamran. He raised his coffee cup in salute and headed back to the Gold Command suite.

Inspector Adams intercepted him. 'I'm going to need more people,' he said.

'Specifically?'

'I've got two support staff monitoring social media and a third collating and passing positive intel to Sergeant Lumley. But they're already overwhelmed.'

'Bring in what you need, Ian.'

'I think I'm going to need another three at least. At the moment there are hundreds of tweets a minute using hashtag ISIS6. Unfortunately a lot of it is just noise. Also, I want to get someone identifying the hostages – ideally get names and addresses and contact numbers. That's going to take manpower.'

'All good, Ian. I don't think anyone is going to be worrying about the overtime bill on this one.'

'And just to let you know, we're having problems on the negotiator front. I'm now calling in officers on days off and most of them don't have their phones on.'

Kamran smiled ruefully. Even the keenest of police officers didn't like having to work their days off so preferred to switch off their phones rather than being put on the spot. He had to admit to pulling the same stroke himself from time to time. 'Put in calls to neighbouring forces, see if we can borrow from them if necessary.'

The inspector nodded and hurried back to his pod. Kamran managed to get back to the Gold Command suite without further interruption and found Lumley talking to a stocky man in his early thirties, casually dressed in a black North Face fleece and blue jeans. His hair was cut short and he had a tan that was starting to peel around his nose. 'This is Captain Murray,' said Lumley. 'SAS.'

'Welcome aboard, Captain,' said Kamran.

'Call me Alex,' said Murray, shaking hands with the

superintendent. 'Anything we can do to help, you just have to ask.' He had a firm grip and the policeman noticed that his nails were bitten to the quick.

'The SAS has a number of men embedded with the various firearms units, right?' said the superintendent.

'Across London, yes. A dozen or so at any one time.'

'Can we get them to the various locations, especially any snipers you have? If you liaise with Marty Windle, he's our tactical firearms commander. And they're to report to the Silver officer at each scene, answerable to them.'

'Understood,' said Murray. 'We've also got a Chinook flying in from Hereford as we speak with a counter-terrorism team on board. Eight men in all. They'll be arriving at the Wellington Barracks in about twenty minutes. I've been told to tell you that we have another four teams on standby if you need them.'

'I think you can take it that they will be needed,' said Kamran. 'We have four incidents already and if there are four, there could just as easily be five. Or six. Or seven. If that happens we're going to be running short of ARVs so we'll need your men.'

'I'll arrange more choppers,' said Murray.

Kamran looked at Sergeant Lumley. 'Do me a favour. Take the captain down to the SCO19 pod and introduce him to Inspector Windle. He can tell him where his men will be best deployed, then you can keep me in the loop.'

'Will do,' said Lumley.

'And no offence, Alex, but no ski masks, please. We got quite a bit of flak last time we had plainclothes armed officers covering their faces. If they're in uniform, masks are allowable, but otherwise let's make do with dark glasses.'

'Understood,' said Murray. The sergeant took the SAS captain into the SOR and along to the SCO19 pod.

Kamran went over to Waterman's workstation. 'Still four?' she asked, without looking up from her screens.

'Fingers crossed,' said Kamran. 'But I've got a feeling there'll be more.'

She sat back in her chair and looked up at him. 'The thing I don't get is why they aren't better co-ordinated,' she said. 'With the Seven/Seven Tube bombers, they all went down at the same time. Why are these attacks spaced out?'

'Good point,' said Kamran. He frowned. 'Can you pull up a map, then ID the locations and times they went active?'

'No problem,' said the MI5 officer. Her hands played across the keyboard and the screen on her left went to black, then was filled with a map of the city. One by one red circles marked the areas where the terrorists had struck. Brixton. Wandsworth. Fulham. Kensington. He stared at the screen. Two south of the river. Two north. All to the west of the city. Times began to appear under the dots. The Brixton siege had started at 10 a.m., on the dot. Wandsworth twenty minutes later.

Waterman grinned. 'Do you see what I see?' she asked, as the final time popped up underneath the dot representing Kensington.

Kamran checked the four times just to be sure. 'They're being dropped, one at a time. They started at Brixton, then drove to Wandsworth, then across the Thames to Fulham and headed east to Kensington. Okay, we need CCTV of the minutes prior to each siege starting. We're looking for a common vehicle, something large. A van, a coach, a bus, something along those lines.'

'I'm on it,' said Waterman.

Lumley returned from the special operations room and walked over to them. 'What's happening?' he asked.

'It looks as if they're being dropped off,' said Kamran.

'So there are going to be more? This is just the start?'

'I'm afraid that's exactly what it looks like,' said Kamran.

One of the phones on Lumley's desk rang and he answered it. 'It's the deputy commissioner, line two,' he said.

Kamran picked up his phone. 'So there's four now?' said the senior officer.

'I'm afraid so,' said Kamran. 'Kensington.'

'How are things in the SOR?'

'All good. A bit frantic, as you can imagine, but we're staying on top of it.'

'We're going to have to hand over more of the operational decisions to you at GT Ops,' said the deputy commissioner. 'I know that generally the SOR takes more of a support role but things are moving too quickly so we need decisions taken centrally.'

'I understand, sir.'

'At the moment you're the only one who can see the big picture, the wood for the trees, if you like.'

'Understood, sir.' Kamran wasn't thrilled about being given operational command on a day when a lot of people could die. Generally the special operations room didn't control incidents: it provided a support structure to Incident Command and helped manage the incident, providing resources, analysing intelligence and co-ordinating communications. Kamran understood the necessity of

taking decisions centrally but he was only a superintendent, and if anything went wrong, shit had a habit of
rolling downhill.

'I know it's a lot of responsibility,' said the deputy commissioner, as if sensing Kamran's unease. 'Just bear with me
for an hour or so. I'm going to fix up an SO15 senior
officer to take over there.'

'No problem, sir,' said Kamran. SO15 was Counter-
terrorism Command, the anti-terrorism squad formed in
2006 by merging the Anti-terrorist Branch with Special
Branch.

'Have the negotiators gone in yet?'

'Not yet, sir. We've got four locations and we're getting
phone numbers as we speak. As soon as we've established
communications we'll have a better idea of what's going
on.'

'Twitter's on fire, as I'm sure you know.'

'We're monitoring it for intel.'

'Well, it sounds as if you've got everything under control,'
said the deputy commissioner.

Kamran smiled to himself. He might well have given
that impression, but it wasn't exactly how he felt. Things
were changing so quickly that he was close to losing any
grip that he had on the situation. He felt like a juggler with
too many balls in the air and more threatening to join them
at any moment. One lapse of concentration and he might
end up dropping them all. But that wasn't something he
could ever admit to the deputy commissioner, or to the
men and women in the special operations room. 'Yes, sir,
we're on top of it,' he said.

MARYLEBONE HIGH STREET (11.52 a.m.)

Faisal Chaudhry sat and stared at the card in his hands, reading the typewritten words for the third time, unable to get his head around what he was being asked to do. Each time he thought about the consequences of the suicide vest going off he felt so light-headed he feared he would pass out.

He jumped as a hand fell on his shoulder. Shahid was behind him. 'It is time,' he said.

'Brother, this is a mistake,' said Chaudhry.

'Just do as you're told and everything will be all right,' said Shahid.

'Brother, I am in Al-Qaeda. I am one of the chosen ones. I have been trained in Pakistan. I was trained in explosives and guns and everything. I'm one of you, brother. I want to kill the infidel, too. But not like this, brother. This is not what I was trained for. I'm a jihadist. I'm a fighter. Give me a gun, give me a knife, and I'll kill with a happy heart. But I can't blow myself up, brother. I can't.'

'This is how you will best serve Allah, brother,' said Shahid, patting him on the shoulder. 'Follow your instructions and six of our brothers will be released. You will leave the country with them and your actions will be a beacon for jihadists all over the world. Now, go and serve Allah.'

The fight went out of Chaudhry. He nodded.

Shahid opened the door. '*Allahu Akbar.*'

'*Allahu Akbar,*' mumbled Chaudhry, as he shuffled towards the door. He climbed out and the door slammed. He walked away and didn't look back.

MARYLEBONE (11.55 a.m.)

The midday rush wasn't far away, thought Kenny Watts, as he looked at the wall-mounted clock. Once it started he'd be rushed off his feet so he figured he had better pop out for a cigarette now rather than try to grab a break later. He caught Bonnie's eye and gestured at the door. 'Just popping out for a fag,' he said.

'Have one for me,' she said, bending down to fill the glass-washer. Two men in suits came up to the bar, one waving a twenty-pound note. 'Get them first, will you?' she asked.

'Sure,' said Kenny, thrusting his pack of cigarettes back into his back pocket. 'What can I get you, gents?'

'Two pints of Speckled Hen,' said the guy with the money. 'Straight glasses.'

Kenny was pulling the second pint when another customer came in. He grimaced, wondering if he'd lost the opportunity for a smoke. It was an Asian wearing a long coat. He had a straggly beard and a hooked nose and looked for all the world like the Kalashnikov-toting nutters he kept seeing on the evening news. The man came up to the bar and stared at his reflection in the mirrored gantry.

Kenny finished pouring the second pint, took the money and gave the man his change. He put his hands on the bar and nodded at the new arrival. 'What can I get you?' he asked.

The man turned slowly to look at him, a slight frown on his face.

'What can I get you?' Kenny repeated.

The man's right hand shot out and grabbed Kenny's arm. Kenny pulled back but the man's other hand appeared and clamped a handcuff around his wrist. 'What are you

doing?' shouted Kenny. He pulled back and the chain linked
to the man's left wrist tightened. The man yanked it and
the metal bit into Kenny's flesh, making him grunt in pain.
The two men Kenny had just served were watching what
was going on, their pints forgotten. 'What the hell are you
doing?' shouted Kenny.

Bonnie stared in horror at the Asian man as he used his
right hand to unbutton his coat and reveal that he was
wearing an explosive-packed suicide vest.

'*Allahu Akbar!*' shouted the man, reaching into his coat
pocket. He pulled out a metal trigger and held it above his
head. 'Everyone do exactly as I say or we all die!'

WELLINGTON BARRACKS (12.02 p.m.)

The Chinook did a slow circle two hundred feet above
Wellington Barracks, then slowly descended to make a textbook landing in the centre of the parade ground. The twin
rotors continued to whir as the back ramp lowered and
eight SAS troopers came out, toting black kitbags.

Major Haydyn Williams was standing at the edge of
Tarmac Square, a line of four black SUVs behind him. The
men jogged over and formed a line in front of him, then
dropped their bags beside them. All eight were part of the
SAS's special projects team, specialising in anti-hijacking
and counter-terrorism.

'For those of you who haven't been watching the news,
there's been a spate of hostage-taking incidents across
London this morning,' said Williams, who had lost most,

but not all, of his Welsh accent during his eight-year stint with the SAS. 'The hostage-takers appear to be linked to ISIS and are wearing suicide vests. In each case the terrorist has handcuffed himself to a member of the public. It's a delicate situation, to put it mildly.'

The Chinook's engines roared and it lifted off, heading back to Hereford. The men kept their heads turned away from the rotor blast and the major waited until the deafening roar had faded before continuing. 'This is how it's going to work,' he said. 'You're to be attached to the various armed police units attending the four incidents around the capital. You will be acting under the orders of the local Silver Commander in each case. For those of you not familiar with the way the cops operate, a Silver Commander is in charge on site. Usually an inspector but not always. He in turn reports to a Gold Commander, who in this case is at the special operations room in Lambeth. The Gold Commander decides overall strategy, the Silver Commander makes decisions on the ground. You do what the Silver Commander says. But I also want you using our own comms to stay in touch with Captain Alex Murray. He's in the SOR so he'll always have the big picture.'

The men nodded. Most of them were chewing gum, the only sign of the building tension.

'Under no circumstances are you even to think of firing your weapon without being ordered to do so by the Silver Commander,' said the major. 'At the moment the cops are running the show so we have to play by their rules.'

'What about if we come under attack, boss?' asked a trooper. Ben Peyton was one of the youngest members of the group, though he had already seen plenty of action in

Afghanistan and Syria. He was the linguist specialist in his four-man patrol, fluent in Arabic and French.

'The intel we have is that the targets are only armed with suicide bombs,' said Major Williams. 'No guns, no knives, just a vest full of explosives. They won't be attacking you. The risk is that they self-detonate and take out everyone close by. At the moment the police are containing them and are preparing to negotiate. Our task is to support the armed police units as they are now stretched thin. We're in a support role in the first instance, but my personal feeling is that will change fairly soon. But until it does, you follow the Silver Commander's orders to the letter.'

The men nodded, their faces impassive.

'As soon as you've deployed, I suggest you all grab some cop kit so that you blend in. We're under orders not to cover our faces so no ski masks or balaclavas. Dark glasses are fine, but the best way of staying below the radar is to blend. Understood?' More nods. 'So, any questions or are we good to go?' The major looked down at his clipboard and began reading out their assignments. As soon as their name was called the troopers would pick up their kitbags and jog over to the waiting SUVs. Five minutes later they were all being whisked across the capital.

LAMBETH CENTRAL COMMUNICATIONS
COMMAND CENTRE (12.05 p.m.)

Joe Lumley twisted in his seat and waved his hand to get Kamran's attention. 'Lisa Elphick from the press office wants to know if you can spare her a minute or two.' He pointed to the large viewing window at the far end of the special operations room. A blonde woman in her mid-thirties in a black blazer and white skirt was standing there. She gave Kamran a small wave when he saw her. He grinned and beckoned her in. She walked quickly over to the Gold Command suite and air-kissed him on both cheeks. Kamran had worked with the chief press officer on several occasions and always admired her professionalism and no-nonsense approach. She was totally trustworthy, which was a breath of fresh air in an organisation where the key to climbing the greasy pole of promotion depended, more often than not, on stabbing someone else in the back. 'Busy day, I gather,' she said.

'You always were a master of understatement,' he said.

'How many now?'

'Five,' said Kamran.

'Twitter's gone into meltdown,' she said. 'We're getting copied into a lot of it so our feed is being overwhelmed. They're letting their hostages tweet, which is a first.'

'A first here, maybe, but it happened during that ISIS attack in Paris. It helps to spread the word.'

'Hashtag ISIS6 is what they're using now. Some of the hostages are even posting selfies.'

Kamran looked over at Lumley. 'Let's get that checked, Joe,' he said. 'See if there are any decent pictures we can use.' He sat down and smiled at Elphick. 'So, how can I help you, Lisa?'

'We've had a request from the media, obviously. They want a pool journo in the SOR. Ideally one TV crew and one print.'

Kamran shook his head. 'No can do,' he said.

'I thought as much, but I had to ask.'

'There's too much operational stuff on the screens,' said Kamran. 'And too much info being shouted about.'

'I already explained that,' she said. 'I said that afterwards, when it's been resolved, we can give them a press conference here and show them around but that's it.'

'That would certainly be doable,' said Kamran.

'I've had requests for interviews with Bomb Squad and firearms spokespeople but I've explained that we're swamped,' said the press officer. 'At the moment they're getting most of their info from social media. I thought it might be helpful if I put a couple of press officers here full time and they can feed information out. Information that you want out there, obviously.'

'That sounds like a plan. But I'd prefer them to run everything through Sergeant Lumley, just to be on the safe side. There's a lot of operation information that we don't want out there.'

'I'll make sure that happens,' said Elphick. 'Now, in terms of talking to the TV, do you want to do that?'

'I won't have time, Lisa. Can't the deputy commissioner do it?'

'I think he's trying to distance himself from the operational side,' she said.

'In case the shit hits the fan?' Kamran grinned. 'Can't blame him, can you? Did he put my name in the frame?'

'He said the best spokesman would be someone involved directly.'

'To be honest, I might be running the SOR but I think the spokesman needs to be at a higher level.'

'It really is a poisoned chalice, isn't it?'

'Unless it gets resolved, in which case they'll all be falling over themselves to talk to the press. Why don't you step up, Lisa? You know how to handle journalists.'

'They want someone in uniform,' she said.

Lumley looked up from his screens. 'We've managed to get a live feed from inside the shopping centre,' he said. 'From inside the actual shop.'

Kamran stood up. 'Duty calls,' he said. 'Sorry.'

'I'll send a couple of press officers over,' she said. 'Don't worry, I'll make sure they keep out of your way. And let me know if you change your mind about going on TV.'

Elphick waved, and as she left Kamran went over to Lumley's desk and peered over his shoulder. There was a black and white CCTV image of a young Asian man handcuffed to an even younger girl. Half a dozen women of various ages were huddled in a corner. Kamran couldn't tell if they were staff or shoppers. The quality wasn't great but it was good enough to see what was going on. The man was holding something in his right hand. The trigger to the explosives, presumably. He was shouting something at the women. Several of them were holding their mobile phones.

'How are we getting this?' asked Kamran.

'The videos in the stores all feed through to a central control room, mainly so they can watch out for shoplifters,' said Lumley. 'After Seven/Seven we started talking to all the centre owners about direct video feeds, and most of them now have it in place.'

'No sound, though?'

'Unfortunately not.' He gestured at the screen. 'Their

tweets are starting to come through now, all with the hashtag ISIS6.'

'Who's Silver Commander there?'

Lumley looked at his notepad. 'Inspector Ross Edwards.'

'Can you get him for me?' Kamran went back to his desk to get his coffee but realised the mug was empty.

Inspector Adams rushed into the suite. 'There's been another, sir. An ARV's on the way. A pub in Marylebone. The Grapes.'

'How many hostages?' asked Kamran.

'We don't know for sure. But a pub at lunchtime. Dozens, maybe.'

Kamran sighed. 'Okay. As soon as you've found out who the Silver Commander is at the pub scene, let me know. In the meantime make sure Fire Brigade and Ambulance know what's going on and where they're needed. And we're going to need one of TfL's traffic experts in here. All those road closures are going to play havoc with the traffic flow.'

'I've had Transport for London on twice now asking if they should close the Tube down.'

'That's not our call,' said Kamran.

'That's what I said and suggested they call the mayor's office. They did and the mayor passed them back to us.'

Kamran's brow furrowed. It looked as if no one wanted to make a decision, which during a crisis tended to be par for the course. No one was ever punished for indecisiveness but plenty of careers had been ended by a wrong decision taken in the heat of the moment. 'I'll talk to him,' he said.

Adams smiled his thanks and left. Lumley stood up. 'Inspector Edwards is holding on line two.'

'Thanks, Joe. Do me a favour and get me a coffee, and as soon as I'm done with Inspector Edwards, see if you can put me through to the mayor.'

Kamran picked up the phone and sat down. 'Ross, long time no see. How's the wife?'

'All good, Mo. The chemotherapy's taking its toll but the doctors are pleased with her progress.'

Kamran had been Edwards's sergeant at Savile Row police station almost a decade earlier and the two men had always got on well together. Their paths had continued to cross, and a few months earlier they'd had a catch-up drink during which Edwards had revealed that his wife had been diagnosed with breast cancer. 'Give her my love, please.'

'I will, Mo. Thanks.'

'So how are things there?'

'We've one ARV and we're waiting for more. The floors have been cleared and within the next five minutes or so we should have the whole centre to ourselves. I'm waiting for a negotiating team and until they arrive we're keeping our distance.'

'We're getting a live feed from the video in the shop. Are you seeing it?'

'I'm in the security centre now. So yes.'

'Looks to me as if there's only the one way in and out.'

'That's right, there's no back entrance to the shops.'

'Are you planning on a face-to-face negotiation?'

'I was going to leave that up to the experts, Mo. There's a phone in the shop we can use. Just be aware there's a lot of glass around. If he does detonate it'll cause mayhem.'

'Okay, we'll be watching on the video feed but keep us posted.'

'How many others are there?'

'Five plus you. The first was in Brixton, then the Southside shopping centre, followed by Fulham, Kensington and Marble Arch. And I've just been told about a pub in Marylebone.'

'This is a fucking nightmare, isn't it?' said Edwards.

'You said it.'

MARYLEBONE (12.08 p.m.)

'Shit! Please tell me we're not the first on the scene,' said PC Connor O'Sullivan, as he brought the patrol car to a halt outside the Grapes. There were half a dozen people standing on the pavement looking at the pub but none of them was wearing uniform and there were no emergency vehicles in the street.

'Luck of the Irish,' said the PC in the front passenger seat, Emma Wilson.

'This isn't funny, Emma,' said O'Sullivan. He had been with the Met just three years and Wilson had even less experience. They had been heading out to offer home-security advice to a couple of pensioners in St John's Wood when the call had come in and there had been no one else to take it. A reported suicide bomber and hostages. O'Sullivan's heart was racing and he fought to stave off the panic that was threatening to overwhelm him. A suicide bomber? A fucking suicide bomber? His hands were shaking as he turned off the engine.

'Where are the ARVs?' he muttered.

'En route,' she said. 'We just have to hold the fort until a senior officer gets here.'

'So we just stay in the car, right?'

'No, Connor, we get out and do our job.' She patted his knee. 'We've been trained for this. We just follow the protocols and we'll be fine.'

'A fucking suicide bomber, Emma.'

She forced a smile. 'It's a major incident and we treat them all the same,' she said. 'SADCHALETS, remember?'

O'Sullivan nodded. He remembered the mnemonic:

S – Survey the scene.

A – Assess the situation and gather information.

D – Disseminate the information to the control centre.

C – Casualties: check the number of dead and injured. Hopefully none, so far.

H – Hazards: identify the existing hazards. Presumably a deranged suicide bomber.

A – Access and Egress for emergency vehicles.

L – Locate: confirm the exact location of the incident.

E – Emergency services and evacuation: list which will be needed.

T – Type: assess the type of incident and its size.

S – Start a log and review safety.

'But there's only two of us. How do two of us do all that?'

'We're just the first. There'll be more on the way. We just start the ball rolling.' She patted his knee again. 'It'll be fine.'

O'Sullivan reached for his hat and opened the door. He pressed his transmit button and spoke into his radio: 'Bravo

Delta Three responding to the incident at the Grapes.'

'I'll clear the area,' said Wilson, as she got out of the car. She hurried over to the onlookers. 'Folks, please clear the area, it's not safe here.'

'They said there's a suicide bomber in there,' said a teenager in baggy sweatpants and Puffa jacket.

'Which means you all need to move away,' said Wilson. 'Now!'

She looked over her shoulder. O'Sullivan was still on the radio, reporting to the control room. To be honest, she felt as out of her depth as he clearly did. They were just PCs and this was a major incident.

'So it's true?' said a young woman with a toddler in a pushchair.

'Yes, it's true,' said Wilson. 'Now come on, move along.'

'Let me get a selfie first,' said the woman, turning so that her back was to the pub. She raised her smartphone and pouted for the camera.

'Folks, you're really going to have to move,' said Wilson. She was close to shouting but no one appeared to be paying her any attention.

O'Sullivan jogged over to join her. 'Fire and Ambulance are on their way.'

A black BMW SUV screeched to a halt behind their patrol car and three armed officers dressed in black ran over. 'What the fuck are these civilians doing here?' shouted a sergeant.

'I was just moving them along, sir,' said Wilson.

'Well, bloody get on with it,' snapped the sergeant. 'You need to establish an inner cordon immediately. Where's the Silver Commander?'

'There's no one else here at the moment,' said O'Sullivan.

'Well, consider me acting Silver,' he said. He lifted his chin and glared at the crowd of onlookers. 'Ladies and gentlemen, you need to clear the area now!' he shouted. 'Anyone still here in ten seconds will be arrested for obstruction. I need you to be at least one hundred yards from here. Move!'

The onlookers scattered like sheep.

'Thank you,' said Wilson.

'What's your name?' asked the sergeant.

'Emma. Emma Wilson.'

'Well, you'll be fine, Emma Wilson. Just organise me an inner cordon and find somewhere for the appliance and ambulances when they arrive.'

'Yes, sir. The JESCC, right?' The Joint Emergency Services Control Centre was where all the emergency vehicles would gather.

'That's it,' said the sergeant. He looked at O'Sullivan. 'And you are?'

'Connor O'Sullivan, sir.'

'Okay, Connor O'Sullivan, I need you to park your car across the road to block it off until we get more officers here.' He pointed at a line of houses overlooking the pub. 'As soon as you've done that, work those houses. Anyone inside, tell them to keep well clear of the windows and warn them that we might have to evacuate them. If you come across anyone who seems especially police-friendly then ask if they'd allow a room to be used as a control centre. A little old lady with a big teapot would be favourite.'

'Yes, sir, th-th-thank you,' stammered O'Sullivan, but the sergeant was already jogging over to his colleagues who had positioned themselves either side of a parked car, their weapons covering the front door of the pub.

LAMBETH CENTRAL COMMUNICATIONS COMMAND CENTRE (12.10 p.m.)

Sergeant Lumley placed a mug of coffee and a couple of plastic-wrapped sandwiches on Kamran's desk. 'Cheese salad and tuna mayo – not much of a choice, I'm afraid.'

'This'll do fine, Joe, thanks.'

'If you want something hot bringing down, let me know. The shepherd's pie is just about okay.' He looked at the clock on the wall. 'The mayor should be calling anytime soon. He was cycling to his office and his assistant said you were at the top of his list.'

A phone on Lumley's desk rang and he rushed over to answer it. He grinned and put his hand over the receiver. 'Speak of the devil,' he said. 'Line three.'

Kamran took the call and the mayor got straight to the point. 'So, Superintendent, do we shut down the Tube or not?'

'It's a tough call, sir.'

'Yes, I'm aware of that, which is why I'm asking for guidance.'

'General policy is to close the Tube only if and when there is a direct attack on it.'

'So I guess my next question has to be, is it likely that they will do that?'

'They haven't yet, sir. And I would have thought that if

they wanted to do a repeat of Seven/Seven then they would have.'

'No Tube stations and no mainline stations have been targeted so far?'

'A church, a shop, a post office, a childcare centre, a coffee shop and a pub.'

'And there's no discernible pattern to the attacks?'

'Not in terms of type of places, no. But there does appear to be a geographical pattern. They started in Brixton and are moving clockwise around the city. We're checking CCTV at the moment to see if we can spot the vehicle we believe dropped them off.'

The mayor was silent for a few seconds. Kamran said nothing, giving the man time to think.

'The problem, Superintendent, is that I'm old enough to remember how the IRA operated,' said the mayor, eventually. 'They would set off a small bomb so that a panic would start. Then they would detonate a second, bigger, bomb to kill those running away.'

'You think they could be trying to drive people down into the Tube system?'

'Multiple bombs above ground causing traffic chaos. They wait until the Tube is packed, then set off multiple devices below ground. Can you think of a more damaging scenario?'

'I can't,' agreed Kamran. 'But my gut feeling is that this isn't about causing casualties. If they'd wanted to kill and maim, they could have just detonated the devices. I think they're serious about wanting these ISIS prisoners freed.'

'So you think this could actually be resolved without casualties?'

'I hope so, yes.'

'Well, we all hope so, Superintendent. I'm asking for your professional opinion.'

Kamran took a deep breath and exhaled slowly. 'They've gone to a lot of trouble to organise this so I do believe that they're serious about their demands. If those demands are met, there is every possibility they will withdraw their threats.'

'Well, I hope you're right. So you're saying we keep everything moving?'

'That would be my advice, sir. Obviously at the first sign of trouble on the Tube we would react accordingly, but until then I would suggest business as usual.'

'And the road closures?'

'Nothing we can do about that, unfortunately. We have to establish an inner cordon and an outer cordon surrounded by a pedestrian zone, and all non-essential traffic has to be excluded from that.'

'The problem TfL has is that even a single road closure can cause havoc with the buses. What we have already is approaching chaos and as soon as they work their way around one incident they get hit with another.'

'I can see if there's any way of limiting the size of the outer cordon, but most of the time our hands are tied,' said Kamran. 'What I can do is allow you to have a couple of TfL people here in the SOR. That way they can see what's happening in real time but also they could give their input re road closures on the spot. That might smooth things along.'

'We'll definitely take you up on that, Superintendent. And as far as the negotiations are going, how likely is it that the ISIS prisoners will be released from Belmarsh?'

'That's a decision only the PM can make,' said Kamran.

The mayor chuckled without warmth. 'Well good luck with that, Superintendent,' he said. 'Without a focus group to guide him, decision-making doesn't come easy to our beloved prime minister. You'll need to watch your back because if this ends badly he'll be looking for someone to blame. Anyway, I'll be in my office until this is resolved. Call me as and when you think appropriate.'

'I will, sir.'

'And good luck. I rather think you'll need it.'

The line went dead and Kamran put down the receiver.

Waterman looked up from her screens. 'Mo, we've got IDs for two of the men now.'

Kamran hurried over to stand behind the MI5 officer. 'What's the story?' he asked.

On her right screen were two photographs, one taken from the CCTV camera within the Southside centre boutique, featuring a bearded Asian man in a long coat. Next to it was a photograph taken from a passport application. 'Mohammed Malik,' she said. 'We've managed to get CCTV from inside the shop via the centre's security system, so the quality's good. Facial recognition says it's a hundred per cent match. He's a second-generation Pakistani Brit. Parents run a curry house in Southall. He went fundamentalist when he was sixteen, just after Nine/Eleven. Went to Pakistan three years ago for six months. Told his parents he wanted to learn something about his culture but we believe he spent half his trip in a training camp on the Afghan border. Since then he's been quiet. That happens to a lot of these kids who go over thinking that jihad is action and adventure. They realise that it's not a game and they come back with their tails between their legs. He works in Halfords, has a clean record and wasn't regarded as a serious threat.'

'And the fact that he was at an Al-Qaeda training camp wasn't considered serious enough to have him watched?'

'If we watched every British Asian who went to Pakistan we'd be overwhelmed. Close to three hundred thousand British Pakistanis go to Pakistan each year. Border Force doesn't check passports on the way out and we don't ask them where they've been or what they were doing when they return, unless they're on a watch list. And Malik wasn't considered a serious threat. As I said, we have no direct proof that he went to a training camp. He was vocal for a while at his local mosque and used to send letters to his local paper accusing the West of wanting to exterminate Muslims, but he's stopped all that.'

On her right-hand screen there were two more photographs, one from the CCTV camera within the Fulham post office showing a second bearded Asian handcuffed to a young woman. The man's suicide vest was clearly visible under his coat, as was the trigger in his right hand. He could have been the twin of the Asian in the shopping centre – dark-skinned, bearded, average height, average build. Nothing out of the ordinary, other than that they were both wearing suicide vests and threatening to blow themselves up. Next to the CCTV picture was another passport photograph. 'This is another hundred per cent match. We're getting a direct feed from the post office and the images are first class,' said Waterman. 'Ismail Hussain. He's more an anti-war demonstrator than a fundamentalist. Was photographed on a few poppy-burning demonstrations and is a member of a group called Muslims Against

Crusades. He was one of the guys screaming at soldiers from the 2nd Battalion Royal Anglian Regiment when they arrived back in Luton after their Iraq tour. He's got one conviction for assault after he attacked an off-duty soldier with a bottle. That was well before the killing of Lee Rigby in Woolwich so he only got community service.'

Lee Rigby was a British soldier who had been stabbed to death in Woolwich, south London, in May 2013, not far from his barracks. His attackers waited for the police to arrive and said that they had murdered him to avenge the killings of Muslims by British soldiers. Both killers were British-born Nigerians who had been raised as Christians but then converted to Islam.

'No overseas training?' asked Kamran.

Waterman shook her head. 'None that we know of,' she said. 'He's a cleanskin. We're aware of him but he's never been on a watch list.'

'So what's happened to trigger him?' asked Kamran. 'How's he gone from burning poppies and shouting to threatening to blow himself up? That's one hell of a jump.'

'We're looking into his background now,' said Waterman. 'Maybe we missed something.'

Kamran peered at the video of the man in the post office, then turned to Sergeant Lumley, who had the same photographs on his screens. 'Hey, Joe. Can you get me a close-up of the trigger?'

'Will do,' said Lumley. He began tapping on his keyboard.

The SAS captain walked into the suite. 'What's happening?'

'We've got IDs on two of the bombers,' said Kamran. 'Joe's just getting me a close-up.'

Murray walked over to watch what Lumley was doing. He bent down and squinted at Lumley's screen. The image focused on the right hand of the man in the post office. 'It's not a dead man's trigger,' said Murray.

'That's what I thought,' said Kamran. 'Joe, check the guy in the boutique. Get a shot of his trigger and see if they're all the same.'

Murray straightened up. 'That's interesting,' he said. 'I would have expected the trigger to operate when it was released. That depends on active pressing. The way things are, we have a chance of taking them out without the vests going off.'

'That's not a risk we can take,' said Kamran. 'Not at this stage, anyway.'

'Sure. I'm not suggesting we go in with guns blazing,' said Murray. 'But the lack of a dead man's switch means a head shot could well neutralise the threat.'

'Unless there's another trigger in place,' said Kamran.

Murray tugged at his ear. 'True. If there's some sort of remote trigger, then all bets are off,' he said. 'What about jamming mobile-phone cells in the area? We've got the gear to do it, and I'm sure Five has, too.'

'That would kill the texting and social media that's going on, and that's obviously a big part of their strategy,' said Kamran. 'Blocking all cell phone activity might provoke a negative reaction.'

Murray shrugged. 'Your call, obviously.'

Kamran nodded. It was his call, and his responsibility, so any decision he made had to be the right one.

'I've got a view of the shop guy's trigger,' said Lumley. The image flashed up on Kamran's centre screen. The trigger was identical to the first. There was a Velcro strap holding it in the man's hand. The trigger itself was a simple metal button with a small protective plastic cage over the top. The cage had to be flipped back so that the trigger could be depressed with the thumb.

'A head shot while the cage is in place would be safe,' said Murray. 'Death would be instantaneous and there would be no chance for the trigger to be pressed.'

'You would need to be able to guarantee a kill, and while they're inside that's not possible,' said Kamran.

'A double shot, one to smash the window followed by a kill shot would do it.'

'Too much of a risk,' Kamran said.

'There is another possibility. If we can get close, a machete would take off the lower arm like slicing a carrot. No arm, no trigger.'

Kamran shook his head. 'If we can get close. There's been no indication that's going to happen. They're not allowing anyone in or out.'

'I'm just giving you your options,' said Murray. 'The sooner we end this, the better.'

'I'd already come to that conclusion,' said Kamran, frostily.

'I wasn't stating the obvious,' Murray said. 'The point I'm trying to make is that these guys have just two options: to talk or to blow themselves and their hostages up. The fact that they have no weapons other than the vests is telling. With a knife or a gun they can increase the threat level bit by bit. Hurt a hostage or single one out to kill. But our guys don't have that option. They talk or they detonate. There's no midway stage. It's all or nothing.'

Kamran exhaled through pursed lips as he realised what the SAS officer was getting at. None of the men were carrying guns or knives. And they didn't appear to be in contact with anyone. That meant there could be only two possible resolutions. Either the jihadists got what they wanted. Or they and their hostages died. There was no middle ground.

TAVISTOCK SQUARE (12.13 p.m.)

Kashif Talpur joined the queue to get onto the bus. He took a quick look over his shoulder. Two police officers were walking along Tavistock Square, deep in conversation. The man in front of him was having trouble with his Oyster card. He kept tapping it against the reader but it didn't seem to work.

'You'll have to get off,' said the West Indian driver.

'It's got ten quid on it, for sure,' said the man. He was in his forties with greasy, matted hair, wearing a green jacket that had once belonged to an East European soldier.

'If it doesn't work you'll have to get off.'

'There's nowt wrong with it,' said the man, and slapped the card against the reader so hard that everyone on the bus heard the thwack. The reader beeped and the man waved his card in triumph.

He moved down the bus and Talpur stepped forward. The driver glared at him from behind his vandal screens. 'Come on, I haven't got all day,' he snapped.

Talpur turned away and looked down the bus. The

passengers reflected the multi-ethnicity of London. Twelve men and women. Half were Asian, four were black, one was Middle Eastern and one was white. The nearest was an Asian woman in a black headscarf holding two carrier bags of groceries. He was supposed to choose the passenger closest to the driver but he knew that she was going to panic and probably scream blue murder. The passenger next to her, closest to the window, was a young black man with headphones, eyes closed, head bobbing back and forth in time to a tune that only he could hear. Talpur would have preferred to use the man but his instructions were clear and he had been told not to deviate from them.

'Oy, are you going to tap your card or not?' said the driver, impatiently.

Talpur grabbed the woman's right hand and handcuffed himself to her. For a few seconds she sat stunned, then screamed at him in Urdu. She let go of her bags and her groceries spilled onto the floor. Apples, oranges, naan bread, a box of eggs. Talpur stepped back and pulled the chain tight. The woman continued to scream at him, peppering his face with spittle. He slapped her, hard, and she immediately went quiet. With his right hand he undid his coat and opened it so that everyone could see the suicide vest. '*Allahu Akbar!*' he shouted. 'You must all do as I say or we will all die here!' He reached into his pocket and pulled out the trigger, slipping the Velcro strap over his palm.

He turned to the driver, who was staring at him open-mouthed. 'Close the door, now!' Talpur shouted. The man did as he was told. Talpur stared at him through the protective glass. 'If you make any attempt to leave the cab, you will be responsible for the death of every single person on this bus. Just stay where you are.'

The driver nodded, wide-eyed.

The woman was sobbing quietly now, her hands covering her face. 'You all need to listen to me!' shouted Talpur.

The man sitting by the window noticed what was happening and took off his headphones. 'What the fuck are you doing?' he asked.

There were footsteps on the stairs and a middle-aged black man peered from the stairwell.

'You have to do exactly as you are told or everybody dies. You are all prisoners of ISIS, the Islamic State of Iraq and Syria. We are demanding the release of six prisoners who are being held in Belmarsh Prison. Anyone who has a phone must start tweeting now. If you can't tweet, send text messages to your friends. Tell everyone that ISIS demands the release of its six brothers in Belmarsh. Do it now. Use hashtag ISIS6.'

No one moved. The only sound was the sobbing of the woman next to him.

Talpur raised his right hand so that they could all see the trigger. 'Start sending the messages now. The ISIS Six must be released by six tonight or everyone dies!' he shouted.

One by one the passengers took out their phones and started tapping away, except for the sobbing woman he was handcuffed to. She continued to bury her face in her hands and cry.

LAMBETH CENTRAL COMMUNICATIONS COMMAND CENTRE (12.15 p.m.)

'I've got the details of the six ISIS guys in Belmarsh,' said Sergeant Lumley. Kamran pushed himself out of his chair and walked around to the sergeant's station. Lynne Waterman joined him. There were six photographs on Lumley's left-hand screen, each made of three images – left side, right side and straight ahead. They were all Asian, dark-skinned, with straggly beards and contemptuous eyes. There were differences between them but they were clearly all cut from the same cloth. 'What's the story?' asked Kamran.

'They've all returned from Syria in the past two months,' said the sergeant. 'The top three are all members of the North London Boys. They signed up with ISIS, probably even before they left the country.'

Kamran nodded. The North London Boys was a network of Muslim fundamentalists, mainly of African and Arab heritage, who funnelled jihadists from London, first to Somalia and latterly to Syria. It was this network that had helped create Jihadi John, the ISIS figurehead who had appeared in numerous videos of savage beheadings.

'The three at the top flew in together from Turkey and were arrested when they arrived at Heathrow,' continued Lumley. 'They'd been in Syria for five months and are known associates of Jihadi John.'

'Known how?' asked Kamran. 'They're always wearing ski masks.'

'They were at school with him,' said Lumley. 'They went to the same mosque, and posted pictures on Facebook while they were in Syria. One of them posted a selfie he'd taken with Jihadi John. They were both wearing masks, but there's no reason to doubt it was him. In another picture he was holding a human head.'

The young men who went out to fight for terrorist organisations like ISIS often behaved as if they were in some crazed video game, Kamran thought. He could barely comprehend how someone born and brought up in Britain could end up hacking off the head of a fellow human being and boasting about it.

'The three at the bottom have been picked up separately over the past month. One came in through Northern Ireland, two on the Eurostar. Again they were on our watch list and were picked up as soon as they entered the country.'

'All British Pakistanis?' asked Kamran.

Lumley shook his head. 'The three at the bottom are Bangladeshis. At least, their parents are. All three were born in Britain and are from the Portsmouth area. They were members of a group called the Britani Brigade Bangladeshi Bad Boys. Dozens of them went out to Syria via Turkey last year. Most are still out there, dead or still fighting. These three came back after a few months. It probably wasn't as much fun as they thought it would be.'

'And what's the story charge-wise?' asked Kamran.

'They've all been charged under section five of the Terrorism Act 2006,' said the sergeant, 'and they're all being held on remand. The CPS is working with the Ministry of Justice to see whether they can be charged with treason.'

Waterman nodded. 'They'll be able to throw away the key if they can do that,' she said.

'Best way forward,' said Murray. 'It's crazy putting these

radicalised kids in prison for a few years, then letting them out again. Prison just toughens them up and makes them even angrier. But put them away for twenty or thirty years and they might just calm down.'

'In addition to these six, there are more than two dozen family members also facing charges, though not all of them are in Belmarsh,' said Lumley.

'What charges?' asked Kamran.

'Engaging in conduct in preparation of terrorist acts, arranging availability of money and property for use in terrorism, failing to disclose information about acts of terrorism.'

'And what about connections between the three from north London and the three from Portsmouth?'

'Nothing obvious,' said Lumley. 'Other than the fact that they all went to fight for ISIS in Syria.'

'If there is a link between them, that might lead us to whoever is organising this,' said Kamran.

'It could just be that they're members of ISIS,' said Waterman. 'That might be the only connection.'

'But what about the family members?' asked Kamran. 'Why not ask for everyone to be released? Why just these six?'

'Because the families are collateral damage, not jihadists,' said Waterman. 'But let me get our people looking for links.'

'And we need to see if there are any connections between these six and the jihadists out there now.'

'I'm on it,' said Waterman, heading back to her work-station.

WANDSWORTH (12.16 p.m.)

Malik peered out of the store, looking left and right. The mall was deserted and had been for the best part of fifteen minutes.

'I need to go to the toilet,' said Zoe. The sales assistant was standing as far away from him as she could get without putting tension on the chain. Each time the chain tightened, Malik would snap it towards him and tell her to stay close. The other sales assistant and the four shoppers who had been there when Malik arrived were now huddled in one of the changing rooms. Malik had told them to stay there and to tell everyone on social media what had happened.

'You will have to wait,' said Malik, moving back into the chair.

'I can't wait.'

'Then you will just have to do it here.'

'You could undo the handcuff. I'll let you put it back on afterwards.'

'Do you think I'm stupid?' snapped Malik. 'If I take that off I'll never see you again.'

'But I have to pee!'

'There's nothing I can do,' he said. 'Now shut up. I need to think.'

Malik wiped his forehead with his sleeve. He was uncomfortably hot but there was no way he could remove the coat while he was handcuffed to the girl. Taking the cuff off wasn't an option because he didn't have the key, but he didn't want to admit that to her.

Tears began to trickle down her face and Malik groaned. 'Girl, pull yourself together.'

'I want to pee.'

'I know. I know. Look, is there a toilet in the back?'

'Just the changing rooms.'

'What about a bucket or something?'

'A bucket?'

'You can pee into a bucket.'

'I'm not peeing into a fucking bucket.'

'I'm trying to help here,' said Malik. He squinted at the name tag, white letters on a black plastic oval. 'Look, Zoe, I know we're in a bad place at the moment but if we stay calm and see this through, everything's going to work out all right.'

'You're not going to blow us up?'

'I don't want to die today, Zoe, and I certainly don't want to die like this.'

'Mohammed, can you hear me?'

Malik stiffened. The shout had come from outside the store. 'Who's that?' he asked Zoe. She shrugged, not sure if he expected her to answer the question.

'Mohammed, I'm with the police and I'm here to talk to you. Can you hear me, Mohammed? Let me know that you can hear me, will you?'

'Is that your name, Mohammed?' asked Zoe.

'No. Well, yes, but no one calls me Mohammed, not even my mum.'

'He wants to talk to you.'

'I've nothing to say.'

'You have to tell him what you want.'

'They know what we want. We want the six ISIS prisoners released.'

'Mohammed, I'm coming up to the front of the shop.

I'm not armed and I'm alone. I just want to talk.'

'Stay the fuck away from me, man!' shouted Malik.

'I just want to talk. I'm almost there now. Come to the entrance and you'll see me. I just want to talk.'

'I've nothing to say to you!' shouted Malik. He took a hesitant step towards the entrance.

'It's just a conversation,' said the man. 'That's all I'm here to do, establish contact so that you have someone to talk to.'

'I don't need to talk to anybody,' said Malik. 'All you have to do is release the prisoners. There is nothing to talk about.' He took another step to the entrance, keeping the trigger held high above his head. He pulled Zoe after him.

The man was about twenty feet away from the entrance. He was wearing a black flak jacket with POLICE in white letters across the front and was holding his hands above his head, fingers splayed. He stopped when he saw Malik, and smiled. 'Mohammed, good to see you,' he said. He was in his thirties with hair that looked as if it hadn't been combed in days and a close-cut beard.

'You need to get the hell away from here, now,' said Malik.

'I just want a quick chat,' said the man, slowly lowering his hands. 'Your name's Mohammed, right?'

'No one calls me that.'

'Mo, then? Is that what they call you, Mo?'

'My name's Sami.'

'Sami Malik? I thought it was Mohammed.'

'Sami's my middle name. That's what everyone calls me.'

'Yeah? Well, I'm Jamie. Jamie Clarke. Is everyone all right in there, Sami?'

'Of course they're not all right. They're all scared shit-less. Now you need to get the fuck away from here before we all die.'

'I just want to talk to you, Sami. That's all.'

'There's nothing to talk about,' said Malik. 'You need to get the ISIS Six released and then everyone can go home.'

'How are you for food? Water? I suppose everyone in there is thirsty.'

'We're fine.'

'I'm thirsty,' said Zoe. 'They can give us water, can't they?'

'See? The lady wants a drink. Why don't I send you in some water, Sami? Maybe some soft drinks. If you wanted pizza we could get you some.'

'I don't want anything!' Malik shouted.

Clarke held up his hands. 'Okay, okay. I just wanted to make sure everyone was comfortable, that's all.'

'I need to go to the toilet!' shouted Zoe.

'I can get a portable loo sent in,' said Clarke.

'You need to get the hell away from here,' said Malik. 'I'm not to talk to anybody.'

'Why not? You need to talk to us, Sami, so that we can understand what it is you want.'

'You know what they want. They want the six ISIS prisoners released. Do that and we can all go home.'

'Who's "they", Sami? Who do you mean?'

'Stop using my name!' shouted Malik. 'You don't know me. You're doing it to show that you're my friend but you're not my friend. Same with the beard. They sent you because you've got a beard, right? Same as me. So I'll empathise.'

'I've had this beard for years, Sami. I had bad acne when I was a kid, and it helps hide the scars,'

Malik saw movement behind the policeman and he stepped to the side. On the far side of the mall, two armed police were crouched by a bench, pointing their guns at him. 'You need to get them away from here!' shouted Malik.

'They're just here to make sure that no one gets hurt,' said Clarke.

'They're pointing their fucking guns at me!' yelled Malik. 'Get them away from here. Everybody needs to stay the hell away!'

'Sami, keep calm. No one's going to hurt you.'

'Yes, they are! If you don't do exactly what they want, we're all going to die! Now get those prisoners released! Just do it!'

Clarke started to back away, his hands still up. 'I'm going to be along the way a bit, Sami. If you want to talk, just call out and I'll come back.'

'I don't want to fucking talk to you or anybody!' shouted Malik. 'Keep your distance or everybody dies.'

Clarke turned and walked away and Malik pulled Zoe back into the shop. 'That bloody idiot is going to get us all killed!' he hissed.

LAMBETH CENTRAL COMMUNICATIONS COMMAND CENTRE (12.18 p.m.)

'Another one's just come in,' said Lumley, standing up. 'A bus in Tavistock Square.'

'Please don't tell me it's a number thirty,' said Kamran.

'I'm afraid so,' said Lumley.

Kamran groaned. There had been four suicide bombs in London on the morning of 7 July 2005. Three had been on Tube trains. The fourth, the final one, was detonated on the top deck of a number thirty double-decker bus in Tavistock Square, close to the headquarters of the British Medical Association, killing thirteen people and injuring dozens more. 'This can't be a coincidence,' said Kamran. 'Not when it happens on the tenth anniversary of Seven/Seven. On the same bloody bus. Bastards, bastards, bastards.' He took a deep breath and let it out slowly, then patted Lumley on the shoulder. 'Liaise with SCO19, Bomb Squad, Fire and Ambulance. And let's get the helicopter overhead. Where is it now?'

'Marble Arch.'

'Move it to Tavistock Square. As soon as you know who the Silver Commander is there, let me know.'

'Will do,' said Lumley, picking up his phone.

Waterman stood up and came across. 'That's a bit of a game-changer, isn't it? A bus. Tavistock Square.'

'Like I said, it can't be a coincidence. But why aren't we seeing them on the Tube? And Seven/Seven was never about hostages, it was about mass killings.'

'This lot are different,' said Waterman. 'This is ISIS and they've always been good at PR. They know that by replaying the Seven/Seven bus they'll get more coverage. People will talk about it, exactly as we're doing now.'

Kamran sighed. 'It's obviously been well planned,' he said. 'Was there nothing to suggest that anything like this was coming?'

'The threat level has been severe for some time, but that's more a reflection on the number of jihadists in the country rather than a specific threat.'

'You'd have thought there'd be something. This number of targets, so many people involved, you'd have thought someone would have talked.'

'Attacks on shopping malls and public places, yes, they're always being discussed. But individual attacks like this across the city, co-ordinated and planned? No, no one knew this was coming.'

Kamran walked out into the main room and headed for the SCO19 pod. The desks were laid out so that eight people could work facing each other. Inspector Windle was on his feet, talking animatedly into his headset. 'I know resources are running thin but we need at least two ARVs in Tavistock Square now.' He took off his headset. 'This just gets worse, doesn't it?'

'How are you fixed for vehicles?'

'We're not. All I can do now is move assets around.'

'Where's Captain Murray?'

'He's a smoker. Haven't you noticed he pops out every half-hour or so?'

'How many of his men do you have?'

'Eight so far. They're two apiece at the first four locations. That's in addition to the six we already had embedded with ARV units. There's another Chinook on the way from Hereford with eight more.'

'And how are they getting on with your people?'

'Good as gold, so far. Our guys do a lot of training with the SAS and while there's a fair bit of healthy competition there's mutual respect too.' He put his hand up to his headset. 'Sorry. I've another call coming in.' He turned his back on Kamran to take it. The main screen was showing Sky News. They had managed to get their own helicopter above Tavistock Square and were transmitting an overhead view of the bus.

Kamran walked to the pods on the far side of the special operations room where the Ambulance and Fire services were based. The officer liaising with the Fire Brigade was a familiar face – a twenty-year veteran called Danny King – but Kamran hadn't met the London Ambulance representatives before and took the time to introduce himself to the two men and one woman sitting there. 'How do we stand?' he asked.

'We've got ambulances and paramedics at each location and they've all made contact with the respective Silver Commanders,' said the senior Ambulance official. His name was Alfie Robins and he was a balding man in his fifties, who appeared to be making copious notes on a clipboard. 'We also have A & E departments at all hospitals in the vicinity on standby,' he said.

Kamran nodded his approval and looked over at King, who wasn't as gung-ho but, then, pessimism seemed to be his regular frame of mind. 'We're stretched,' King said glumly.

'Do you have an appliance at each location?'

King pulled a face. 'Not exactly,' he said. 'We're really stretched in the West End so what we've done is paired up the locations and sited the appliances midway. We have one between Brixton and Wandsworth, another between Fulham and Kensington. Then we have individual appliances at Marble Arch and Marylebone. And we're en route to Tavistock Square.'

'What's the story with the Southside centre?'

'Actually, Southside is the least of our problems,' said

King. 'It's now been evacuated and they have a state-of-the-art fire-control system in place. Worst possible scenario and the bomb detonates, the immediate damage will be confined to the shop area and the sprinklers will come on automatically. We've had a look at the building plans and there's no danger of damage to the floors above or below. If the blast spreads sideways, the sprinklers will kick in. Also there's no gas in the building, so other than the initial blast, damage will be minimal. The church in Brixton is also not much of a fire risk. There isn't much flammable inside and no gas on the premises. The bus is a bugger but it's outside and the square is in the process of being evacuated. If you recall the bus that exploded there in 2005, there was very little collateral damage. Everyone remembers the bus with the top blown off. Catastrophic damage, but confined to the vehicle.'

King picked up a bottle of water and took a swig. 'That's the good news. Or, at least, the less bad news. The really bad news is that the four other locations are absolute bastards. They're all part of terraces and all have gas plumbed in. The childcare centre has apartments above it, as does the coffee shop in Marble Arch. There are shops around the post office in Fulham and the pub in Marylebone, all full of flammable stuff and with gas mains. An explosion in any of those four could set off a devastating chain reaction.'

'So we need as many appliances as we can get on standby,' said Kamran.

'I hear you, and we're doing what we can, but we've suffered cuts as deep as you guys have. And we still have to maintain our regular coverage. Two or three events like this and we wouldn't have a problem. But seven?' He grimaced.

As Kamran headed back to the Gold Command suite he saw Murray returning, a transceiver pressed against his ear. Kamran waved him over and the SAS captain finished his call and headed towards him. 'There's another one, in Tavistock Square. A bus.'

'Same as Seven/Seven,' said Murray. 'That can't be a coincidence.'

'Marty says you have eight more troopers on the way.'

The captain looked at his watch, a rugged Breitling with several dials. 'ETA fifteen minutes.'

'What else can you offer us in the way of manpower? I don't think we've seen the last of them.'

'There's a major training exercise going on in the Brecon Beacons so we've got a chopper going out to pick up another eight. But they'll have to be taken to Hereford to re-equip so it'll be a couple of hours before they're on the ground.'

'Just keep them coming,' said Kamran. 'I suspect that before this is over we'll need every man you can send us.'

FULHAM (12.20 p.m.)

Ismail Hussain peered through the window. The street was deserted except for two police cars about fifty yards to the left and another two to the right. Beyond them were an ambulance and a paramedics' vehicle. He sensed movement across the street and scanned the first-floor windows. He stiffened when he saw that one was open and something was sticking out of it. The barrel of a rifle. He took a step back and bumped into the woman who was handcuffed to him. 'Get back! Get back! They've got guns,' he said.

She was in her late twenties and he hadn't realised how pretty she was until after he'd slapped the handcuff on her wrist. He hadn't even looked at her face: she'd been the last in the queue so was the obvious target. She hadn't screamed, she hadn't shown any fear, just turned to him, held up her right arm and asked him what he was playing at. Even when he had ripped open his coat and revealed the suicide vest she hadn't seemed scared. If anything, she appeared distant, as if her mind was elsewhere. As the hours had passed he'd come to realise that she wasn't scared in the least. But she wasn't calm either. There was a tenseness about her, like a coiled spring that was set to burst free at any moment. Her hair was dark brown, an almost chocolaty colour, greasy as if she hadn't washed it for a few days. Her eyes were dark green but the whites had reddened as if she'd been crying and there was a sickly pallor to her skin. She was wearing a sheepskin jacket a couple of sizes too big for her over a man's shirt, faded blue jeans that were ripped at the knee and brown Ugg boots.

'They won't shoot you,' she said, as she moved over to the counter with him.

'How do you know?' barked Hussain.

'You're wearing a suicide vest,' she said. 'They can't shoot you. Don't you watch TV?'

'They might shoot me in the head,' said Hussain. He checked that where he was standing wasn't overlooked by the marksman.

'Not through a window,' she said. 'Everyone knows that. And you've locked the door so they can't get in. Anyway, they'll send a negotiator. They always do.'

A telephone began to ring. It was on the other side of the counter, behind the screens, where three post-office workers were sitting. Two were Asian and one was black. Like the dozen customers who were now sitting on the floor by the back wall, they were busy on their smartphones. The black guy looked over his shoulder at the ringing phone.

'Don't answer it!' shouted Hussain.

'It'll be the negotiator,' said the pretty woman. 'You have to talk to them.'

'How do you know who it is?' asked Hussain.

'That's what they do. They call you and ask you what you want. Then they negotiate.'

'They know what we want,' said Hussain. He waved at the hostages by the wall. 'That's why I told them to use their phones. They can tell everyone what we want.' He waved his trigger above his head. 'Don't forget to put hashtag ISIS6 on every message.'

'They'll still want to talk to you,' said the woman.

'There's nothing to talk about,' said Hussain. 'They release the prisoners or everyone dies.' The phone stopped ringing. 'See? They don't need to talk.'

'They'll call back,' she said.

He stared at her for several seconds and she met his gaze unflinchingly. 'Why aren't you scared?' he asked eventually.

She frowned but continued to look into his eyes. 'What makes you think I'm not?'

'You don't look scared.'

'Well, I am. I'm terrified. But screaming and crying aren't going to do me any good, are they?'

'I suppose not.'

She smiled thinly. 'You suppose not? Don't you know? You're the one running the show.'

'I wish that were true,' he said.

'What do you mean?'

'Nothing,' he said. 'But trust me, I want this to be over as much as you do.'

'So take off the handcuffs and go outside. Then it'll be over.'

'They have to release the prisoners.'

'You really think they'll do that?'

'They'll have to. Or we all die.'

'You'd kill yourself, and us, just to get some idiot jihadists out of prison?'

'What do you mean, idiots?'

'Oh, come on. Anyone who gives up a halfway decent life in the UK to go out to Syria and hack the heads off charity workers isn't right in the head. You have to realise that, surely.'

'They're fighting for what they believe in. That doesn't make them stupid.'

'What's your name?'

'Why do you care?'

'I don't, not really, but I'd like to know who I'm handcuffed to.'

'Ismail. My name is Ismail.'

The woman grinned. 'Seriously? Ishmael?'

She spelled it out for him and he shook his head. 'I-S-M-A-I-L,' he said. 'It means "heard by Allah".'

'It's also one of the most famous opening lines in literature,' she said. '"Call me Ishmael." That's how *Moby-Dick* starts.'

'*Moby-Dick*?'

'You've heard of *Moby-Dick*, surely. The novel by Herman Melville. About Captain Ahab, the whaler, and his hunt for the great white whale?'

Hussain shook his head. 'I don't read much,' he said.

'That's your loss,' she said. 'So tell me, Ismail, do you believe that nonsense about getting seventy-two sloe-eyed virgins in Heaven if you kill us infidels?'

'That's what it says in the Koran.'

'And you believe that God wants you to grow that ridiculous beard and not eat bacon?'

His eyes narrowed. 'Why are you being so disrespectful?'

'You handcuff yourself to me and threaten to blow yourself up, and I'm the one being disrespectful? You know what, Ismail, you are a fucking idiot.' Hussain opened his mouth to speak but he jumped when the phone began to ring again. 'You really should answer that,' said the woman.

LAMBETH CENTRAL COMMUNICATIONS COMMAND CENTRE (12.25 p.m.)

Sergeant Lumley jumped up from his workstation and waved at Kamran. 'Got it,' he said excitedly. Kamran hurried across and looked over the sergeant's shoulder. 'It's a white van. It was outside three of the four locations. Haven't seen it at the Brixton church but there isn't much in the way of CCTV in that street.'

'Same van? You're sure?' asked Kamran.

Lumley pointed at his left-hand screen. It was divided into four and in three of the four sections there were close-up shots of the number-plate of the white van, two from the front, one from the rear. They matched.

'Who owns it?'

'According to the DVLA, it belongs to a company up in Birmingham.'

'Get the Birmingham cops around to see the owner,' said Kamran. 'And find out where the van is now. Run a search through all the number-recognition databases, but focus on north and north-east London.'

'I'm on it, sir,' said Lumley.

BRIXTON (12.28 p.m.)

Father Morrison reached inside his vestments, pulled out a bright red handkerchief and mopped his brow. 'I'm going to need my medication,' he said to the man chained to his wrist.

'Medication? For what?'

The priest chuckled ruefully. 'Where do I start? High blood pressure, diabetes, gout. The flesh is failing, my son. I'm in my seventh decade, you know.'

'Statins?'

The priest nodded. 'Oh, yes.'

'My doctor put me on them last year. They make my legs ache.'

'Mine too. But at least the blood pressure comes down.'

'They told me to stop smoking.'

The priest smiled. 'Me too. Chance'd be a fine thing. It's one of the few vices that we priests are allowed.'

'And where is your medicine?'

Father Morrison waved towards the back of the church. 'In the sacristy.'

'What's that?'

'It's the room where we change into our vestments. Over there, by the altar.'

'We have to stay here.'

'One of my parishioners can get it.'

'Everyone stays here,' said the man. 'I need to be able to see everyone.'

The priest dabbed his forehead again, then blew his nose before slipping the handkerchief back into his pocket. 'Why are you doing this, my son?'

'You know why. They want the six ISIS prisoners released.'

'And why are they in prison?'

'Because they are jihadists. They were in Syria, fighting for ISIS.'

'I can never remember what that stands for,' said the priest. 'It always sounds like an insurance company. What does it stand for? ISIS?'

The man shook his head. 'I don't know.'

'You don't know? You're prepared to die for them and you don't even know the name of their organisation?'

'They are jihadists and they fight in Syria. Now they're in prison. That's all I know.'

'And by threatening innocent people you think they'll be released?'

The man nodded.

'And you do this in the name of religion? You do this for God? Your God?'

'You need to shut up, priest.'

Father Morrison took out his handkerchief again and mopped his forehead. 'What's your name, my son?'

'I'm not your son. You're not my father.'

'I've already told you my name. It's Sean. Listen, we're human beings, aren't we? Can't we at least treat each other with some civility?'

The man sighed. 'Fine,' he said. 'If it'll shut you up. My name is Rabeel.'

The priest smiled. 'See? That wasn't too difficult. Now at least we know who we are.' He put the handkerchief away. 'And you are a Muslim?'

Rabeel sneered at the priest. 'What sort of question is that? Of course I'm a Muslim. One look at me and you know I am.'

'Because of your beard? I have parishioners with beards. Because of the colour of your skin? Look at my parishioners, Rabeel. Most of them are of colour. This is Brixton, remember. I am the minority here.'

Rabeel gestured at the explosives and wires in his vest. 'How many Catholics do you see wearing vests like this?'

The priest forced a smile. 'Admittedly not many. But the Catholic Church has had its fair share of martyrs in the past. Do you want to be a martyr? Is that why you're here?'

Rabeel shook his head fiercely. 'I don't want to die. Not today. Not like this.'

'Then take off the vest. Walk outside with me.'

Rabeel shook his head again. 'I can't.'

'Yes, you can. You have free will. A man's life is made up of the decisions he takes.'

'You don't know what you're talking about.'

'I know that your God wouldn't want you desecrating a house of worship. Islam and Catholicism are not that far apart.'

'Of course they are,' snapped Rabeel. 'Have you forgotten about the Crusades, when you Christians waged war on Islam? Millions died.'

'But we have moved past that, Rabeel. Different religions can live together. We can worship our own gods and respect the right of others to worship theirs.'

'Father Sean, please, just shut the fuck up, you're doing my head in.'

'Maybe that's because you're starting to realise the enormity of what you're doing,' said the priest. 'You know this is wrong. Of course you do. Do you have a wife, Rabeel?'

'Yes. I have a wife.'

'And children?'

'Two daughters.'

'So you're a family man. Do you want your family to live without you, Rabeel? Do you think it's fair to them for you to be behaving like this? Is it how you want your family to remember you?'

'You don't know what the fuck you're talking about,' said Rabeel. He sighed. 'Okay, fine, you can have your medicine if that's what it takes to shut you up.' He gestured at the parishioners in the front rows of the pews. 'Tell one of the women to go and get it. One of the old women.'

'Thank you,' said Father Morrison. 'Mrs Brooks,' he called, to an elderly West Indian lady in a large black hat with a sweeping brim. 'Mrs Brooks, could you do me a special favour?'

She stood up.

'Be an angel. Go into the sacristy and get my medicine, will you? It's in my bag. The white ones. And the blue and white capsules, bring them too. Actually, bring them all. The more the merrier.'

LAMBETH CENTRAL COMMUNICATIONS COMMAND CENTRE (12.30 p.m.)

Lumley put down his phone and waved a hand to attract Kamran's attention. 'The Bomb Squad chief is here, sir,' he said. 'Tony Drury.'

The main door to the special operations room opened and a man in a grey suit stood there, looking around uncertainly as if not sure where to go. Lumley went over to him and brought him to Kamran's workstation. Drury was in his forties, with short grey hair and piercing blue eyes. He walked with his back ramrod straight, the sign of a military background, and he had a firm handshake.

'I'm going to drop you in at the deep end and ask you to give me a view on the vests these guys are wearing,' said Kamran. One by one he brought up CCTV photographs of the jihadists.

Drury nodded thoughtfully as he studied the pictures. 'How many are there?' he asked.

'Seven so far,' said Kamran. 'They're the same, right? At least, they look the same.'

'They're the same design and seem to be using the same components,' agreed Drury. 'I'd say each has between ten and twenty-five pounds of explosive. The trigger is a push button so I'm assuming a simple circuit. Push the button and the vest explodes. From the look of it something has been wrapped around the explosive. I would guess ball bearings or nails, to create shrapnel.'

'Similar to what was used on the London Tube?'

Drury shook his head. 'No, the Tube bombs were in backpacks. I'd say these vests would be more lethal.'

'How lethal?' asked Kamran. 'Suppose one went off in a shop.'

'It's difficult to say,' said Drury. 'A lot depends on how many people are nearby, how close they are. Bodies absorb shrapnel so if you have a few people close to the site of the explosion they would take the brunt of the blast.'

'But people further away might survive?'

'Sure. It all depends on the type of shrapnel, the velocity, and what's there to absorb it. Plenty of people survived the London Tube bombings. There were some people in the carriage where the bombs detonated who were completely unscathed. They were the lucky ones, of course. What locations do we have so far?'

'A coffee shop. A nursery. A post office. A bus. A church. A pub. A shop.'

'So no pattern, then? Not like Seven/Seven when all four bombers went down the Tube.'

'This is a different situation,' said Kamran. 'The Tube bombings were about causing maximum casualties and spreading terror. These men want something. The bombs are a negotiating technique.'

'What do they want?'

'Prisoners released from Belmarsh and a plane out of the country.'

'I'm guessing they're going to be disappointed,' said Drury.

'Is there any way of neutralising the vests at a distance?'

Drury shook his head. 'No, you have to remove the detonators or cut the wiring. They're actually very simple circuits.' He grimaced. 'Sorry not to be more helpful.'

'I just need to know where we stand,' said Kamran. 'Now, do you think the trigger is significant?'

'Push to detonate? That's pretty standard.'

'We were thinking that a dead man's switch would have made more sense.'

'It depends on the environment,' said Drury. 'A dead man's switch means that you can't take out the man without the bomb going off. But the downside is that the operator can set it off by mistake.' He peered at one of the pictures. 'Looks as if they're using Velcro strips to keep the triggers in the palm.'

'Have you seen that before?'

'It's a technique used in Israel, by Palestinian suicide bombers, especially the ones who board buses and coaches. It means if they're rushed they won't drop the trigger.'

'If the hand was chopped off? At the wrist or the elbow?'

'You'd be taking a chance,' said Drury. 'If the thumb was on the trigger you might get a muscle contraction that would close the circuit.'

'And that would go for a head shot, too?'

Drury flashed him a tight smile. 'The SFOs keen to have a go, are they?'

'The SAS raised it as a possibility,' said Kamran. 'If they get the chance of a clear head shot, what's the downside?'

'The downside is that, despite what you see in the movies, death is rarely instantaneous,' said Drury. 'You might blow the brain apart but the heart will still pump and muscles can still contract. The headless-chicken thing. I wouldn't like to bet that a bullet to the brain would stop the trigger being depressed.'

'Do you have any suggestions?'

'If you could cut the wires to the trigger, that might do it. I'm not seeing a secondary circuit. That doesn't mean there isn't one, of course. And there could be a remote trigger, too.'

'How would that work?' asked Kamran.

'They use them in Iraq when they're not sure how committed a jihadist is. They give him a trigger but they have a remote switch as well, triggered by a mobile phone. You make a call, the circuit closes and bang.'

Kamran sighed. It wasn't what he wanted to hear. 'So what's the SOP with a suicide bomber?' he asked.

'To be honest, most of our procedures are for after the event – dealing with the crime scene, making the area safe, procedures like that. In terms of dealing with bombers in situ, that's generally left to the negotiators.'

'What about minimising the damage if there is an explosion?'

'We just make sure that everyone is kept well away.'

'What about bomb-disposal officers wearing bomb suits?'

Drury shrugged. 'The suits we have provide pretty good protection against a vest bomb,' he said. 'The top-of-the-range Kevlar, foam and plastic jobs weigh more than thirty-five kilos and would provide pretty good protection. Except for the hands and forearms, of course. They're left unprotected so that the officer can use his hands to defuse the device.'

'I was thinking of using them to disarm the men,' said Kamran.

'I don't see that being possible,' said Drury. 'The suits inhibit movement and they'd be seen coming a mile off.'

'Is there definitely no way that the vests can be disabled at a distance?'

'I'm afraid not,' said Drury. 'That's down to whoever's going to be negotiating with them.'

Kamran rubbed the back of his neck. He was starting to get a headache. A bad one. 'The way things are going, that will probably be me,' he said.

MARBLE ARCH (12.33 p.m.)

The man who had handcuffed himself to El-Sayed's son was watching the television anxiously. A blonde presenter was detailing the latest suicide bomber who had locked himself into a pub in Marylebone, not far from the coffee shop.

'How many is that?' asked the man, almost as if he were addressing the newsreader. Then he turned and glared at Hassan. 'How many?'

'S-s-s-seven,' stammered Hassan. 'It was five, then you, and then the pub.'

'Can I get you something to drink, brother?' El-Sayed asked the man. 'Water, perhaps. Or a fruit juice?'

'No,' said the man, who was now staring out of the window. There were two armed police, sheltering behind a car, aiming rifles in his direction. He shouted to one of the waitresses, 'You! Yes, you!' She looked at him and pointed at her chest. 'Yes! Stick some newspaper over the window so that they can't see us.'

The woman left the counter and picked up a copy of *The Times*. Another waitress gave her some Sellotape and she went over to the window to begin sticking the sheets onto the glass.

'I've got to go home and feed my dog,' said a woman sitting at the table next to El-Sayed. She was one of the few non-Asian customers in the shop, in her thirties and wearing a green parka with a fur-lined hood over an Adidas tracksuit. Her mousy brown hair was pulled back in a tight ponytail and she had applied too much blusher. Her lipstick was also a slapdash affair and she had smeared some across her top teeth. 'I can't stay here all day.'

'Madam, that is a suicide vest he is wearing,' said El-Sayed. 'If he presses that trigger in his right hand, it will detonate and everyone here will die and then there will be no one to feed your dog. Now, please, be quiet.' He turned to the man again. 'What about something to eat? You must be hungry.'

The man shook his head.

'May I know your name, brother?' asked El-Sayed.

He shook his head again. 'My name doesn't matter.'

'It matters to me, brother. We are both men, are we not? We are in this situation together. My name is Imad El-Sayed. That is my only son, Hassan.'

'You need to stay quiet,' said the man. 'If you want to talk, talk on Twitter and Facebook. Tell people that we want the six warriors released from Belmarsh.' He waved his right arm around. 'All of you, do it now. Keep sending messages to all your friends. Keep telling them what is happening here. And use hashtag ISIS6 with every message.'

Customers and staff began taking out their phones.

El-Sayed smiled. 'I never use Twitter,' he said. 'I never really understood the point of social media. People need to talk to each other. They need to connect, face to face, or at the very least to hear each other's voices. I call my friends and family, I don't text them.'

The man said nothing.

'At least let me get you a drink, brother,' said El-Sayed. 'Some water if nothing else. You must be thirsty.'

The man didn't look at El-Sayed, but he nodded.

El-Sayed waved at a barista and clicked his pudgy fingers. 'You, bring him a water. Quickly.'

The barista hurried over with a bottle, twisted off the cap, put it down in front of the man, then scurried back behind the counter.

The man used his left hand to lift the bottle to his lips. El-Sayed smiled and sipped his coffee, then smiled encouragingly at his son. Hassan's face was bathed in sweat and El-Sayed could smell the boy's fear. He wanted to tell him that everything was going to be all right, but he had to take it one step at a time.

LAMBETH CENTRAL COMMUNICATIONS COMMAND CENTRE (12.34 p.m.)

'We've identified four of them now,' said Waterman. She tapped on her keyboard and four pictures flashed up on her screen. All bearded Asian men, all in their twenties or thirties, they could have been cousins, if not brothers. 'Top left, Mohammed Malik. Top right, Ismail Hussain. We talked about them earlier. Bottom left, Rabeel Bhashir, bottom right, Mohammed Faisal Chaudhry. Rarely uses the Mohammed as a Christian name.' She pulled a face. 'Whoops. Can't say that, obviously. Anyway, we're reasonably sure that Bhashir is in the church in Brixton. Chaudhry is the bomber in the pub in Marylebone.'

'What do you mean you're reasonably sure about Bhashir?'

'Facial recognition isn't an exact science,' said Waterman. 'A lot depends on the material we're working with. One of the hostages posted a picture of him on Twitter but it was a side-on view. But even so we're looking at an accuracy prediction of eighty per cent. We're more sure about Chaudhry.'

'And are either of them known?'

'They're both known, both on our watch lists, but at a low level.'

'Then how could this happen?' asked Kamran. 'If they were being watched, how did they get suicide vests?'

'There's a difference between being watched and being on a watch list. They were considered possible threats, not direct threats.'

'I'd say this was a pretty direct threat, wouldn't you?'

asked Kamran. Captain Murray joined them, holding a cup of black coffee.

Waterman held up her hands. 'Please, Superintendent, don't go shooting the messenger here. At any one time we have literally thousands of British Asians on our watch lists. Just visiting a relative in Pakistan is enough to get them red-flagged, or posting on a jihadist website or tweeting in support of ISIS. But we don't have the resources to put every one of them under full-time surveillance.'

'So they were known to be potential problems, but not considered a serious threat?'

'That's the situation, yes.'

'So what can you tell me about the latest two? What are we dealing with?'

The MI5 officer gestured at the bottom left photograph. 'Rabeel Bhashir. He's the oldest of the group by far. Forty-six next month. He came to the UK with his wife and two young daughters about twelve years ago. They claimed to be Afghan refugees but they are almost certainly Pakistanis. Arrived on a BA flight having burned their passports on the plane and flushed the ashes down the toilet. They were granted refugee status and five years later they all became citizens.'

'You mean we can't even tell what country they're from?' asked Kamran.

'The border area between Pakistan and Afghanistan is porous at best,' said Waterman. 'You get a family saying they're Afghans fleeing the Taliban and it's hard to prove otherwise. They've destroyed their passports so where do you send them back to?'

'Presumably they showed their passports to get onto the

plane,' said Captain Murray. 'If they showed Pakistani passports, ship them back to Pakistan.'

'It's not as simple as that,' said Waterman. 'There's a whole industry geared to getting asylum-seekers accepted and settled. Anyway, Mr Bhashir was in the news last year when his daughters ran off to become jihadi brides in Syria. One was sixteen, the other fifteen.'

'I remember that,' said Kamran. 'He blamed MI5 and the cops for not tipping him off that his daughters were leaving the country. Blamed the school for not keeping track of them. Then it turned out he was at a few flag-burning protests with one of the men who murdered Lee Rigby. One was outside the Israeli embassy and there's a video of Bhashir screaming that all Jews should be killed.'

'Was he arrested for that?' asked Murray.

'Not that I recall,' said Kamran.

'There were a lot of protesters and it would have been seen as inflammatory to start making arrests,' said Waterman.

'And what was the Lee Rigby connection?' asked Murray.

'One of Rigby's killers, Michael Adebowale, was at one of the demonstrations with Bhashir, as was Anjem Choudary, the hate preacher.'

'And despite that he wasn't considered a threat?' asked Murray, in disbelief.

'They were at the same demonstration, so it's only guilt by association,' said Waterman.

'But the fact that his daughters went to join ISIS should have been a red flag, surely,' said the SAS captain.

'As I said, he played the injured father perfectly. Blaming everyone else but himself. It was several months later that he was identified in the flag-burning episodes. I think it was the *Mail* that broke the story.' Waterman pointed at the final photograph. 'Mohammed Faisal Chaudhry. British born. Spent three months in Pakistan in 2014, we think for Al-Qaeda training but unfortunately we have no evidence. He returned to London at the end of the year and has been quiet since. He was a minicab driver before he went to Pakistan but has been on benefits since he got back. Runs a fundamentalist website but he's careful to stay within the law.'

Kamran folded his arms and stared at the four photographs. 'So we've got four men, none of whom was considered a direct threat. On the same day they all decide to put on suicide vests and take hostages. Someone is running them, right? Someone is pulling their strings.'

'No question of that,' said Waterman. 'But so far we haven't found anything that connects them personally. They are all Muslim men, all physically fit, three of them youngish and one middle-aged, all under fifty anyway, but other than that and the fact they live in London there doesn't seem to be anything that ties them together.'

'Except they're all wearing explosive vests and seem prepared to blow themselves to kingdom come,' said Murray, sourly.

CAMBERWELL (12.35 p.m.)

Roger Metcalfe, OBE, really didn't enjoy meeting the great unwashed, but his majority was under threat from a growing switch of his electorate to the United Kingdom Independence

Party, which meant that his biweekly MP's surgeries were more important than ever. If he could help a constituent with a planning application or write a letter in support of a visa application for a family member, hopefully that constituent would vote for him and, even more importantly, spread the word. The problem was, he wasn't sure that he could help most of the people who came to the surgeries, and when he did help, he never seemed to get the credit. He could count on the fingers of one hand the number of times a constituent he'd helped had written to thank him.

He sipped his coffee and waited for his assistant to bring in the next contestant, as he liked to think of them, because, more often than not, the consultation would turn into a battle. It always started the same way, with a smile and a handshake, but once they had outlined their problem and grasped that there wasn't much Metcalfe could do to help them, their true natures were revealed. Metcalfe had been sworn at, slapped, spat at and had his life threatened more times than he could count. It was the sense of entitlement that he found so worrying. Men who had never worked a day in their lives felt they were entitled to a larger house for their families. Parents who spoke next to no English themselves, despite having lived in the UK for years, felt their children were entitled to teaching staff who spoke their home language. Obese women in disgustingly short skirts would bang on his desk and demand that the NHS pay for their gastric bands or boob jobs. Former asylum-seekers who had only just been granted citizenship would jab their fingers at him and demand that their newly discovered wives and children be allowed to join them in the UK. Metcalfe always promised to do what he could but there wasn't much that was within his gift, these days. He'd been an MP for the best part of twenty years and had never felt so powerless. He was giving serious consideration to packing it in at the next election. The pay was bad and the public scrutiny was soul-destroying; he was treated as a punch-bag by his constituents and as voting fodder by the leaders of his party. He'd earn more money and have more respect if he went back to his former career – accountancy.

The door opened and his assistant, a recent political science graduate called Molly, who was prepared to work for a pittance to gain experience at the cutting edge of politics, opened the door and ushered in an elderly woman with white permed hair and skin the texture of parchment. The constituents who wanted to see him waited in an outside room until it was their turn to be brought in. Metcalfe had tried meetings where he addressed groups but they never went well and it didn't take much to turn an unhappy bunch into a lynch mob. At least one at a time they could be controlled. She was wearing a cheap wool coat and had a black plastic handbag clasped to her chest. She sat down and perched the bag on her lap. 'This is Mrs Ellis,' said Molly. 'She's having problems with the council with regard to her spare bedroom.'

'Bedrooms,' said Mrs Ellis, primly. 'They say I have two spare bedrooms even though one of them is a sewing room.'

'It's a council house, is it, Mrs Ellis?' asked Metcalfe, his heart sinking as he anticipated exactly how the conversation would go. Thousands of council tenants had been hit by changes to housing benefit introduced in the Welfare Reform Act of 2012, which basically reduced the amount of money given to those who lived in homes larger than they actually needed.

She nodded and tightened her grip on the handles of her bag. 'They want to cut my housing benefit,' she said. 'By twenty-five per cent. If they do that, I can't live there any more. I just can't afford it.'

'Well, as I'm sure you know, the councils are trying to get the maximum use from their housing stock.'

'But this is my house. I moved in there with my husband forty years ago, God rest his soul. Forty years, Mr Metcalfe, and now I'll have to move out.'

'No one is saying you have to move out, Mrs Ellis. The council is just asking you to pay for the rooms you don't need.'

'But that doesn't make any sense. Why should I pay for something I don't need?' Metcalfe was struggling for an answer when the door burst open. A young, bearded Asian man stood there, with a look of confusion on his face, as if he wasn't quite sure where he was.

Molly jerked out of her iPhone reverie but he had walked in before she had even got to her feet.

'I'm sorry, there's a queuing system,' said Metcalfe. 'We deal with people one at a time. You talk to Molly here and she'll take your details.' He smiled but the man didn't appear to be listening. He walked up to the table and Metcalfe caught a whiff of stale sweat. There were flecks of white lint in the man's straggly beard and hair and the whites of his eyes were threaded with tiny burst veins. Metcalfe wondered if he might be high on drugs. He stood and held up his hands defensively as the man continued to swivel his head from side to side. 'Look, please, you really need to wait outside in the other room. I will get to you eventually.'

The man mumbled something and spittle peppered the table. Metcalfe caught a strong whiff of garlic. He looked at Molly and started to tell her to call the police but the man grabbed him by the wrist, his nails digging into the MP's skin. Then something metallic flashed and Metcalfe yelped, fearing a knife. He ducked away but the man's grip held firm and something fastened around Metcalfe's wrist. The garlic smell was almost overpowering now.

'*Allahu Akbar!*' the man shouted. 'Everyone do exactly as I say or we will all die here today!'

Metcalfe began to tremble. His face reddened with embarrassment as he felt the warm liquid around his groin and realised that he'd wet himself.

LAMBETH CENTRAL COMMUNICATIONS COMMAND CENTRE (12.40 p.m.)

'Bad news on the white-van front,' said Sergeant Lumley. 'The Birmingham police have spoken to the owner. In fact, they've seen the van. It's still up in Birmingham, complete with the name of the plumbing firm on the sides.'

Kamran grimaced. 'So they cloned the number?'

Lumley nodded. 'Looks like it. And the even worse news is that number-plate recognition hasn't turned it up. But the van is still out there.' He pointed to his left-hand screen. Where there had been three CCTV shots of the white van, now there were four. The registration number of the fourth was different. 'This van dropped off the bomber who is now holed up in the coffee shop near Marble Arch. According to the DVLA, this belongs to another firm up in Birmingham.'

'They changed plates? Terrific.'

'I've got both numbers flagged on number-plate recognition, but if they switched twice they can switch again.'

'Which means we're looking for a white van in London,' said Kamran. 'Needle in a haystack doesn't even come close.'

Lumley's phone rang and he answered it. He stiffened noticeably, then put his hand over the receiver. 'It's Downing Street,' he said. 'The prime minister.'

Kamran frowned. 'What?'

'The PM wants to talk to you.'

Kamran held up his hands. 'He needs to talk to the commissioner. Or the deputy commissioner.'

'No, he wants you. Asked for you by name.'

Kamran pointed at the receiver in Lumley's hands. 'Is that him? Actually on the line?'

Lumley smiled tightly.

Kamran sighed. 'Better put him through, then.' He took a deep breath to steady himself. His phone buzzed.

'Line one,' said Lumley.

Kamran took another deep breath and picked up the phone. 'Superintendent Kamran,' he said.

'What's the state of play, Superintendent?' asked the prime minister. 'Where do we stand?'

'We have seven incidents now, sir,' said Kamran. 'The latest is a bus in Tavistock Square.'

'I heard,' said the prime minister. 'That has echoes of Seven/Seven, doesn't it?'

'That may well be why that particular bus was targeted,' said Kamran.

'This is a nightmare,' said the prime minister. 'And getting worse by the minute.'

Kamran said nothing.

'Their demands haven't changed?' asked the prime minister, eventually.

'No, sir. They want the six prisoners released from Belmarsh and an aircraft fuelled and ready at Biggin Hill.'

'That's out of the question, obviously,' said the prime minister.

'The problem is there doesn't appear to be any negotiating,' said Kamran. 'It's take it or leave it. We accept their demands by six p.m. or they will all detonate their vests.'

'Presumably you have snipers in position?'

'All the bombers are inside, sir. I can't guarantee that shooting will end the sieges without casualties.'

'So what do you suggest, Superintendent?'

Kamran gritted his teeth. He had no suggestions to make. He was all out of ideas. 'We have to start talking to them,' he said. 'Face to face.'

Waterman began to wave excitedly at Kamran. 'We've identified the guy on the bus,' she said. 'You're not going to believe this!'

'I have to go, sir,' said Kamran. 'It's a bit hectic here, as you can imagine.'

'I'm heading into an emergency meeting of the Joint Intelligence Committee, Superintendent. I shall be in touch once we're done.' The JIC was composed of the country's top intelligence experts, including the directors of MI5, MI6, GCHQ, plus the chief of the Defence Intelligence

Staff, with representatives from the Ministry of Defence and the Foreign Office. Kamran figured the PM could probably do with all the advice he could get.

The prime minister ended the call and Kamran went over to Waterman's workstation. Murray was already peering over the MI5 officer's shoulder. 'What's the story?' asked Kamran. 'He's known?'

'He's known all right,' said Waterman, sitting back. 'He's one of yours.'

'One of mine?'

'Kashif Talpur. He works for the National Crime Agency's undercover unit.'

Kamran's jaw dropped. 'What are you telling me?' he asked.

'I don't think I can be any clearer,' said Waterman. 'He's a cop.' She pressed a button and a picture flashed up on her screen. A caption gave his name as Kashif Talpur and he was wearing the uniform of a Metropolitan Police officer.

For only the second time that day Kamran cursed. He looked at Lumley. 'Joe, find out who Talpur's governor is and get him in here right away,' he said. 'He needs to see what's going on.'

SOUTHWARK (12.50 p.m.)

The lunchtime rush was in full swing and Calum Wade was worked off his feet. To be honest, he preferred it that way. Working in a restaurant that wasn't busy could be soul-destroying: the minutes ticked slowly by and you were always looking for things to do. But the hours between twelve and two always seemed to whizz by, taking orders, filling glasses, carrying food from the kitchen and empty plates back to be washed. Wade always thought of himself as a people person, which was the main reason he had chosen to work in the restaurant business. And it had been a deliberate choice, too. Most of his fellow waiters were doing it as a fill-in before they found the job they really wanted, but it had long been his first choice as a career. Wade loved restaurants, and had done since his parents had first taken him into Harry Ramsden's fish and chips emporium in Blackpool. It had been the first time he had been served food by a waiter and he'd never forgotten the man who had put down the plate of fish, chips and mushy peas in front of him, with a sly wink.

Wade had studied computing at university, more to satisfy his parents than from any interest in the subject, and during all his holidays he had worked as a waiter. When he'd finally graduated – with a decent degree because, despite his lack of interest, he was actually quite good at the keyboard – he'd gone straight to London and found a job in a bistro in Southwark.

Wade loved the front-of-house part, the bit where he got to deal with customers. He didn't enjoy cooking, and could think of nothing worse than standing in front of a stove all day. He enjoyed the company of chefs, especially drinking with them after hours or tasting something they had created, but he'd never had any desire to work alongside them. Chefs never really got to see the customers enjoying the fruits of their labour: full plates went out and, hopefully, empty ones came back, but they missed the whole process in between. That was the part Wade liked – watching people enjoy themselves, and sharing in the experience. He didn't plan to stay a waiter for ever, though. His ambition was to be a maître d' in one of the capital's best restaurants. The Ivy, maybe, or Scott's, but that was for the future. Today he was just happy to be busy.

He had finished taking the order of table eight, three suited businessmen he'd persuaded to try the sea bass special and upsold on the wine, when he saw the Asian man walk in through the door. He was young, brown-skinned, bearded, and wearing a cheap raincoat. Wade was pretty sure he was looking for work. At least a dozen people a day dropped in their CVs, but he still smiled professionally in case the man was a customer. 'Do you have a reservation, sir?' he asked.

The man didn't say anything but he looked around as if searching for someone.

'I'm sorry, we're totally full,' said Wade. 'Or are you here to meet someone?' The man didn't seem to be listening. He was still looking around, deep furrows in his forehead. Wade heard someone behind him calling for a new bottle of wine. 'We're full,' he said again. 'We might have something in an hour, but I can't promise.'

The man's right hand lashed out and grabbed Wade's. Then he clamped something metallic around Wade's wrist. 'What the fuck?' shouted Wade. 'Get the hell away from me.'

He pushed the man in the chest and he staggered back but the chain linking them snapped taut.

'What have you done?' Wade yelled. The man began to unbutton his coat but Wade yanked his arm with the chain. 'Get this off!'

'I can't. I don't have the key,' said the man. He continued unbuttoning his coat and Wade stared in horror as the suicide vest was revealed. 'Don't push me again,' said the man. 'I don't know what it takes to set this thing off.'

'It's a bomb,' said Wade, his eyes widening.

The man nodded and finished unbuttoning his coat. 'Yes, it's a bomb, and if you and everyone else in here don't do exactly as I say, everyone will die.' His right hand slid inside his coat pocket and emerged holding a trigger with a Velcro strap. The man wiggled his fingers so that the strap slipped over his hand and the trigger nestled in his palm. 'Just do as I say and everyone will be all right. Do you understand?'

Wade nodded slowly, dumbstruck, unable to take his eyes off the explosives and wires attached to the canvas vest under the man's coat.

The man held up his right hand and shouted, at the top of his voice, '*Allahu Akbar!* Everyone stay exactly where they are. If anyone gets up everyone here will die! Listen to what I have to say and this will soon be over!'

LAMBETH CENTRAL COMMUNICATIONS
COMMAND CENTRE (12.51 p.m.)

Kamran walked over to the SCO19 pod, carrying two coffees. 'How's it going, Marty?' he asked, as he handed him a mug.

Marty Windle smiled his thanks and sighed. 'We're stretched tight, Mo. Bloody tight. We get another one and we're buggered, frankly.'

'How many SAS men do you have now?'

'Eight more have arrived and they're on the way to

support the ARVs. I do worry that we've got so many of them. I mean, we need as many guns as we can get but there's a danger that they'll take over. I'm not sure how well trained they are for hostage situations like this. They prefer to go in with guns blazing. As you know, we like to resolve our situations without firing a single round.'

'They know it's a Met operation,' said Kamran. 'They're here in a support role.'

'Yeah, so far,' said Windle. 'But that could well change as the deadline gets closer.' He groaned. 'I'm getting a bad feeling about this, Mo.' He stood up and looked at the large screen on the wall that mapped out all the hostage locations. 'Seven,' he said, 'and nothing linking them. Do you think they've been chosen at random?'

'I can't see how that can be because everything else has been so well planned,' said Kamran.

'But look at the range of places,' said Windle. 'A church in Brixton, a shopping centre in Wandsworth, a post office in Fulham, a childcare centre in Kensington, a coffee shop in Marble Arch, a pub in Marylebone, a bus in Bloomsbury. There's no pattern at all.'

'The geographical location is the pattern,' said Kamran. He sipped his coffee. 'They dropped the first one off at Brixton, then headed clockwise around the city. One every fifteen minutes or so.'

'Which means one vehicle, obviously. But why do that? Why limit yourself? Why not have seven vehicles? Why not have the bombers all strike simultaneously like they did on Seven/Seven?'

'This way is more efficient, maybe.'

Windle shook his head. 'This way is more risky. Suppose

something had gone wrong at the start. They'd all have been caught. Seriously, why put all your eggs in one basket?'

Kamran nodded thoughtfully. What Windle was saying made sense. A simple road traffic accident could have derailed the entire plan. If one of the vests had malfunctioned and detonated prematurely, all the bombers would have died. It would have made far more sense for them to travel separately. And there wasn't much sense to the locations. The bus in Tavistock Square was perhaps a reference to the Seven/Seven attacks on London, and a church made religious sense. But a childcare centre? And a coffee shop just down the road from Paddington Green, one of the most secure police stations in the country? A post office? Yes, they were soft targets, but if this was an attack on Britain then why not pick targets that reflected that? There was nothing political about the locations that had been chosen and they did seem to be random. But, again, Windle was right – why go to all the trouble of planning a multiple suicide-bomber attack, then choose targets at random?

Sergeant Lumley hurried over, looking worried. 'There's another one, sir. An MP's surgery in Camberwell. A couple of people managed to get out before he locked the door but the bomber's holding the MP hostage.'

For the third time that day, Kamran swore.

FULHAM (12.52 p.m.)

The phone behind the counter started to ring again and the three post-office workers turned to look at it. 'Do you want me to answer it?' asked the Indian woman in a head-scarf, who was the closest employee to Ismail.

'No,' he said. 'Let it ring.'

'You should talk to them,' said the woman he was chained to.

'I've nothing to say.' He glanced at the clock on the wall. 'They have just over five hours in which to release the ISIS prisoners. If they don't . . .'

'If they don't, we all die?'

Hussain heard a vehicle arrive to the left and craned his neck to look out of the window. A large Mercedes van had pulled up behind two police cars, which were blocking the road to the left of the post office. The rear doors opened and uniformed police piled out. He saw movement at the window of one of the offices overlooking the post office and ducked back.

'I told you, they won't shoot through the window,' said the woman scornfully.

The phone stopped ringing. It had rung more than a dozen times since Hussain had been in the post office.

The black guy sitting behind the counter took a photograph of Hussain with his iPhone, then tapped away on his screen.

'You don't care that they're taking your picture?' asked the woman.

'People need to see what's happening here,' said Hussain. 'The pictures will show that we're serious.'

'Make sure you tell them my name,' she called, to the man who'd taken the picture. 'Rebecca Nicholls. Nicholls with two *l*s. And his name is Ismail Hussain. Tell them that!'

'You think this is funny?' Hussain hissed. 'You think this is a game?'

'It is what it is,' she said. She tilted her head back and looked down her nose at him. 'Why did you choose me, Ismail?'

'Choose you?'

'Why did you handcuff yourself to me?'

'You were at the end of the queue. The nearest to the door.'

'And that was the only reason?'

'Why do you ask?'

She smiled. 'Because you chose the one person who doesn't care if she lives or dies.'

Hussain's eyes narrowed. 'What do you mean?'

'You know nothing about me, Ismail. You've handcuffed yourself to me and threatened to kill me, but you don't know the first thing about me.'

'You're just a hostage. A body.'

'That's right. That's all I am to you. Well, my name's Rebecca. My friends call me Becky.'

Hussain shrugged.

'Up until a week ago I was a wife and a mother. My husband's name was William and my daughter's name was Ruth.'

'They died?'

'Why, thank you for asking, Ismail,' she said, her voice loaded with sarcasm. 'Yes. They died.'

'How?'

'A stupid, senseless car crash. I wasn't feeling great so William agreed to do the school run. Took Ruth and one of her classmates to school. Some bastard in a truck didn't see that they'd stopped at a red light and ploughed into the back of them. The girls died immediately. They spent more than an hour trying to save William but he bled to death in the car. It was a Volvo. They say a Volvo is the safest car in the world but when a truck smashes into the back of you . . . Anyway, Ismail, every morning I wake up and wonder if today is the day I'm going to join my husband and daughter. I've got the tablets saved up. They'll do the trick, with a couple of glasses of wine.'

'You want to kill yourself?'

'What do I have to live for? Do you have any idea what it's like to lose the two people you love most in the world? I wish I'd died with them. In the car. Instead I was sitting at home watching some crap TV show and drinking coffee.' She shuddered, then a slow smile spread across her face. 'Maybe that's why your God has sent you here today. Maybe this is the sign I've been waiting for. This way I don't have to take the tablets and lie down. Maybe this is a better way to go.' She nodded at the trigger in his hand. 'You press that and it's like flicking a light switch, isn't it? Press it and the lights go out, just like that. Like the blinking of an eye.'

'What are you talking about?'

Her smile widened and he saw the craziness in her eyes. 'I want you to press it, Ismail. If there is a Heaven, then I want to be with William and Ruth. And if there isn't, if there's just an empty blackness, then fuck it, I want to be with them there, in the darkness.' She leant towards him. 'Press it, Ismail,' she hissed. 'Just press it.'

'You're fucking mad!' he said, trying to pull away from her.

She shook her head. 'No, I'm not. I'm the sanest person

here. And the way it's going, Ismail, if you don't press that trigger, I might just do it myself. You think about that. When you're not looking, when you're distracted, I might just reach over, grab your hand and squeeze it.'

Hussain backed away from her until the chain tightened.

She laughed at his discomfort. 'Now who's scared, Ismail? Now who's fucking scared?'

MARBLE ARCH (12.53 p.m.)

Inspector Richard Horton, a twenty-five-year veteran of the Metropolitan Police, had been appointed as Silver Commander at the Marble Arch incident. He was based at Paddington Green station, less than half a mile away down Edgware Road, and had arrived outside the coffee shop within six minutes of getting the call. It wasn't his first major incident by any means. In 1994 he had been a beat constable when a car bomb had exploded outside the Israeli embassy in London, injuring twenty people. He had been a sergeant in April 1999 when a neo-Nazi with mental problems carried out nail-bomb attacks in Soho, Brixton and Brick Lane. And he was still a sergeant on duty on 7 July 2005 when four suicide bombers had attacked the capital, and two weeks later when four copycats had tried and failed to bring havoc to London's transport system.

He had been an inspector since 2010 and had taken part in several major incident rehearsals and had hit the ground running at Marble Arch. The role of Silver Commander was basically to take charge of the scene and to implement the strategies of the Gold Commander. It was clear from the speed of events that the Gold Commander had yet to have any strategy in place – everyone was simply reacting to events. Horton's first tasks had been to manage the scene and establish the necessary cordons. They had to be set up promptly to protect the public, keep onlookers away and to ensure that the emergency services had the access they needed. He already had sixteen constables and had requested more. They had set up inner and outer cordons around the coffee shop, and a traffic cordon to prevent unauthorised vehicle access to the scene. As the coffee shop was close to one of the busiest intersections in London, where Edgware Road met Bayswater Road, the closures had already caused traffic chaos. Two ARVs were on the scene, with two SAS snipers, who were wearing borrowed police clothing. Horton wasn't happy about having special-forces soldiers mixed in with his armed-response teams, but that had come down from Gold Command so he had no choice in the matter.

A marshalling area had been set up at the junction of Edgware Road and Bayswater Road where most of the emergency vehicles were parked. Horton walked towards a new arrival at the scene – a white DAF truck with only police markings on it. If necessary, magnetic signs could be reversed to reveal the van's bomb-disposal role but generally it stayed in covert mode so as not to alarm the public and to avoid becoming a target for attack.

A dark-haired woman was getting into an ABS – an advanced bomb suit – assisted by an older man in a fluorescent jacket. He was helping her into the crotchless Kevlar trousers that would protect her legs. Horton greeted her with a smile. 'Richard Horton,' he said. 'I'm Silver here.'

'Charlie,' said the woman. 'Charlie Kawczynski.' She nodded at her companion. 'Peter here's my dresser.'

'You don't sound Polish,' said Horton.

'Neither does my husband,' said Kawczynski. 'But he was born here, too.'

'Sorry, no offence.'

Kawczynski grinned. 'None taken.'

Peter helped her on with the Kevlar jacket. It would protect her chest and groin but it left her forearms and hands exposed. She would be free to work on any devices but would lose her hands and arms in the event of an explosion. Horton tried to blot the image out of his mind as he explained what he needed her to do.

'The problem we have, Charlie, is that we can't see inside the coffee shop and there's no CCTV we can access. He's covered the windows with newspaper so we can't see what's going on inside. I need you to go to the window and see if you can spot anything. Ideally get us some pictures we can analyse.'

'Got you,' said Kawczynski.

'No need to make contact,' said Horton. 'Just see what you can and pull back.'

'Not a problem. We've got a camera in the truck,' said Kawczynski.

They finished fastening the jacket and Peter began putting the ballistic panels in place. He worked slowly and methodically, checking and double-checking that everything was as it should be. If anything went wrong and the device exploded, the suit was the only thing that would save her from certain death.

CAMBERWELL (12.54 p.m.)

The man was sweating and a vein was pulsing in his fore-head. He kept looking at the window. He was in his late twenties, Metcalfe figured, and conformed to the racist stereotype of a suicide bomber, straggly beard and all. He had taken Metcalfe to the outer office and had slipped the bolts on the main door so that no one could enter or leave. The window overlooked the street. They were on the first floor, over the main constituency office.

A dozen people were sitting on hard-backed chairs, most of them elderly. The man stood with his back to the bolted door and told his hostages to stand up and move to the front office where Metcalfe had been taking his meetings. They filed through one by one and stood in the far corner, huddled together and whispering fearfully.

'Shut up and listen!' the man shouted. 'You are all prisoners of ISIS. You are to send text messages to your friends and family to tell them what is happening. Use Twitter and Facebook, if you can, and use hashtag ISIS6. Tell everyone that you are being held hostage and that the government must release the six ISIS fighters who are being held in Belmarsh Prison. Do you understand?'

A stick-thin West Indian woman, wearing a shapeless hat and a herringbone coat, raised a hand. 'I'm sorry, what is a hashtag?' she asked, her voice trembling.

'That thing that looks like a noughts and crosses game,' said the man.

The woman's frown deepened. 'I don't know what that is,' she said to the man next to her.

'I'll help you,' said Molly. She smiled at the bomber. 'Don't worry, I'll get them to do it.'

The man pointed at the far corner of the room, away from the window. 'Everyone sit down there. Just do as you're told and everyone will go home.'

The hostages obeyed, though several were quite elderly and had to be helped onto the floor. Molly fussed around them, making sure they were comfortable and explaining what they had to do.

'What's your name?' asked Metcalfe. The man frowned at him, as if he hadn't understood the question. Metcalfe repeated it slowly, enunciating every syllable carefully. He could still smell garlic but it wasn't as overpowering as when the man had handcuffed him.

'I'm not fucking retarded,' snapped the man. 'What – you think cos I'm Asian I don't understand English? I was born here, mate. I'm as British as you are.'

'I'm sorry, I thought you hadn't heard me,' said Metcalfe.

'No, you thought I'd just got off the bloody boat, that's what you thought. You condescending prick.'

'Seriously, no. I'm sorry. I just wanted to know your name, that's all.'

'Why do you give a toss about who I am?'

'Because you're handcuffed to me, that's why. And if things go wrong and that vest goes off then yours will be the last face I see and that's about as personal a relationship as you can have, so I just wanted to know who you are.'

'This isn't personal,' said the man.

'You came here deliberately, though. You chose me. You could have gone anywhere but you came to my surgery and handcuffed yourself to me, so it is personal. It's very personal. You know I have a lot of Muslim constituents, don't you? I've visited all the mosques here and have always been welcomed.'

'You talk too much, mate,' said the man.

'I'm just saying, you're attacking the wrong person here. I do a lot of work on behalf of Muslim constituents.'

'What's done is done,' said the man. 'You've got a phone, right?'

Metcalfe nodded.

'Then start tweeting. Hashtag ISIS6. Tell your government to release the prisoners and you'll be released too.'

'The government doesn't negotiate with terrorists,' said Metcalfe.

'You'd better pray that they do, because otherwise we'll all die today.'

Metcalfe rubbed his face with his free hand. He was sweating profusely and his hand came away wet. 'And what are you? Al-Qaeda? ISIS? Who do you represent?'

'I don't represent anyone, mate.'

'But you want the ISIS prisoners released, right? That's what you told everyone?'

The man nodded. 'If the prisoners are released, we all get to go home,' he said. He wiped his forehead with the sleeve of his right arm.

'Do you want some water?' asked Metcalfe. 'We've got bottled water in the fridge.'

The man nodded again. 'Yeah. Okay. Thanks.'

Metcalfe gestured at his assistant and she got up off the floor and went over to the fridge. She took out a bottle of water, unscrewed the cap and gave it to the man, then sat down again with the rest of the hostages. The man released his grip on the trigger, though the Velcro strap kept it in place in his palm as he drank greedily. He put the bottle down and thanked her again.

'My name is Roger,' said Metcalfe.

'Ali,' said the man. He forced a smile. 'Pleased to meet you.'

Metcalfe smiled despite himself. 'I'd say I was pleased to meet you, and under other circumstances that might well be true, but . . .' he gestured at the vest '. . . that scares me, you know that?'

'You and me both, mate.'

'You know who I am? I'm the local MP.'

'Yeah. I know.'

'So the thing is, Ali, I'm a pretty valuable hostage. You'll get a lot of media attention because of me. I'm in the government.'

'You're a very important man, I get it,' said Ali, his voice loaded with sarcasm.

'No, I meant that you need to be talking to the police. You need to start negotiating.'

Ali nodded at the dozen or so constituents, who were now sitting on the floor with their backs to the wall, tapping away on their phones. 'That's what they're doing. They're putting the word out.'

'You want those men in Belmarsh released?'

'That's what this is about. If they're released, we can all go home.'

Metcalfe frowned. 'We?'

'I don't want to die today.'

'Then you need to talk. You need to negotiate. You need to show them that you've got me as a hostage. I'm an MP.

I know the prime minister. They won't want anything to happen to me.'

Ali said nothing.

'You heard what I said? They need to know that I'm handcuffed to you.'

Ali gestured at the constituents. 'They'll explain what's happened. I don't need to talk to anyone.'

Metcalfe winced as his soaked trousers scraped across his flesh. 'I need to change my trousers,' he said.

'Why?'

'I wet myself.'

'You what?'

'I wet myself when you started shouting.' The MP pointed with his left hand at the door to the office. 'I've an overnight bag in there,' he said. 'There's a change of clothes.'

'I have to stay here. By the door.'

'My assistant can get the bag.'

Ali shook his head. 'Everyone has to stay here.'

'She can leave the door open. You can see everything she does.' Metcalfe waved at the damp patch at the front of his trousers. 'You can't leave me like this. It's disgusting.'

'You're the one who pissed himself,' said Ali.

'Yes, because I was scared. Now, please, I'm begging you, let Molly get me my trousers.'

Ali stared at him for several seconds, then gestured with his chin at Molly. 'Go in there and get his bag. Come straight back.'

Molly did as she was told and returned a few seconds later with Metcalfe's overnight bag. 'There's a clean pair of trousers in there, and underwear,' said Metcalfe.

She took them out and handed them to him. Metcalfe

looked at Ali. 'Can you do me a favour and ask everyone to turn around while I change?' he asked.

'Just fucking do it,' snarled Ali. 'No one gives a fuck about the colour of your underpants.'

'I'll stand in front of you, if that'll help,' said Molly.

LAMBETH CENTRAL COMMUNICATIONS COMMAND CENTRE (12.56 p.m.)

Kashif Talpur's boss was a thirty-five-year-old inspector with the National Crime Agency. His name was Mark Biddulph and he arrived at the communications command centre in a leather jacket and jeans. 'Day off,' he explained. 'I was at the dentist's about to have a tooth drilled.'

'Sorry to drag you away but we're in the middle of a shit-storm,' said Kamran. 'We've got eight would-be suicide bombers at various locations around London.'

'I saw it on the TV at the surgery,' said Biddulph. 'But what do you need me for? I'm not in anti-terrorism.'

'One of the bombers seems to be your man – Kashif Talpur.'

Biddulph's jaw dropped. 'No fucking way,' he said. 'Excuse my French, sir, but Kash is one of my best men.'

'There's no way he could have fundamentalist leanings?'

'He's third-generation British,' said Biddulph. 'Grandparents came over just after the Second World War. His dad's a teacher, mum's a nurse. He supports West Ham, for God's sake.'

Kamran tapped on his keyboard and Talpur's face filled one of his screens. 'Is that him?'

Biddulph stared at the picture taken from the CCTV camera on the bus.

'Mark?' prompted Kamran.

Biddulph stammered for a second or two, then shook his head fiercely. 'Yes, that's him. At least, it looks like him. But it can't be.'

'Can you call him?'

'Sure.' Biddulph took out a mobile and called a number. 'Straight to voicemail,' he said. He put the phone away. 'Where is he?'

'On a bus in Tavistock Square, threatening to blow himself to kingdom come if we don't release six ISIS fighters from Belmarsh.'

'That's impossible,' said Biddulph. 'I don't mean unlikely, I don't mean out of character, I mean one thousand per cent impossible.'

'Where is he supposed to be today?'

'Brentford. That's where the gang operates, mainly,' said Biddulph. 'He's been doing a great job. There's a group of two dozen Asians, minicab drivers most of them, that have been seducing the girls, passing them around and prostituting them. He infiltrated the gang but it soon became clear they were also involved in big-time drugs smuggling. The investigation has grown and grown but we're almost ready to move in.'

'And what does he do when he's undercover?'

'Hangs out with the Asian gang. Works part-time in a kebab house in Brentford. Almost four months now.'

'So what's he up to? Could this in any way be part of the case he's on?'

Biddulph shook his head. 'These Asians are Muslim, but

in name only. They drink, they smoke dope and they screw underage girls. They go to mosques but maybe once a week, if that.'

'But Talpur is a Muslim?'

'Well, again, yes, but you don't see him in the office face down on a prayer mat. And he drinks. Always buys his round. He can handle his booze, too.'

'Could he have been hiding all this time?' asked Biddulph.

'What – you mean concealing fundamentalist leanings so that he could penetrate the Met?' He shrugged and sighed. 'Look, he's a bloody good undercover cop so, yes, I suppose that's possible. But if he was involved in some long-term penetration of the Met, why throw it all away to lay siege to a bus? Surely there'd be better ways of sticking it to us.' He held up his hands. 'But that's just crazy talk. As I said, Kash is a bloody good officer, one of my best men.'

'So what's he doing on that bus?' asked Kamran.

'I have absolutely no idea,' said Biddulph. 'All I can think of is that he's had some sort of breakdown.'

'At the moment he's got a trigger in his hand and he's refusing to let anyone off the bus,' said Kamran. He thought for a few seconds, then reached a decision. 'You need to get out there and see if you can talk to him.'

Biddulph nodded. 'No problem.'

Kamran turned to Lumley. 'Joe, arrange a car for Inspector Biddulph. We need to get him out to Tavistock Square ASAP. Blues and twos.' He looked back at Biddulph. 'Is he married? Kids?'

Biddulph shook his head. 'Three siblings. You're thinking a tiger kidnapping?' It was a common tactic used in robberies where a family member was kidnapped to force the relative to co-operate with the robbers. But the technique had been refined by the IRA, who had used tiger kidnappings to force civilians to plant car bombs, sometimes losing their lives in the process.

'If you're sure he's not turned fundamentalist, maybe he's being pressured,' said Kamran. 'Give me a list of family members before you go and I'll get someone to check that no one has gone missing.'

MARBLE ARCH (1.05 p.m.)

The helmet weighed just three and a half kilos but it absorbed outside sounds so all Charlie Kawczynski could hear was her own soft breathing. Her heart was pounding but she was able to control her breathing, slow and even. She hadn't bothered to use the optional cooling system that came with the suit. It had a network of capillaries sewn into it and connected to a four-pint reservoir but it wasn't usually needed for short periods and Kawczynski figured she'd be done in less than half an hour. There was a microphone and ventilation system built into the helmet, along with a battery pack using standard nine-volt batteries that would run for five hours. All the wiring was built into the fabric of the suit so that it couldn't be snagged. Walking wasn't easy but she'd been in the Bomb Squad going on three years so she'd had plenty of practice. It was looking down that was the problem. The ballistic panel that covered the neck and the lower part of the helmet meant that she couldn't see her feet so the trick was always to know what was on the ground ahead of her.

She looked up to her left and saw a sniper at the window of an office overlooking the coffee shop. And in the far distance two police cars were blocking off the road. Beyond them was a fire engine and beyond that a van belonging to Sky News with a large white satellite dish on the roof.

She walked down the middle of the road. The suit wasn't designed for concealment and it certainly didn't allow for running. 'Slowly but surely': that was the Bomb Squad's mantra. Bomb disposal was all about technique, about working out the safest method of making a device safe. And that was what made suicide bombers so difficult to deal with – the human element made them unpredictable. She was always much happier looking down at an IED or approaching a car bomb than a human being.

She reached the coffee shop, paused, then turned to face it. Newspapers had been plastered across the glass but there were gaps between the individual sheets. In her right hand she was holding a small digital camera.

She looked back at the van, raised her hand and waved to Peter. He waved back. The suit's wireless system used a very low level of RF radiation to minimise the risk of activating IEDs, but they had decided against using it to be on the safe side.

She walked towards the shop, calculating how many steps she had to take before she reached the pavement. She stepped up, steadied her breathing, and walked towards the window. The largest gaps were at the edge closest to the door and she moved towards it, holding up the camera. She squinted at the small screen on the back. She could just about make out figures so she pressed the button several times. Then she moved to the right to another gap and fired off a few more shots.

She saw movement and put her helmet closer to the window. Somebody was moving around but she couldn't make out what was happening. She put the camera up to the gap between the sheets of newspapers and took more photographs.

Something slammed against the window and she flinched. An eye pressed itself to the glass and she took a step back. A hand ripped away part of the newspaper and then reappeared. It was holding a trigger. Kawczynski raised her hands and stepped away. 'I'm going, I'm going!' she shouted, even though she knew that the suicide bomber couldn't hear her. She stepped off the pavement and walked back to the van, slowly but surely.

LAMBETH CENTRAL COMMUNICATIONS COMMAND CENTRE (1.30 p.m.)

Sergeant Lumley's phone rang and he picked up the receiver. It was Inspector Richard Horton, Silver Commander at the Marble Arch scene. 'We have some pictures of the inside of the coffee shop,' said the inspector. 'I can download them now if you want.'

'Ready when you are, sir,' said Lumley.

'Let me have your email address and I'll send you the link.'

The inspector stayed on the line until Lumley had the photographs on his left-hand screen. 'The quality isn't great,

I know,' said the inspector. 'There's glare off the window and everyone was standing well back.'

'I can get our tech boys to tinker with them,' said Lumley, but he knew that the inspector was right. The pictures were blurry and even the best of the bunch were half obscured by the newspaper.

The final photograph of the series was a close-up of an Asian face, bearded with glaring eyes, partly obscured by a hand holding a metal trigger. A piece of newspaper had been torn away, just enough to reveal part of the face.

'This last one, the guy saw what was happening?' asked the sergeant.

'He went to the window and the Explosive Ordnance Disposal officer backed off immediately,' said Inspector Horton. 'How are things there?'

'Hectic,' said Lumley.

'We're still waiting for a negotiating team here,' said Horton. 'Can you tell Gold?'

'He knows,' said Lumley. 'The problem is, even where we have negotiating teams on site, the bombers are refusing to talk to them. All communication is through social media at the moment.'

'Four and a half hours left until their deadline,' said the inspector. 'Has a decision been taken on the Belmarsh prisoners yet?'

'That's all well above my pay grade, sir.'

'Mine too, thankfully,' said the inspector. 'It's not a decision I'd want to make. That guy in there looks perfectly prepared to blow himself up and take everyone in the shop with him, if he and the other bombers don't get what they want.'

TAVISTOCK SQUARE (1.35 p.m.)

Two uniformed constables held up their hands to stop Mark Biddulph's car at the outer cordon around Tavistock Square. Biddulph climbed out and showed them his warrant card. 'Where is Silver Commander?' he asked.

The older of the two, a man in his forties with a beer gut the size of a late pregnancy, nodded towards the BMA headquarters. 'They've taken an office on the ground floor, sir.'

Biddulph thanked the man and headed over to the BMA building. There was another uniformed constable outside and Biddulph flashed his warrant card as he walked by. The office was to the side of Reception. A uniformed inspector was talking into a mobile phone and frowned at him until Biddulph held out his warrant card. He ended the call and looked at Biddulph expectantly.

'Silver Commander?' asked Biddulph.

'That would be me,' said a uniformed inspector.

Biddulph flashed his warrant card again. 'Mark Biddulph, National Crime Agency. Gold Commander has sent me along.'

'Alistair McNeil, good to meet you.' They shook hands. 'What's the NCA's involvement?' he asked.

'The man in there is one of mine,' said Biddulph.

'A CI?'

'Unfortunately he's not a confidential informant, no. He's a detective. Undercover.'

McNeil's jaw dropped. 'Run that by me again.'

'He's supposed to be undercover penetrating an Asian drugs gang. Where do we stand?'

'I've an inner cordon and an outer cordon set up, there's an ambulance and a fire appliance on standby. One ARV here and I'm told there's another on the way. I've put in a call for a negotiating team and the Bomb Squad but resources are obviously stretched pretty thin. This is number seven, right?'

Biddulph nodded. 'One every twenty minutes or so. Things are getting a bit frantic in GT Ops.'

'Yeah, they said they can't guarantee I'll be getting a negotiator.'

'That's why Gold wants me here.'

'You think he'll talk to you?'

'I've known him for the best part of two years, so I don't see why not.'

'If you know him, do you think he'll blow himself up? Do you think he'll press that trigger?'

'The Kash I know wouldn't be there in the first place. He's not your typical Muslim. He's one of the guys. He stands his round in the pub, eats bacon sarnies with the lads. Sure he looks the part but he's what the fundamentalists call a coconut.' The inspector frowned, not getting the reference. 'Brown on the outside, white on the inside. I know, it's the sort of talk that'd get you turfed out of the Met, but that's what he was called at school, to his face and behind his back. Kash is as British as you or me. He's not the sort to go fundamentalist. Not without there being warning signs first. I saw him for a debrief three days ago and he was as right as rain then.'

'Well, something's happened, because he's on that bus threatening to blow it up with everybody on it.'

'I need to talk to him.'

'No can do, I'm afraid. No one is allowed within fifty feet of the bus.'

'I need to know why he's there.'

'I understand that, but I'm in charge here and if anything were to happen to you it would be down to me.'

'He's my man.'

'And this is my crime scene and the SOP is quite clear. I have to keep everyone well away from the immediate danger, and at the moment that immediate danger is the bus. If he detonates, there'll be glass and shrapnel spraying all over the square. If anyone gets caught in the blast that will be my responsibility.'

'So how do you plan to set up lines of communication with him?'

'We're waiting for the Bomb Squad,' said McNeil. 'Once we have someone with the appropriate protective gear we can see about getting a landline over.'

Biddulph sighed, knowing that the Silver Commander was right. But what was happening made no sense, no sense at all. And the only way of answering the riddle of why Kash was on the bus was to speak to the man himself.

LAMBETH CENTRAL COMMUNICATIONS COMMAND CENTRE (2.00 p.m.)

Sergeant Lumley put his hand over the phone he was holding. 'Sir, you might want to take this. Guy on the line says he wants to talk to the man in charge about the demands of the suicide bombers.'

'Are you sure he's not a crank?' asked Kamran. 'They'll all be coming out of the woodwork today.'

'He seems to know what he's talking about. Design of the vests, location of the bombers.'

'Anyone who's watching Sky would know most of the details,' said Kamran.

'He sounds like the genuine article, sir.'

Kamran wrinkled his nose, then took the phone from the sergeant. 'Who is this?' he said.

'My name is Shahid – at least that's what you can call me. You are?'

'Superintendent Kamran.'

'And you are the Gold Commander?'

'Yes. For now. I'm expecting a more senior officer at any moment.'

'But you're the acting Gold Commander?'

'Yes.'

'Then you are my point of contact from now on. I'll talk to you and no one else. Do you understand?'

'I'm not the best person for that. I'm not a trained negotiator.'

'You're my point of contact. I won't be talking to anyone else in future. Do you understand?'

'Yes,' said Kamran.

'Good. Now what's your first name?'

'Mo.'

'Mo is short for Maurice?'

'Mohammed.'

There was a silence for several seconds. 'You are fucking shitting me?'

'That's my name. Mohammed Kamran. Superintendent Mohammed Kamran.'

'You're a Muslim?'

'Very few non-Muslim boys get to be called Mohammed.'

'Don't fuck around, Mo. Are you a Muslim or not?'

'Yes. I am.'

'A good Muslim?'

'I try to be.'

'You pray five times a day, you plan to visit Mecca one day, you give ten per cent of your earnings to charity?'

'Like I said, I try to be a good Muslim. I do the best I can.'

'And they fast-tracked you, did they? Because you're Asian and a Muslim?'

'I wish,' said Kamran. 'I walked a beat for five years and drove around in a Territorial Support Group van as a sergeant for three. I've been lucky, but I didn't get preferential treatment. I worked for my rank. Why? Do you have a problem with Muslim police officers, Shahid?' Lumley was grinning and giving him a thumbs-up.

'I just think it's one hell of a coincidence that you're in charge, on today of all days.'

'I've had experience in policing major events,' said Kamran. 'But, as I said, a more senior officer will be taking over shortly.'

'No, you tell everyone that I'm only talking to you from now on. You're my point of contact and only you. Make that clear to one and all, right, Mo?'

'If that's what you want, Shahid. You're the one calling the shots.'

'Then we're on the same wavelength, Mo. You and me, we're going to get along just fine, I can tell.'

Sergeant Lumley stood up and punched the air. He picked up a phone and started talking animatedly.

'So what is it you want, Shahid?' asked Kamran, keeping his voice as calm as he could. By the look of it the sergeant had managed to trace the call.

'What I want is the six brothers released from Belmarsh. Can you handle that, Mo?'

'How do I know you have any connection to the incidents?' said Kamran.

'One of them is in a childcare centre in Kensington,' said Shahid.

'That's been on television,' said Kamran. 'Everyone knows that.'

'I will arrange for the children to be released,' said Shahid. 'Our quarrel is not with innocents. I shall arrange for their release, then call you back. But I need a direct line for you, Mo. From this point on I will talk with you and no one else.'

Kamran started to give him a landline number but Shahid cut him short. 'Your mobile, Mo. Your personal mobile. It's that or nothing.'

Kamran gave him the number of his mobile. Shahid repeated it once, then cut the connection.

Lumley put down the phone. 'We've got a location,' he said. 'Brixton. There are two ARVs en route as we speak. Well done on keeping him talking as long as you did.'

'It wasn't down to me,' said Kamran. 'I couldn't shut him up.'

'Well, we've got him now, that's the important thing.'

KENSINGTON (2.02 p.m.)

Mohamed Osman flinched as the mobile phone in his waist-pack buzzed. He was sweating and wiped his forehead with the back of his sleeve. The phone buzzed again. The girl was standing as far away from him as she could and the chain linking them was taut. He had to step towards her to reach into the waistpack but as soon as he moved she backed away from him. He tried to smile. 'I have to answer the phone,' he said.

'What phone?'

'In my pack. Someone is calling me. I have to use my left hand.' He held up his right hand and showed her the trigger. 'I have to keep hold of this. You understand?'

The girl nodded fearfully. Osman took a step towards her and this time she didn't move. He unzipped the pack and took out the phone. He pressed the green button to accept the call and put it to his ear.

'Are you well, brother?' It was Shahid.

'I just want to go home,' said Osman. 'What we're doing is wrong.'

'You are part of jihad, brother, you should be proud. Now, listen to me and listen carefully. You are to release the children. But only the children. You are to take the children to the door and allow them to leave, in single file.

If you allow even one of the adults to escape, I will detonate the vest. Do you understand?'

'Please, this isn't fair. I shouldn't be here. I'm a good Muslim. I have a mother and a father and they need me. They depend on my money. I should be at work today. This isn't—'

'Brother, if you carry on like this I will detonate the vest. Is that what you want?'

'No!' said Osman.

'Then do as I say. Let the children go. But the adults must stay. Do you understand?'

'Yes.'

'Then do as you are told, brother, and know that you are serving Allah the best you can.' The line went dead. Osman put the phone away and zipped up the waistpack with a trembling hand. He tried to smile at the girl. 'What is your name, madam?' he asked.

'Sally,' she said, her voice trembling. 'Sally Jones.'

He forced a smile, trying to put her at ease. 'Sally, you have to help me,' he said. 'We are going to let the children go.'

'Really?'

He nodded. 'Can you gather them all together? And then we will take them to the door. The police will be outside to meet them.'

'What about me?'

'The adults have to stay inside.'

'Why can't you let us all go?'

'I can't. But the children can go.'

'Are you going to kill us?'

'I don't think so,' said Osman. 'Not if we all do as we're told. Now gather them together.'

Sally closed her eyes, took a deep breath, then opened

them. 'Right, children, listen to me,' she said. 'It's time to go outside so I want you all to stand up and hold hands. We're going to go for a walk.'

'What's happening?' asked Laura.

'He's letting the children go,' said Sally.

'What about us?'

'We have to stay.'

Laura was close to tears.

'Madam, the children can go now,' said Osman. 'If the prisoners are released, you will be able to go, too. Now, please, get the children organised.'

The children were standing up and looking around, confused.

'Children, I want you all to hold hands in a long line,' shouted Sally. 'Hold hands with the friend next to you.'

'What about us?' Laura said to Osman. 'You should let us all go.'

'I can't,' he said. 'If any adults leave, the vest I am wearing will explode.'

'This isn't fair,' said Laura.

'I know, madam. I am sorry. But, please believe me, if any of the adults try to leave, the bomb I am wearing will explode and everybody will die.'

'Just because you want your friends released from prison?'

'They are not my friends, madam. Now, please, get the children ready.'

Some of the children had split into twos. 'No, children, form a line,' shouted Sally. 'Hold hands with the friends either side so we make a long line, like a snake.'

Laura went over to help the children. Several had realised that something was wrong and had been crying.

'It's all right, children!' shouted Sally. 'Your mummies and daddies are outside.' She realised what Max Dunbar was about to do and she yelled at him, 'Max, I swear to God, if you bite Henrietta I'll slap you into the middle of next week.'

The boy's jaw dropped and he stared at her in astonishment.

'I'm serious, Max. You do as you're bloody well told for once in your life!'

BRIXTON (2.05 p.m.)

Ben Peyton gripped the handle above his head to steady himself as the tyres of the BMW X5 screeched against the tarmac and the vehicle swung to the left. He would have preferred to be driving but he was SAS and a guest of the Met so he had to sit in the back, grin and bear it. There were two armed officers in the car and so far they seemed decent enough guys, though both admitted to never having fired a shot in anger. Even their range time was minimal compared with what passed for normal in the SAS. Peyton couldn't even begin to count the number of rounds he fired during training in an average year. Twenty thousand? Thirty thousand? It would be several hundred rounds each training session, and when he wasn't on active duty he'd often train twice a day. The cops trained but they tended to do it without actually pulling the trigger, which, to be fair, was the way they went about their work on the streets. The whole point of the Met's armed police seemed to be geared towards *not* firing a shot. If shots were fired and anyone was hit, the officer was immediately suspended pending an investigation, which, more often than not, seemed to assume that the officer was guilty of a crime.

It was a set-up that Peyton found difficult to understand. In the SAS he was trained to kill, then sent out to do just that. In fact, he would be doing a crap job if he didn't kill people. He had killed a fair number during the ten years he'd been in the SAS, and he could remember every single one. But the guys he was riding with had never killed, never wounded, and in all likelihood they never would. There were two of them. Phil Hall was a sergeant, thirty-something, as bald as a cue ball but with a spreading moustache. Hall was in the front passenger seat, handling the comms and the satnav. The driver was Tom McGuirk, a few years older than Hall but still a constable, albeit one with more than ten years' experience. Both men were dressed in black fireproof coveralls. They had put on their bulletproof vests and Kevlar helmets before getting into the SUV.

Peyton was wearing jeans and a black denim jacket. He had a Glock in a nylon holster on his hip and the cops had lent him a flak jacket and a helmet.

'The phone's in Wiltshire Road, next to Max Roach Park,' said Hall. 'We're assuming it's in a vehicle. We're coming in from the north. Trojan Two Five One is approaching from the south. We're going straight in. We don't have time to fuck about. Ben, get the guns ready, will you?'

Peyton unhitched two SIG Sauer 516 assault rifles from their rack. He left the third where it was. He preferred to stick with his Glock because it was clearly going to be up close and personal.

'Two minutes,' said Hall.

They weren't using lights or sirens but it was a marked car so McGuirk had no problem cutting through the traffic and they had been lucky with the lights. A woman with a pram was getting ready to use a zebra crossing but McGuirk flashed his lights and beeped his horn to let her know he wasn't stopping. From the look on her face she was cursing him something rotten and McGuirk mouthed, 'Sorry,' but kept going.

'One minute,' said Hall.

Peyton had the rifles on his lap. Hall took a quick look over his shoulder. 'Okay?' he asked Peyton.

Peyton nodded. 'Good to go.'

'We're going in hot, there's every chance he'll have explosives.'

'Understood,' said Peyton.

'Not quite the same as Afghanistan,' said Hall.

'Not as much sand here,' said Peyton.

McGuirk took a quick left, the tyres screeching.

'Almost there,' said Hall.

The SUV turned right. There was only one vehicle parked in the road by the park – a white van. Hall was already on the radio, reading out the registration number as McGuirk brought the car to a halt. Hall put his hand up to his earpiece, then nodded. 'That's the van that dropped the bomber at the Camberwell location.'

The second ARV came around the corner ahead of the white van and stopped with a squeal of brakes.

Peyton was out of the SUV first and handed the rifles

to Hall and McGuirk before pulling his Glock from its
holster. He followed the two cops as they headed towards
the van, shuffling forward with their rifles shouldered. He
kept to the right, making sure that neither of his companions crossed his line of fire.

Three armed cops fanned out of the ARV ahead of the
van, guns at the ready.

'Phil, maybe move to the left a tad,' said Peyton.

Hall and McGuirk crossed the road to the pavement,
taking themselves out of the other group's field of fire.
Peyton followed them.

There were no pedestrians in the vicinity and any traffic
would be held up by the police SUVs parked across the
road.

Peyton peered at the offside mirror. He couldn't see
anyone in the front. He was about to tell Hall but then he
flinched as something went bang, but it was a reflex and
his trigger finger stayed where it was. The bang hadn't
sounded like a shot, more like a car backfiring. But one of
the armed cops from the other vehicle didn't agree and
yelled, 'We're under fire!' He immediately fired a shot at
the van and the windscreen exploded in a shower of glass
cubes. His two companions also started firing and within
seconds dozens of rounds were slamming into the vehicle.

'Hold your fire!' shouted Peyton, but the armed cops
couldn't hear him.

Rounds continued to slam into the white van. One by
one the tyres burst and the van lurched from side to side
as it settled. Eventually the three officers stopped firing.

The stench of cordite drifted over and Peyton's eyes
watered. Hall motioned for them to move forward and

McGuirk and Peyton followed him to the rear of the van. The only sound now was the barking of a dog in the distance and the trickling of water from the ruptured radiator. People were starting to emerge from their homes and most of them were taking videos with their smartphones.

Hall reached the rear of the van and stepped to the side as he pulled open the door on the right. McGuirk and Peyton rushed forward, their guns covering the van's interior. It was empty, except for a mobile phone lying on the floor along with several number-plates.

The three cops from the other van ran to the side doors and pulled them open, then stepped back. 'Shit,' said one.

'I heard a shot,' said another. 'I swear to God, I heard a shot.'

'It was a car backfiring,' said Peyton, as he holstered his Glock. 'Easy mistake to make.'

LAMBETH CENTRAL COMMUNICATIONS COMMAND CENTRE (2.10 p.m.)

Lumley took the call, then relayed the message to Kamran. 'The van was empty. Abandoned. The phone was in the back.'

'It would have been too easy for Shahid to still be there,' said Kamran. 'Get Forensics all over the van and the phone.'

'The kids are coming out,' said Waterman. The MI5 officer was standing at the door, looking at one of the big screens on the wall in the special operations room. The feed was coming from one of the police cameras, a close-up of the main door to the childcare centre. A blonde woman was holding the door open and ushering the children out. They filed out in a long snake, all holding hands, as if they were playing a game.

'There's Osman. Can you see him?' said Kamran. The suicide bomber was standing behind the woman. 'They're handcuffed, right?'

'Looks like it,' said Murray, coming up behind him.

'Joe, get a close-up of her and see if we can ID her. How many kids are out so far?'

'Twelve,' said Waterman. 'Thirteen. Fourteen. Fifteen. Sixteen. That's the lot.'

Police were breaking up the snake and taking the children away in twos. The worried parents were being kept back by officers in fluorescent jackets but at the sight of their children they forced their way through. The police resisted at first but then stood back and let the parents scoop up their kids.

'Get them away from there!' shouted Kamran. 'That's still a live bomb inside. Get everyone away.'

Lumley relayed Kamran's instructions over the phone.

'So who's still inside?' asked Kamran.

'Two teachers, two office staff. Everyone else got out.'

'So four hostages. That's an improvement anyway.' Kamran's mobile rang. He rushed over to his desk. The caller was withholding his number but he answered. 'So you have your children, Mo.' It was Shahid. Kamran waved at Lumley and mimed for the sergeant to trace the call. On the screen the police were ushering the parents and their children away from the building. Armed police were still covering the main entrance.

'Do you know what Shahid means, Mo?'

'"Martyr", I think.'

'It's more complicated than that. It's an Arabic word that means "witness". But you are correct. In recent times it has become the word that describes someone who dies for their faith. So today I am Shahid and my nine fellow warriors are also Shahids. But whether or not they become martyrs depends on you. You have seen our demands.'

'We need to talk to you, Shahid. We need to discuss this.'

'There is to be no discussion. You have the names of the six warriors we want released. They are to be taken to Biggin Hill airport. There is to be a jet there, fuelled and waiting. The warrior brothers will leave the country with the nine Shahids. And then it will be over.'

'It's not as simple as that, Shahid.'

'It is very simple, Mo. It is either-or. Either the warriors are released or the suicide bombers become martyrs. It is now ten past two. You have less than four hours to release the warriors and get them to the airport. The plane must leave at six o'clock this evening.'

'There isn't enough time,' said Kamran.

'There is all the time you need,' said Shahid. 'You call the prime minister. You tell him that, if he does not agree to our terms, the bombers and their hostages will meet their maker in four hours. It will be on his head. Call him now, and I will call you back.'

The line went dead. Kamran looked at Lumley. He could see from the sergeant's face that he'd had no luck in tracing the call.

'Nowhere near enough time,' said Lumley. 'Sorry.'

'Looks like he's serious about using me as the sole point

of contact,' said Kamran. He ran his hands through his hair. 'Thing is, I'm not trained for negotiation.'

'You're doing fine, so far as I can see,' said Waterman. 'But I might know someone who can help.'

'Any assistance gratefully received,' said Kamran.

'We have a guy over at Thames House at the moment. He's running a few training courses for us. Former cop but for the last ten years he's been working as a private-sector hostage negotiator. He did a lot of work in the Horn of Africa when the Somalian pirates were at their peak. Chris Thatcher. He's one of the best negotiators around.'

'Get him here as soon as you can,' said Kamran. 'I'm starting to feel out of my depth.'

'Something else I might be able to help you with,' said the MI5 officer. 'Twitter has gone into overdrive on this, as you know. Sergeant Lumley's got a team combing through social media for intel, but I think it's fair to say they're overwhelmed at the moment. Hundreds of ISIS, Al-Qaeda and assorted jihadist accounts are retweeting everything and a big chunk of them are claiming responsibility for what's happening. On the other side of the fence we have hundreds of anti-Islamic sites pouring out their bile, all with the hashtag ISIS6. We've got to the stage where we can't see the wood for the trees.'

'So how can you help?'

'What I'd like to suggest is that we handle all social media through Thames House. We've got the manpower and the technology.'

'Sounds good, and can someone there liaise with Sergeant Lumley? Make sure that I'm kept in the loop?'

'Absolutely,' said Waterman. 'And if it's all right with you, I think we should go more pro-active.'

'In what way?' asked Kamran.

'We can make direct contact with the hostages who are online,' she said. 'We can talk to them directly and ask them for intel and photographs. It would help us immensely.'

'I wouldn't want the hostages put at risk,' said Kamran.

'To be frank, they're already at risk,' said the MI5 officer. 'And they have been encouraged to use social media. This would be an extension of that.'

'I worry that if they got caught talking directly to MI5 or the police there might be repercussions.'

'Not a problem. We'll use dummy accounts. We have people who are experts at this sort of thing.'

Kamran nodded. 'Okay, run with it. But at the first sign of trouble, shut it down.'

TAVISTOCK SQUARE (2.15 p.m.)

Mark Biddulph patted the ballistic panel that would protect his chest and groin from any explosion – hopefully. 'It's bloody heavy,' he said.

Robin Greene grinned over at him. 'I'd like to say you get used to it, but that'd be a lie. It's almost forty kilos and the longer you wear it the heavier it gets.'

Biddulph held up his hands. 'It seems so wrong that the hands aren't protected,' he said.

'We need the flexibility,' Greene said. 'But it's not like

the movies. We're not in there deciding which wire to cut while the clock ticks away.'

Biddulph had arrived with a Bomb Squad team at just before two o'clock. The van had POLICE on the side but there was no indication that it was involved in bomb disposal. Inspector McNeil had given Greene a briefing in the Silver Command office, which was when Biddulph had asked if he could go on the recce. McNeil hadn't been happy but Greene had said that, providing Biddulph wore a suit and didn't get any closer than twenty feet to the bus, the risk of injury was minimal.

The recce was to establish contact with the bomber and to get a close-up view of the inside of the bus, and after confirming with Gold Command at Lambeth that the risk was acceptable, Inspector McNeil reluctantly gave the go-ahead.

Two other members of the Bomb Squad helped Greene and Biddulph suit up while another technician prepared a field phone that they would try to persuade the bomber to use.

'So this guy, he's been working undercover?'

Biddulph nodded. 'For the NCA. It started as a sexual-predator case with Asians grooming underage white girls, then it became obvious they were big-time drug importers.'

'But there was no terrorism involvement?'

'None that Kash reported.'

'Kash?'

'That's his name. Kash, with a K. Well, his nickname, I guess. Kashif Talpur. He joined three years ago, did a couple of years pounding a beat in Wandsworth, and then we co-opted him into the NCA. Bright lad.'

'Lad?'

'He's only twenty-three but looks younger.'

'And no one suspected he'd turned fundamentalist?'

'I still can't believe it's him,' said Biddulph. 'I'm hoping that when I get up close I'll realise that it just looks like him and that the facial-recognition system has screwed up.'

'People change.'

'Yeah, but not that quickly. I saw him just three days ago and he was as right as rain. Had a couple of pints and a curry, chatted about the football more than the case.'

'Pints? He drinks?'

'Likes his beer. Was going out with a very pretty blonde girl before she got fed up with his hours. I've even seen him buy pork scratchings in the pub.'

'But he's a Muslim, right?'

'Same way that I'm a Christian. I'm in church for funerals and weddings and I've broken most of the Ten Commandments. Kash is third-generation British. He can speak Urdu but that's because his mum and dad insist on it at home. But Kash is . . .' He shrugged, lost for words.

'Well, let's see what he has to say for himself,' said Greene. He indicated a metal box with a phone handset on the top and a coil of wire clipped to the side. 'You'll be carrying the field phone. We'll try to persuade him to take it onto the bus so that we can get negotiations started.' He gestured at a small video camera that had been clipped to his protective jacket, just under his chin. 'I'll be recording everything and the video will be uploaded to Gold Commander in GT Ops so if there's anything you'd rather keep private . . .' He tapped the side of his nose with his finger.

'Thanks for the heads-up,' said Biddulph. The man who

was helping him dress began adjusting the collar that would protect his neck. 'You do this a lot?'

'Suicide bombers? Nope, this is a first for me. To be honest, most of what we do involves old war munitions. Unexploded bombs and the like. And meth labs, we do a lot of them. But since the IRA went quiet we don't have many terrorist-related bombs. We were there on Seven/ Seven, but after the event, obviously.'

'And these suits will protect us, one hundred per cent?'

'There's always a chance that a piece of shrapnel might hit you, but it won't be anywhere vital. You'd be bloody unlucky to get a scratch.'

Biddulph grinned. 'Good to know.'

'It'd be a different story for anyone on the lower level of the bus, though,' said Greene. 'What they usually do with those suicide vests is wrap wire and nails and bolts around the explosive. The actual bang isn't what does the damage, it's the shrapnel. Now you and me, outside the bus, wearing these suits, we'll be fine and dandy. And the passengers on the upper level, they'll mostly be okay. But everyone else – they'll be ripped to shreds.'

Biddulph nodded. 'Got it,' he said.

'So we go in slowly, try to keep him calm. If there's any sense that we're making him agitated, we back away. We don't want to be the trigger for anything happening. If he wants to talk, we tell him to use the phone. We give him the phone, gather intel, then leave.'

'All good,' said Biddulph.

'We won't be using the radios in the suits to talk until we're sure what detonating system he's using, but providing we're close together we should be able to hear each other.'

Biddulph's heart was racing and he took several deep breaths to calm himself down.

Greene grinned and patted him on the shoulder. 'You'll be fine,' he said. 'That Kevlar will stop most things.'

'It's not me I'm worried about,' said Biddulph. 'It's Kash.'

MARBLE ARCH (2.20 p.m.)

The waitress who had been sticking more sheets of newspaper over the window looked at the man in the suicide vest. 'Is that enough?' she asked. 'I can't see any gaps.'

The man peered at the sheets and nodded. 'Get back behind the counter,' he said. 'And, everyone, you need to keep texting. Hashtag ISIS6.'

'Do you want me to text, too?' asked Hassan.

'Sure,' said the man. 'The more the merrier.'

'And what do you expect this texting to do?' asked El-Sayed. 'You think the government cares about texts?'

The man glared at him. 'If there are enough of them, yes.'

'So why do you cover the windows? Isn't it better publicity for the outside world to see what's going on here?'

'Shut the fuck up,' snarled the man.

El-Sayed held up his hands. 'Brother, I am merely curious,' he said. 'You want publicity, you want the world to know what is happening, but you hide behind newspapers.'

'Because there are snipers out there,' said the man. 'And they might be stupid enough to think that if they shoot me in the head the bomb won't go off.'

Something buzzed at the man's stomach and he flinched. El-Sayed's eyes widened in horror, but then he realised it wasn't the vest: it was something in the pack he had around his waist. The man unzipped it and took out a cheap mobile phone. He held it to his ear with his left hand, which meant Hassan had to stand closer to him. Hassan glanced fearfully at his father and El-Sayed smiled, willing the boy to stay calm.

'I don't know. I saw movement at the window, pulled back some of the paper and there was a bomb-disposal woman there. She backed off and now I'm covering the window again.'

There was a pause as the man listened. 'I think she was taking photographs,' he said eventually. 'She had a camera in her hand.'

Another pause, longer this time. 'Okay, okay, I understand.'

A short pause. 'Yes. I understand.'

He put away the phone and looked up at the television screen. It was showing a view of Edgware Road from a helicopter overhead.

'What is the problem?' asked El-Sayed.

'Shahid saw the bomb-disposal woman on TV,' said the man, quietly. 'He wanted to know what was going on.'

'Shahid? Who is Shahid?'

'What's it to you?' said the man, glaring at him again. 'You need to shut the fuck up.'

'Brother, if someone is organising this, if there is a man in charge, then maybe I should talk to him.'

'Maybe you should shut the fuck up. Maybe that's what you should do.'

'Brother, please, stay calm. We have never met before,

we are strangers, we don't know each other, but there is a very good chance that I might be able to help you. But for that to happen, I need to talk with the man in charge. This Shahid. Can you call him back?'

The man shook his head. 'I can't call out on this phone. He can only call me.'

El-Sayed nodded thoughtfully. 'Then we must wait for him to call you again. But when he does, I beg you, let me speak with him.'

LAMBETH CENTRAL COMMUNICATIONS COMMAND CENTRE (2.30 p.m.)

'We have a match on the man in the Kensington childcare centre,' said Waterman. 'Not one hundred per cent but it looks good to me.'

Kamran walked over to the MI5 officer and stood behind her. On the middle screen there were two photographs, one taken from outside the nursery as the children were being released, the other a full-face picture taken from either a driving licence or a passport. The man was black, his head shaved. In the CCTV image he was tall and thin, probably over six feet, his runner's physique covered with a parka. In the head-and-shoulders shot he had a gaunt face with dark patches under his eyes.

'Mohamed Osman, born in Somalia, came over with his parents nine years ago. They were all granted British citizenship in 2011. Osman is Muslim but relaxed about it. Doesn't attend a mosque that we know of, no fundamentalist leanings that we know of, has a job as a courier. Never been abroad.'

'So why is he known to you?' asked Kamran.

'He isn't,' said Waterman. 'He's on the Police National Computer. He was accused of rape two years ago. An underage Somalian girl claimed he'd raped her in the back of his van. There was no physical evidence, he had an alibi, and eventually the girl dropped the charges.'

'But nothing terrorism-related?' asked Kamran.

'Definitely not,' said Waterman. 'A true cleanskin. He's come out of nowhere.'

Kamran rubbed his chin thoughtfully. 'So we've got four Pakistani Brits and one Somalian Brit. No connections between them, except that today they've decided to become suicide bombers.'

Murray smiled thinly. 'Strictly speaking, they only become suicide bombers when they press the trigger. Until then they're just terrorists.'

'We can't link Osman to any Pakistanis, never mind the ones wearing suicide vests today,' said Waterman. 'He's always stayed within his own community, so far as we know.'

'So who the hell has put this together?' asked Kamran. 'Why would a Somalian with no apparent interest in fundamentalism be willing to kill himself to get ISIS terrorists released?'

Waterman and Murray shrugged. Kamran sighed in exasperation. Asking the questions was easy. It was getting answers that was driving him to distraction.

'This is probably a dumb thing to say, but is there any significance that so many of them are called Mohammed?' asked Murray.

'It's the most common name in the UK for male newborns,' said Waterman. 'Has been for some time. There are various ways to spell it, but put them all together and it's the most popular name by far.'

'It's the tradition for Muslim families to name their boys Mohammed,' said Kamran. 'The vast majority don't use it in everyday life, but it's on all their official documents. I'm quite unusual in that my parents always used it. They still do. I got called Mo at school but at home I'm still Mohammed and always will be to my mum. But the answer to your question, Alex, is no. It's just an indication that they're Muslim, nothing more.'

Waterman transferred the picture of Osman to the screen where she had lined up the photographs of the six bombers they had already identified. Kamran stared at the faces on his screen. Mohammed Malik. Ismail Hussain. Mohamed Osman. Rabeel Bhashir. Mohammed Faisal Chaudhry. Four British Pakistanis. One Somalian. And Kashif Talpur, an undercover cop. One middle-aged, the rest relatively young. Six men with no obvious link between them, other than that they had chosen that day to put on suicide vests and hold the city to ransom. There had to be a connection, but he couldn't for the life of him figure out what it was. Someone had brought the six of them together, trained them, equipped them, and dropped them off at their present locations. There had to be a link between the men, and that link would lead to whoever was behind it.

Sergeant Lumley's phone rang and he answered it. 'Your negotiator is here,' he said to Waterman.

'I'll go and get him,' said the MI5 officer. She left the Gold Command suite and returned a few minutes later with a man in his mid-sixties with a close-cropped grey beard. He was wearing an expensive suit with a sombre tie and a perfectly starched white shirt, though his hair was in disarray and he was patting it down with his left hand. In his right he was carrying a slim leather briefcase. 'This is Chris Thatcher,' said Waterman, and Kamran shook his hand, catching a glimpse of gold cufflinks.

'Sorry if I seem a bit flustered,' said Thatcher. 'They put me on the back of a high-powered motorbike and whizzed me through the streets at something like a hundred miles an hour.' He grinned. 'That's what it felt like, anyhow.'

'Can I get you a coffee?' asked Kamran.

'Caffeine is the last thing I need right now,' said Thatcher. 'But I'd love a camomile tea.'

'I'll get it,' said Lumley, heading out of the suite.

Thatcher looked out over the special operations room appreciatively. 'This is impressive,' he said. 'You're getting live CCTV feeds from around the city?'

'Everywhere we can,' said Kamran.

'We've been watching it on TV at Thames House. One hell of a day.'

'And it's getting worse by the minute,' said Kamran. He gestured at a chair. 'Make yourself comfortable while I bring you up to speed.'

WANDSWORTH (2.45 p.m.)

'Sami, I really have to go to the toilet,' said Zoe. She was jiggling from foot to foot. 'I'm going to piss myself.'

'There's nothing I can do,' said Malik. 'Sorry.'

'You want to be handcuffed to someone who's wet themselves?'

'You can pee on the floor.'

'Then it'll spread everywhere. Ask them for a bucket or something.'

'What?'

'A bucket. I'll pee in a bucket. And the kids need something to eat and drink.' She nodded at the changing rooms. The two toddlers had been crying non-stop for the past fifteen minutes and no amount of shouting from Malik had quietened them down. 'That's why they're crying, Malik. Kids cry when they're hungry. You said they've got until six to free the prisoners. That's more than three hours. Do you want kids crying for the next three hours?'

Malik bit his lower lip. She was right. The crying was doing his head in and it was getting worse. 'Okay, okay,' he said. 'Come on.' He pulled the chain and they walked slowly towards the shop entrance. 'Jamie?' he shouted. 'Jamie, are you there?'

'I'm here, Sami,' shouted the negotiator. He sounded far away, at the other end of the shopping centre, maybe. 'Do you want me to come over?'

'No, stay where you are. There's a girl here who needs to go to the toilet. You have to get me a bucket or something.'

'Okay, Sami, I can do that.'

'And there are two kids. They need food. And something to drink.'

'How old are the kids?'

'I don't know. Young.'

'They're two and a half!' shouted the woman in the changing room.

'Two and a half,' repeated Malik.

'I'll get something fixed up. What about you, Sami? Are you hungry?'

'No.'

'I could bring a pizza or something.'

'I don't want a fucking pizza!' shouted Malik.

'I could eat pizza,' said the woman in the changing room.

'We're not here to eat fucking pizza!' yelled Malik.

'It's almost three o'clock and I haven't had any lunch.'

Malik groaned. 'Jamie, send in a pizza as well.'

'No pineapple,' shouted the woman. 'I hate pineapple.'

Malik muttered under his breath. 'No pineapple on the pizza, Jamie. A bucket. And something for the kids. That's all.'

'I'll get it sorted, Sami,' shouted the policeman.

'And I want some fags,' said the woman in the changing room. 'I'm gasping.'

'You can't smoke in here,' said Zoe.

'I need a fucking cigarette, darling,' said the woman.

'He's got explosives strapped to him and you want to light a cigarette?' Zoe looked at Malik and shook her head in disgust. 'Some people, huh?'

LAMBETH CENTRAL COMMUNICATIONS COMMAND CENTRE (3 p.m.)

'Chief Superintendent Philip Gillard is on his way up,' said Sergeant Lumley. 'SO15.'

'Finally,' said Kamran. Acting as Gold Commander had

been challenging but it had been the most stressful few hours of his life and he was looking forward to handing over the reins. He went out to the special operations room and met the chief superintendent at the entrance. Gillard was wearing a dark blue suit with a red and black striped tie, his black hair glistening as if it had been gelled. He was wearing black-framed spectacles and carrying a scuffed leather briefcase, and looked for all the world as if he had arrived to sell them life insurance. He shook hands with Kamran. His fingers were stained with nicotine and there was a wedding band on his left hand.

'We've not met before, but I was at a presentation you gave on major incident procedure last year at Hendon,' said Gillard. 'It was good stuff.'

'Thank you,' said Kamran.

'This is our first time, so a few ground rules. When it's just the two of us I'm Philip, or boss or governor, if you prefer. You're Mohammed, right?'

'Mo is fine,' said Kamran.

'So when it's just the two of us I'll call you Mo, if that's okay with you. In front of the troops we use our ranks.'

'Sounds good,' said Kamran.

'So what do I do desk-wise?'

'We're in the Gold Command suite,' said Kamran. He took Gillard through to the room. 'This is the Gold Commander's station.' He pointed at the desk he had been using.

'What about you?'

'I'll take this one,' said Kamran, gesturing at the work-station to the right of the Gold Commander's. 'Sergeant Lumley has been assisting me and is using that desk.'

Lumley nodded. 'Sir,' he said.

Chris Thatcher was sitting opposite Sergeant Lumley, studying a CCTV feed of the Wandsworth shop.

'Bloody hell – Chris Thatcher!' Gillard exclaimed.

Thatcher's jaw dropped. 'Phil?' He stood up and the two men embraced and patted each other on the back. 'Must be, what, fifteen years?'

'More like twenty,' said the chief superintendent. He released his grip on Thatcher. 'Chris and I were in the Flying Squad in the nineties,' he said. 'Snatcher Thatcher he was known as then.'

'Chief Inspector Thatcher, actually,' said Thatcher. He grinned. 'And I seem to remember you being just a sergeant at the time, so a little respect is in order.'

'Chris is a security consultant, these days,' said Kamran. 'He was over at Thames House so we've just pulled him in.'

Lynne Waterman stood up and introduced herself. Gillard shook hands with her, then swung his briefcase onto the desk, hung his jacket over the back of his chair and sat down. He steepled his fingers under his chin. 'Right, Mo, bring me up to speed.'

Kamran spoke for the best part of fifteen minutes and the chief superintendent didn't interrupt once. He nodded, he smiled occasionally, but most of the time he remained impassive as Kamran went through what had happened and detailed who was doing what in the special operations room.

'Looks as if you've got everything on an even keel,' said Gillard, when Kamran had finished.

'There's one wrinkle,' said Kamran. 'The only point of

contact we have is this guy Shahid and he'll only talk to me. That's why Chris is here. I'm not trained in negotiation and his skill set will be helpful.'

'How does Shahid get in touch?'

'He calls my mobile.'

Gillard frowned. 'How did that come about?' he said. 'Protocol is to make contact through a landline and record.'

'He came through to the SOR, and after our first conversation he said he'd only talk to me. He insisted on a mobile number.'

The chief superintendent grimaced. 'That's unfortunate.'

'I agree, but he was adamant.'

'And he said he'll only talk to you?'

Kamran nodded.

'Why do you think that is? Because you're a Muslim?'

'I don't think so. If anything, he seemed perturbed by the fact I was Muslim. He was asking all sorts of questions about how often I prayed, stuff like that. In fact he was so busy interrogating me that we managed to get a location of the mobile he was using.'

'That was when the van got shot up?'

'Unfortunate. They heard a car backfire.'

Gillard rubbed his chin. 'Right. A few basic necessities I need before I get stuck in. I'm a smoker. I'm guessing the front of the building is out of bounds.'

'There's a terrace outside the canteen on the third floor,' said Kamran. 'Most of the smokers gather there.'

'And how do we go about getting coffee here?'

'Sergeant Lumley can fix you up,' said Kamran. 'But the canteen is open twenty-four/seven.'

Gillard smiled at the sergeant. 'White, two sugars. And

if there are any biscuits going, I'd be a very happy bunny.'

Lumley headed out.

'He's good?' asked Gillard.

'First class,' said Kamran.

'So here's how we'll play it,' said Gillard. 'I'm Gold Commander, but you stick close to me and we'll share the load. I get the feeling this is going to get worse before it gets better. When Shahid calls, you answer and you talk to him. But talk to our tech boys and see if we can get the conversations recorded. I'd also like to listen in when you're on to him. And so should Chris, obviously.'

'I'll get that sorted.'

'When you spoke to him, what were your impressions?'

'He's organised. Confident. He knows what he's doing. He asked for Gold Commander and it was his suggestion to release the kids in the childcare centre, as if he knew that was what I was going to ask for.'

'But the fact you were a Muslim threw him?'

'I think so. He wasn't expecting it.'

'And what about his voice? What could you tell?'

'Do you mean could I tell if he was a Muslim? Not from his accent. South London, maybe. Essex. Twenties or thirties. Well educated.'

'Why do you say that?'

'His vocabulary. His manner. There was no real emotion during the conversation. Like I said, there was a confidence about him. He seemed totally unfazed by what was happening.'

'Okay, so what were you planning to do next?'

'To be honest, I was waiting for him to call. I don't see that we gain anything by negotiating with the bombers themselves. I don't think the individuals on the ground have any negotiating power. They're just the tools. Even if we do talk to them, I don't think there's anything they can do.'

'And the guys on the ground? How are we getting on ID-wise?'

'Fairly good progress on that front,' said Kamran. 'I'll pull up the guys we've identified.'

Kamran sat down and tapped on the keyboard. Gillard stood behind him. Kamran called up six photographs on his left-hand screen and he pointed at them one by one. 'Rabeel Bhashir is in the church in Brixton. Mohammed Malik is in the shop in the Southside shopping centre in Wandsworth. Ismail Hussain is in the Fulham post office. Mohamed Osman is in the Kensington nursery. Faisal Chaudhry is in the pub in Marylebone. All are cleanskins, pretty much. Never red-flagged as terrorist threats in this country, no evidence of ISIS membership.'

'And this one?' asked Gillard, pointing to the final photo-graph.

'I'm saving the best till last,' said Kamran. 'He's a cop. An undercover cop with the National Crime Agency.'

TAVISTOCK SQUARE (3.02 p.m.)

As soon as they got within twenty feet of the bus, Biddulph could see that it was Kashif Talpur. There was no question about it. There was also no doubt that he was wearing a suicide vest packed with explosives. 'What the fuck are you playing at, Kash?' Biddulph muttered to himself.

Talpur was standing next to the driver and on his left side was a woman who had clearly been crying earlier on but now had a blank look on her face as if she had emotionally shut down. The woman's right hand was chained to Talpur's left and in his right Talpur was holding what was obviously the trigger for the vest.

Greene stopped and Biddulph almost bumped into him. He moved to Greene's right side. Both men slowly raised their hands to show that they weren't armed. 'Kash! It's me, Mark!' shouted Biddulph.

There was no reaction from Talpur, though several of the passengers had already spotted them and were peering through the windows. Biddulph realised that his voice wasn't carrying through the helmet.

'Kash!' he shouted, louder this time, but there was still no reaction. He was side on to them, saying something to the driver. Biddulph looked at the upper floor of the bus. Two black schoolboys were looking down at him. And further along he saw a young mother cradling a baby and rocking back and forth.

Biddulph began to remove his helmet but Greene realised what he was doing, put a hand on his shoulder and shook his head. 'No way,' said Greene.

'I have to talk to him,' said Biddulph.

'That's what the phone's for,' said Greene.

'I've known Kash for years,' said Biddulph. 'There's something not right about this.'

As he was speaking, Talpur turned and spotted them. Biddulph saw the man's mouth open and close but he couldn't hear anything. He picked up the field phone with his left hand, held it up and pointed at it with his right, but that seemed to make Talpur even more agitated

'I have to talk to him face to face,' said Biddulph. 'He can't see who I am with the helmet on and he can't hear a word I'm saying.'

'If you take your helmet off and he detonates . . .'

'If he was going to detonate, surely he'd have done it already.'

'Your call,' said Greene. 'But it'll be on your head.' He grinned. 'No pun intended.'

Biddulph put the phone down, straightened up, then slowly removed his helmet. It snagged on something and Greene had to help him wiggle it off. As soon as the helmet came free, Biddulph heard Talpur screaming at him: 'Get the fuck away! Both of you!'

Biddulph put the helmet down next to the field phone. Greene was using the digital camera on video mode.

Biddulph held up his hands and took a step towards the bus. 'Kash, it's me, Mark!'

'Fuck off!' shouted Talpur. 'Just get the fuck away before we all die!'

Biddulph took another step towards the bus. 'Kash, mate, whatever the problem is, we can talk it through. I'm here to help.'

Talpur said something to the driver and a few seconds later the door rattled open. Talpur stood in the doorway, glaring at Biddulph. 'Listen to me and listen to me good!' he shouted. 'You coming here is putting everyone at risk. Do you not understand that? You need to go away – get the hell away from here – because if you don't this vest will go off and everyone dies.' He turned and spoke to the driver and the door closed.

'Looks like he doesn't want to talk,' said Greene. 'But leave the phone where it is, in case he changes his mind.'

Biddulph picked up his helmet and the coil of wire attached to the field phone. The two men walked back to the cordon with Biddulph playing out the wire behind him.

LAMBETH CENTRAL COMMUNICATIONS COMMAND CENTRE (3.04 p.m.)

Sergeant Lumley stood up and waved over at Kamran. 'ISIS have just posted a propaganda video on YouTube, claiming responsibility for what's happening,' he said. 'Dozens of fundamentalist Twitter accounts are now tweeting about it.'

'Can you put it up on the big screen?' asked Kamran.

'No problem,' said the sergeant. He tapped on his keyboard and the YouTube main page appeared on the screen. Kamran stood up and Gillard joined him.

Shahid was dressed in black and was wearing a black ski mask. Behind him was the black and white flag of the Islamic State of Iraq and Syria. He stood with his arms folded. 'ISIS is prepared to do whatever is necessary to force the British government to release the ISIS fighters it is currently holding in Belmarsh Prison,' he said.

The flag disappeared and was replaced with a view of an Iraqi street. A man was walking towards an American checkpoint while soldiers in desert camouflage aimed their weapons at him. Shahid was obviously standing in front of a green screen and the image was being superimposed behind him. He pointed at the man and as he did so he exploded and the checkpoint was destroyed.

'ISIS suicide bombers are now in place at nine locations around London,' said Shahid.

The suicide-bomber footage was replaced with a TV news shot of the Brixton church where the first bomber had struck.

'There is an ISIS warrior at this church, and if the six ISIS freedom fighters are not released by this evening, the warrior will destroy the church and everyone in it.' On cue, the church exploded.

Kamran flinched even though he knew it was only a CGI special effect.

A map appeared on screen with nine cartoon bombs dotted around the capital, marking the location of the suicide bombers. 'Other warriors are around the city, ready to give their lives in order to force the government to release the ISIS prisoners,' said Shahid, folding his arms.

The background became a rapid series of images of the effects of the Seven/Seven bombings in London – images of bodies on stretchers being carried from Underground stations, of damaged Tube carriages and the bus blown apart in Tavistock Square.

The camera went in close on Shahid's mask. 'What happens next is in the hands of the prime minister,' he said. 'If he releases the ISIS Six, lives will be saved and he will have proven himself to be the better man. But if he insists on unjustly imprisoning the ISIS warriors, his citizens will die. He knows what needs to be done.' Shahid raised a clenched gloved fist above his head. '*Allahu Akbar!*' he said. 'Allah be praised.' The screen went black and then the ISIS flag appeared, wreathed in flames. It stayed on the screen for almost a minute as background chants of '*Allahu Akbar*' grew louder and louder.

'Two hundred thousand hits already,' said Gillard, as the video came to an end. He looked at Lumley. 'Can we talk to YouTube and get them to take it down?'

'I can make the call, but even if we get them to take it down it'll be copied and back up within minutes,' said the sergeant. He peered at his computer screen. 'It's already on five other sites. Make that six.'

'They really know how to use social media,' said Kamran. 'Videos of beheadings, video tutorials on how to sign up and what life is like as an ISIS soldier, all professionally done.'

'They shouldn't be allowed to post inflammatory videos like that,' said Gillard.

'Almost impossible to stop, unfortunately,' said Kamran.

'Twitter's going crazy with it,' said Lumley. 'Hundreds of retweets of the video URL. And they're growing exponentially.'

'Bastard,' muttered Gillard, under his breath. 'He's got us by the short and curlies and he knows it.'

MARBLE ARCH (3.07 p.m.)

One of the baristas raised his hand. He was in his twenties, olive-skinned with a carefully tended goatee beard.

'What?' snarled the man in the suicide vest. 'What do you want?'

'I need to use the bathroom.'

'Where is it?'

The barista pointed at a door opposite the end of the counter. 'I really need to go.'

'Then go,' said the man. 'But leave the door open.'

The barista smiled his thanks and dashed to the toilet. One of the men sitting at the table behind El-Sayed also raised his hand. 'I need to go, too.'

'You can take it in turns,' said the man. 'But don't even think about fucking with me.' He raised his right hand above his head and opened his palm so that they could all see the metal trigger attached to the black Velcro strap. 'Anybody tries anything, I press this and we all die!' he shouted.

'Nobody wants to die here today,' said El-Sayed, calmly.

'And nobody has to,' said the man. 'So long as they release the ISIS prisoners.'

'But what if they do not, my friend? Will you kill us all?'

'I will,' said the man.

'And what will that achieve?'

The man frowned. 'What do you mean?'

'If you don't get what you want, and we all die, who benefits? Do you? No, you are dead.' He waved an arm around the café. 'Do we? No, we are also dead. Have the ISIS fighters benefited? No, they are still in prison. So who benefits?'

'They will do as they are told,' snapped the man. 'They will not allow so many hostages to die.' He nodded at the television. The shot was of a studio with two newsreaders, a middle-aged man with blow-dried greying hair and a young Asian girl, talking to each other in front of a map of London on which had been marked the locations of the suicide bombers. 'They cannot possibly allow that many bombs to go off across London.'

El-Sayed shrugged. 'Maybe. Or maybe not. Do you think this government cares about individual citizens? About me? Or my son?' He sneered. 'Of course they don't. Look around you, brother. How many white faces do you see? We are all Arab, Asian and African in this part of London. You think they care about the likes of us? You chose the wrong place to attack, brother.'

The man stared at him but didn't answer. He jumped as the phone in his waistpack buzzed.

El-Sayed pointed at the waistpack. 'If that is Shahid, then I must speak with him.'

'He won't talk to anyone. Just me.' He fumbled for the zip.

'He will want to talk to me, brother. Trust me on that.'

The man took his phone out of his waistpack with his left hand and put it to his ear. He mumbled into the phone, listened and mumbled again.

El-Sayed waved for the phone. 'Let me speak to him,' he said.

The man on the phone flashed him an angry look. 'Shut up!' he said.

'Tell him I want to speak with him. Tell him I will make it worth his while.'

The man turned his back on El-Sayed and continued to mumble into the phone. El-Sayed stood up. His son shook his head frantically. 'Dad, sit down! You'll get us all killed.'

'I must talk to Shahid,' said El-Sayed. He stepped forward and put his hand on the man's shoulder. The man yelped and whirled around, his thumb on the trigger. The baristas screamed and dropped behind the counter.

El-Sayed immediately released his grip on the man and stepped back, his hands in the air. 'Brother, I just need to talk to Shahid. I mean you no harm.'

'Stay away from me or we all die!' shouted the man.

'I understand,' said El-Sayed, quietly. He sat down and folded his arms.

The man put the phone back to his ear and gritted his teeth as he listened, barely able to contain his anger. 'Someone keeps saying he wants to talk to you. One of the hostages. He insists.' He listened again and nodded. 'He is the father of the man I have handcuffed myself to. An Arab.'

'I am Lebanese,' said El-Sayed.

'He's Lebanese,' said the man.

'Tell Shahid I can help,' said El-Sayed.

The man glared at El-Sayed but then he repeated the message to Shahid. He listened, then handed the phone to El-Sayed. 'Shahid says he will talk to you.'

El-Sayed took a deep breath to compose himself, then put the phone to his ear. '*As-salamu alaykum,*' he said. Peace be upon you. The Arabic greeting that was used around the world.

'I do not have much time,' said the voice at the other end of the line. 'What do you want?'

'My name is Imad El-Sayed. You are Shahid, yes?'

'What do you want, Imad El-Sayed? As you can imagine, I am busy just now.'

'I want you to return my son to me.'

'The best way to achieve that is to call for the government to release our six brothers in Belmarsh. If they are released then everyone can go home.'

'Killing my son, my only son, will not help you in the fight against the infidel. But there is perhaps something I could do to help you.'

'I doubt that.'

'At least let me try,' said El-Sayed. 'Shahid, my friend, I wish you well in your struggle, I really do.'

'You are not my friend. And you are wasting your breath.'

'Shahid, we are on the same side here. I am the same as you. I want what you want.'

'I doubt that,' said Shahid.

'Do you know what *hawala* is, brother?'

'I'm not stupid,' snapped Shahid. 'Of course I know what *hawala* is.'

'I do not mean to be patronising, brother,' said El-Sayed, 'but perhaps you are not aware that I am one of the largest *hawala* brokers in London.'

'So?'

'So I am a big supporter of Al-Qaeda. One of the biggest.'

'I'm nothing to do with Al-Qaeda.'

'I understand that,' said El-Sayed, hurriedly. 'But we are in the same fight here.'

'The same fight? What do you mean? What fight?'

'The fight against the infidel,' said El-Sayed. 'Brother, please listen to me. Listen to me and listen well. I am on your side. We are fighting the same fight. I helped to fund the glorious attacks in London on the seventh of July 2005.'

'Bullshit.'

'I am telling the truth, brother. I used my own funds. And even this very morning I moved money to Syria to help the fight there. Somalia, too. I am on your side, brother, you need to understand that.'

'You are a money man, that's all.'

'I am more than that, brother. Much more.'

'Bullshit.'

'I am telling you the truth, brother. We are fighting the same fight. We are on the same side.'

'I don't believe you.'

'You must, brother, for it is the truth, may Allah strike me dead if I lie. I move donations from London to ISIS in Syria and Iraq. And I move funds for ISIS into this country.'

'What funds?'

'You do not know, brother? ISIS is the richest terrorist organisation in history. They make more than two million dollars a day from the oil fields they control. They make millions from ransoms, they raid banks in the territories they take over. They tax all businesses that operate in their lands. And they are selling antiquities they seize. They used to destroy them but I persuaded them to get them out of the country and sell them in Europe. Brother, ISIS is worth billions and I play a part in moving their money around the world. Tell me, brother, you have heard of Jihadi John, surely?'

'Of course,' said Shahid.

'Well, I have supported Jihadi John, and the North London Boys, from the start. Financially and with advice and contacts. I have helped them send jihadists from London to Somalia and Syria. Hundreds of fighters. I am on your side, brother. I am fighting the good fight with you.'

There was a long silence.

'Are you there, brother?' asked El-Sayed, eventually.

'There is nothing I can do,' said the man.

'There is, brother. You can allow us to cut my son free. Your man can simply walk out of here. Or I can find someone else to take my son's place.'

'Why should I agree to that? One hostage is the same as the next.'

'Exactly,' said El-Sayed. 'It doesn't matter who you use as a hostage. So why not let my son go and use someone else?'

'Why would I do that?'

'Because we are on the same side, brother. We both want the same thing.'

'If that is true, you should be proud of your son's contribution to the struggle.'

'My son can fight in other ways, *inshallah*. He can help me with fundraising and financing. He is already doing that, brother. He is more useful working for me as a *hawaladar*.'

'I don't think so,' said Shahid. 'I have wasted enough of my time talking to you.'

'Wait, please,' said El-Sayed. 'How about this? How about I contribute to your fight?'

'Contribute in what way?' asked Shahid.

'Money,' said El-Sayed. 'All the money you need. Delivered to you or your people, anywhere in the world. All I ask is that you release my son.'

'How much were you thinking?' asked Shahid.

'A hundred thousand pounds?'

Shahid laughed harshly. 'You insult me,' he said.

'How much, then?' asked El-Sayed. 'How much for my son?'

'How much is he worth to you?' asked Shahid.

'He is the world to me,' said El-Sayed. 'He is my only son.'

'And yet you insult him by offering so little?'

El-Sayed mopped his sweating brow with a handkerchief. 'A million,' he said. 'A million pounds.'

'Five million,' said Shahid.

'Five million?' repeated El-Sayed.

'It is up to you,' said Shahid. 'If your son is not worth five million pounds then I am wasting my time talking to you.'

'Yes, okay, yes. Five million. Yes.'

'You will transfer the money for me now?'

'Yes. Yes, I will.'

'I shall phone you back,' said Shahid. The line went dead.

LAMBETH CENTRAL COMMUNICATIONS COMMAND CENTRE (3.10 p.m.)

Kamran put down the phone, amazed. 'Well. Inspector Biddulph is on the spot and he confirms that Kashif Talpur is on the bus. Unbelievable.'

'Has he spoken to him?' asked Chief Superintendent Gillard.

'He's tried but as soon as he gets anywhere near the bus Talpur starts shouting that they're all going to die. They shot some video close up and they'll send it over. There's a field phone near the bus now but no one expects him to use it. Oh, and there are children on the bus. Two school-kids and a baby.'

Gillard shook his head. 'How the hell does something like this happen? How do we end up with a suicide bomber working on the Met? What the hell's going on with human resources? Don't they look for signs that something's not right?'

'Inspector Biddulph said that Talpur was as straight as a die. Never put a foot wrong. And certainly wasn't a fundamentalist. I'm checking to see if his family is okay. Give me a minute.' He picked up a phone, rang through to Inspector Adams and asked him to come through to the Gold Command suite. Adams was there within a minute and Kamran introduced him to the chief superintendent. 'Any joy with Talpur's nearest and dearest?' asked Kamran.

'All present and accounted for,' said Adams. 'His parents run a shop out in Southall and they're both fine. His sister is a nurse and she's halfway through her shift, one brother is at university and the other's at school.'

'And we've had sight of all of them?' asked Gillard. 'There's no possibility of coercion?'

Adams nodded. 'They've all been spoken to, face to face. They're fine. And none of them believe that it's him. He's shown no signs of fundamentalist leanings, not one.'

'Maybe he just did a great job of hiding it,' said Gillard. 'He's an undercover agent. That's what he's good at.'

'But it doesn't make sense, boss,' said Kamran. 'If you were ISIS or Al-Qaeda or whoever these guys are, and you had an asset like Talpur, you'd use him to your best advantage. You'd walk him into a police station or even Scotland Yard with a vest and you'd take out a dozen or so top cops. Why waste him on a bus?'

The chief superintendent lowered his head and looked

at Kamran over the top of his spectacles. 'Bloody hell, Mo, I hope you don't ever go rogue on us.'

Inspector Adams chuckled but stopped as soon as Gillard turned to him. 'What do you think, Inspector?' asked Gillard.

'You wonder why he won't talk to his governor,' said Adams. 'If he's gone fundamentalist, wouldn't he want to say something? Make a statement?'

Gillard nodded. 'There's something very wrong about this, that's for sure.' He turned back to Kamran. 'So, that's six accounted for. Three to go. What's the situation with the one at Marble Arch?'

'It's a coffee shop and he's plastered the window with newspapers. There's no CCTV footage of the inside of the premises and nothing usable outside.'

'There's CCTV all along that part of Edgware Road, especially around Paddington Green,' said Gillard. 'It's long been known as a terrorist hot-spot – they even call it Little Arabia.'

'There are cameras aplenty but he had his head down or turned away as he entered the shop. We have footage of the van dropping him off, but nothing to help with facial recognition. I asked the Silver Commander to see if they can get someone from the Bomb Squad to get close and take pictures. They did, but the quality isn't great so we're getting the pictures tweaked as we speak. We do know that there are at least fifteen hostages in the coffee shop.'

'And the MP in Camberwell?'

'Some decent shots taken inside the surgery by the hostages so we're hopeful we'll get something soon,' said Kamran.

'And the restaurant in Southwark?'

'Some clear council CCTV footage. If he's in the system, hopefully we'll find him.'

'That's the problem,' said Waterman. 'They're cleanskins. Not one of them was regarded as a threat.'

'And what about links between them?' Gillard asked. 'Please tell me there's something. A mosque, a website, a school they went to, a sport they all did, something that brought them together.'

'There's nothing so far,' said the MI5 agent. 'We can't connect any two of them, never mind find a common denominator.'

'But there has to be something, doesn't there? This can't be random. It just can't be.'

WANDSWORTH (3.15 p.m.)

The toddlers were taking it in turns to cry. One would bawl for a minute or so, then stop and the other would take over without skipping a beat. Malik had given up asking the mother to quieten the kids because all he got in return was a torrent of abuse. He looked at his watch for the hundredth time, wondering what was taking the negotiator so long. They were in a shopping centre, for fuck's sake. How hard could it be to get a pizza, a bucket and some food?

'Sami, are you there?' Clarke was calling from outside.

Malik smiled to himself. Where the fuck did the cop think he'd gone? 'Yeah, I'm not going anywhere!' he shouted back.

'I've got the stuff you wanted. I'll walk along and leave it outside the store and you can get it.'

'You think I'm stupid? If I come out there, they'll shoot me.'

'No one's going to shoot you, Sami. Not while you're wearing that vest.'

'You lot shot that Brazilian electrician on the Tube, remember? You thought he was a suicide bomber and you shot him.'

'That was a mistake,' said Clarke. 'Lessons were learnt. No one is going to shoot you, Sami. You have my word.'

'Yeah, well, your word's not worth much, truth be told,' said Malik. 'Bring it to the entrance and push it inside. Then walk away.'

'Sure, I can do that,' said the negotiator. Malik and Zoe backed away from the door. A couple of minutes later they heard a soft footfall and Clarke appeared holding a bucket on top of which were two pizza boxes, some crisps, fruit and bottles of water and fruit juice. 'Is everything okay?' asked Clarke.

'Just bring the stuff in and put it down,' said Malik. 'Don't even think about trying something.'

'I'm not going to be trying anything, Sami,' said Clarke. 'We just want everyone to walk away from this safe and well. No one is going to put you under any pressure. We just want to help you.'

'You do like to talk, don't you?' sneered Malik. 'Just put the stuff down and go.'

Clarke bent down slowly and placed everything on the floor, then straightened, holding up his hands, fingers splayed. 'If you want anything else, just shout,' he said. 'We're not far away.'

'We won't want anything else,' said Malik.

'What about the children?'

'What about them?'

'Just let the kids go. This is no place for kids, you know that.'

'They're hostages, and all the hostages have to stay put,' said Malik.

'They're kids.'

'Look, mate, the best thing you can do is to tell your bosses that the sooner they release the prisoners in Belmarsh the sooner everyone gets to go home. Now fuck off.' He waved the trigger in his right hand to emphasise the point.

'No problem, Sami. Just shout if you want anything else.' Clarke backed away a few steps, then turned and headed down the centre.

Malik and Zoe went over to the pile. Malik picked up the pizza box with the rest of the food and drink, while Zoe grabbed the bucket. They walked together to the changing rooms. There were three girls in one, and the mother with the two crying kids was in the other with the second shop assistant. Malik gave the snacks and the drinks to the woman with the children, and one of the pizzas. He gave the other pizza to the three girls but they put it on the floor, unopened.

'Where's the smokes?' asked the mother.

'They wouldn't let us have cigarettes,' lied Malik.

'Bastards,' said the woman. She unscrewed the cap from a bottle of orange juice and gave it to one of the children, a bottle of water to the other. They stopped crying as she opened the pizza box and shoved a piece into her mouth.

Malik took Zoe back into the shop. She was still holding

the bucket. 'I'm sorry, I can't undo the cuffs,' he said. 'I can look the other way, if that helps.'

'Over there,' she said, nodding at a circular rack full of items on sale. 'I can duck inside and do it.'

'Are you sure?'

'Can you think of anything else? Because I can't and I'm fucking bursting.'

LAMBETH CENTRAL COMMUNICATIONS COMMAND CENTRE (3.20 p.m.)

Virtually everyone in the special operations room was watching the woman squat over the bucket in the shop. The CCTV camera was looking down on her so gave a full view of what was taking place, even though the man she was chained to couldn't see her through the rack of clothes.

'Take it down, Joe,' said Gillard. Sergeant Lumley tapped on his keyboard. The CCTV feed disappeared from the large screen and was replaced by the scene outside the childcare centre in Kensington. 'Mo, did we know this was happening?' asked Gillard.

'Inspector Edwards is Silver and he didn't mention it,' said Kamran.

'Have a word, will you?' said Gillard. 'Explain to him the error of his ways.'

'Joe, get me Inspector Edwards ASAP,' said Kamran, as he walked back to his desk. He sat down and stared at his screens as he waited for Lumley to put Edwards through.

'Line three,' said Lumley.

Kamran picked up the receiver and pressed the flashing button to take the call. 'Ross, what's happening there? We've just seen one of your people delivering food.'

'Yes, sir. One of the hostages needed to use the bathroom and they wanted something to eat.'

'That's not SOP, Ross,' said Kamran. 'You should know that. You told me you were going to use the phone.'

'It was the negotiator's idea,' said Edwards. 'He said we should initiate contact at the earliest opportunity. He did that and commenced negotiations.'

'And if it had been a ploy to get a senior officer up close so that he could be killed in the blast, what then?' asked Kamran. The inspector didn't reply. 'Who's leading the negotiating team?'

'A guy called Jamie Clarke. He seems to know what he's doing.'

'Ross, you're Silver Commander there. You're in charge. You need to explain to this Clarke that a suicide bomber is a different scenario from a man with a knife or a gun. You don't send in an officer to talk face to face. The way to establish contact would be to call the in-store number. Or, if that doesn't work, to see if they'll accept a landline. But anyone who approaches the line of fire needs to be in full ABS gear.'

'Understood, sir. Sorry.'

'Not a problem, Ross. But you need to keep us informed in the SOR before you make contact again.'

'Yes, sir.'

'Now, did your contact produce any intel? Anything at all that might be useful?'

'Unfortunately not, sir. Oh, he uses the name Sami.'

'Sami? We have him as Mohammed Malik.'

'That's right, sir, but he said his middle name was Sami and that's the name he goes by.'

'That's good to know. Thank you.'

'Sir? I'm not a hundred per cent sure what I should be doing next.'

'You're doing just fine,' said Kamran. 'The centre is evacuated, right? You have the area contained? Armed police are on the scene?'

'Yes, sir.'

'Then that's all good,' said Kamran. 'Now we wait and see what their next move is. In the meantime, your priority is to keep your people out of harm's way.' He put down the phone and went over to Gillard, who was standing behind Chris Thatcher, watching a video on the left-hand screen. It took Kamran several seconds to realise what they were looking at. It was a jerky view of the bus in Tavistock Square. The vehicle seemed to be swinging from side to side so the camera must have been attached to the bomb-disposal man's jacket. Talpur was standing at the front of the bus, beside the driver, handcuffed to a female passenger. He was screaming and swearing, his eyes wide and his lips curled back, like a snarling dog's.

The camera swung to the side and Inspector Biddulph's face filled the screen. He had removed his helmet.

'Well, that's not SOP, is it?' said Gillard. 'Bloody idiot.'

They could hear Talpur screaming, though his voice was muffled by the closed doors. 'Get the fuck away! Both of you!'

Biddulph put the helmet on the ground and then raised his hands. 'Kash, it's me, Mark!'

'Why is everyone seemingly so keen to throw away the safety manual today?' asked Gillard.

The camera swung back to show the bus. 'Fuck off!' shouted Talpur. 'Just get the fuck away before we all die!'

'Kash, mate, whatever the problem is, we can talk it through. I'm here to help,' they heard Biddulph shout, but the camera stayed on the bus.

Talpur said something to the driver and a few seconds later the door rattled open. Talpur stood in the doorway, glaring at Biddulph. 'Listen to me and listen to me good!' he shouted. 'You coming here is putting everyone at risk. Do you not understand that? You need to go away – get the hell away from here – because if you don't this vest will go off and everyone dies.' He spoke to the driver again and the door closed.

Thatcher clicked his mouse and the picture froze. He clicked again and went back to after the doors had just opened. 'Watch this closely,' he said. Kamran and Gillard peered over his shoulders and Waterman walked around to join them. Thatcher replayed the moment that Talpur had started shouting through the open door.

'Listen to me and listen to me good! You coming here is putting everyone at risk. Do you not understand that?'

Thatcher clicked the mouse and the picture froze again. 'His choice of words is important here. Everyone is at risk, he says. He's including himself with the hostages. He does it twice.'

He clicked the mouse and played out the next part. 'You need to go away – get the hell away from here – because if you don't this vest will go off and everyone dies.'

The bus door rattled shut and Thatcher froze the picture.

'He puts himself with the hostages,' said Thatcher. 'It's not him against them, it's him with them. Usually hostage-takers do everything they can to disassociate themselves from their hostages. They treat them as objects, or as animals, not as human beings. But this guy, it's as if he's one of them. Everyone dies, he said. Not "they'll all die" or "I'll kill them". He regards himself as equally vulnerable.'

He clicked on the mouse and went back to the moment the bus doors had opened. He froze the picture once more. 'And look at his face. Look at the eyes, the mouth, the way the lips curl back. That's not anger, or aggression. That's fear. He's scared.'

'But that's to be expected, surely?' said Gillard. 'He's a suicide bomber. He's well aware of the consequences of his actions.'

'But he's in control, supposedly,' said Thatcher. 'He's the one with his finger on the trigger so he's the one with the power of life or death. It's his decision. He's in control.' He pointed at the screen. 'But does that look like the face of a man in control?'

'He's terrified,' Kamran said.

'So what's scared him?' asked Thatcher.

'He thinks they're going to attack him?' suggested Kamran.

'But they're in ABS suits and they're clearly not armed. And they can't move quickly enough to rush him, he must be aware of that. And, let's not forget, he opened the doors.'

'So what are you saying?' asked Gillard.

'At the moment all I'm saying is that he isn't behaving the way I'd expect a suicide bomber to behave,' said Thatcher. 'Generally they're in control and their anger is directed outwards. They are the focal point and everyone else is a victim. By killing them he wins his place in Heaven. Talpur isn't behaving like that. He's as scared as his hostages.'

'So that means he's not in control,' said Kamran. 'Or, at least, he doesn't feel as if he's in control.'

'So who is?' asked Waterman from behind them. 'Shahid?'

'It could be,' said Thatcher. 'It could be that Shahid is in total control, and that it'll be his decision and his alone whether they detonate.'

'Let's hope he calls soon,' said Kamran. He glanced at the digital clock on the wall. It was 3.25 p.m. Only two and a half hours to go before they reached the deadline. 'What do you think, boss?' he asked Gillard. 'Do we just flat-out refuse to release the Belmarsh prisoners?'

'That's not our call. You spoke to the PM, what did he say?'

'His knee-jerk reaction was to say that they wouldn't negotiate with terrorists. He said he was going into a Joint Intelligence Committee meeting and that he'd call me once they'd reached a decision. That was nearly three hours ago.'

'They can't release the prisoners, surely,' said Murray. The SAS captain had walked in without anyone realising it.

'It's one of a number of options being considered,' said Gillard.

'They can't let the terrorists win,' said Murray.

'The choice is what, though?' said Kamran. 'Nine suicide bombers detonate in the capital, killing dozens of innocent civilians. Would you want to be the prime minister who allows that to happen on his watch?'

'What if they tell the pilot to fly over central London and they all detonate then?' said Murray. 'Everyone on the plane dies but how many hundreds will be killed on the ground? I don't see how they can ever be allowed on a plane, do you?'

Gillard grimaced. The SAS captain was right. However they resolved the situation, allowing the terrorists onto a plane was not an option.

No one answered and Murray shrugged. 'If it was my call I'd take them out now. We end it rather than them taking the initiative. If we go in and people die, the public will understand. But if we do nothing and people die, the armchair warriors will start looking for someone to pin the blame on. If it were my call, I'd be authorising simultaneous head shots and sending our guys in before things go any further.'

MARBLE ARCH (3.35 p.m.)

Al Jazeera was rerunning the footage they had shot of the two bomb-disposal officers approaching the bus in Tavistock Square. It was the third time they had shown the video but everyone in the coffee shop was watching.

'Brother, do you know that man?' El-Sayed asked the man who was handcuffed to his son.

'Why do you want to know?'

'I assumed you would be friends, that you had planned this together.' El-Sayed spread out his hands. 'If I'm wrong, I apologise.'

'You talk too much.'

'I am scared, brother. When a man is scared, he tends to babble.'

'Providing everyone does as they are told and the prisoners are released, there is no need to be scared, old man.'

'Then answer me this question, brother,' said El-Sayed. 'You want the prisoners released from Belmarsh. That is a noble aim and you have my support. But why are you not talking to the police?' He gestured at the screen. 'Your colleague on the bus, he had the chance to talk to them but he shouted at them to go away.' He pointed at the newspaper-covered window. 'And you have done everything you can to blot them out. Why aren't you talking to them? Why don't you tell them face to face what it is you want?'

'Shahid is doing that,' said the man. 'He is making sure that our demands are met.'

'And what sort of man is he, this Shahid? I could tell nothing from his voice, though he speaks English as if he was born here. Is he young, is he old, is he here in London?'

'Old man, you ask too many questions.' The man's phone rang and he answered it, then passed the phone to El-Sayed. 'He wants to talk to you.'

It was Shahid. 'Do you still want to help the fight, brother?' asked Shahid.

'Yes, of course,' said El-Sayed. 'Nothing would make me happier.'

'And you are prepared to commit five million pounds to the cause?'

'Yes,' said El-Sayed. 'If it means you will return my son to me, I will.'

'And you are in a position to do that now?'

'I can do it over the phone,' said El-Sayed. 'That is how *hawala* works.'

'I know exactly how it works,' said Shahid. 'You make a call to the designated location. You give a codeword and an amount. No matter who turns up at the location, if they have the codeword they get the money. What I was asking is, do you have the money to transfer right now?'

'I do.'

'I have spoken to my colleagues and they have decided that, provided you make the transfers now, we can release your son and replace him with another hostage.'

'*Al-hamdu lillahi rabbil'alamin*,' said El-Sayed. 'All praises be to Allah, the Lord of the Alamin.'

'I will give you five locations. And five codewords. The money is to be available immediately. If it is not, the deal is off and I do not talk to you again.'

El-Sayed waved at the barista to bring him a pen and paper. 'I will make the transfers now,' he said. He nodded at his son and smiled. Everything was going to be all right, he knew it now.

LAMBETH CENTRAL COMMUNICATIONS COMMAND CENTRE (3.40 p.m.)

'How long do you think the Joint Intelligence Committee is going to take to reach a decision?' Kamran asked Gillard. He gestured at the clock on the wall. 'It's three forty. Two hours and twenty minutes to go.'

'My guess is that they're trying not to reach a decision

because whatever they decide is going to be wrong. Alex hit the nail on the head. There's no way we can put nine bombs on a plane.'

'But we need to hear that from the horse's mouth, don't we? It's not our call to make.'

Gillard nodded. 'I hear you, Mo. But I can hardly phone the PM and tell him to make up his mind, can I?'

'The commissioner could.'

'He could, but haven't you noticed the deafening silence from his office? He knows that this is going to end badly, one way or the other, so he's already distancing himself. The PM will make the decision. I'm organising the operation. The SAS are on site. No matter what happens, no one is going to be pointing the finger at our beloved commissioner.'

'We need a decision, though,' said Kamran. 'And soon. I need to be able to tell Shahid something when he calls.'

Lynne Waterman waved at Chief Superintendent Gillard. 'We've identified two more,' she said.

'Excellent,' said Gillard. He pushed himself out of his chair and went over to the MI5 officer's workstation. Kamran followed and they stood either side of her as they looked down at her screens.

On her left screen was a photo taken from the MP's surgery in Camberwell. It showed a bearded Asian man in his late twenties, who appeared to be staring directly at the camera. Next to it was a passport photograph, though in that picture the man was clean-shaven. 'Mohammed Ali Pasha,' said Waterman. 'Dad was a boxing fan, I kid you not. Twenty-six years old, London born, went to a comprehensive in Tower Hamlets, did a year at college studying computer science before he dropped out. He's never been out of the country, never been remotely involved in jihadism so far as we can tell. Isn't a regular at any mosque, doesn't have any jihadist friends.'

'So another cleanskin?' said Kamran.

'Yes, but he is known to the police. He was arrested two years ago after a long-running investigation into an underage sex ring in Tower Hamlets. A dozen or so Asian men were grooming underage white girls, getting them hooked on drugs and alcohol before having sex with them.'

'So why isn't Mr Pasha inside?'

'That's a very good question,' said the MI5 officer. 'And one that the *Sunday Times* investigation team was asking a year or so ago.'

'I remember this,' said Kamran. 'Didn't they accuse the CPS of having a mole or something?'

'Or something,' Waterman said. 'The journalists didn't come up with a name but they alleged that all the evidence pointed to someone within the CPS tipping the gang off. The initial investigation involved three girls, but as soon as the CPS was given the file one of the girls vanished and the other two had a sudden change of heart, which may or may not have had something to do with the fact that one family had an arson attack on their home and the other found their pet cat gutted outside their front door. The detectives kept on the case and came up with two more girls, one of whom had contracted HIV. The files went to the CPS and, again, the families of the girls were threatened. Actually, worse than threatened. Someone threw bleach into the face of the mother of one of the girls, almost blinding her. Again they refused to give evidence.'

'It does seem pretty conclusive that someone within the CPS was passing information to the gang,' said Kamran.

'No argument there,' said Waterman. 'But it all got very racially charged, as you can imagine. There are a fair number of CPS staffers who are of Pakistani heritage and all sorts of allegations got thrown about. Several lawyers started alleging racism and the Met had to back off. A few of the CPS people took the paper to the Press Council but they found in favour of the journalists. At the end of the day the investigation was allowed to wither on the vine, as it were.'

'So the big question is, how does a child molester end up holding an MP hostage with a waistcoat full of explosives?' said Gillard.

'And you might very well ask the same question of Mohammed Tariq Masood, the man in the restaurant in Southwark,' said Waterman, turning her attention to the centre screen on her desk. There were another two photographs there. One was a CCTV shot of a bearded Asian man walking along the pavement, the other a police mugshot. 'He's another cleanskin. No terrorist involvement, isn't a regular at a mosque and actually applied to join the army when he was eighteen. He was turned down on medical grounds. He had a detached retina, which was fixed when he was twelve but that's a barrier to joining the forces. He got a job in the family business, importing rugs and textiles, and was a model citizen until last year. He was in a car with three Asian friends and they got into an argument with a couple of Romanian women in west London. The women were gypsies selling the *Big Issue*, words were exchanged and the four guys beat the women senseless.

They were arrested and charged and they're due in court next month. The case has taken time because after they left hospital the women went back to Romania. But they've been interviewed and will come back to give evidence.'

'So yet again no terrorist involvement. But known to the police.' Gillard rubbed the back of his neck 'What the hell is going on here?'

'They're cleanskins, but they're not innocents,' said Kamran. 'Is that what's happening? Someone has recruited them because they're not on MI5's radar?'

'It's possible,' said Waterman. 'But how do you persuade someone with no history of fundamentalism to become a suicide bomber?'

MARBLE ARCH (3.45 p.m.)

El-Sayed's heart was pounding. His head was moving constantly, his attention switching between the television on the wall and the pack around the man's waist. According to Al Jazeera there were now nine suicide bombers spread around London. Most of the attention seemed to be devoted to a bus in Tavistock Square and an MP who was being held hostage in Camberwell. There was the occasional shot of the coffee shop but there wasn't much to be seen now that the windows had been covered with newspaper. From the little El-Sayed did see, the street had been closed off and the only people moving around were armed police officers. They had shown the ISIS propaganda video twice, so at least now El-Sayed had some idea of who Shahid was. Asian, for sure, probably London born, like many of the fighters he had sent to Syria and Somalia.

He looked at his watch. It was worth more than fifty thousand pounds but he would happily have given away a hundred of them to get his son released. He could always make money, he could always replace things, but he had only one son.

The phone buzzed in the man's waistpack and El-Sayed flinched. The man fumbled for the phone, answered it, then handed the phone to El-Sayed. 'You are a man of your word,' said Shahid.

'That is how *hawala* works,' said El-Sayed. 'Your word means everything. All transfers are done on trust.'

'We have the money. We thank you for that.'

'And you will release my son?'

'Like you, we keep our word. But my man will need a hostage. You must find someone there to take his place.'

'And when that is done, my son can leave?'

'No one can leave until it is over,' said Shahid. 'But I will tell my man to allow you and him to go upstairs, out of the way. You can both stay there.'

'I appreciate this, my brother. You have done a good thing today.'

'I will have done a good thing when the brothers are released from Belmarsh,' said Shahid. '*Inshallah*. Now pass the phone back to my man.'

El-Sayed did as he was told and reached over to pat his son's arm. 'It's going to be okay,' he said. 'You are to be freed.' He looked at a group of four men sitting at a nearby table, staring up at the television screen. A senior uniformed police officer was being interviewed by a reporter, saying that negotiations were continuing. El-Sayed suspected that was a lie. No one had even tried to negotiate with the man who was chained to his son.

'My friends,' El-Sayed said to the men, 'I have a favour to ask of you. Is there one of you who would be willing to help me in my time of need? For a price, of course?'

LAMBETH CENTRAL COMMUNICATIONS COMMAND CENTRE (3.50 p.m.)

Kamran's mobile phone rang. He hurried over to his desk and checked the screen. It was showing number withheld. 'I think this is him,' he said to Gillard.

The chief superintendent went over to Chris Thatcher's workstation. Thatcher had run a wire from the earphone socket of Kamran's phone to a grey metal box with a line of small lights on the top and sockets on the side, from which ran leads to four sets of headphones. Thatcher had already put on one set and Gillard, Waterman and Murray followed his example. The grey box contained a hard drive that would record both sides of the conversation, and the headsets would allow them to listen in without Shahid knowing.

'Remember, take it slowly,' said Thatcher. 'There's always a tendency to rush. Big breaths every time you speak.' He had a small whiteboard in front of him and a black marker so that he could write messages for Kamran if necessary.

Kamran looked at Sergeant Lumley, who was already working to trace the incoming call. Lumley flashed him a thumbs-up and Kamran pressed the green button to accept the call. 'Superintendent Kamran,' he said.

'You took your time, Mo,' said Shahid. 'Are you trying to make me sweat?'

Kamran took a breath and exhaled. 'It's hectic here, Shahid, as you can imagine. And you're the one who's been keeping us waiting. It's more than an hour and a half since we last spoke. The ball's in your court. Has been from the start.'

'I've got a lot on my plate too,' said Shahid. 'Time is running out, Mo. Just a little over two hours to go.'

'I know, I know. You need to give us more time. There's a lot to arrange.'

'Are the prisoners being prepared for release?'

'It's under consideration.'

Thatcher held up his whiteboard. He'd written two words in block capitals. DON'T LIE.

'By who?'

'The prime minister. He's discussing it with the Joint Intelligence Committee as we speak.'

'He does realise that the clock is ticking? If those six men are not released by six p.m., all the brothers will detonate their bombs.'

'He understands that, Shahid. We all do.'

'Then you need to hurry him up, Mo. Or you'll have blood on your hands. A lot of blood.'

'Once the prisoners have been released, what then?' asked Kamran.

'What do you mean?'

'What happens to your people? With the bombs?'

'They are to be taken to the airport, of course. I told you that last time. They are to fly out with the brothers from Belmarsh.'

'You want me to arrange that?'

'No, they can call cabs. Are you fucking with me, Mo? Of course you need to arrange that.'

Thatcher held up his board again. SLOW DOWN. BREATHE.

Kamran realised he had speeded up and took a deep breath.

'Did you hear me, Mo?'

'Yes, I heard you. I'll arrange it. But, Shahid, we need a gesture of good faith from you.'

'I have already released the children. You can take the credit for that. You don't need more.'

'It's not about taking credit, Shahid. As you said, this isn't about hurting innocents. And there are children on the bus. A baby and two schoolchildren. Can you let them off?'

'Are you fucking with me, Mo?'

'I just want the children out of there. Men don't kill children, Shahid. You know that.'

'When the prime minister announces that the brothers are being released, I will release the children on the bus. But your time is running out, Mo. At six o'clock, my people will sacrifice themselves and their hostages.'

'And there are two children at the shopping centre in Wandsworth. Two toddlers. Can you let them go, too?'

'How do you know there are kids in there? The centre was evacuated.'

'We sent in food for the kids. They were crying.'

'You did what?'

'The kids were crying, we sent in food . . .' began Kamran, but Shahid had already cut the connection.

MARBLE ARCH   (3.51 p.m.)

The man's name was Mohammed. That was all El-Sayed knew, though, to be honest, he cared nothing for the man or what he was called. All El-Sayed cared about was that the man was prepared to take the place of his son. The agreed price had been a hundred thousand pounds, which El-Sayed had arranged for the man's daughter to collect from a *hawala* agent in Shepherd's Bush, and the watch, which was now on Mohammed's wrist. The man was nervous, but committed. It hadn't taken much convincing to persuade Mohammed to take Hassan's place – he was clearly in need of money and, as El-Sayed had explained, if the suicide vest were to go up then it wouldn't matter if he was sitting at the next table or was chained to the bomber: the result would be the same. 'At least by helping me, you will be helping your family. I truly believe that this situation will be resolved without bloodshed, but if not . . .' El-Sayed had shrugged. 'Well, at least you will have provided for your family.'

Mohammed had originally asked for a million pounds but had settled for a hundred thousand and the watch. He stared at the glittering gold and diamond timepiece on his wrist as the man unlocked the handcuff that was attaching him to Hassan. Hassan scurried over to his father as if he was scared the man would have a change of heart. Mohammed held out his right hand, still staring at the watch on his left wrist, though he flinched as the handcuff snapped shut.

'Thank you,' El-Sayed said to Mohammed. Then he nodded at the man wearing the suicide vest. 'And thank you for giving me back my son.'

'Don't thank me,' said the man sourly. 'This is nothing to do with me. Just go. Get the hell away from me.'

El-Sayed stood up. 'This way,' he said to his son, and ushered the boy up the stairs, which led to an office overlooking an alley at the back of the building. There was a desk and two metal filing cabinets, boxes of coffee and a couple of chairs.

'Now what?' asked Hassan.

'Now we wait,' said El-Sayed. 'We wait for this to be over.' He looked out of the window and saw two armed police crouched in the alley. They were dressed all in black with military-style helmets and bulletproof vests, and the guns they were holding looked like something that belonged in the hands of a soldier. One of them glanced up at the window and El-Sayed stepped back. He twisted his wrist to look at his watch, then smiled ruefully when he remembered he had given it to Mohammed. 'What time is it?' he asked his son.

'Almost four,' said Hassan. 'Why?'

'Because the deadline is six p.m. What happens then is the will of Allah. But at least you are safe, my son, and that is all that matters.'

LAMBETH CENTRAL COMMUNICATIONS
COMMAND CENTRE (3.52 p.m.)

Chris Thatcher took off his headphones. 'Well, that was interesting,' he said to Sergeant Lumley. 'I'm thinking he ended the call before we could get any meaningful trace.'

'He knows how long it takes to get a fix on a mobile.'

'That's not why he ended the call, though.'

'What do you mean?' asked Gillard, taking off his headphones and putting them on the desk.

'It threw him that we'd made contact with his man in Wandsworth. He didn't know that had happened. Hardly surprising because there are no TV cameras in the shopping centre. You told him something he didn't know and that unsettled him.'

He stood and began to pace slowly up and down as he gathered his thoughts. 'You see, up until then he was totally in control. You could hear it in his voice. Some tension, yes, but not fear. He sounded like a man in control. We heard it all the time when we were dealing with the Somalian pirates. They know the score, they know that the ships are insured, so it's almost as if they're following a script. They play their part and we play ours. The money is handed over and the ship and the crew are released. The pirates would sound angry but it was an act. They knew how it would end. They were never scared because they knew that no one would be attacking them.'

'So Shahid knows he's going to win? Is that what you mean?' said Gillard. 'He's confident?'

Thatcher stopped pacing. 'He's calm, as if he knows how this is going to end.'

'Well, I wish I did,' said Gillard. 'Because the way things stand, I've no idea how it'll pan out.'

'Perhaps I should rephrase that. He thinks he knows how it will end. Everything is going to plan. At least, it was until he discovered that you had spoken to his man in the shopping centre.' He went over to his desk, picked up his cup of camomile tea and discovered it was empty. He put it down. 'Shahid clearly knows what he's doing. Everything has been planned down to the smallest detail, which is why that small deviation from his plan threw him. The question is, what is he working towards? What is he so confident will happen?'

'Presumably that the prisoners will be released and his men fly off to who knows where,' said Gillard.

'So why is he concerned about you making direct contact with the bombers?' said Thatcher. 'We saw that, too, when Inspector Biddulph tried to make contact with his man on the bus. There was real fear, then, remember? And the man in the coffee shop in Marble Arch, papering the window so that he can't be seen. This has all been about isolating the bombers so that we have to negotiate with Shahid.' He nodded thoughtfully. 'Maybe Shahid is the only one who knows what's happening. It's completely his show. The bombers are the chess pieces and he's masterminding the game.'

'You mean he hasn't told the bombers the full story?' said Kamran.

'It's possible they don't know what he's planned, yes.' He took off his spectacles, pulled a handkerchief from his pocket, and began to polish the lenses. 'This is what concerns me,' he said. 'Shahid is confident that everything is going exactly as he planned. You can hear that in his voice. My worry is that what he's planned isn't the release of the prisoners, but that right from the start his aim has been to kill as many people as possible.' He finished polishing his glasses and put them back on before forcing a smile. 'I just hope I'm wrong,' he said.

WANDSWORTH (3.53 p.m.)

The pack around Malik's waist vibrated and he jumped. 'What's wrong?' asked Zoe, as he groped for the zip.

'It's okay, it's the phone.' He took it out and pressed the red button to accept the call. 'Brother, what the fuck did I tell you?' It was Shahid.

'What?'

'You were talking to the police. I told you, you talk to no one.'

'I didn't talk to him. He walked up to the shop. I couldn't shut him up.'

'He sent in food?'

'There are two kids here and they were playing up. And one of the shopgirls needed to go to the toilet.'

'What?'

'She was close to pissing herself. So they sent in a bucket.'

'A bucket?'

'To piss in. And a couple of pizzas.'

'For fuck's sake, Sami, what part of "don't talk to anyone" didn't you understand? Do you want me to detonate that vest now? Because I fucking will. Do you want to fuck off and lie with the seventy-two virgins, is that it? You're not getting laid on earth so you're in a rush to do it in Heaven?'

'Bruv, no, I wasn't—'

'I told you, no talking to anyone. I do the fucking talking.'

'I know, bruv—'

'You know what's sitting on the table in front of me? It's a phone, mate. And there's a number on speed dial. I call that number and five seconds later – bang! It's so long and good night for Mohammed Sami Malik and anyone within fifty feet of him.'

'Bruv, I was doing what you said—'

'I said no talking to anyone. To anyone, Sami. You want me to press this button, Sami? Do you? You want it to end now? Just say the word, Sami, and I'll do it. It means fuck all to me. I press a button and it's over for you.'

'No, bruv, please! Please, bruv! It was a mistake, okay? I know it, and I won't do it again, I swear! I swear on my mother's life! Please!'

Shahid stayed quiet for several seconds.

'You still there, bruv?' asked Malik, eventually.

'Yeah. I'm here. Okay, look, let the woman with the kids go. But you don't talk to anyone, do you hear? Just tell her to take the kids and get the fuck out of there. But you remember what I said, Sami. You so much as open your mouth to the cops one more time and you and everyone there will be blown to bits.'

'I won't talk to anyone, I swear.'

'Just do as you're told, and this will soon be over and everyone can go home,' said Shahid. '*Inshallah.*'

'*Inshallah,*' repeated Malik. If Allah wills.

The line went dead. 'What's happening?' asked Zoe, fearfully.

'He's mad at me for the bucket and the pizzas,' said Malik. 'But he says we can let the kids go.'

'Who is he? Who were you talking to?'

'The man who's organising all this. His name's Shahid.'

'But who is he?'

Malik shook his head. 'You ask too many questions,' he said.

LAMBETH CENTRAL COMMUNICATIONS
COMMAND CENTRE (3.54 p.m.)

Kamran stared at the digital clock on the wall. It clicked over to 3:55. In a few minutes there would be just two hours left before the deadline expired. 'He'll call back,' said Gillard.

'But when he does, we've nothing to tell him,' said Kamran. They were sitting at Gillard's workstation. Lumley had gone off to the canteen with Thatcher. On the right-hand screen were photographs of the six men the bombers wanted released from Belmarsh. On the left-hand screen were the photographs of the bombers. Peas in a pod, thought Kamran. All were young, bearded Asians with the exception of Osman, the Somalian, and Bhashir, the forty-six-year-old father.

'We play for time,' said Gillard.

'We don't have time, that's the problem,' said Kamran. 'Two hours and that's it. And what Alex said earlier was bang on – no pun intended. There's no way we can put nine bombers on a plane. And sooner or later Shahid is going to realise that.' He ran his hands through his hair. 'Maybe he knows that already. Maybe he's just waiting for the deadline, knowing that the whole world is watching. That way he gets the maximum exposure.'

'If that's true, there's nothing we can do,' said Gillard.

'There is one thing,' said Kamran. 'We can give him what he wants.'

WANDSWORTH (3.55 p.m.)

Inspector Edwards wanted a cigarette but even though the shopping centre had been evacuated he figured the NO SMOKING signs still applied. He looked longingly at his cigarettes and lighter, sitting on the counter of the sports shop they had commandeered as a forward base.

'I know how you feel,' said Sergeant Clarke, catching his look.

'I suppose we could pop out for a quick one,' said Edwards. 'It's not as if there's much happening. Mick and Paul can hold the fort.' Mick Hecquet and Paul Savage were the other two members of the negotiating team, but they had done nothing except keep watch since they had arrived.

'Just a quick one, then,' said Clarke, picking up his pack of Rothmans.

'Sir, there's somebody coming out,' said Hecquet.

The two armed officers had their rifles up at their shoulders.

Edwards and Clarke rushed over to the entrance and peered cautiously out. There was a woman walking purposefully towards them, pushing a double buggy with two toddlers in it. One was munching a slice of pizza.

'Armed police, hands in the air,' shouted one of the armed officers.

'Fuck off, I'm coming through!' yelled the woman, increasing her pace.

Edwards stepped out of the shop.

'Stop where you are and raise your hands!' roared the second armed officer, a woman with short blonde hair.

Both officers were dressed in black with Kevlar vests and helmets.

'What – are you shooting fucking housewives now?' shouted the woman.

Edwards knew it was standard operating procedure to stop and search everyone leaving a hostage situation, but even a quick glance showed him that the woman wasn't carrying any explosives. 'It's okay, guys, let her through,' he said.

The two armed officers lowered their weapons.

Edwards ushered the woman into the sports shop. 'Are you okay?' he asked her.

'Of course I'm not fucking okay. I've been held hostage by a fucking suicide bomber! Would you be okay?'

'Why did he let you go?'

'He didn't say. He got a phone call and then he said me and the kids could go.'

'A phone call? On the shop phone?'

The woman shook her head. 'He had a mobile in his bumbag. That thing around his waist. He answered the call and then he said we could go.'

'And, just to confirm, how many hostages are still in there?'

'The poor girl he's handcuffed to. Another shop assistant. And three customers. He's keeping them in the changing rooms.'

'What's your name, madam?'

'Stella. Stella Duffy.'

'What we're going to do, Stella, is get you to a safe place and have a chat with you about what's happened.' He waved over a female officer. 'Can you take Mrs Duffy out to the Joint Emergency Services Control Centre, please?'

'Will do, sir.'

'He says you're not to talk to him,' said Mrs Duffy.

'Who? Sami?'

'He just said that if you try to talk to him again, everyone will die. He says you're not to go anywhere near him. He said I was to tell you that and to make sure you understand.'

'How does he seem?' asked Sergeant Clarke.

'What do you mean, how does he seem? He's threatening to blow himself up, how do you think that seems? He's a fucking nutter, that's what he is. Now who do I see about compensation? Criminal Injuries and all that. I need compensating for what me and the little ones have been through.'

'This lady will deal with all that,' said Edwards.

The officer took the woman and her children away. 'What do you think, Chris?' asked Edwards.

'It's not usually how it works, is it? We offer them something and ask for something in return. He sent out the kids for no good reason – he already had the food and the bucket.' The sergeant grinned. 'Maybe he just got fed up with her. You saw how mouthy she was.'

'Or maybe he didn't want the kids in the firing line. But when we spoke to him, he didn't seem to care much.' Edwards took out his mobile. 'I'll give GT Ops a call and let them know what's happening.'

'And what do we do?' asked the sergeant.

'You heard what she said. He doesn't want to talk so we just wait and see if he changes his mind. At least we got three of the hostages out.'

LAMBETH CENTRAL COMMUNICATIONS COMMAND CENTRE (3.56 p.m.)

Superintendent Kamran's stomach growled and he realised it had been almost four hours since he had eaten anything. He glanced at Sergeant Lumley, but he was busy on the phone, so he took the lift up to the third floor, visited the toilet then headed to the canteen. As soon as he pushed the door open he saw Captain Murray out on the terrace, smoking. Kamran went to join him.

The terrace ran almost the full length of the building and looked north towards the river. Off to the left was Lambeth Palace, the home of the Archbishop of Canterbury, and beyond it the Houses of Parliament. Directly in front of them was the top of the London Eye. Off to the right was the eighty-seven-storey glass skyscraper known as the Shard. It was one of the best views in London and a prime location for watching the riverside fireworks on New Year's Eve, as Kamran knew from experience. He had been on duty the two previous years and both times had managed to catch the displays.

'Not a smoker are you, Mo?' asked the captain.

'Gave up years ago,' said Kamran. 'You okay?'

'All good,' said Murray. 'Just getting my thoughts together. That basement gets bloody claustrophobic at times.'

'It's because it's underground, no natural light,' said Kamran.

Murray nodded. 'Hell of a day.'

'Yeah, you can say that again.'

'You've never seen suicide bombers up close and personal, have you?' asked the captain.

'Thankfully, no,' said Kamran. 'You?'

'Once in Iraq and three times in Afghanistan. They're difficult to figure out.' He blew smoke up into the air and the wind whipped it away. 'It's like they want to die. No fear at all. Their sole aim is to blow themselves up and take as many people as they can with them.'

'How did you deal with them?'

'You kill them. That's the only way. You can't talk to them, you can't reason with them. All you can do is slot them before they blow themselves up.'

'I think we have a different situation today,' said Kamran. 'I don't think it's about killing people.'

'You can't be sure of that,' said Murray. He blew more smoke up into the air. 'My second tour in Afghanistan, there was a young kid who hung around our base. We called him Wrigley because he was always asking for chewing-gum. His dad was a metalworker and he made these pens out of machine-gun casings. Sold them as souvenirs at a dollar apiece. I bought a couple. We let him wander around the base, do odd jobs, practise his English, that sort of thing. Then one day he turned up wearing a different jacket. Bigger than his usual one. He got to within about fifty feet of our main command tent before we realised what he was up to.' Murray shuddered and his hand shook as he took another pull on his cigarette.

'A suicide vest?' said Kamran, quietly.

Murray nodded. 'The wind lifted the jacket. There were tubes of explosive wrapped around his body, studded with dozens of his father's pens. My mate Bunny Warren saw it first and shouted a warning. We both fired but I'm not sure who got the killing shot in. Either way we blew his head off and the bomb didn't detonate. If it had done,' he shrugged, 'well, I probably wouldn't be here telling you the story.'

'I can't imagine how horrific that must have been,' said Kamran.

'Yeah, it's certainly up there in my top ten,' said Murray. 'The kid was, what, twelve years old? Not even a teenager. We liked him. And we thought he liked us. But at the end, when he thought he was about to kill us, he was smiling. Can you explain that to me? The little bastard was smiling. And he was still fucking grinning when we blew his head off.'

'He might have been drugged. Brainwashed, maybe.'

'Or maybe he hated us so much he was happy to die if it meant we would die too. That's what we're up against with these people. They're not like you or me. It's a completely different mindset.'

Kamran nodded. 'I hear what you're saying, but the men in London, they're British. They were born here.'

'It's not about where they were born. It's about the mindset. And until you know their frame of mind, you can't assume anything. It could be they're getting ready to detonate come what may. And if they do, I don't see there's anything we can do to stop them.'

'So what do you suggest, Captain?'

Murray flicked what was left of his cigarette over the side of the building. 'Get your retaliation in first, as my old rugby coach used to tell me. Take them out before they get the chance to do it themselves.'

'Even if it means hostages will die?'

'Face facts, Mo. They're probably going to die anyway.'

Murray's mobile rang and he walked along the terrace as he took the call. Kamran went back into the canteen and paid for a tray of coffees, teas, sandwiches and fruit and took it down in the lift to the basement.

Gillard grinned when he saw Kamran walk into the Gold Command suite. 'Excellent,' he said, helping himself to coffee and a cheese sandwich. Kamran put the tray down on his desk.

Thatcher grabbed a cup of camomile tea. 'You're a life-saver,' he said.

Gillard took his coffee and sandwich over to the doorway of the suite where he looked at the large map of London and the red lights marking the positions of the nine suicide bombers. Kamran helped himself to coffee and an apple and joined him. 'You know, getting them to the airport might not be a bad idea,' he said to the chief superintendent.

Gillard wrinkled his nose. 'We can't let them on a plane,' he said.

'We don't let them get on a plane. We don't let them anywhere near a plane. We take them to a hangar where we can isolate them.'

'How does that help us?' asked the chief superintendent.

'Numbers,' said Kamran. He gestured at the map. 'Between them they've got, what, a hundred hostages? Maybe more. But if we pick them up in a coach, they won't get all of them on. In fact they're more likely to go on board with just the ones they're handcuffed to, right?'

'That's an assumption,' said Gillard. He took a bite of his sandwich.

'But a realistic one,' said Kamran. 'And if there were just

nine bombers and nine hostages, well, we've improved the situation quite a bit.'

'What if they insist on taking on all the hostages?'

Kamran shrugged. 'We use a small coach. Coaches can run from, what, twenty-eight seats up to fifty plus? So we come along with a twenty-eight-seater. Even if they fill the thing, we've still vastly reduced the hostage situation.'

'What about the ISIS prisoners?' asked Gillard.

'We're not going to release the ISIS guys, that's a given. And as soon as they realise that, it's all over and everyone dies.' Kamran took a sip of coffee. 'This way at least we can save some lives, and make sure if anything happens it happens well away from the TV cameras. We can take them to Biggin Hill and we can make sure the airport is secure. But instead of taking them to a plane, we drive them into a hangar. Then we tell them it's over.'

'And if they kill everyone?'

'They're going to do that anyway,' said Kamran. 'At least this way we limit the number of casualties and the damage.' He drank some more of his coffee. 'Remember Operation Kratos?'

'That was discontinued in 2008,' said Gillard.

'The name, maybe. But the tactics still hold good.'

Operation Kratos had been developed soon after the Al-Qaeda suicide attacks on 11 September 2001, when suicide bombers seized commercial jets and killed almost three thousand people by flying them into the World Trade Center in New York and the Pentagon. For the first time police agencies around the world realised they were vulnerable to suicide attacks and the Metropolitan Police sought advice from the three countries with the most experience of fanatics who were prepared to die for their cause – Israel, Sri Lanka and Russia. They concluded that shooting suicide bombers in the chest was almost certain to detonate the explosives and suicide bombers were likely to blow themselves up when discovered. By 2002 the police had decided that the best way of dealing with them was covertly and that the bombers had to be incapacitated immediately so that they had no opportunity to self-detonate. They released their new operating procedures under the banner Operation Kratos and it quickly became national policy.

'Any confrontation should be in a secluded location to avoid risk to police officers and members of the public,' said Gillard, frowning as he tried to remember the official wording.

'Can't get much more secluded than an airport hangar,' said Kamran.

'What else did Kratos say? Covert police officers should fire on suicide bombers without warning, aiming at the head?'

'Exactly,' said Kamran. 'Multiple shots at the brainstem to minimise the risk of detonation. This would be textbook Kratos, except we'll be using the SAS. Who, thankfully, are not governed by the Police and Criminal Evidence Act.' He took another sip of his coffee. 'And, just as importantly, we deny the terrorists the PR coup of having nine simultaneous bombings in London on TV.'

Gillard knew that Kamran was talking sense. Terrorism in the twenty-first century had become as much about social media and YouTube as it had about the acts themselves. 'What about the driver? Assuming we do this, who's going to drive the coach?'

'I can ask my men for volunteers,' said Murray.

Kamran looked incredulously at the SAS captain. 'For a suicide mission?'

'We'll see what we can do to protect the cab, and he can bail as soon as the coach is in the hangar.'

'Do you think Shahid will go for it?' Gillard asked Kamran.

'If he thinks he's won, why not?' said Kamran. 'We'll be telling him that he's getting what he wants. How can he not take that as a victory?'

Gillard peered at the clock. It wasn't a decision he could take on his own. It would have to come from the top. Number 10. But they were rapidly running out of time. The phone rang and Lumley answered it, then waved at Kamran. 'Inspector Edwards for you,' he said.

Kamran went over to his desk and took the call. 'Hi, Ross,' he said.

'Have you been watching the CCTV footage?' asked Edwards. 'From the shop?'

'Sorry, no, we've a lot of feeds coming in just now.'

'Sami has released a hostage. A woman with a couple of kids.'

'Did you promise him anything?'

'He didn't even talk to us. Still won't.'

'Do you have any idea what triggered the release?'

'None, sir. Since our last conversation, we've had zero contact.'

Kamran ended the call and asked Sergeant Lumley to pull up the Wandsworth CCTV. 'Three hostages have just been released from Wandsworth,' he called over to Gillard. 'A woman and her two children.'

Lumley had the CCTV feed up from the store but all they could see was the suicide bomber and the salesgirl he was handcuffed to standing at the edge of the picture. Gillard walked over to stand by Kamran. 'Why would that have happened, do you think?'

'It must have been Shahid. I told Edwards to minimise contact.'

'It's Shahid moving to maintain control,' said Thatcher, coming up behind them. 'He tells his man to release hostages, and you have to acknowledge that he's in charge. And the fact he did it before hearing whether or not his demands have been agreed to is significant. It's an ego thing. And that could be a weakness. I think Shahid has something to prove and he didn't like it when you took the initiative.'

'You think we should make contact with the other bombers?' asked Kamran.

'I think that might be unproductive,' said Thatcher. 'He might see it as a challenge to his authority. The first time it worked and hostages were released. He might not be so accommodating next time.'

'So that leaves us with Mo's plan,' said Gillard. 'Get the bombers isolated with the minimum number of hostages. Where's Tony Drury? We need an EOD expert on this.'

'He's over at the SCO19 desk,' said Sergeant Lumley. 'I'll get him.'

Gillard turned to Murray. 'What do you think, Alex? If we can get the go-ahead to isolate them at the airport, could your men handle it? I don't see it being resolved peacefully so it might be best if your men were there.'

'To do the dirty work, you mean?' The SAS captain

grimaced and waved an apology. 'Sorry, that came out wrong. Yes, of course, if this turns into a shoot-out then our guys are better equipped to deal with it. Your armed cops bend over backwards not to fire their weapons whereas we're trained to keep shooting until the problem is neutralised. There's another Chinook en route from Hereford as we speak. It could easily be diverted to Biggin Hill.'

'Do that now so we're ahead of the game,' said Gillard. 'I don't want to be chasing up resources closer to the deadline. We've only got two hours as it is.'

Murray took out his radio and moved to the far end of the suite as Lumley returned with Drury. 'Tony, we need to pick your brains,' said the chief superintendent.

Drury leant against a desk and folded his arms. 'Pick away.'

'We're thinking of isolating the bombers on a coach, driving them to Biggin Hill airport and placing them in an isolated building, like a hangar. It'll minimise the number of hostages and confine any damage. It also means that whatever happens will happen away from the public eye. So my first question would be, what if just one of the bombs detonates. Will they all go off?'

Drury nodded. 'In close proximity like a coach, almost definitely. I suppose it's possible that if it was right at the front or at the back it might be confined to a single explosion, but even then . . . A lot would depend on the type of explosive, and we still don't have intel on that. But even if it was super stable like C-4, one device going off a few feet away is almost certainly going to detonate the ones closest to it. And you'd get a ripple effect.'

'And presumably that would be unsurvivable.'

'You remember what happened to the bus on Seven/ Seven,' said Drury. 'That was just one device. It blew the roof clean off and killed a lot of people. You'd get nine times that.' He scratched his ear thoughtfully. 'Actually, that's not, strictly speaking, true,' he said. 'The whole would actually be less than the sum of the parts, because you would get some cancellation effects. You'd have opposing forces meeting with the bus, and you'd have shrapnel smacking into other shrapnel thus absorbing some of the force. But that's purely technical and would make sod all difference to anyone on the coach.'

'And outside it?'

'As in the Seven/Seven bus bombing, most of the blast would be directed upwards. The bodies and the sides of the coach would absorb a lot of the sideways blast and shrapnel but the roof is generally just thin metal. You'd have a problem with flying glass, of course.'

'Can we minimise that?'

'The glass? Sure. We could fit anti-blast film. Maybe reinforce the sides of the coach with ballistic panels.'

Gillard looked up at the clock again. 'We might have time to fit anti-blast film but not much else,' he said.

Murray walked back over, putting his transceiver away. 'The Chinook's being diverted,' he said. 'Should arrive at Biggin Hill in about twenty minutes. What was that about anti-blast film?'

'We're looking at ways of minimising the damage if the bombs should detonate on the coach.'

'Makes sense, but you need to be aware that if we do have to fire, we'll be firing through the windows, obviously.

Anti-blast film generally isn't bulletproof but it'll make it that much harder.'

Gillard turned to Drury and the EOD expert nodded. 'He's right.'

'If we shoot and don't kill, there's a good chance they'll detonate immediately,' said Murray.

'But the problem there is that if one goes off they all go off,' said Gillard. 'In which case we need to minimise the glass that's flying around.'

'We can make sure that our men are protected,' said Murray. 'We'll have time. Personally I'd rather leave us with the option of shooting through the glass.'

Drury shrugged. 'Six of one, half a dozen of the other,' he said. 'This is all uncharted territory. But as far as flying glass goes, yes, that'll all be outward so if your guys can protect themselves it shouldn't be a problem.'

'What about the driver?' asked Gillard. 'Alex is going to come up with a volunteer but we'd like to protect him as much as possible.'

'If we can get a coach to Drummond Crescent we could see about fitting ballistic panels to the driver's seat,' said Drury.

Gillard looked over at Lumley. 'Can you get the coach sorted, Sergeant? The smaller the vehicle, the better.'

'I'm on it, sir,' said Lumley, picking up his phone.

It had just passed four o'clock, Gillard saw. 'We need to talk to the prime minister now, JIC meeting or no JIC meeting.'

'I can probably get my boss to interrupt it,' said Waterman.

'Please, Lynne,' said the chief superintendent. 'We need to talk with him now.'

MARYLEBONE (4.06 p.m.)

The Sky News presenter was a young Asian woman with too much make-up. Faisal Chaudhry shook his head in disgust. She was a Muslim by the look of her, so why wasn't she covering her head? The only reason he was looking at her was because he wanted to know what was happening around London. According to the woman, three hostages had just been released from the Southside shopping centre in Wandsworth. The picture then cut to a shot of the child-care centre in Kensington where a group of small children had been let go earlier.

'Does this mean you're letting us go?' asked the man that Chaudhry had handcuffed himself to.

Chaudhry shook his head. 'No one's going to be allowed out until the prisoners are released from Belmarsh.'

'What's so important about them?'

'I don't know,' said Chaudhry.

The man frowned. 'Why don't you know? You're doing all this and you don't know why they're important?'

'Just shut up,' said Chaudhry. He glared at the staff and customers, who were all sitting on the floor by the toilets. 'And you lot, keep texting. Hashtag ISIS6. Tell everyone that if the six prisoners aren't released, this pub will be destroyed with everyone in it.'

'What's your name? I'm Kenny.'

'Faisal.'

'You're Al-Qaeda, right?'

'I'm a Muslim.'

Kenny nodded. 'My girlfriend's a Muslim.'

'Like fuck she is,' spat Faisal.

'Her name's Nura. It means "light".'

'I know what Nura means.'

'She was born here, mind, but her parents were born in India.'

'And they're Muslim? You sure? Not Hindu? They're not the same.'

'I know they're not the same. I'm not stupid,' said Kenny. 'Muslims don't eat pork but they'll eat beef and stuff. Hindus won't touch beef because of their cow thing. Nura's family are Muslims. They pray to Allah and all that. I've been to their mosque and everything. Might even convert, you know.'

'You work in a bar. You can't be a Muslim and serve alcohol.'

'Nura's parents drink wine. They're good people.'

'And they're okay with a *kafir* going out with their daughter?'

'Why not?'

'Then they're not true Muslims.' Chaudhry scowled. 'No true Muslim would let their daughter associate with an unbeliever.'

'Like I said, they're cool.'

Chaudhry saw movement outside the windows and he pulled Kenny with him as he went to see what was happening. It had been almost four hours since any traffic had gone by. There had been shouted commands through a loudspeaker, telling everyone to clear the area, but after another hour it had been quiet outside.

He bent double as he approached the leaded windows. 'What is it?' whispered Kenny.

'Shut the fuck up,' said Chaudhry. He peered through

the glass. Two policemen dressed in black were crouched behind a car, their rifles trained on the pub. To the right, another two armed police were looking down on the pub from an office window opposite. Chaudhry backed away, almost bumping into Kenny.

'Why don't you let a few hostages go, like that guy did at Southside?' said Kenny.

'No one's being released until the ISIS soldiers are free,' said Chaudhry. He sat down at a table in the middle of the pub. Kenny pulled up a chair and sat down next to him.

One of the waitresses, a young blonde girl, raised her hand. 'Sir?' she said.

'What?' barked Chaudhry.

'Everyone's getting thirsty. Can I hand out some bottles of water and soft drinks?'

Chaudhry's first instinct was to say no, but then he realised how dry his mouth was. 'Okay, but move slowly. And, remember, if anyone tries anything we'll all die.'

The girl stood up and went behind the bar.

'I could do with a beer,' said Kenny.

'What?' said Chaudhry.

'A beer. This is a pub – don't sound so surprised.'

Chaudhry laughed. 'You're fucking mad,' he said.

Kenny shrugged. 'It was worth a try.'

Chaudhry waved at the waitress. 'Bring me a water, and a beer for this idiot.' He shook his head. 'Some Muslim you're going to be.'

LAMBETH CENTRAL COMMUNICATIONS COMMAND CENTRE (4.10 p.m.)

Lynne Waterman was as good as her word. She phoned her boss and he phoned the director-general, and at exactly ten minutes past four the prime minister was on the line to her. She explained that Chief Superintendent Gillard was now Gold Commander and put the call through to him. Gillard put it on speakerphone so that everyone in the suite could hear what was said.

'Sir, before we start, I just want to let you know that with me here in the Gold Command suite are Lynne Waterman from MI5, Superintendent Kamran, whom you spoke to earlier, Captain Alex Murray from the SAS, Tony Drury from the Bomb Squad and Sergeant Lumley,' said Gillard.

'And can I just thank you for all your excellent work at a most trying time, gentlemen – and lady,' said the prime minister. 'I understand your need for a decision, Chief Superintendent. The problem is that all the outcomes we have before us are just too awful to consider. I'm sure you've realised that even if we release the ISIS prisoners there is no guarantee that any lives will be saved. And that if we allow the bombers onto a plane, even more lives will be lost.'

'We have a possible way forward,' said Gillard, 'but it does involve letting the prisoners out of Belmarsh. If we do that, the bombers will also be moved to the airport. That will reduce the number of potential casualties and allow us to deal with the terrorists away from the public eye.'

'Deal in what way, Chief Superintendent?'

'The idea is to confine them to a secure area at the airport and tell them that the only option is surrender. The SAS will be there and it will be made clear that there is no alternative.'

The prime minister was clearly worried and they heard constant whispering around him over the speakerphone.

'We can't be seen to be negotiating with terrorists, obviously,' said the prime minister, eventually. 'Or, at least, not giving in to their demands.'

Murray frowned and shook his head.

'We're not giving in to their demands. We're using the negotiation as a way of getting the bombers into a safer environment,' said Gillard.

'But it could be seen that we're giving in to their demands,' said the prime minister. 'We would all much prefer it if that wasn't part of our strategy. Captain Murray, what are our options in terms of ending this in situ?'

'Limited, sir,' said Murray. 'We can storm any of the locations but they would see and hear us coming. We'd never be able to guarantee that they wouldn't detonate. Plus we'd have to hit all nine locations at exactly the same time. I'm sorry, but I don't see armed assaults taking place without casualties.'

They heard more whispers on the speakerphone.

'Chief Superintendent, what about continuing to negotiate? Is that a possibility?'

'The problem is that there is no negotiation,' said Gillard. 'We have their demands and they haven't deviated from them. One of the problems is that the man I'm talking to isn't himself in any danger. He isn't one of the bombers so he has nothing to lose personally. And the bombers have no way of escalating the situation.'

'I don't follow you.'

'In a negotiation like this, you'd expect them to raise the stakes. To increase the pressure. We don't give them what they want so they kill a hostage, then threaten to kill more. But that isn't happening in this case. They don't appear to have guns or knives, or any way of hurting the hostages other than blowing them up. We either do what they want or we don't. They either detonate or they don't. There isn't any room for negotiation that I can see.'

'You mean it's all or nothing? There is no middle ground?'

'I'm afraid it might be worse than that, Prime Minister. They might have gone into this planning to detonate the bombs but to put the blame on you. They can tell the world that they gave you the opportunity to save the hostages, but your refusal left them with no choice. Whereas in fact they knew from the start that they wouldn't get what they wanted. The plan all along might have been to get the world's media watching so that the explosions all go out live. ISIS are masters at using video and social media to promote their cause.'

They heard more whispering on the speakerphone.

'Prime Minister, I have to warn you that we're running out of time,' said Gillard. 'They've set a deadline of six p.m. and they haven't deviated from that. If we don't get the ISIS prisoners to Biggin Hill by that time, I fear the worst.'

'Is that your advice, Chief Superintendent?'

'I'm not offering advice, sir, I'm simply explaining the situation as I see it. We have a deadline of six p.m. We can wait and see what happens if we don't meet that deadline but there is a possibility, and I would say it's a strong one, that all nine bombers will detonate. For all we know, the bombs could be detonated remotely. And again we come back to the fact that the man we're talking to is in no immediate danger himself.'

'And we don't know who or where this man is?'

'He calls in on a different phone each time and he's never on long enough for us to trace him. We've managed to locate the nearest mobile-phone antenna each time but all that shows us is that he's moving around.'

'This is an absolute nightmare,' said the prime minister. 'Awful business. Truly awful.'

Gillard said nothing, but it was clear from the look on his face that he was in full agreement. It was a nightmare. But not one that they would be waking up from anytime soon.

'Do you have any sense of how likely it is that they'll detonate at six p.m. if we don't do what they want?'

'I don't, sir. I really don't. The one saving grace is that they do have demands. They didn't just blow themselves up. If this had been a repeat of Seven/Seven we'd be looking at dozens of dead, possibly hundreds. The fact that they gave us demands does suggest there is a possibility that this can be resolved without casualties.'

'Unless you're right and this is a set-up to make it look like it was our fault,' said the prime minister. 'They ask for something they know we can't give so that when we refuse they can kill the hostages and blame us.'

'On a more positive note, from the conversations we've had with their man, it does at least appear that he wants to achieve his objectives,' said Gillard. 'He isn't shifting the goalposts. He made his demands clear at the start and hasn't wavered.'

'He has released some hostages, though.'

'Children, Prime Minister. And I think that was always part of their plan. Why send a bomber into a childcare centre if you were concerned about putting children at risk? I think they deliberately targeted the nursery in Kensington so that they could then appear to gain the moral high ground by letting the children go.'

'Moral high ground?' snapped the prime minister. 'I hardly think so.'

'An unfortunate choice of words, my apologies,' said Gillard. 'What I meant was that by offering to release the children they appeared to be doing the humanitarian thing, even though it was their actions that put the children at risk. I have to say he was less happy about the idea of releasing the children from the bus.'

'Is there anything else we can do to get more of the hostages released?' asked the prime minister.

'He has said that once he's assured the ISIS prisoners are being transferred to Biggin Hill, he will release the children on the bus.'

'How many?'

'So far as we can see, two schoolkids and a babe-in-arms.'

'That's not much of a concession, is it?'

'He's not making concessions, Prime Minister. I think he just appreciates that killing children is bad PR. Look, sir. If we can isolate the bombers on a coach and then at the airport, we can drastically reduce the number of hostages at risk. From close to a hundred to hopefully nine or so.'

'And at no point will the ISIS prisoners be set free?'

'They will remain on the prison transport van at all times under armed guard,' said Gillard. 'They will still be in our custody and that won't change.'

'Is there any way of doing this without the media being aware of what's happening?'

'I'm afraid not, sir,' said Gillard. 'The man we're talking to has already said he wants to see the prisoners on TV. Once he sees that the prisoners are on the way to the airport, he'll arrange for the bombers to follow them.'

The prime minister sighed. He was clearly frustrated at the way he'd been backed into a corner, but Gillard sensed he had already decided what he had to do. 'So far as the world is concerned, the terrorists will have won,' said the prime minister.

'Once we have the bombers in a controlled environment, the prisoners will be taken straight back to Belmarsh,' said Gillard.

'And this is the best way forward?' asked the prime minister. 'There's no alternative?'

'I don't see one,' said Gillard. 'Worst possible scenario, we drastically reduce the number of casualties. Best possible scenario, they realise there's no way forward and they surrender.'

'Do you think the latter is at all likely?'

Gillard could hear the hope in the man's voice and he didn't want to dash it by being too honest. 'It's a possibility,' was the best he could do.

'Please God,' said the prime minister. 'Well, Chief Superintendent, it looks as if we have no choice. Go ahead and pick up the prisoners from Belmarsh. I shall speak to the home secretary now. I'll leave it to you to make the announcement. Obviously keep me informed.'

The line went dead. Gillard sat down and sighed.

'That we-never-negotiate-with-terrorists line annoys the hell out of me,' said Murray. 'Not only did they negotiate with the IRA, they let the bastards get away with murder.'

Gillard ignored him. 'At least now we have a plan,' he said. 'Alex, you need to get a secure environment ready at Biggin Hill. Tony, do what you can with a coach in the time available. Sergeant Lumley, track down Lisa Elphick from the press office. Oh, Alex, did you find a driver for the coach?'

'We had a dozen volunteers.'

Gillard shuddered. 'Rather them than me.'

'Just a thought,' said Kamran. 'What about getting a similar coach to Biggin Hill now? It'd give your guys something to rehearse with.'

'Excellent idea,' said the SAS captain.

'I'll arrange that,' said Kamran, reaching for his phone.

Inspector Adams popped his head around the door, but before he could speak Gillard waved at him. 'Ian, the prisoners are being moved to Biggin Hill airport as soon as possible. Make contact with Belmarsh. We need a high-security van to transfer them, and make sure it's real prison officers and not GS4 muppets.'

BIGGIN HILL AIRPORT (4.20 p.m.)

Biggin Hill airport was fourteen miles south east of London, a six-minute helicopter ride from the city centre that made it the airport of choice for the tycoons and oligarchs who called the capital home. As the unmarked grey Chinook helicopter came in to land, three large private jets were lined up ready to take off.

The helicopter touched down on a helipad some distance away from the main aviation terminal, where a white minibus and a black saloon car were parked. The back ramp came down as the twin rotors continued to turn. Eight men walked out, all casually dressed and carrying black nylon kitbags. They were led by a fifteen-year veteran of the SAS, Sergeant Pete Hawkins. He waited until all the men were off before jogging over to the vehicles. A pretty brunette in a beige jacket over a dark blue dress climbed out of the car to meet him as the Chinook lifted into the air and headed back to Hereford.

She turned her face away from the rotor draught and put up her hand in a vain attempt to stop her hair whipping about. Hawkins was still grinning when she turned back to face him. 'Plays havoc with the hairdo,' he said. He held out his hand. 'Pete Hawkins.'

'You don't look like SAS,' she said, shaking it.

'We scrub up well,' he said.

'I thought you'd be, you know, bigger.'

'SAS.' He laughed. 'Short And Stupid.'

She grinned. 'Paula Cooke. I'm in charge here today. I'm told to offer you any support you need and then to keep well away from you.'

'Sounds perfect to me,' said Hawkins. 'We need a hangar where we won't be disturbed.'

'The biggest is over by the terminal,' said Cooke.

'Size isn't that important, and the further away from the terminal the better,' said Hawkins.

'We have a smaller one that's being used to respray a jet,' said Cooke. 'It wouldn't be a problem to move it out.'

'And could we get to it without going close to the terminal?'

Cooke nodded.

'In that case you don't have to evacuate the terminal. But all non-essential personnel will have to be moved out. I suppose you've already been told that the airport has to close?'

'We've got four flights coming in within the next thirty minutes or so but all flights after that are being diverted.' She looked at her watch, a slim Cartier on a leather strap. 'Do you have any idea how long this is going to take?'

'It's open-ended, I'm afraid,' said Hawkins. 'But, trust me, we want to get it resolved as quickly as possible. Have you been advised about the media?'

'We're to keep them off the airport,' Cooke said. 'We've increased security at the gate and no one is getting in without prior authorisation.'

'Sounds like you've got everything covered,' said Hawkins. 'Do you think you could show me and the guys this hangar?'

LAMBETH CENTRAL COMMUNICATIONS COMMAND CENTRE (4.30 p.m.)

Kamran and Gillard stared at the main screen showing Sky News. Lisa Elphick was talking to an earnest young man in a dark grey suit. Across the bottom of the screen a headline moved slowly by: 'ISIS PRISONERS TO BE

RELEASED'. From where he was standing Kamran could barely hear what was being said, but he knew the gist. The prisoners were being released so that the sieges around the city could be brought to an end peacefully. The prime minister's office had wanted the Metropolitan Police to issue the statement and the commissioner had suggested that the announcement came through the press office. It was clear that no one wanted to take responsibility for the decision, and Kamran could understand why. The reporter began asking Lisa questions but her answer was always the same – that there would be a press conference later that day, and while the operation was ongoing only a limited amount of information could be made public.

She was good, very professional and at the same time personable, smiling a lot, but then her job wasn't on the line if anything went wrong.

Gillard looked at the clock on the wall. 'Ninety minutes,' he said. 'This is going to be close.'

'Presumably the deadline will be lifted once he sees the prisoners arrive at Biggin Hill,' said Kamran.

'I hope so,' said the chief superintendent. 'But I do worry that he intends them to blow themselves up, come what may.'

'Have we given any thought to where we're going to hold the prisoners at the airport?' asked Kamran.

'I was assuming we'd keep them in the van,' said Gillard. 'Then, once the coach is there, we run them straight back to Belmarsh.'

'I was wondering if we should take them to RAF Biggin Hill,' said Kamran. 'It's a separate enclave within the airport and it's well away from the main terminal. There's a chapel there, the former station headquarters and a number of barrack blocks. Most of the buildings are empty.'

'Good idea,' said Gillard. 'Can you arrange that? And make sure the ARVs stand guard every second the van is at the airport.'

Kamran's mobile rang on his desk. Number withheld. 'It's Shahid,' said Kamran. Gillard and Thatcher hurried over to put on headphones. Waterman joined them.

Kamran waited until they were all listening before pressing the green button to accept the call. 'There now, that wasn't so hard, Mo, was it? Did you notice how the prime minister is avoiding responsibility for releasing our brothers? No mention of it being a political decision.'

'Okay, Shahid, you've won,' said Kamran. 'There's no need to gloat. The prime minister has agreed to your terms, so they'll be on the plane with your people. You need to tell us where the plane will be flying to. We have to file a flight plan.'

'No,' said Shahid. 'The pilots will be told of their destination once everyone is on board. Just make sure that it's fully fuelled.'

'It will be,' said Kamran. 'We want to send a coach now, to pick up the men, okay?'

'Have the warriors been released? I mean, actually released from the prison?'

Kamran hesitated, not wanting to lie. 'I'm not sure,' he said.

'I want to see them being released on television,' said Shahid. 'And not just on Sky. On the BBC. I want to see them leaving the prison. Then you can send the coach.'

'I'm not sure we can do that at such short notice,' said Kamran.

'Then I suggest you try,' said Shahid. 'If not, everyone dies.'

'What about the children on the bus? The prime minister has agreed to free your men. You said you'd let the children go.'

'And I'll keep my word, Mo. Make sure you do the same.'

The line went dead and Gillard looked at Kamran. 'We have to start moving,' said the chief superintendent. 'We need the prisoners driven out of Belmarsh and we need the TV cameras there.'

'Do they have to actually be in the prison transport?' asked Waterman. 'The van could be empty for all the cameras will see.'

'We don't know where this Shahid has people,' said Gillard. 'For all we know he could have someone in the prison. No, we put them on the transport. In fact, let's allow the cameras to get a shot of them being loaded on. I tell you what, Mo, I'll call the governor of Belmarsh while you arrange the TV and press coverage through Lisa.'

Captain Murray had been talking into his radio and came over as he tucked it into his jacket. 'My men have a suitable hangar at Biggin Hill, and all non-essential personnel are in the process of being evacuated,' he said.

'Is there any way we can fix up a video feed?' asked Kamran.

'I'll talk to the airport to see what's available. I'm sure we can rig something up.'

'Liaise with Sergeant Lumley to get the feed into the SOR,' said Kamran.

'How are you fixed for manpower here in London?' Gillard asked the captain.

'We're at all the sites, and we still have men in Wellington Barracks. Why do you ask?'

'We're going to start the transfer from Belmarsh soon,' said Gillard. 'It would be helpful if we had a couple of cars with your guys in the convoy. There'll be plenty of ARVs and motorcycle outriders but I'd feel happier if the SAS was in the mix.'

'I'm on it,' said Murray.

'I've had a thought,' said Kamran, as the SAS captain left. 'We're setting the hangar up as an SAS operation but, no matter what happens, it'll be a crime scene at some point. Plus we'll have to send emergency services, ARVs, Bomb Squad, followed by forensic teams. The full monty. Might be better to get a Silver Commander on the scene now. If nothing else, we're going to need inner and outer perimeters, a JESCC, a scene-access control, a multi-agency marshalling area, and the sooner we start on that the better.'

'How about Adams? He's a safe pair of hands. He's been here all day and knows what's what. With blues and twos he could be there within the hour.'

Kamran looked up at the clock. 'That'd only give him thirty minutes to spare.'

'We could send someone from Croydon or Bromley but they'd have to be brought up to speed. The only closer alternative would be Kent Police. Send him. But we should be liaising with Kent Police, see what they can offer us in the way of resources.'

Gillard picked up his phone to call the deputy commissioner while Kamran went over to his briefcase. He took out a copy of the *Major Incident Procedure Manual* and went off in search of Inspector Adams.

He found him at one of the workstations in the middle of the SOR, wearing a headset and talking to someone animatedly. He finished the call, took off his headset and looked at Kamran expectantly. 'You'll be glad to know that Chief Superintendent Gillard wants you as Silver Commander out at Biggin Hill,' said Kamran.

'Me? Really?'

'You've done a great job here throughout the day but we're entering the end phase and we need someone who knows what they're doing at the airport,' said Kamran.

Adams looked worried. 'I haven't been in charge of a major incident this big before, sir. It might be too much for me.'

'It's not as daunting as it sounds,' said Kamran. 'The SAS will be in charge of the hangar. But no matter how the situation is resolved it will be a crime scene and they're all the same. You'll need to safeguard it and make sure that all the evidence is protected. But your first order of business is to do what we do at every major incident. Set up an inner cordon, which will be the hangar, obviously. Then an outer cordon. It's an airport so you probably won't need a traffic cordon. Make sure logistical support is lined up, arrange an RVP, a marshalling area, a multi-agency marshalling area, a multi-agency holding area, and a Joint Emergency Services Control Centre.'

Kamran fought back a smile as he saw the confusion on the inspector's face. He gave Adams the manual he was holding. 'Have a look at that in the car,' he said, 'and if you need any help, just give me a call. You'll be fine. Really.'

'Thanks, sir.'

'You've done a great job today, Ian. It's only right that you're in at the finish.'

Adams smiled thinly. 'I won't let you down, sir.'

Kamran patted him on the shoulder. 'I know you won't,' he said. 'Now, off you go. The clock's ticking.'

He went back to the Gold Command suite, just as Chief Superintendent Gillard was coming off the phone. 'The prisoners are prepared for transit, Mo. Can you get a helicopter overhead to track the transport all the way to the airport? The one thing we do not want is to lose those guys.'

TAVISTOCK SQUARE (4.33 p.m.)

Kashif Talpur jumped as something buzzed at his waist. For a frantic few seconds he feared that the vest was about to explode but then he realised it was the mobile phone in his waistpack. He went to open it with his right hand but that would mean letting go of the trigger so he used his left instead. He pulled out the phone, his heart racing, and held it to his ear. 'It is Shahid, brother. You are doing well. I am proud of you.'

'I just want off this bloody bus,' said Talpur.

'Soon, brother, soon. We are talking to the authorities and I expect our brothers to be released soon. But right now I need you to do something for me. I want you to let the children go.'

'The children?'

'Anyone under sixteen can leave the bus. But do it carefully, brother. Explain that you are releasing the children and only the children. Do you understand?'

'Yes.'

'Only the children. If I see any of the adults getting off, I will detonate the vest.'

'Okay, I hear you. But I don't see any children.'

'They are upstairs,' said Shahid. 'Two schoolkids and a baby.'

'A baby? What about the mother?'

'What mother?'

'Holding the baby. She has to stay with the baby, right? The baby can't get off on its own. It's a baby.'

'Yes, the mother can take the baby. But no other adults. If I see any other adults getting off – well, you know what will happen.'

'Yes,' said Talpur.

'Then do it now, brother. I will call you back later.'

The line went dead and Talpur put the phone away. Talpur pointed at a middle-aged black man in overalls. 'Hey, bruv, go upstairs and tell the woman with the kid to come on down. And the schoolkids.'

The man went upstairs. He reappeared a minute later with the mother, a woman in her twenties, her eyes wide and fearful, holding her baby. He motioned for her to join him at the front of the bus. The two schoolboys clattered down the stairs. Talpur waved them over. 'You can go.'

'What about me?' said the man who had fetched them. 'This is nothing to do with me. I'm a Muslim.'

'Me too!' shouted a middle-aged woman in a headscarf. 'I'm a Muslim too. You should let the Muslims go. This isn't anything to do with us.'

Within seconds everyone on the bus was imploring Talpur to release them, and virtually all of them were shouting that they were Muslims.

'Shut up!' he roared. 'Seriously, all of you, just shut the fuck up! This isn't about who's Muslim and who's Christian or who believes in Santa Claus. It's about the kids. It's about letting the children go.'

'She's not a child!' shouted the woman in the headscarf. 'She's as old as I am.'

'She's holding the baby,' said Talpur.

'I've got children at home,' said the woman. 'I've got five children waiting for me.'

'And be grateful for that,' said Talpur. 'Now listen to me. The driver's going to open the front door. She gets off with the baby. Then the two kids get off. Then the driver closes the door. If anyone else tries to get off, this vest explodes and we all die.'

'This isn't fair!' hissed the woman in the headscarf. 'I hate the *kafirs* as much as you do.'

Talpur pointed the trigger at her. 'You need to be quiet,' he said.

The woman glared at him, muttering under her breath. Talpur nodded at the driver. 'Open the front door,' he said.

The driver did as he was told and the door hissed open. 'Thank you, thank you, thank you,' whispered the mother, as she clutched her baby to her chest and stepped off the bus. 'God bless you.'

'Just go,' said Talpur. He waved at the two schoolkids. 'You two, off the bus. Now.' They scrambled past him. As the second went by, Talpur grabbed him and whispered something to him. The boy frowned at him, shook his head, then jumped off the bus.

'Close the door!' Talpur shouted at the driver. He watched through the window as police officers in fluorescent jackets rushed towards the woman and the children and hurried them away.

LAMBETH CENTRAL COMMUNICATIONS COMMAND CENTRE (4.40 p.m.)

The massive gate that guarded the entrance to Belmarsh Prison rattled back and the prisoner transport vehicle pulled out. Virtually everyone in the special operations room was watching the screen on the wall showing the feed from Sky News. One of the shots was from a helicopter and the news team had been given permission to fly over the prison so they could film the six prisoners being loaded onto the van, each handcuffed to a burly prison officer.

There were two ARVs escorting the van, one in front and one behind, along with half a dozen police motor-cyclists.

'I have two cars en route,' said Murray. 'Make sure the ARVs are expecting them. We don't want a friendly fire incident.'

Kamran glanced at Lumley, who nodded. 'They've been briefed,' he said.

'How long to drive from Belmarsh to Biggin Hill?' asked Gillard.

'With no traffic should be forty-five minutes, but we've

told them to take it slowly,' said Kamran. 'It should take them an hour with an ETA of seventeen forty. We're using motorcycle police to keep the roads clear.' He turned to Lumley. 'Joe, can you call up the route for me?'

Lumley clicked his mouse and a map filled his left screen, showing the route the police van would take from the prison, down the A206, A205, A208 and B263 to Bromley, then south to the airport on the A21 and A233.

'As soon as they get to the airport they'll drive to RAF Biggin Hill and park by the main block there,' said Kamran.

Kamran's mobile rang. It was Shahid. 'It is time to take my people to the airport,' he said. 'You have the coach?'

'It's ready when you are,' said Kamran.

'I need the windows to be blacked out.'

'Blacked out? We never discussed that.'

'I'm discussing it now. I need the windows blacked out.'

'Why?'

'So that no one can see inside. I don't want one of your armed cops shooting one of my people.'

'They won't do that, Shahid. I swear,' said Kamran. 'We don't want anyone getting hurt. We just want this to be over.'

'It will be,' said Shahid. 'Soon. Is the coach ready?'

Kamran looked at Drury, who nodded.

'It's ready,' said Kamran.

'Then start to pick up the warriors,' said Shahid. 'Pick them up in the order they went out. Brixton. Wandsworth. Fulham. Kensington. Marble Arch. Marylebone. Tavistock Square. Camberwell. Southwark. Then drive south to the airport.'

'It will be quicker if we collect the warriors individually and take them to the coach,' said Kamran.

'You will do as you are told, Mo. Do you understand me? If you deviate one iota from your instructions, everyone will die.'

'I understand,' said Kamran, quickly. 'I just wanted to make things easier.'

'All the warriors will be taken in the same coach, along with their hostages. The windows will be blacked out. I will be watching, and if at any point during the journey to the airport you try to gain access to the coach or hinder its progress in any way, it will be destroyed. Are we clear?'

'Yes, Shahid. We are clear.'

'Then send the coach to Brixton. The clock is ticking, Mo. Tick, tock. Tick, tock.' The line went dead.

BIGGIN HILL AIRPORT (4.43 p.m.)

Pete Hawkins's mobile buzzed and he took it out of his pocket. It was Alex Murray. 'How's it going, Jim?' asked Murray. Hawkins had been given the nickname 'Jim' on his first day at SAS Selection by a grizzled sergeant major who had recently reread *Treasure Island*.

'The coach is here and we're running through as many scenarios as we can. Is there any way we can make that emergency door at the back easier to open?'

'I'll see what I can do,' said Murray. 'What about a video feed?'

'A couple of the airport's technical guys are rigging something up as we speak. They've already spoken to a guy called Lumley in the SOR.'

'Excellent,' said Murray. 'In the meantime, here's another wrinkle for you. They're insisting on the windows being blacked out. On the positive side, that means they won't know they're in the hangar until it's too late.'

'And on the downside, we'll be shooting blind,' said Hawkins. 'Shit.'

'I know. The thing to remember is that in all cases the hostage is on the left side of the bomber. So on the port side the hostage will be next to the window. On the starboard side, the hostage will be on the inside.'

'I'm not sure that helps if the windows are blacked out,' said Hawkins. 'I was never happy at shooting through the windows anyway.'

'How are you getting on there?' asked Murray.

'The bottleneck is the door, obviously,' said Hawkins. 'If the door is open we can get a man in straight away but he then blocks the men behind him. He can take out the first two targets immediately but it's at least a second before he can get to the next row. Flash-bangs might slow things down but that slows us getting in, too. If we can get in through the back emergency exit, we can have a man there take out the rear two. But we haven't been able to get through that door in less than three seconds. Best will in the world, at the moment we're looking at four seconds to neutralise all nine targets and we both know that's not good enough.'

'Keep at it, Jim. See if you can shave off a second or two. At the moment the hope here is that, once they see there's no way out, they'll surrender.'

'They're fucking jihadists, Captain. It doesn't work like that. These idiots want to die. And the more they take with them, the more credit they get.'

'I hear you, Jim. But let's stay optimistic, shall we?'

'The lads had a couple of thoughts, boss. Any way we could rig up some knock-out gas, pump it into the coach and put everyone to sleep?'

'It was discussed but there isn't enough time and even if there was we'd be putting the driver to sleep, too.'

'It could be activated once they'd parked in the hangar,' said Hawkins.

'But nothing works instantaneously and if they realised what was happening they'd probably detonate.'

'Okay. What about arming the driver? We're using one of our guys, right? Give him a gun, he could take out the bad guys on the starboard side as we move down the aisle shooting port. It might shave some time off.'

'My worry would be that if one of the bombers searched the driver and found a gun that could create its own set of problems.'

'To be honest, without that extra gun I think we're screwed.'

'Okay, I'll get that sorted,' said the captain. 'Start rehearsing with an armed driver and see how it works out.'

Hawkins put the phone away. Arming the driver would give them an edge, but he knew that, no matter how often they rehearsed the scenario, there was no way they could take out all the suicide bombers before at least one would have the opportunity to press the trigger. And if that happened, everyone on the bus would die, including the SAS troopers. All the men in the hangar knew the risks, but if they were given the order to storm the coach with guns blazing, that was what they would do.

TAVISTOCK SQUARE (4.44 p.m.)

Alistair McNeil, Silver Commander at Tavistock Square, agreed to allow Biddulph to sit in while he interviewed the three hostages who had been released from the bus. They were being kept in rooms on the second floor of the British Medical Association building. The woman, Christine Melby, was feeding her baby with a bottle while a female officer looked on. The two schoolboys were being cared for in an adjoining room.

McNeil went to see the woman first. He introduced himself and told her that Biddulph was a sergeant with the National Crime Squad.

'Why can't I go home?' she asked.

'You can, absolutely you can,' said Inspector McNeil. 'We'd just like to ask you a few questions first, if that's okay?'

'I've had one hell of a day,' she said. 'And my husband's going to be wanting his tea.'

'I've asked for a car to run you home,' said McNeil. 'In the meantime, how did he seem, the man with the bomb?'

She frowned, not understanding the question.

'Was he tense?' asked McNeil. 'Did he seem preoccupied? Focused?'

'He was angry. He kept shouting at us. Why don't you just shoot him? He's going to kill all the people on the bus if you don't.'

'We're trying to resolve this so no one gets hurts, Mrs Melby.'

'He's a nutter,' said the woman. 'Threatening innocent people like that. You need to throw away the key.'

'I'm sure they will do,' said McNeil. 'Did he say anything about ISIS?'

'ISIS?' she repeated.

'The group the terrorists belong to. Did he talk about them? What they wanted? What they planned to do?'

'He didn't say much. Just kept saying that so long as we all did as we were told, no one would get hurt.'

'Did he sound scared?' asked Biddulph. 'Or scary?'

The woman tilted her head to one side as she studied his face. 'He was scared,' she said eventually. 'I think he was more scared than the woman he was handcuffed to.'

McNeil and Biddulph moved to the room next door where the two schoolboys were being given soft drinks and crisps by a female officer. The two boys seemed nervous and uncomfortable, which wasn't surprising under the circumstances. Their names were Luke Young and Peter Okonkwo. Their parents had already been contacted and were on their way.

'Are you two lads okay?' asked McNeil.

'I just want to go home,' said Luke. 'I've got five-a-side tonight.'

'Your mum's coming to pick you up,' said McNeil.

'I don't need my mum,' said the boy. 'I'm twelve.'

'We'd just be happier if she was here to take care of you,' said McNeil. 'You've both been through a very trying experience.'

'Do you think he's going to blow up the bus?' asked Luke.

'We hope not,' said McNeil. 'Now, the man, did he say anything to you, anything at all?'

Luke shook his head. 'He just said we were to do as we

were told. We were on the top deck so we didn't see much. He's a Muslim, right? He wants to kill anyone who isn't. That's what this is about, right?'

'It might be,' said McNeil. 'Did he say anything about that? Did he talk about Islam?'

'He didn't say anything, really. Not to us, anyway. Like I said, we were upstairs.'

'What about when he let you off?' asked McNeil. 'Did he say anything then?'

Luke shook his head again.

Biddulph noticed that the other boy seemed uncomfortable, staring at the floor and fidgeting. 'What about you, Peter?' asked Biddulph. 'Did he say anything to you?'

'Not really,' said the boy.

'Are you sure? Nothing at all?'

'I don't want to say.'

Biddulph frowned. 'What do you mean?'

The boy shrugged. 'He's a pervert,' he said, his voice barely a whisper.

'A pervert?'

'He was asking me about condoms.'

Biddulph and McNeil stared at each other in astonishment.

EUSTON (4.45 p.m.)

The police sergeant put his phone away and went over to the man who was going to be driving the coach. 'Gold Command says it's time to go,' said the sergeant.

The SAS man had given his name only as Terry. He was in his thirties and, to the sergeant, he didn't look much. He was about five-eight with close-cropped greying hair, wiry rather than muscled, and had a chewing-gum habit that saw him popping a fresh piece between his lips every ten minutes or so. He wore a light brown leather jacket over brown cargo pants and a handgun in a nylon holster under his right arm. The sergeant had seen much tougher men in his twenty years in the police but there was a quiet confidence to Terry that he had rarely come across.

Terry nodded. There was a group of technicians in the coach inserting Kevlar plates in the driver's seat and in the backs of the first few rows of the passenger seats. Two more had just finished putting black film over the side windows.

'Guys, you're going to have to stop now,' shouted the sergeant. 'We need to get this show on the road.'

The technicians filed off the coach. The senior man, a former army bomb-disposal officer, went up to Terry. 'I'm not sure how much good it'll do if nine bombs go off in a confined space,' he said. 'There'll be some protection for your back but your neck and your head are going to be exposed.'

'Hopefully it won't come to that,' said Terry. 'Anyway, I brought a protective helmet with me.' He pulled a flat cap from his pocket and placed it on his head. 'What do you think?'

'I think you've got one hell of a set of balls on you, lad,' said the technician. 'Good luck.'

As he walked away, Terry climbed into the driving seat, took a quick look at the controls and turned on the engine.

'Just follow the bikes,' said the sergeant.

'How far is it to Brixton?' asked Terry.

'Six miles, give or take. Normally it would take half an hour to drive but the roads have been cleared so you'll be able to keep your foot down. Should be there in less than ten minutes. The bikes know the route so just follow them.'

Terry nodded. 'Thanks for your help, Sergeant. Now please get the fuck off my coach.'

BRIXTON (5.00 p.m.)

The pack around Bhashir's waist vibrated and Father Morrison gasped. 'It's a phone,' Bhashir said to the priest. 'Don't worry.'

'Did I look worried?' said the priest. He took out his handkerchief, mopped his brow, then put it away.

Bhashir used his left hand to unzip the waistpack and take out the phone. 'It is time to go, brother,' said Shahid. 'The brothers have been released from Belmarsh. In five minutes there will be a coach outside to take you to the airport. You are to take only the hostage you are handcuffed to. The rest can stay behind.'

'It's over?' asked Bhashir.

'It soon will be,' said Shahid. 'They have agreed to our demands. There is a plane waiting at Biggin Hill airport.'

'To take us where?' asked Bhashir.

'Away from this country. To a place of safety.'

'But this is my country,' said Bhashir.

'Then you can stay. But first you must go to the airport.

The coach will be outside in five minutes. In five minutes' time you are to open the main door and walk out of the church with your hostage. You are to get into the coach. But be vigilant. I will be watching. If I think that the police are up to anything, all the vests will detonate.'

'Please do not do that, brother. I do not want to die, not like this.'

'Providing everyone does as they are told, no one will die,' said Shahid. He ended the call and Bhashir put the phone back in his waistpack, then zipped it up.

'We are to leave in five minutes,' said Bhashir. 'The government has released the prisoners.'

'So you got what you wanted?' asked the priest. 'You can release us?'

'Your parishioners will be freed when we go. But you have to come with me to the airport.' He raised his left hand and jiggled the chain that connected them. 'I don't have the key for this.'

'What will happen when we get onto the plane?' asked Morrison. 'Will you let me go?'

'I don't know,' said Bhashir.

The priest frowned. 'How can you not know?'

'It's not my decision.'

'I don't understand,' said Morrison. 'Surely once you have the plane and the prisoners, you just let us go, right? And you fly off to where you're going.' He took out his red handkerchief again to mop his brow. 'And where is it you're going?'

Bhashir shrugged but didn't reply.

'You don't know?'

'Priest, you ask far too many questions,' said Bhashir. He sighed. 'I want a cigarette so badly.'

The priest grinned. His hand disappeared into his vestments and reappeared with a pack of Benson & Hedges and a cheap disposable lighter. Bhashir stared at the cigarette greedily. 'I told you it was one of the only vices I'm allowed,' said Father Morrison. 'But I suppose the question is, how safe are we smoking while you're wearing that bloody thing?'

'I don't think a cigarette will set it off,' said Bhashir.

'You're probably right,' said the priest. He flicked open the pack and offered a cigarette to Bhashir. He took it and smelt it as Father Morrison took one for himself and slid it between his lips. The priest lit Bhashir's cigarette, then his own, and the two men contentedly blew smoke up at the ceiling. 'This is against the law, you know,' said Father Morrison. 'The church is classed as a place of work so smoking is forbidden.'

'With all that has happened today, no one is going to be charging us with smoking,' said Bhashir.

The two men chuckled. Father Morrison noticed that one of the parishioners, a black man in his seventies, was looking at them longingly and he waved his cigarette. 'Do you want one, Mr Donaldson?' The man nodded. 'Mr Donaldson is a three-pack-a-day man,' the priest said to Bhashir. 'Do you mind if he lights up? We often have a cigarette together outside after the service.'

'Why not?' said Bhashir.

'You're a good man, Rabeel,' said the priest. He held his cigarette above his head. 'Mr Bhashir has kindly agreed that the smokers among you may light up,' he called. 'If you do light a cigarette, please respect those who do not smoke and move away from them.'

Three of the men, including Mr Donaldson, and one of the women took out their cigarettes and shuffled along the pews to the far side of the church before lighting up.

The priest tried to blow a smoke-ring but failed. He smiled. 'Just a thought, Rabeel. If that does go off, do you think I will go to my heaven or yours?'

'That's a good question, Father Sean. There are supposed to be seventy-two virgins waiting for me.'

'You see now, that's my problem, Rabeel. Most of the virgins I come across are nuns and, truth be told, you wouldn't want to be spending eternity with them.' He took a last drag on his cigarette and flicked it away. 'Okay, let's get this show on the road.'

'What show?'

'It's an expression.' He crossed himself and took a last look around his church, wondering if he would ever see it again.

The two men walked to the door. Bhashir undid the bolts and pushed the large oak doors open. There was a white coach parked in the road, the engine running. The front door was open. All the side windows had been blacked out. Just in front of the coach were six white police motor-cycles and another four behind it.

To the left, crouched behind a police car, two armed officers were sighting down rifles at them. Beyond them were more vehicles and a cluster of policemen in fluorescent jackets. One was holding a megaphone. 'Please move to the coach,' boomed an electronic voice. 'You are in no danger.'

'Easy for you to say,' muttered the priest.

To their right, close to a large white van, there were two

men in bomb suits. They both pointed at the coach.

Bhashir headed for it, the priest following. The driver looked down at them. 'We're on a tight deadline so if you could hurry up I'd appreciate it,' he said. Bhashir nodded and went up the stairs, his left hand behind him. The priest followed. 'Come on, come on,' said the driver.

Bhashir went to sit on the seat behind the driver but he shook his head. 'Not that close. Move down. And get a move on.' Bhashir walked down the coach and sat on the right-hand side, next to the window, the priest beside him. The driver closed the door. The motorcycles switched on their flashing lights, giving everyone on the coach a bluish tinge. The coach lurched forward as if the driver wasn't used to the controls. They quickly reached forty miles an hour. Traffic had been diverted from the route and they sailed through any red traffic lights as they headed north to Wandsworth.

LAMBETH CENTRAL COMMUNICATIONS COMMAND CENTRE (5.05 p.m.)

Kamran looked up at the main screen on the wall. It was showing a feed from Sky News, a helicopter shot of the police transport van driving down a deserted road, police motorcyclists leading a convoy of marked and unmarked vehicles. Across the bottom of the screen a headline read, 'RELEASED ISIS PRISONERS HEADING TO BIGGIN HILL AIRPORT.'

'They'll be there by six,' said Gillard, as if reading his

mind. 'The roads are being cleared along the route. Did you get the RAF sorted?'

'All non-essential personnel have been moved out,' Kamran confirmed. 'There's a parking area they can use to wait in.'

'What will happen to the TV news helicopter? Will they be allowed to fly over the airfield?'

'We're closing the airport as of five thirty, so in theory there'd be no problem allowing it, but I don't want Shahid seeing what we're doing. If he spots the van parking at the RAF base he might realise we're up to something.'

Gillard nodded. 'Talk to Lisa Elphick. They can have news crews at the entrance to the airport showing the van and the coach arriving, but make it clear the helicopters have to stay away from the airport itself. The only chopper allowed above Biggin Hill is our own.' He looked at the SAS captain. 'Alex, your men are going to have to start thinking about moving their coach out of the hangar.'

'How long have we got?' asked Murray. 'The more they rehearse, the better.'

'What do you think, Mo?' asked Gillard.

Kamran rubbed his chin. 'Eight to pick up but we're clearing the roads so an hour and a half until they're ready to head to Biggin Hill. Southwark to Biggin Hill is about half an hour on a regular day, maybe twenty minutes with the roads cleared.'

'That takes us past the six o'clock deadline,' said Murray.

'The ISIS prisoners will be at Biggin Hill by six,' said Kamran. 'We're assuming that's the deadline that has to be met. I'd suggest your men continue to rehearse until six thirty.'

Chris Thatcher stood up and waved a hand apologetically. 'I don't want to rain on anyone's parade, but have you considered that this might be a way of them attacking the SAS?'

'We've considered that,' Murray said. 'If they do detonate at the same time in the hangar, there's a chance they could take out a dozen SAS men.'

Gillard turned to Kamran. 'Could that be what they've got planned?'

'It doesn't seem to be how ISIS or Al-Qaeda operates,' said Kamran. 'They want to inspire terror so they go for civilians wherever they can. The old IRA was a different kettle of fish. They tended to attack military targets. But these jihadists are looking for shock value and they would have got that by blowing up nine different locations in London at the same time.'

'We need to do as much as we can to protect your people, obviously,' Gillard said to Murray.

'We've got sandbags in place and our guys will stay behind them for as long as they can,' he replied. 'But obviously if we have to storm the coach, all bets will be off.'

Kamran's phone rang and he answered it. It was Mark Biddulph. 'We've spoken to the three passengers released from the bus,' he said. 'Something weird came up that I thought I should run by you.'

'I'm listening.'

'One of the kids says that Kash whispered something to him about condoms as he got off the bus.'

'Condoms?'

'I know, it's bloody weird, right? But the boy swears blind that Kash said he wanted to know if the boy had a condom. A Durex, specifically. He asked him twice.'

'Just as the boy was getting off?'

'Yeah, he grabbed him and whispered in his ear.'

Kamran looked up at one of the screens on the wall, showing the feed from Tavistock Square. 'It wasn't "Durex" he was saying, Mark,' said Kamran. 'It was "duress". He's under duress. Somehow he's been forced into this.'

WANDSWORTH (5.10 p.m.)

Malik heard his name being called. 'Sami! It's me, Jamie. Can you hear me?'

'I told you, I've nothing to say to you!' shouted Malik. 'Leave me alone.'

'The coach is here to take you to the airport.'

'What coach?'

'The Belmarsh prisoners have been released,' shouted Clarke.

'It's true,' called Laura, from the changing rooms. 'It's all over Twitter. They've let the prisoners go and they're on the way to the airport.'

'It could be a trick,' said Malik. 'They could be lying.' He walked slowly to the entrance of the store, pulling Zoe with him. He peered out and saw three armed policemen pointing their weapons at him. He pulled back. 'They're going to shoot me,' he said to Zoe.

The phone buzzed in his waistpack and he flinched. Zoe gasped, then they both smiled ruefully as they realised it wasn't the vest. Malik used his left hand to pull out the phone and take the call.

'Sami, my brother,' said Shahid. 'It's time to leave.'

'They've agreed to let them go?'

'Of course they have, brother. There was never any doubt. Now this is what you have to do next. You and your hostage will be taken downstairs and put onto a coach with the rest of the brothers. I will be watching, so stay alert and focused. For this to work, everyone must be on the coach, do you understand?'

'Yes,' said Malik. 'But if you have the ISIS prisoners, why can I not remove the vest now?'

'Everyone must go to the airport, Sami. Everyone. Once there and once the prisoners are on the plane, then, and only then, will it be over. Do you understand?'

'I suppose so,' said Malik.

'There is no suppose so,' said Shahid. 'You must do exactly as I say. Disobey me and everyone dies. We are close to finishing this, Sami. We will get what we want, but you have to follow my instructions to the letter. Go with your hostage to the police. Keep the trigger in your hand and show them that you are willing to press it. Take the stairs down to the coach. Do not let them put you in the lift. Tell them to keep their distance. At least ten feet from you at all times. And even when you are on the coach, do not relax. Stay vigilant.'

'What happens when we get to the airport?' asked Malik. 'I don't want to leave the country.'

'One step at a time, Sami,' said Shahid. 'Just take your hostage down to the coach.' The line went dead.

'What's happening?' asked Zoe.

Malik put the phone away. 'It's over,' he said.

'You're letting me go?'

Malik shook his head. 'No, you are to come to the airport with me. You will be released there.'

'I can't,' she said. 'I'm seeing my boyfriend tonight. He'll be really pissed off.'

'There's no choice,' said Malik. 'You have to come. But it should all be over by six. You can still see your boyfriend. And you can text him and tell him you'll be late.' He walked towards the shop entrance, tugging at the chain so that she followed. He raised his right hand in the air. 'Jamie, we're coming out! Don't shoot!'

'No one's going to shoot you, Sami!' shouted Clarke. 'Just walk slowly and keep your hands where we can see them.'

'We're not to use the lifts,' shouted Malik.

'That's not a problem,' said Clarke. 'We can take you down the escalators.'

Clarke was standing next to another officer, both wearing black bulletproof vests with POLICE across the chests. Standing next to them was a figure in a green suit with a mask like a spaceman's helmet.

'This man will take you down,' said Clarke. 'His name's Rick. He's with bomb disposal.'

Malik stopped and waved the trigger over his head. 'Don't come near me!' he shouted.

Clarke held up his hands. 'It's okay, Sami. Stay calm. He's just here to escort you to the coach.'

'Tell him to keep his distance!' shouted Malik. He pointed at the armed police who still had their weapons trained on him. 'And tell them to get back, too.'

'No one is going to hurt you, Sami,' said Clarke. 'We're here to help, that's all.'

'You can help by keeping away from me,' said Malik.

Several more police officers emerged from the shop behind Clarke, all wearing black vests.

'I'm serious!' shouted Malik. 'All of you, keep your distance!'

The man standing next to Clarke said something to the other officers and they all went back into the shop. Malik moved to the middle of the walkway. He could see inside the shop the police were using. It sold sports gear. There were more than a dozen people there, some in uniforms and some in regular clothing, but they were all wearing protective vests.

He and Zoe moved to the centre of the walkway. They looked over the railing at the lower level. There were more than a dozen officers in fluorescent jackets. 'You all need to keep well away from me!' he shouted.

He took Zoe to the escalator and they stood together as they went down to the ground floor. He held the trigger up in the air and shouted for them to stay back.

Jamie Clarke appeared at the top of the escalator. 'Sami, I'm coming down!' he called. 'I'll lead you out to the coach.'

Malik and Zoe moved away from the escalator and waited until Clarke had come down. He pointed off to their left. 'This way,' he said.

Malik glanced up. The armed police officers were looking down at them, their rifles at their shoulders.

'Tell them to put their guns away,' Malik told Clarke.

'It's standard procedure,' said Clarke. 'They won't shoot. Their fingers aren't on the triggers.' He started moving towards the car park. 'Come on, let's get you on the coach.'

Malik walked slowly, constantly looking around, fearful

that at any moment the cops would rush him, but they all kept their distance.

'Sami, they're more scared of you than you are of them,' whispered Zoe.

'I'm not scared,' he said.

'It's nothing to be ashamed of,' she said. 'I'm scared, too. We're all scared. Nobody wants to die.'

'I'm just worried they might fuck up,' said Malik. 'Cops shoot people all the time.'

'Yeah, but they know that if they shoot you the vest will still explode. They'll have been told not to fire.'

'It only takes one idiot to make a mistake,' he said.

'It'll be okay,' she said. 'Just so long as we all stay calm.'

Malik forced a smile. 'I'm glad I chose you,' he said.

Zoe snorted softly through her nose. 'I wish I could say the same but, to be honest, I wish you'd chosen anyone but me. No offence.'

'None taken,' said Malik. They reached the coach and Malik went up the stairs first, Zoe close behind him. He frowned when he saw the priest sitting next to an Asian man in a suicide vest. The priest was wearing purple and white robes and dabbing at his face with a red handkerchief.

The Asian was staring straight ahead. Like Malik, he had a trigger in his right hand.

Malik took the seat opposite the priest, then realised that Zoe had to go in first. She took the window seat and he slid in after her.

The door closed and the coach moved off. Malik leant forward to get a better look at the Asian man sitting next to the priest. 'All right, brother?' he asked.

The Asian turned to him. 'No, I'm not all right,' he said.

'On what fucking planet could this be considered all right?'

'Brother, I was just trying to make conversation,' said Malik. He sat back in his seat.

LAMBETH CENTRAL COMMUNICATIONS COMMAND CENTRE (5.12 p.m.)

'Duress? He definitely said he was under duress?' Chief Superintendent Gillard stared at Kamran over the top of his glasses.

'The boy heard it wrong. He thought Talpur said "Durex". But I think he was getting a message to us through the boy. Duress. He's being forced into this.'

'But we ruled out a tiger kidnapping, didn't we?'

Kamran nodded. 'All his close relatives are accounted for. But they could be applying pressure in other ways. Threats, perhaps.'

'They threaten to kill a family member unless he helps? Would he believe that? Wouldn't he be more likely to ask for protection?'

'I don't know,' said Kamran. 'Maybe it's something else. Maybe it's not something we can protect him from.'

Gillard sighed. 'Which doesn't help us much, does it? Even if he's acting under duress, it doesn't change the situation we're in, does it? The ISIS prisoners and the bombers are heading for the airport and nothing is going to change that.'

'The fact that he tried to get a message to us suggests that he thinks there is something we can do,' said Kamran. 'But for the life of me I can't think what that might be.'

BIGGIN HILL AIRPORT (5.20 p.m.)

Sergeant Hawkins was studying the handle on the emergency exit at the rear of the coach when his mobile phone rang. It was Captain Murray. 'How's it going, Jim?'

'I wish I could be more optimistic, boss, but this is a bloody nightmare.'

'Keep at it, Jim. There's still a chance we can negotiate this to a peaceful ending.'

'Suicide bombers tend not to negotiate, in my experience,' said Hawkins. 'They're usually in a rush to get to their seventy-two virgins.'

'I hear you, but this whole thing has been weird from the start. Anyway, two things you need to know. The coach should be arriving close to eighteen thirty hours so you really need to be getting the practice coach out by eighteen thirty hours. And until we know for sure that we're going in, keep your men behind the sandbags.'

'That would be the royal "we", would it, boss?'

Murray chuckled. 'Believe me, Jim, I'd much rather be there than here, trust me. The good news is that Terry McMullen will be driving the coach. That will give you an edge, but you're not going to be able to communicate with him before he gets there so we've locked in his contribution. At the first sign that the coach is being boarded, he'll take out the terrorist directly behind him. And the one behind him. Then he'll play it by ear.'

'Please don't tell me he's wearing his lucky hat?'

'Hey, whatever makes him happy. Anyway, keep on doing what you're doing. Just make sure the hangar is clear by six thirty.'

'What about the negotiations, boss? Are they sending a negotiator down?'

'There'll be a negotiating team on site but at the moment they'll be told to keep away from the hangar. The negotiations, such as they are, have so far been handled through the SOR here and it looks as if that's going to continue.'

'And one more thing, boss. A few of the lads aren't that happy about the camera.'

'Not much I can do about it, Jim,' said Murray. 'The cops need to be able to see what's going on.'

'They just don't want it plastered all over YouTube. If we end up slotting the bastards, there'll be others out for revenge.'

'I'll make sure the video doesn't get out,' said the captain. 'But to be on the safe side, do whatever you have to do to conceal your identities. And, Jim, be bloody careful, okay? We need to get the hostages out but it could very easily go tits up.'

'I hear you, boss.'

LAMBETH CENTRAL COMMUNICATIONS COMMAND CENTRE (5.23 p.m.)

'Chief Superintendent Kamran?' A pretty black girl with bright red lipstick was looking down at him. Kamran didn't recognise her and didn't recall seeing her in the special operations room before. She sensed his confusion and smiled. 'Sorry, I'm Rose Taylor, with Transport for London.'

Kamran stood up. 'It's Superintendent Kamran,' he said, 'but please call me Mo.'

'We were wondering, now that the situation has been resolved at Brixton and Wandsworth, are we okay to open the roads? The closures are causing chaos, what with it being rush-hour and all.'

'We should be able to cancel the outer and inner perimeters straight away,' he said. 'The premises themselves will remain as crime scenes but I don't think we need the roads blocked off.'

'Who do I talk to about that? We're being told that the roads have to stay closed.'

'I'll handle it, Rose.'

'How soon after each bomber has gone can we open the other roads?'

'Pretty much straight away,' he said. 'I'll talk to the Silver Commanders of all the scenes.'

She frowned. 'Silver Commanders?'

He smiled. 'I'm sorry. The man in overall charge today is the Gold Commander, Chief Superintendent Gillard. At each scene there is a senior officer in charge and he's called the Silver Commander. He has Bronze Commanders reporting to him.'

'That sounds awfully complicated.'

'Actually, it makes things much simpler. There's no doubt who is in charge at any point, no matter what ranks or services are present.'

She laughed. 'I think we could do with a system like that at TfL,' she said. 'Lots of chiefs there and no one who wants to do any real work.'

'All bureaucracies are the same,' said Kamran. 'They

grow to the point where they lose sight of what their purpose is. The Gold-Silver-Bronze system does help streamline things.' He peered up at a screen showing a map of the coach's progress through west London. It was about to arrive at the Fulham post office.

FULHAM (5.25 p.m.)

Hussain heard the coach pull up in front of the post office. He went over to the window. The armed police were still there but the cars that had been blocking the road to their left had been moved. 'It's time for us to go,' he said to Rebecca. She glared at him sullenly. 'We're going,' he said. 'We're going to get on the coach. The prisoners have been released. It will be over soon.' She stared at him but her face was a blank mask.

Hussain turned to the rest of his hostages, sitting up against the far wall. 'It's over, you can go back to your families!' he shouted. '*Allahu Akbar*, Allah be praised!'

The hostages started whispering to each other. One woman began to cry. Hussain opened the door. There were six police motorcyclists in front of the coach, more behind. The coach door hissed open and the driver, a man in his thirties wearing a bomber jacket and a flat cap, waved at him to get on board. The windows had been blacked out and all Hussain could see was his own reflection. He pulled the chain to get Rebecca to follow him, but she wouldn't move. 'Come on, come on,' he said. 'The sooner we get to the airport, the sooner this will be over.'

Rebecca ignored him and turned to look at the armed police. 'Just shoot the Paki bastard!' she screamed. 'Come on, I don't care. Just put a bullet in the bastard's face!'

'Madam, please get onto the coach!' shouted the armed cop nearest the post office. 'Everything is under control!'

'Like fuck it is!' she shouted. 'He's got a fucking bomb under his coat and he was threatening to kill us all. Shoot him now and I'm the only one who gets killed and I don't give a fuck. So shut the fuck up and shoot him. Now, while he's out in the open! I don't even think he'll press the trigger – he's more scared than I am. Shoot him in the fucking head and he'll drop like a stone. Do it!'

'What is your problem, lady?' hissed Hussain.

She whirled around. 'My problem? My fucking problem? You handcuff yourself to me and threaten to blow me to bits and you ask me what my problem is? Fuck you, Call-Me-Ismail. Fuck you and fuck all Pakis like you.'

'Why are you saying this? Why are you being so aggressive?'

'Madam, please board the coach!' shouted the armed cop. 'You're putting everyone's lives at risk here.'

Rebecca ignored him and stared at Hussain. 'You want to know why, Call-Me-Ismail? You want to know why I hate Pakis like you? Because it was one of you that killed my family. A Paki bastard just like you, beard and all, slammed his car into my husband's and killed him and killed my little girl. Was he insured? Was he fuck. Did he have a driving licence? Did he fuck. Did he stay and face the music? Did he fuck. According to the cops he was out of the country the next day and is now probably living it large in Paki-fucking-stan. He killed my William and he killed my Ruth and the one thing I want right now is to be with them and if I can do that and kill you at the same time then I'll be one very happy woman.' She glared at him and he could see the madness in her eyes. 'I want you dead, Call-Me-Ismail. I can't get the Paki bastard who took my family from me but I can sure as hell take you with me.' She grabbed at his right hand, trying to get at the detonator.

He held it away from her and pushed her with his left hand. 'You're fucking crazy!'

'Madam, please, will you stop resisting!' shouted the armed cop. 'Just get on the coach!'

Rebecca turned to him. 'Do your fucking job, why don't you? Shoot the fucker. He's a fucking terrorist and he deserves to die so do your fucking job and shoot him.'

'Lady, please stop this,' said Hussain. 'I'm sorry about what happened to your family. But it wasn't my fault.'

Rebecca spat at him. 'No, but this is your fucking fault. You handcuffed yourself to me, you chose me, so fuck you.' She grinned. 'Maybe your God is fucking with you the way my God fucked with me. Do you get that, Call-Me-Ismail? Maybe your God wanted you to choose me. He does move in fucking mysterious ways, doesn't he?'

'Lady, please stop this,' said Hussain. She lunged at his right hand again and he kept it well away from her. 'If we don't get on the coach, everyone will die,' he pleaded.

'Don't care,' she said.

'Everyone on the coach will die, too. And there are hostages on it. And a driver. They'll have families, too. Do you want to hurt their families the way you've been hurt?'

'Don't care,' she said again, but less vehemently this time.

'Lady, really, I'm sorry,' said Hussain. 'I'm so, so sorry about what happened to your family. The bastard who did it should burn in Hell. And shame on him for running away. But that has nothing to do with what's happening here.'

'Madam, please get on the coach now!' shouted the armed cop.

'Shut the fuck up!' screamed Hussain. 'Can't you see she's in pain?' He put his face closer to the woman, but kept the trigger behind his back. 'Lady, please, just help me do this. I don't want to be here any more than you do. I just want to go home.'

Tears were running down the woman's face. 'I miss them.'

'I know you do,' said Hussain. 'And I'm sorry.'

Rebecca began to howl and before he knew what he was doing, Hussain had stepped forward and embraced her. He felt her press against the explosives strapped to his chest, and gently patted her on the back. 'I'm sorry,' he whispered.

'I want my husband and my daughter back,' she sobbed.

The armed police officers looked at each other, not sure what to do.

'You have to get on the coach with me,' he said. 'Nothing bad is going to happen. I promise you.'

'It's already happened,' she said. 'I want to die. Just press the fucking button and end it for me. Please.'

'I can't,' he said. 'It's not up to me. And if we do what we're supposed to do, then everyone goes home.'

'I don't want to go home,' she said. 'Please, please, please, end it for me now.'

'You have to be strong for your husband and daughter,'

he said. 'You have to keep their memories alive. Do you think they would want you to die? Of course they wouldn't. They'd want you to enjoy every minute of your life here. And then, when it's your time, you can join them in Heaven. But now's not the time. You don't have to die and I don't have to die, and the people on that coach don't have to die.' He patted her on the back again. 'Now come on, walk with me. One step at a time.' He put his left hand around her waist and guided her towards the coach, keeping his right hand held high so that the police could see it.

He got her to the coach door, then went up the stairs backwards so that he could lead her up. She kept her head down as she sobbed.

'Come on, we haven't got all day,' snapped the driver.

Hussain stared at him with dead eyes. 'You need to stay quiet,' he said. 'She's not well.'

The driver gazed back at him, then nodded slowly. 'Okay. But we're on a tight deadline. Please try to hurry her along.'

Hussain put his left hand out and she took it. He led her down the coach. There were two Asian men wearing suicide vests, one sitting next to a young woman, the other beside a robed priest.

Hussain sat down behind the man next to the priest and smiled up at Rebecca. 'Please sit down,' he said.

She sniffed and did as he asked. The priest twisted around in his seat and offered her a red handkerchief. She took it, thanked him, and dabbed at her eyes.

Hussain saw the driver watching him in the rear-view mirror. Hussain nodded and the driver nodded back. The door closed and the coach lurched forward.

LAMBETH CENTRAL COMMUNICATIONS COMMAND CENTRE (5.27 p.m.)

'What just happened there?' asked Gillard, who was watching the screen showing the Sky News feed from the news crew outside the Fulham post office. The coach was pulling away, flanked by police motorcyclists.

'It looked like the hostage was freaking out,' said Kamran. 'Hardly surprising, considering the stress she's under.'

The Sky News feed was replaced by an overhead view from one of the Met's helicopters showing the police van en route to Biggin Hill.

'I just hope everyone stays calm,' said Gillard. 'At least until we get them to the airport.'

'Sir, we have a feed from the hangar now,' Lumley called, from the Gold Command suite. 'It's only black and white and there's no sound but the picture's clear.'

Kamran and Gillard walked back to the sergeant's station. The feed was on his left-hand screen. The camera had been put up near the roof and was looking down at the centre of the hangar, focused on a coach that was a match to the one that was picking up the bombers and their hostages. 'Make sure we have everything recorded, in duplicate, if possible,' said Gillard. Murray appeared at the door to the suite and Gillard waved him over. 'You might like to see this, Alex,' he said. 'Your guys are rehearsing taking the coach.'

As the captain joined them, three SAS troopers ran up to the front of the vehicle and two approached the rear. Unlike the coach that was being used to collect the bombers and the hostages, the windows were clear and they could see a single figure sitting in the driver's seat.

'That's Jim Hawkins,' said Murray. 'He's a sergeant.'

The two men at the rear of the coach had the door open and they charged inside, holding handguns. At the exact moment they entered the coach, the first of the three troopers at the front launched himself up the stairs. The driver stood up, twisted and aimed a gun down the coach. Almost immediately the second and third troopers piled in. They were all waving handguns. Then they stopped. Murray was frowning. 'Two and a half seconds,' he said. 'It's good but it's not good enough.'

The troopers filed out of the coach. The two at the back closed the door, then moved out of view. Sergeant Hawkins sat down again.

'Do you think it's doable?' asked Kamran. 'Can they shoot all the bombers quickly enough?'

Murray screwed up his face. 'Hand on heart, I don't see how it's possible,' he said. 'You have to take out all nine before any of them has time to press the trigger.'

'What about snipers shooting through the windows?'

'When they're blacked out? They'd be guessing. And if they missed they'd risk hitting the hostages.'

'Is there anything else we can do?' asked Kamran.

'You can hope they just surrender,' said Murray. 'Because if we have to storm the coach . . .' He shrugged and left the sentence unfinished.

'What about those night-vision goggles you guys some-times use?' asked Waterman. 'Wouldn't they work?'

Murray shook his head. 'The passive ones wouldn't see through the blacked-out windows, and the infrared type wouldn't work because glass is very effective at blocking infrared. Why? What were you thinking?'

'Shooting through the windows, maybe. If you could see where everyone was you could shoot through the glass.'

'It wouldn't work,' said the SAS captain. 'Our only way in is through the two doors, unfortunately. Hopefully the lads can shave some more time off it.'

Gillard focused on the screen showing the feed from the helicopter. The van had almost reached the main gates of Biggin Hill airport.

'Sergeant Lumley, can you get the TV news feeds up on screens? Let's see what Shahid can see.'

Within seconds two screens on the main wall began showing feeds from Sky News and BBC News. Sky was showing a view from its own helicopter, at an angle because they had been forbidden to enter Biggin Hill airspace. The BBC was showing a shot of the road outside the prison. The flashing blue lights of the motorcycles leading the way were visible in the distance. Across the bottom of the BBC screen was a scrolling headline: 'FREED ISIS PRISONERS ARRIVING AT BIGGIN HILL AIRPORT.'

'Strictly speaking, they haven't been freed,' said Kamran. 'Just moved.'

'Hopefully, it'll satisfy Shahid,' said Gillard. 'I really don't want them out of the van, even under armed guard.'

The picture being transmitted by Sky changed to show a view similar to the BBC's. Six motorcyclists flashed by, then a police armed-response vehicle, the prison transport van, another ARV and more motorcycles. Bringing up the rear were two black SUVs with darkened windows. 'Please tell me they're your men, Alex,' Kamran said.

Murray laughed. 'Yeah, they're Sass.'

The convoy drove straight into the airport and a pole barrier came down behind them.

Both TV feeds now had reporters talking to the camera, explaining what had just happened.

Kamran glanced at the clock on the wall. 'We made it with half an hour to spare. How are we getting on with the pick-ups?' he asked Lumley.

'Three on board,' said the sergeant. 'En route to Kensington to collect number four.'

MARYLEBONE (5.32 p.m.)

The Sky News presenter with too much make-up was talking to a grey-haired man in a suit who was some sort of terrorism expert. He was trying to explain what ISIS was and what they wanted, but the woman kept interrupting him. 'Let him talk, woman,' muttered Chaudhry, under his breath.

'She likes the sound of her own voice, doesn't she?' said Kenny.

'She probably only got the job because she's Asian,' said Chaudhry, contemptuously.

Kenny laughed. 'Funny thing to say, you being Asian and all.'

'Hey, mate, I've had to fight for everything I've done. No one ever gave me a break because I'm a Pak.'

'Is it okay to say that?' asked Kenny.

'Pak? Hell, yeah. Paki's an insult, but I'm a Pak and proud of it.'

'But you were born here, right?'

'Sure. So was my mum. My dad is the only one who lived in Pakistan.'

'So you're British, right?'

'Same as you.'

'So why do this?' He nodded at the suicide vest. 'I mean, that's a bit fucking extreme, isn't it?'

'It wasn't my idea, believe me,' said Chaudhry.

'What do you mean?'

'Nothing. Forget it.'

'But you're ISIS, right?'

'ISIS? Fuck, no. They're nutters, ISIS. Have you seen those videos? They're fucking animals.'

'Now I'm confused.'

'Yeah, tell me about it,' said Chaudhry. 'I'm a supporter of Al-Qaeda. Have been since the invasion of Iraq and all the shit that went on there. You can't be a Muslim in the world today and not feel threatened.'

'That's how you feel?'

'Fuck me, yeah. You can see what the Americans want, right? They want every Muslim dead. We have to stand and fight.'

'But what you're doing is about ISIS, right? And you've won.' He gestured at the TV. 'You got them released and now they're picking up you guys to take you to the airport.'

'That's the plan, yes.' He took a sip from his bottle of water. 'You seem very calm, Kenny.'

'I smoked some dope before I started my shift. That's probably helped. But generally, you know, if it happens, it happens. I'm not a worrier.'

'Easy not to worry when you're white,' said Chaudhry.

'Mate, I've not had it easy either. Don't go thinking that.

My mum ran off with my uncle when I was still in nappies and my dad brought up three boys on his own. I went to a shit school and managed one year at uni before I bailed, and now I'm working in a pub for minimum wage. I'm not exactly living the life, you know.' He raised his almost-empty glass. 'But, assuming I get through this in one piece, I should be able to sell my story to the papers, right?'

'I hadn't thought of that,' said Chaudhry.

'Aye, it's an ill wind,' said Kenny.

'What the fuck does that mean?'

'It's an expression. It's an ill wind that blows no good. It means most things work out well for somebody.'

'Yeah, well, I don't see that anything that's happened today helps me at all. It fucks me up, big-time.'

'What happens to you?' asked Kenny. 'You'll be on the plane with the ISIS lads, right?'

'Fuck that,' said Chaudhry. 'I live here. I'm not fucking off to Syria for nobody. Have you been there? It's a shit-hole.'

'Have you? Been there?'

Chaudhry shook his head. 'I've been to Pakistan, and I was over the border in Afghanistan, but trust me, mate, they're shit-holes too. You want to stay well clear.'

'But you'll have to leave the UK after this, right? I mean, you've won, but they're never going to forgive you.'

The TV was showing a shot of a coach with blackened windows driving through Kensington. 'Kenny, mate, will you shut the fuck up? You're really starting to depress me.'

LAMBETH CENTRAL COMMUNICATIONS
COMMAND CENTRE (5.34 p.m.)

'What the hell is wrong with those people?' asked Kamran, staring up at the large screen that was showing the Sky News feed. The pavements were crowded with people filming the coach on their phones as it went by. 'Don't they realise there are bombs on that coach? If it goes up there'll be shrapnel and broken glass everywhere.'

'We've told people to stay away but they're just not listening,' said Gillard. 'And we don't have the manpower to clear the pavements.'

'This could be Shahid's plan, right from the start,' Kamran mused. 'Get all the bombs on the coach, then detonate among the crowds. Even if it went off now, with just three bombs on board, they'd kill and maim dozens. By the time the last bomber is on there'll be nine, and if that went up in south London . . .' He shuddered.

'You're right, Mo,' said Gillard. 'We need to make sure that doesn't happen.' He waved at Sergeant Lumley. 'We need to clear the streets on the route,' he said. 'Get as many police as you can out there and move everyone off the pavements. And I mean everyone.'

'I'm on it, sir.'

'The roads to the airport are going to have to be cleared,' said Gillard.

'It's not the roads that are the problem,' said Kamran. 'It's the pavements. The gawkers. The idiots who want a selfie as the coach goes by. Can you talk to Lisa? She needs to make sure the media are pumping out warnings. People need to understand just what will happen if those bombs go off on the coach.'

Kamran picked up his phone and dialled the press officer's mobile. It went straight through to voicemail so he left a message. As he was talking, he looked up at the clock. It was twenty-five to six. He put the phone down and went over to Gillard. 'You know, the bombers will pretty much all be on board at six,' he said. 'If Shahid has been planning a spectacular all along, that would be the time to do it.'

'What are you thinking?'

'I don't know, but as the clock hits six we want as few people near that coach as possible.'

KENSINGTON (5.35 p.m.)

'I'm hungry,' said Sally. 'I haven't eaten since this morning. Nobody has.' She was sitting with her back to the wall, her legs drawn up to her chest. Osman was standing next to her, his left hand at his side to keep the tension off the chain that linked them.

'There's nothing I can do about that, madam,' said Osman. 'I'm hungry too. I haven't had food since last night.'

'There's stuff in the kitchen. We give the children lunch so there are sandwiches and fruit.'

'Everyone has to stay here,' said Osman.

Sally pointed with her left hand. 'That's the kitchen there. Just open the door and there's food.'

Osman's stomach growled. He looked at the five hostages sitting by the wall at the far end of the room. 'Is everyone hungry?'

They all nodded. 'I'd like a drink,' said a middle-aged woman. 'I have to take my cholesterol tablets and I need water for that.'

'You can stand up and go into the kitchen,' Osman said to her. 'Leave the door open and stay where I can see you. Bring out some food and water.' The woman pushed herself up and went to the door. As she reached for the handle, the mobile phone buzzed in Osman's waistpack. 'Wait!' shouted Osman. She froze. He used his left hand to take out the phone and put it to his ear.

'We have won, brother,' said Shahid. 'The ISIS prisoners are being taken to the airport as we speak.'

'It's over?' asked Osman. He grinned, bobbing up and down excitedly.

'Almost, brother. A coach is pulling up outside. You are to take your hostage out with you. It will take you to the airport.'

'I don't want to go to the airport,' said Osman. 'I want to go home.'

'Once the prisoners are on the plane, you can go home,' said Shahid. 'Go outside now. Speak to no one. Just get onto the coach.'

Osman opened his mouth to say something but the line went dead. He fumbled the phone back into the waistpack. 'We are to go outside,' he said.

'Who?'

'You and I.'

'You're letting us go?' asked Sally.

'Not yet,' said Osman. 'We have to get on a coach.'

'A coach? Why?'

'We have to go to the airport.'

She frowned. 'Why?'

'We just do.' He gestured at the door. 'Come on, please, madam. We have to go.'

'I don't want to. You go. You've got what you wanted. You don't need me any more.'

'Madam, even if I wanted to let you go, I couldn't. I don't have the key.'

'How can you not have the key?'

Osman smiled thinly. 'You have many questions, madam, but I'm afraid I have very few answers.' He tugged at the chain that connected them. 'Please come with me. At least then the others can go home.'

She looked at him earnestly. 'Are you going to kill me?' she asked.

He smiled. 'No, madam. I am most definitely not. You have my word on that. Like you, I just want to go home to my loved ones.'

She stared at him for several seconds. 'Okay,' she said. 'Let's go.'

He took her over to the door that led to the corridor and pushed it open. The corridor was empty but through the glass doors to his left he could see the street. There was a coach parked there, its windows blacked out, police motorcycles in front of it, blue lights flashing. The door was already open and the driver was looking down at them, his hands on the steering-wheel.

'I really don't want to get on the coach,' she said.

'There's no choice,' said Osman. He went up the steps

first. The driver flashed him a smile and Osman smiled back. 'Don't sit in the front row,' said the driver.

'Yes, sir,' said Osman.

Six of the seats were occupied. There were four sitting to his left and two to his right. Three Asians and three hostages. A priest, a young woman and an older woman, who was dabbing at her eyes with a red handkerchief. The men and their hostages stared at Osman. The fact that they were on the coach meant that it would soon be over. Shahid had won. The ISIS prisoners had been released and were on the way to the airport. Once the prisoners were on their plane, Osman would be free. He smiled but no one smiled back. He moved down the middle of the coach and moved to sit on the right-hand side, then realised that Sally would have to go in first. 'I'm sorry, madam, after you,' he said, nodding for her to take the window seat.

She slid along and he sat next to her. 'Why have they covered the windows?' she asked.

'I don't know,' said Osman.

The Asian man sitting in front of Osman twisted around in his seat. 'It's so they can't shoot us,' he said. 'If they can't see us, they can't shoot us. *Inshallah*.'

'*Inshallah*,' repeated Osman. 'Thank you, sir.'

'Where are you from, brother?' asked the man.

'I'm Somalian.'

'You're a long way from home, brother.'

'No, sir, England is my home.'

The door closed and the coach pulled away from the kerb.

LAMBETH CENTRAL COMMUNICATIONS COMMAND CENTRE (5.45 p.m.)

Kamran contemplated his mobile phone. 'You're wondering why he hasn't called,' said Chris Thatcher. The negotiator was standing at the door to the Gold Command suite, looking at the main screen in the special operations room, which was showing the view from the Met's helicopter, looking down on the coach containing the bombers.

'The ISIS prisoners are already at the airport, I would have thought he'd be asking about a plane by now.'

Thatcher nodded. 'Everything else has been planned to perfection, hasn't it?'

'He's either assuming the plane is in place or he doesn't care either way. And, frankly, it's a big assumption to make. You'd expect him at least to want to know what sort of plane it is.'

Chief Superintendent Gillard stood up at his desk and rubbed the back of his neck. 'Anyone got any ibuprofen or paracetamol?' he asked. 'My head's throbbing.'

'I've got ibuprofen, sir,' said Sergeant Lumley, handing him a strip of tablets.

Gillard swallowed two and washed them down with water. 'You have to wonder why he hasn't asked about the plane, don't you?' he said.

'It could also be that the plane was never an issue,' said Kamran. 'My worry is that he intends that coach to blow up in London with the world watching.' The clock on the wall was showing just after a quarter to six. 'I suppose we'll know soon enough.'

MARBLE ARCH (5.50 p.m.)

The Al Jazeera newsreader said that they were going live
to a reporter outside Biggin Hill airport. It was a middle-
aged man with a Welsh accent, explaining that the airport
had now been closed and that the six ISIS prisoners were
awaiting the arrival of the bombers and their hostages.

Mohammed nodded enthusiastically. 'You have won,
brother. They have given in. The British always do. They
talk tough but they are weak. They ran away from Afghanistan
and they ran away from Iraq.' He slapped a hand on the
table. 'This is going exactly as you planned, isn't it?'

The man shrugged.

'What is your name, brother?' asked Mohammed.

'Zach,' said the man. 'Zach Ahmed. You?'

'Mohammed.'

'A good name,' said Ahmed. 'Where are you from?'

'Sudan. I am claiming asylum.'

'Good luck with that,' said Ahmed.

'And you, brother? Where are you from?'

'London, mate. I was born here.'

'You are lucky. You are a citizen from birth. That is worth
more than gold.'

Ahmed nodded at the chain linking them. 'That why
you wanted that man's money?'

'I have none,' said Mohammed. 'They give me a little
but it's not enough to live on. They won't let me work. But
being poor here is still better than being rich in Sudan.'
He held out his left hand and showed Ahmed the glittering
watch on his wrist. 'How much do you think I can sell this
for?'

'I don't know, but it's expensive, I'm sure.'

Mohammed nodded. 'That's what I thought.'

'How did you get to London?' asked Ahmed.

'I crossed the border into Libya. I reached Italy on a small boat and travelled overland to Calais. After three months there I hid in the back of a lorry and got to England.'

'When was that?'

'Four years ago. I claimed asylum on the first day I got here but it takes time. The money El-Sayed gave me will help my family.'

'Your family are still in Sudan?'

Mohammed nodded. 'I have two wives and six children,' he said. 'I had to tell the authorities here that they were killed in the fighting, but they are alive and well, and once I am a citizen I will bring them to join me. They already have the money that El-Sayed sent. That will help.'

'Sounds like you have it all worked out,' said Ahmed.

'Everybody knows what you have to do and say to get asylum in England,' said Mohammed. 'It is a game that everyone plays.'

'And how do you know El-Sayed?'

'Everyone here knows him. He is a big man and a good man. A true Muslim. True to his faith and true to his friends. As he said to you, he is on your side.'

'My side?'

Mohammed leant closer and lowered his voice. 'He is a money man for Al-Qaeda. He sends funds to them and helps pay their people here. Everyone knows.'

'I didn't.'

Mohammed nodded enthusiastically. 'He is a good man. And he loves his son.'

Ahmed smiled. 'That was clear,' he said.

'I have often used him to send money back to my family,' said Mohammed. 'Small amounts, not like today. Sometimes he would not even charge me for the transaction. He said that he understands how difficult it is for new arrivals.' He took a sip from a bottle of water. 'Can I ask you a question, brother?'

'I can't promise to answer it, but go ahead.'

'Why did you choose this place? This coffee shop?'

'I'm not sure.'

He waved his left hand. 'There are so many Muslims here. Why not choose a place with more *kafirs*? Look around you, brother. Most of the customers are Muslim, like you. And most of them support ISIS.'

'You think so?'

Mohammed smiled. 'I know so. I come here often, I listen, I talk. The brothers in Syria and Iraq are fighting the good fight. If I was younger I would be there myself. And one day, *inshallah*, they will bring the fight to this country.'

'Why do you say that?' asked Ahmed. 'This country is offering you asylum. Why would you want to change it?'

'I'm here because getting asylum is easy. And because I have many friends here. A Sudanese lawyer helps me and a Sudanese landlord rents me a room. I can talk my own language and eat my own food. But I am a Muslim and I want this country to be a Muslim country. ISIS can bring that about and, *inshallah*, they will, one day. Maybe not in my lifetime but in the lifetime of my children, I hope it will come true.'

Ahmed's waistpack buzzed and he took out his phone. It was Shahid. 'The coach is outside. Good luck, brother.'

Ahmed put the phone away and stood up. 'It's time,' he said.

He took Mohammed over to the window and pulled away one of the sheets of newspaper. Outside there was a white coach with blacked-out windows. The driver had already opened the door and was staring straight ahead, his face blue from the flashing lights of the half-dozen motorcycles parked ahead of him. To their left was a black BMW SUV, and two police marksmen dressed all in black were sighting their weapons along the bonnet.

'Do you think they will kill us?' asked Mohammed.

'They will be too scared that the vest will explode,' said Ahmed.

'They could shoot you in the head.'

'Let's try and look on the bright side, shall we?' said Ahmed. He opened the door. Edgware Road had been cleared of traffic, other than police and emergency vehicles, but there seemed to be a lot of onlookers standing behind yellow and black police tape, many of them holding up mobile phones. Ahmed kept his head down and his right hand above his head as he and Mohammed walked to the coach. Ahmed went up the steps first. The windows were blacked out and it was only when he reached the top of the steps that he saw who was inside. There were eight passengers, four sitting behind the driver and four on the other side.

Ahmed walked down the aisle, Mohammed staying close behind him. He went right to the back of the coach and sat on the driver's side, close to the emergency exit.

Mohammed sat next to him. 'Do you think we will go on the plane?' Mohammed asked Ahmed.

'I've no idea,' said Ahmed.

'I've never been on a plane.'

'It's no big deal,' said Ahmed.

The coach door closed and they drove off, following the six police motorcyclists.

'I can't leave England,' said Mohammed, suddenly worried. 'They said I'll lose my asylum appeal if I leave the country.'

'I'm sure if you just explain that, they'll let you stay.'

'Do you think so?'

Ahmed shook his head contemptuously. 'Mate, I really don't give a fuck.'

LAMBETH CENTRAL COMMUNICATIONS COMMAND CENTRE (5.55 p.m.)

Kamran looked over at the clock on the wall. Six o'clock was fast approaching and there had been no call from Shahid. The coach had left the coffee shop in Marble Arch and was on its way to the Marylebone pub, less than a mile away.

The main screen in the special operations room was showing the feed from the Met helicopter that was tracking the coach and its convoy. The road ahead was clear of traffic but there were still onlookers at most of the inter-sections.

'If they detonate now, they're going to kill a lot of people,' said Kamran.

'We're doing our best to keep the rubberneckers away but the TV isn't doing us any favours,' said Gillard. 'They keep showing the route the coach will likely take and everyone wants their own video to put on Facebook or YouTube.'

'That might be Shahid's plan. He lets the great British public do all the publicity work.'

'I hope you're wrong, Mo,' said Gillard.

'You and me both,' said Kamran.

Captain Murray came into the Gold Command suite, putting away his mobile phone. 'They've got the timing down to two and a half seconds but that's about it,' he said.

'What do you think?' asked Gillard. 'Is that enough?'

'I wish I could say it was, but two and a half seconds is still a long time when all they have to do is press a button,' said the SAS captain.

'What about stun grenades?' asked Kamran.

'They're a double-edged sword,' said Murray. 'They'll likely stun all the occupants but it will increase the time it takes to clear the vehicle. Our driver will be affected, also. The question is whether we can stun them quickly enough and long enough to take them out before they get a chance to detonate. The problem is that flash-bangs don't detonate instantly. The bad guys will see the canisters a fraction of a second before they go off and, unfortunately, a fraction of a second is more than enough time to press a trigger.'

'Just a thought,' said Chris Thatcher. 'Do you have a negotiating team at the airport?'

'I had assumed we'd be talking to Shahid,' said Gillard.

'That's been the way it's gone so far, but once we have the bombers isolated in the hangar there'd be an opportunity to talk to them direct.'

'Shahid has gone out of his way to make sure that we only talk to him,' said Kamran. 'I don't think he's going to change his SOP.'

'I was thinking of not giving him the choice,' said Thatcher. 'They'll be isolated, Shahid won't be able to see them. It might be an opportunity to make direct contact.'

Gillard looked at Kamran. 'What do you think, Mo?'

'When they've had the opportunity to negotiate, they haven't taken it. In fact, other than at Wandsworth, they've gone out of their way to avoid it. Having said that, we should be covering all bases. It wouldn't hurt to have a team there.'

'What about you, Chris? Do you want to go? We could bike you there.'

'I think I'm probably most useful here,' said Thatcher. 'Mo's right. Shahid is the main point of contact. I just think it might be helpful to have someone on the ground with negotiating skills.'

'We have half an hour,' said Kamran. 'I could talk to Bromley, see if they have any negotiators on call.'

'Go for it,' said Gillard.

Kamran looked up at the clock again.

'That six o'clock deadline's worrying you, isn't it?' said Gillard.

'That was his deadline from the start,' said Kamran. There was just a minute to go. He went to the door and looked at the main screen in the special operations room, which was showing the feed from the Met helicopter. The coach was approaching the Grapes pub in Marylebone.

Murray had followed him and put a hand on his shoulder. 'It wouldn't make sense to detonate before they're all on board.'

'I hope so,' said Kamran. He found himself holding his breath as the seconds ticked off. The second hand reached twelve, then ticked past. On the big screen, the coach continued to power along the road, flanked by police motor-cycles, their blue lights flashing. Kamran sighed with relief.

'Don't relax yet, Mo,' said the SAS captain. 'The crunch is half an hour away, when Shahid realises his people aren't getting on a plane. That's when the shit is going to be heading fan-wards.'

MARYLEBONE (6.02 p.m.)

The Asian Sky News presenter with too much make-up was describing the police van that was driving towards Biggin Hill airport at the centre of a convoy of police vehicles and motorcycles. She seemed to be struggling for words and was constantly correcting herself, so Chaudhry figured she wasn't reading from a script.

'What happens to us when the prisoners are at the airport?' asked Kenny. 'You let us go, right?'

'I'm not sure.'

'What do you mean, you're not sure?' Kenny gestured at the TV screen. 'It's almost over. You got what you wanted.'

The picture changed on the TV screen. Now it was showing a white coach with blacked-out windows driving through the streets of London, flanked by police motor-cycles. The pavements were thronged with onlookers, many of whom were holding up their mobile phones. The picture was from a helicopter flying overhead. According to the presenter, the coach was now heading east, presumably towards the Grapes.

'It's coming here, mate,' said Kenny. 'It's coming to collect you.'

Chaudhry's waistpack buzzed. He took out the phone and answered. It was Shahid.

'The coach is on its way, brother,' said Shahid. 'As soon as it pulls up outside, leave with your hostage. The police have been told to stay well back. All you have to do is get on the coach.'

'And when can I go home?' asked Chaudhry.

'Soon, brother, soon. Once the ISIS warriors are in the air.'

'Do I have to go with them?'

'You can decide that at the airport, brother. It will be your choice.'

'I just want to go home.'

'Then, *inshallah*, you shall.'

The line went dead and Chaudhry put the phone away. 'Who was that?' asked Kenny. 'Was it the police?'

Chaudhry shook his head. 'No. Not the police.' He stood up and looked at the TV screen. The coach was driving down Marylebone Road, not far from the pub. All the traffic had been diverted but there was nothing the police could do to keep onlookers away. There were hundreds of people on the pavements, most of them filming on their phones. Other spectators were crowded at the windows overlooking the street, pointing and grinning as if it were a parade they were watching. 'We need to get ready, Kenny.'

'Can I ask you a favour?'

'Sure.'

'Can I take a selfie with you?'

Chaudhry's jaw dropped. 'Are you fucking serious?'

'Mate, if the papers interview me they'll pay a lot for a picture like that.'

Chaudhry sighed. 'Go on, then.'

'You're a star, mate,' said Kenny. He had to use his left hand to pull his mobile out of his back pocket. He put it in camera mode, leant his head close to Chaudhry's and took a picture. He checked the screen. 'You're not smiling,' he said.

'Why would I be smiling?'

'Because you won.' He put the phone away. Kenny looked up at the TV screen. 'Bloody hell, there's the pub,' he said.

Chaudhry followed his gaze. The coach had just pulled up in front of it. It was flanked by police motorcycles and there were two police cars behind it. 'Time to go,' he said. He turned to the rest of the hostages. 'Ladies and gentlemen, I'm happy to be able to tell you that it's over. I'm leaving with Kenny here and the rest of you can go home.'

The hostages stared at him blankly, not sure how to react.

'It's over,' Chaudhry repeated. 'For you anyway.' He stood up and Kenny followed suit. They walked to the main door and Chaudhry pushed it open. There were several armed police aiming their guns from across the road. Off to his left he saw more police cars, two ambulances and a fire engine.

'Please board the coach right away!' boomed an amplified voice. A uniformed officer was standing among the armed police with a megaphone. 'Move straight to the coach.'

The door was already open. Chaudhry and Kenny walked towards it. Kenny grabbed his phone again and began taking photographs. 'You are fucking mad, mate,' said Chaudhry.

He walked up the steps, holding his left hand behind him and keeping his right hand up so that they could see the trigger.

'Put that fucking camera away!' shouted the driver, when he saw the phone in Kenny's hand. Kenny did as he was told but the driver continued to glare at him.

Chaudhry looked down the coach. The windows had all been blacked out but there were small lights on near the roof. Six people were sitting on the left side behind the driver and four on the right. Most of the men wearing the suicide vests were in their twenties but one, sitting next to an elderly priest, was older, in his fifties maybe.

'Sit down. We've got to be on our way,' snapped the driver. He closed the door and revved the engine.

Chaudhry nodded for Kenny to sit by the window of the second row, in front of a young Asian man handcuffed to a pretty blonde girl. Kenny grinned at the girl. 'How are you doing?'

She forced a smile. 'As well as can be expected.'

'I'm Kenny.'

'Zoe.'

'You got a boyfriend?'

'Have you?'

Kenny laughed, but stopped when Chaudhry glared at him. 'Mate, you need to focus,' said Chaudhry. 'This is no fucking joke.' The coach moved off and Chaudhry took slow, deep breaths, trying to calm his racing heart.

MARBLE ARCH (6.05 p.m.)

Imad El-Sayed and his son came down the stairs cautiously. El-Sayed pushed open the door to the coffee shop and flinched when he saw two armed officers with carbines held across their chests. When they saw him they shouldered their weapons and aimed at his chest. 'Armed police, hands in the air!' shouted one.

'We are civilians!' shouted El-Sayed, throwing up his hands. 'Don't shoot, don't shoot!' He looked over his shoulder. 'Hassan, put up your hands.'

'Shut up and move forward!' shouted the armed officer.

El-Sayed stepped forward with his hands up, Hassan behind him. One of the officers quickly patted them down. Satisfied that they weren't armed, he nodded at his colleague. Both men lowered their weapons. 'Who are you?' asked the older of the two.

'My name is Imad El-Sayed, and this is my son, Hassan.'

'Where were you?'

'We were hiding upstairs.'

'You work here?'

El-Sayed shook his head. 'We are customers. We hid while the bomber was here. I run a bureau de change down the road. Can I show you my business card?'

'Go ahead,' said the officer.

El-Sayed slowly reached into his robe and pulled out his wallet. He took out a card and handed it to the officer, who studied it. 'Okay, Mr El-Sayed.' He gestured at the policemen in fluorescent jackets who were talking to the customers. 'Please talk to one of these officers before you leave. They have a few questions for you.'

'Is it over?' asked El-Sayed. 'Have the ISIS prisoners been released?'

The officer gestured at the television on the wall. 'You can watch it while you wait,' he said.

TAVISTOCK SQUARE (6.15 p.m.)

The coach parked across the road and its door opened. Kashif Talpur's phone buzzed and he took it out of his waistpack. 'You are to leave the bus, brother,' said Shahid.

'I'm not your brother,' snarled Talpur.

'Just do as you're told. This will soon be over,' said Shahid.

'I want to leave the woman behind,' said Talpur. 'She's a pain in the arse.'

'You are to take the hostage on to the coach. She will be released at the airport.'

'What's happened to the ISIS prisoners?'

'They're already at the airport,' said Shahid. 'Now move over to the coach. You know what will happen if you do not comply.'

The line went dead and Talpur cursed. He put the phone back into the waistpack. 'Open the door,' he said to the driver, then turned to address the passengers. 'Ladies and gentlemen, I'm about to leave the bus. Please stay where you are until the police arrive. Do not, I repeat do not, attempt to leave the bus. There are a lot of armed police out there and I'd hate for them to shoot any of you by mistake.'

The door opened. 'You have to come with me,' Talpur said to the woman he was handcuffed to. She opened her mouth to protest but he pointed a warning finger at her. 'Don't even think about giving me a hard time,' he said. 'I've had a shitty twenty-four hours and I don't want you making it worse.'

'I'm a Muslim woman and you have no right to do this to me,' she said.

'It's not about you being a Muslim,' said Talpur. 'You were just in the wrong place at the wrong time.' He headed for the door and yanked the chain to get her to follow him.

More than a dozen armed police were covering him with their carbines. In the far corner of the square a cluster of emergency vehicles included a fire engine and two ambulances. Dozens of police officers in fluorescent jackets were holding back onlookers, most of whom were taking videos and photographs on their phones.

'Kash, we need to talk to you!' Talpur looked to his left. Mark Biddulph was standing behind two armed officers, wearing a bulletproof vest over his leather jacket.

'Get the hell away from me,' shouted Talpur.

'If you're being forced into this, we can help you.'

'Seriously, Mark, you're putting everyone's life on the line by talking to me,' Talpur yelled. He pulled at the chain to hurry the woman up. She cursed him in Arabic.

'Just tell me what's happening, Kash,' shouted Biddulph. 'Why are you doing this?'

Talpur ignored him and climbed onto the coach, pulling the woman after him. As she climbed up, Talpur looked over his shoulder and saw Biddulph staring at him, his brow furrowed. Talpur forced a smile, then mouthed, 'I'm sorry.'

'We haven't got all day,' growled the driver.

Talpur turned to him. The driver stared back impassively. 'Sit down and be quick about it,' he growled. 'We're on a deadline.'

Talpur looked down the coach. Six bombers and six hostages were watching him. He moved towards the seat directly behind the driver. 'Not there,' snapped the man. 'Further back.'

Talpur headed towards the back of the coach as the driver closed the door. He told the woman to sit by the window at the back on the right-hand side, then sat next to her. 'Why are you doing this?' she hissed.

'You wouldn't believe me if I told you,' said Talpur.

SOUTH LONDON (ten hours earlier)

Kashif Talpur kept his breathing slow and even. The hood had been over his head when he woke, and he quickly realised that the faster he breathed, the more uncomfortable it was. He had stuck out his tongue and pressed it against the hood and it felt soft and rough. Sacking maybe. He was sitting on something hard and his hands were tied behind him.

He had no idea how long he'd been tied to the chair, or what time it was. The last thing he remembered was walking back to his flat. He'd seen a man waiting on the pavement ahead of him. Something about him had seemed off so Talpur's defences had been up. But he was so busy concentrating on the man ahead of him that he never even heard the one behind him. Something sweet had been clamped over his mouth and, within seconds, he had lost consciousness. Talpur had no idea how long ago that had happened. It could have been an hour, it could have been a day.

He listened intently. He could hear scraping sounds, and a soft footfall. An occasional grunt. After a while he lost all sense of time. The ripping off of the hood came as a shock, intensified by the fluorescent lights overhead that stung his eyes. He blinked away tears as he tried to focus. There was something on his head, covering his face, though there were holes for his eyes and mouth. A ski mask, he realised. He was wearing a ski mask.

There were men in front of him, wearing ski masks and tied to chairs. He looked to his left. More masked men. He twisted his head to the right. More men. They were sitting in a circle, facing inwards. All men, so far as he could see. All masked. All tied. He blinked faster, trying to clear his vision. Then he saw something that made him catch his breath. The man directly opposite him had a canvas vest under his coat. The vest had pockets containing what looked like greyish blocks of Plasticine and, running from pocket to pocket, there were wires, some red, some blue. Talpur knew that he was looking at a suicide vest. He blinked and glanced at the man to his left. He was wearing an identical vest. So was the man next to him. They were all wearing suicide vests. He looked down at his own chest and gasped when he saw the grey blocks and wires tucked into the canvas vest. He began to struggle but the bonds held him tight and all he could do was rock the chair from side to side.

CAMBERWELL (6.30 p.m.)

Ali Pasha put away his phone. 'It is time to go,' he said. He smiled. 'The ISIS prisoners have been released and are on the way to the airport.'

Roger Metcalfe frowned. 'That's impossible,' he said. 'The government's policy is never to negotiate with terrorists.'

Pasha grinned. 'Maybe they changed it when they found out that I had a Member of Parliament as my hostage.'

'Is that why you chose me?' asked Metcalfe. 'Because I'm an MP?'

'I didn't choose you,' said Pasha. 'But someone did and maybe it was because you were an MP that you were chosen. Come on, we must go. There is a coach outside.'

'What do you mean, a coach?'

'We are to go to the airport. You and I. Everyone else can go.'

'Which airport?'

'I don't know. Please, we don't have time to talk. We have to go.'

'It's true,' said Molly, who was sitting, back to the wall, with the rest of the hostages. 'It's all over Twitter. They've let them go. All six of them.'

'Ali, listen to me,' said Metcalfe. 'You've won. You've got what you wanted. You don't need me to get on the coach with you. Please. I have a family. I need to get back to them.'

'We have no choice,' said Pasha. 'I was told to get on the coach with you and I have to do exactly as I am told. If I disobey, the vest will explode.'

Metcalfe frowned. 'You mean someone else can detonate it?'

Pasha scowled. 'I've said too much already. Come on. We must go.'

'You're telling me that someone else can set the bomb off? That it's not up to you?'

Pasha glared at the MP. 'If you continue to talk like this, we could all die. Do you want to die, Roger? I don't. Not today.' He headed for the door.

'They could shoot us,' said Metcalfe.

'They won't,' said Pasha. 'They've released the prisoners. They're letting us go to the airport. They don't want anyone hurt.'

'They make mistakes sometimes,' said Metcalfe. 'Remember that Brazilian electrician they shot in the Tube after Seven/Seven?'

'That won't happen again,' said Pasha. 'They have rules. That is why the police here are so weak. They have to follow them, no matter what.'

'But you don't. Is that what you mean?'

Pasha ignored the question and opened the door. He stepped out into the corridor. A man in a green bomb-disposal suit was standing some fifteen feet away to his left. He pointed to Pasha's right. 'Down the stairs,' he said.

Pasha and the MP went along the corridor and down the stairs to the street. Armed police were aiming their weapons at them. At the roadside a white coach with the windows blacked out was waiting. They climbed on board and found free seats close to the back on the driver's side. Pasha had to take the window seat. Metcalfe was sweating profusely and had started to shake. 'Breathe deeply,' said Pasha. 'You will have a heart attack.'

'I don't want to die. I have a family.'

'We all have families,' said Pasha. 'But we have to stay calm. If we are lucky, we will all get out of this alive. *Inshallah.*'

'*Inshallah*? What does that mean?'

'It means "God willing". It means that everything that happens is the will of Allah.'

The coach door closed and they pulled away from the kerb.

'But this isn't Allah's doing, is it? This is you.' Metcalfe gestured at the men sitting in front of them. 'And them. You're doing it. You're making this happen.'

Pasha shook his head. 'No, we're not.'

SOUTH LONDON (ten hours earlier)

Talpur stopped struggling. Nothing he did loosened his bonds. He looked around the circle. Most of the men were slumped in the chairs. One was crying. 'What the fuck's going on?' he shouted. 'Where the fuck are we?'

There were pigeons roosting in the girders of the warehouse and several fluttered to the roof, but they soon returned to their posts and began cooing softly.

'Stay quiet,' said a voice. 'Anyone who talks will be gagged.'

A man moved into view from Talpur's left. He was wearing blue overalls and his face was covered with a ski mask.

Behind him a large metal screen hung from chains attached to a girder. At the far end of the building there was a pile of disused machinery, much of it rusting and covered with cobwebs. The oil stains on the concrete floor suggested that the building had once been a thriving business.

The man moved into the centre of the circle. 'My name is Shahid,' he said, brandishing a gun over his head.

'What the fuck is this about?' yelled a captive.

Shahid pointed his gun at the man and pulled the trigger. The bullet thudded into the wall. The sound of the shot echoed and the pigeons scattered in fright. Talpur could smell the cordite and his ears were ringing.

'I will kill the next person who speaks,' said Shahid. 'This is what is going to happen. You will notice that you are each wearing a raincoat. Under the raincoat is a vest containing explosives and detonators, with screws, nuts and bolts to serve as shrapnel when the vest explodes. You each have written instructions in your left-hand pocket. You are to read those instructions and follow them to the letter. You will be hooded again and delivered to a specific place where the hood and mask will be removed. You will then follow your instructions. At all times you will be watched. If at any point you deviate from the script you have been given the explosives you are wearing will detonate. The vests cannot be removed. If you attempt to remove the vest, it will explode. It has been booby-trapped. Believe me, any attempt to take it off will end badly so, please, do not even try.'

One of the men began shaking his head. 'This is fucking evil, man. Fucking evil.'

'What I am now about to tell you is the most important

thing you have to remember,' said Shahid. 'In the right-hand pocket of the raincoat there is a trigger for the vest, which you will keep in your right hand at all times. There is a Velcro strap to keep it in place. The trigger must be visible at all times. But the trigger will not detonate the vest. The vest can only be detonated by phone.' He reached into a pocket of his overalls and pulled out a cheap phone. He held it above his head. 'If I call your vest it will explode. Only I can make that call, and until I do, the vest is safe. But if I do call the number – you and everyone nearby will die.'

'This is fucking sick, man!' shouted the man, rocking his chair back and forth.

'You need to shut the fuck up, bruv,' said Shahid, waving his gun at the man's face.

'You can't be doing this to people,' said the man.

'You'll do as you're told or you're dead.' Shahid put away the mobile phone.

'I'm not even a fucking Muslim!'

'Muslim or not, you follow the instructions or you'll be dead.'

The man threw back his head and screamed up at the roof, a blood-curdling howl of frustration and pain.

Shahid walked over to him and slapped him across the face. The man stopped screaming and stared up at him. 'You will do this,' he said. 'You will follow the orders I give you.'

'I can't. I fucking can't. You need to let me go.'

One of the other captives shouted, 'Just do it, man. Just do it as he says. Don't make him mad!'

'Fuck you! I ain't doing this. They'll kill us, man. We go

out in these vests and they'll fucking shoot us like mad dogs.'

'If you follow instructions you won't get hurt,' said Shahid. 'Everything will end peacefully, you have my word.'

'Fuck your word!' screamed the man. 'You can't do this. You have to let us go!'

Shahid backslapped the man again, then shoved the gun into one of the pockets of his overalls and grabbed the chair. He tipped it back and dragged it with its occupant across the concrete floor. The man struggled but there was nothing he could do to stop Shahid moving him. The chair's rear legs scraped across the concrete as Shahid dragged it behind the metal shield that was hanging from the girder. The man was crying now, his body shuddering with every sob.

Shahid came out from behind the metal screen. He was holding the mobile phone again. The bound man was begging for help now, pleading with Shahid to let him go.

Shahid held the mobile phone above his head. 'Let's be clear about this, just so there is no misunderstanding!' he shouted. 'You will do as you're told. Or you will die. There is no middle ground.' He ran his thumb over the keys, then held up the phone into the air. A second later, there was a loud explosion on the other side of the screen. Blood and body parts spun into the air and splattered onto the ground.

All of the bound men were staring in horror at the screen, which was swinging to and fro, and the bloody carnage around it. Panicking pigeons were hitting the roof, their wings flapping frantically.

'If anyone else wants to refuse, let me know and I'll deto-nate their vest here and now.' Shahid looked around the circle. 'Anyone?' he shouted, waving the phone above his head.

The bound men shook their heads.

'I will say this one more time,' said Shahid. 'You follow the instructions you are given, and you will live. Disobey me, stray from your instructions, and your vest will be detonated. Do you all understand?'

The bound men nodded.

Talpur was nodding, too. His ears were still ringing from the sound of the explosion and he couldn't take his eyes off a training shoe that had hit the far wall of the warehouse. It had landed the right way up, an inch or two of splintered bone protruding from it. Talpur's heart was pounding so hard it was as if it was trying to burst out of his chest, and he was finding it hard to breathe. He was still gasping for breath as the hood was pulled over his head again.

He lost track of time. There were noises. Muffled voices. Movement. Then the sound of a vehicle being driven into the warehouse, doors opening and closing. More movement. Footsteps. Then he felt someone untie him and drag him by the collar to a van. Hands helped him inside and into a seat. 'If you want to get out of this alive, stay quiet and do as you're told, brother,' Shahid hissed, then patted him on the back.

SOUTHWARK (6.45 p.m.)

'It's time to go,' said Masood, slipping his mobile phone into his waistpack. He picked up a bottle of water and took a drink. His hand was shaking and water trickled down his beard. He put down the bottle and wiped his beard with his sleeve.

'Go where?' asked Wade.

They were sitting at a table by the window. It was the table Wade always saved for his big-tipping regulars, with a good view of the street outside but in a corner that cut down on the traffic flow around it. 'The airport,' said Masood. 'The prisoners have been released. Now we have to join them.'

'I don't want to go to a fucking airport,' growled Wade.

'You have no choice,' said Masood. He raised his left hand and jiggled the chain. 'I don't have the key.' He stood up and squinted out of the window. Outside the restaurant, armed police officers had taken position. Helicopters were flying overhead. Two. Maybe three. As he and Wade walked to the door, a uniformed officer, crouching behind a police car, put a megaphone to his lips. Wade was hanging back and Masood pulled the chain to bring him closer. 'Stay next to me,' he muttered.

'They're going to shoot you,' said Wade, his voice trembling.

'They won't shoot anyone, not with the TV and press here,' said Masood. He pointed down the road. Off in the distance there was a white van with 'BBC' on the side and next to it a similar van with the Sky News logo. Both vans had large satellite dishes on their roofs. He pulled open the door. 'And if they do shoot me, the vest goes up and it won't matter how close to me you are. So stick with me.'

He stepped out onto the pavement and Wade followed him. They both gazed up at the two helicopters hovering high overhead. 'What are they doing?' asked Wade. 'They wouldn't shoot from a helicopter, would they?'

'That one on the left is a TV chopper,' said Masood. 'They're filming us.' He nodded at the second. 'That's the police. They're just following us. Surveillance.'

A megaphone crackled. 'Please proceed to the coach as quickly as possible,' said the officer.

'Why have they covered the windows?'

'I don't know,' said Masood. 'Come on.'

They walked slowly towards the coach. The armed police tracked them as they moved.

'They're going to fire,' said Wade.

'They're not,' said Masood.

'Then why are they pointing their guns at us?'

'Because they're scared,' said Masood.

'They're scared? Fuck me, I'm the one who's pissing himself.'

'I'm scared, too, but they won't shoot us. They'll take us to the airport, that's all.'

'And then what?' asked Wade. 'What happens then?'

'I don't know,' said Masood. 'We'll find out when we get there.' He pointed at the coach. 'Come on, we're keeping them waiting.'

LAMBETH CENTRAL COMMUNICATIONS COMMAND CENTRE (6.47 p.m.)

Kamran and Gillard looked up at the screen as the coach pulled away from the Southwark restaurant. 'That's it. The last one's on board,' said Kamran.

The coach headed south, preceded by six police motorcycles with flashing lights, a police van and an armed-response vehicle, half a dozen police vans and the two black Range Rovers that contained the SAS.

'It's looking good,' said Murray, who was standing behind the two police officers. 'In terms of numbers, we're well ahead of the game now. Worst possible scenario, if the bus goes up we only lose nine hostages and my man.'

'Let's hope it doesn't come to that,' said Gillard.

'You and me both,' said Murray. 'I'm just saying that we've gone from having close to a hundred civilians at risk to just nine. That's bloody good going.'

'I'm not sure the great British public will see it that way if the coach goes up in flames,' said Kamran.

The helicopter tracked the convoy south towards Croydon. The police were using motorbikes to keep the road ahead clear. It was causing traffic chaos but they had no choice. Anything other than a clear run to the airport would put lives at risk.

'How long before they reach Biggin Hill?' asked Murray.

'It's fifteen miles,' said Kamran. 'Usually it would take about an hour but we've cleared the roads so it shouldn't take much more than twenty minutes. Your men are ready to go?'

'Locked and loaded,' said Murray.

'We're still negotiating, remember that,' said Kamran.

'Absolutely,' said the SAS captain. 'But this time we'll be negotiating from a position of strength.'

'We've sent a negotiating team from Bromley. Have they arrived yet?'

'They've just got in. We're keeping them outside the

hangar with the rest of the police until we're sure we have the situation in hand.'

'I understand that, Alex, but I have to stress that we need to talk to them before we move in. We have to give them the option of surrendering.'

'We'll do that, but I won't be holding my breath.'

NEAR BROMLEY (6.54 p.m.)

Talpur looked at his watch. They had been driving south for less than ten minutes so, assuming they were taking the direct route to Biggin Hill, they must be somewhere near Bromley. Only the front windows had not been blacked out but he was so far back he couldn't see much in the way of road signs. He could see the police motorcyclists ahead of the coach. He leant closer to the woman sitting next to him. 'What is your name?' he asked.

She sneered and said something to him in Arabic. He didn't understand the words but the meaning was clear enough.

'Listen to me carefully,' he whispered. 'I'm a police officer and I need your help.'

She spat in his face and turned away.

'Thank you so much,' said Talpur. He wiped his face with his sleeve. He turned to the man sitting on the other side of the aisle.

'What is your name, brother?' he asked.

'We need to sit quietly,' said the Asian man sitting by the window.

'What's your name, mate?' Talpur asked him.

'Zach. Zach Ahmed.'

'Well, Zach, I'm a cop.'

'You don't look like a cop,' said Ahmed. 'Not with that beard.'

'I'm undercover.'

'Like fuck you are,' said Ahmed. 'Show me your warrant card.'

'Undercover cops generally don't carry warrant cards. It'd sort of negate the whole point of being undercover,' said Talpur. 'Look, we're all in the same boat here. We all saw what happened this morning. But the windows are blacked out so Shahid can't see what we're doing.' He nodded at the man sitting next to Ahmed. 'What's your name, mate?'

'Mohammed.'

'Where are you from, Mohammed?'

'Sudan.'

'Okay, Mohammed from Sudan, I need you to check how this vest is fastened. I'm going to turn around and I want you to reach inside my coat and see if you can work out how it's fastened. There might be a lock or it might just be tied.'

'Are you fucking stupid?' said Ahmed, leaning forward to stare across the aisle at him. 'We were told not to try to take the vests off. He said they'd explode, remember?'

'I'm not taking it off, I'm just trying to find out how it's fastened. He might have been bluffing.'

'Bluffing? You remember what happened to that guy who didn't do as he was told? He's in pieces. Remember?'

'Yes, I remember,' said Talpur. 'But those blacked-out windows mean Shahid can't see what we're doing.'

'You don't know what he can or can't see,' said Ahmed. 'But you need to stop fucking about. You're going to get us all killed.'

'What is your problem, mate?' asked Talpur.

'My problem is that I know what will happen if Shahid finds out we're not following his instructions. We're nearly done, the ISIS prisoners are already at the airport, we'll be there soon. Then we'll be released.'

'You have a lot of faith in Shahid,' said Talpur.

'He's kept his word so far,' said Ahmed. 'The prisoners have been released so he's got what he wants. Once they're on a plane he won't need us any more.'

'Exactly,' said Talpur. 'So what's to stop him just blowing us all the fuck up?'

'We have to trust him,' said Ahmed.

'I don't,' said Talpur. He patted Mohammed's leg. 'Check under my raincoat. Just reach inside and pat my back gently . . .'

'Mohammed, you so much as touch him and I will break your fingers!' hissed Ahmed.

'This is nothing to do with you, mate,' said Talpur.

The man sitting directly in front of Talpur twisted around in his seat. 'He is right, sir,' he said quietly. He was darker-skinned than the other men, and taller, from Africa maybe. He had a thick scar across his cheek. 'Better we sit quietly.'

Talpur shook his head in frustration. 'You're all making a big mistake,' he said.

'It is in the hands of Allah,' said the man in front of him as he turned away.

LAMBETH CENTRAL COMMUNICATIONS COMMAND CENTRE (7.07 p.m.)

Kamran was watching two screens on the main wall of the special operations room. One was showing Sky News. Their helicopter had got as close to the airport as it had been allowed but they had lost sight of the coach and the channel was broadcasting now from the gates of the airport. Police were stopping anyone going in but they had allowed the news crews and photographers to set up a short distance away.

The second screen was showing the live feed from the police helicopter, which had been authorised to fly over the airport. The overhead view showed the coach a few hundred yards away from the airport entrance. Kamran twisted around and called over to Gillard, 'They're arriving at the airport now, Philip.'

The chief superintendent stood up and joined him at the doorway. The convoy was powering along the road, blue lights flashing. The lead police motorcycles turned into the airport and drove through the gate, followed by an ARV, then the coach.

The Sky News screen showed a close-up of the driver, who was turning his head away from the camera, then the blacked-out windows flashed by.

A third screen showed the feed from the hangar, where the SAS were waiting behind walls of sandbags, weapons at the ready. All eyes in the SOR were on the black and white view inside the hangar.

BIGGIN HILL AIRPORT (7.09 p.m.)

Hawkins heard the coach in the distance. 'Here we go,' he said. He was standing behind a stack of sandbags arranged at the side of the hangar. There were four more troopers behind another sandbag wall to his left.

The negotiating team from Bromley were waiting in the main terminal with the Silver Commander, Ian Adams. They had seemed relieved when Hawkins had asked them to clear the area. He'd gained the impression they were more used to dealing with domestic disputes and weren't at all comfortable with the idea of negotiating with nine jihadists prepared to kill themselves and their hostages.

'Everybody stay behind the bags until I say otherwise,' said Hawkins. 'It could be they're after the SAS so let's not give them the satisfaction.'

The engine growl got louder and then there was a squeal of brakes. The coach reached the open hangar doors and turned in. Hawkins peered over the top of the sandbags and caught a glimpse of Terry McMullen at the wheel, wearing his lucky flat cap. The coach reached the centre of the hangar and stopped. There was a wheeze of the air brakes being applied and everything went quiet. After a few seconds the door opened, but then everything was quiet again.

LAMBETH CENTRAL COMMUNICATIONS
COMMAND CENTRE (7.10 p.m.)

'The door's open,' said Gillard. Kamran's mobile rang on his desk and he dashed over to it. Number withheld. 'It's Shahid.' He waited for Gillard, Thatcher and Waterman to put on their headphones before he picked up the phone and accepted the call. 'Yes?' he said.

'Mr Kamran?'

Kamran frowned. It was a man, but not Shahid. 'Speaking.'

'Do you have a pension, Mr Kamran?'

'A pension?'

'You might not be aware of the fact but the regulations regarding the monetisation of pension funds changed recently and we are in a position to offer you a package . . .'

'You're trying to sell me financial advice?' asked Kamran.

'We're not trying to sell you anything, Mr Kamran, but I'm sure you would like to maximise the income from any pension fund you have, wouldn't you?'

'Don't use this number again,' said Kamran. He ended the call. Gillard, Thatcher and Waterman took off their headphones. Kamran looked at Thatcher. 'Why isn't he calling?' he asked the negotiator.

Thatcher shrugged. 'Maybe he's trying to build the tension,' he said.

'Well, it's working, all right,' said Waterman.

'The prisoners are there and so are the bombers,' said Kamran. 'And we don't know what he wants us to do next.'

'On the bright side, from now on we'll be the only

ones who'll see what's happening,' said Waterman. 'From a PR point of view, they've just gone several steps backwards.'

'Maybe it's not about PR,' said Kamran.

'But what, then?' asked Gillard. 'What the hell does he want? And why won't he tell us?' He looked up at the screen. 'What do we do now? Wait or send in the negotiators?'

'I'd recommend waiting,' said Thatcher. 'Shahid has planned this perfectly so far. He must have something in mind.'

'I just wish he'd let us know what,' said Gillard.

BIGGIN HILL AIRPORT (7.12 p.m.)

Talpur moved his head to the left, trying to look out of the door but there were too many people blocking his view.

'What's happening?' said the woman in front of him.

'I don't know,' said the man sitting next to her.

Talpur craned his neck to look out of the front windscreen but all he could see was the wall of the hangar. Why weren't they getting off the bus? Why wasn't anything happening?

'Driver!' he shouted. 'Can you see what's happening out there?'

The driver didn't react but several people in front of Talpur turned to him.

'Driver, can you see anything?' shouted Talpur, standing up.

'Shut up, man,' hissed Ahmed. 'You'll get us killed.'

'We need to know what's happening,' said Talpur. 'The prisoners have been released, we're at the airport, so why aren't they releasing us? Shahid said we'd be released.'

'He also said that if we deviated from his instructions, we'd all die.'

'Brother, we know that only Shahid can detonate these vests. And if we're sitting in this coach, he can't see us. The windows are blacked out.'

Another of the Asians turned. 'Just sit down and shut up.'

'You want to sit here like sheep and wait to see if Shahid will allow us to live or die?' Talpur took a step towards the driver. 'Driver, what's happening out there?'

The driver twisted in his seat. 'Sit the fuck down!' he shouted at Talpur.

Talpur raised his hands and let the trigger lie in the flat of his right palm. 'I'm not holding the trigger,' he shouted. 'I'm not going to press it. My hand is open. Look.' He took another step forward and pulled the chain so that the woman slid across to his seat.

The driver's eyes tightened. 'Sit the fuck down or I swear I'll shoot you in the head.' He had a gun in his hands now and he was pointing it at Talpur's face.

'My name is Kashif Talpur and I work for the National Crime Agency. I'm a cop.'

'Sit the fuck down now!' shouted the driver, his finger tightening on the trigger.

'You have to listen to me! We can't detonate the vests. They can only be detonated by phone. You have to get them off us now!'

The Asian man sitting next to the priest stood up and screamed at Talpur, 'You're going to get us killed!'

The driver pointed the gun at the man. 'You, sit the fuck down! Everyone, sit down, now!'

Talpur heard footsteps outside the coach. 'Please, everyone, just keep calm!' he shouted. 'We can get out of this if we all stay calm.'

'Go back to your seat now!' shouted the driver.

'No! You have to listen to me. No one here is going to press the trigger. The triggers don't work.'

'What's happening in there?' someone shouted from outside.

'If we were going to detonate, we'd have done it already!' shouted Talpur.

Two more Asians at the front of the bus got to their feet at the same time and began shouting. The driver took a step back, trying to cover the two of them with his gun by swinging it from side to side.

'We're not going to hurt you. Can't you see that?' yelled Talpur.

He heard a noise behind him. The emergency exit door opened and he caught a glimpse of two men in leather jackets with handguns.

'Don't shoot!' shouted Talpur. 'I'm a cop! I'm a fucking cop!'

There were more sounds at the front of the bus, dull thuds. He whirled around and saw another man with a gun at the door, next to the driver.

'Listen to me!' shouted Talpur. 'I'm a police officer. No one here can detonate their vest. They are remotely controlled. We are not a threat. I repeat, we are not a threat!'

LAMBETH CENTRAL COMMUNICATIONS COMMAND CENTRE (7.13 p.m.)

'What's going on? Who told the SAS to go in?' said Gillard. He turned to Murray. 'What's happening?'

'I've no idea,' said Murray, staring up at the large screen showing the feed from the Biggin Hill hangar. SAS troopers were at the back of the coach and the front. Two of the SAS men had gone inside, Jim Hawkins leading the way.

'Were shots fired?' asked Kamran. The feed was silent so he had no idea whether the troopers had used their weapons or not.

'I don't think so,' said Murray.

'They've opened the rear door,' said Gillard. 'What the hell is happening?'

Kamran frowned at the screen as the seconds ticked off. It didn't make any sense. If the vests were going to detonate, what was taking so long? Were they trying to lure the SAS in so that they would be caught in the blast?

'They shouldn't have gone in without negotiating first,' said Gillard.

'Something must have happened,' said Murray.

'Then do us all a favour and find out what,' said Gillard.

BIGGIN HILL AIRPORT (7.14 p.m.)

Jim Hawkins kept his MP5 trained on the face of the man standing in the aisle. His finger was tense on the trigger and the slightest increase in pressure would put a slug virtually instantaneously into the man's skull. 'Drop the trigger,' he said.

'I can't,' said the man. 'It's held in place with the Velcro strap. I couldn't drop it if I wanted to.'

'What do you want?' asked Hawkins.

'I want off this fucking coach,' said the man. 'We all do. Listen to me, I'm a cop. My name is Kashif Talpur. We are all here under duress. We can't detonate these vests. They can only be detonated by remote control. You need to get them off us.'

Hawkins frowned. He looked over at McMullen. 'What do you think, Terry?'

'I think if they were going to detonate, they already would have.'

'He's telling the truth,' said the Asian man standing by the priest. 'This is not our doing.'

All the men wearing the vests began to talk at once, proclaiming their innocence and pleading to be allowed off the coach.

'Shut the fuck up!' shouted Hawkins. 'Sit down, shut up, and put your hands on your heads.'

LAMBETH CENTRAL COMMUNICATIONS COMMAND CENTRE (7.16 p.m.)

Captain Murray put down his mobile phone. 'The terrorists have surrendered,' he said. 'They're saying they acted under duress.'

'Duress? How?'

'They're claiming that the vests can only be detonated by remote control. The triggers don't work.'

'Then we need to get the vests off them immediately,' said Gillard. He looked up at the screen showing the feed from the hangar. The SAS men were taking the bombers and hostages off the bus. One of the troopers had a pair of bolt-cutters and was using it to sever the chains. 'Alex, get the hostages and bombers separated straight away. The bombers can be kept in the hangar but our men can take care of the hostages right now.' He nodded at Kamran. 'Mo, can you talk to Silver and make that happen? And get him to send in bomb disposal to sort the vests out.'

'Will do,' said Kamran, heading for his desk.

'What the hell is going on?' asked Gillard, looking at the screen again.

'We've won,' said Murray. 'We've released the hostages, the would-be bombers have surrendered and we still have the ISIS prisoners. It's a win-win-win situation.'

'But why?' asked Gillard. 'Why did Shahid just throw in the towel?'

'Maybe something happened that we're not aware of,' said Kamran. 'Maybe he thinks he's won.' He picked up his mobile phone and called Inspector Adams at Biggin Hill. 'Ian, the ISIS prisoners. Where are they right now?'

'Over at the RAF base.'

'You're sure?'

'Last I heard, that's where they were. Still under guard in the van.'

'Okay. I need you to go over there right now and see for yourself. With your own eyes. Open the door and check that they're all there.'

'You think they're not? You think they've gone?'

'Ian, nothing would surprise me right now. All we know is that we haven't heard from Shahid and the bombers have given up. If we still have the ISIS prisoners in custody then I don't understand what has happened.' Kamran ended the call. 'Inspector Adams is going to check on the prisoners now,' he said to Gillard.

'Please God they'd better still be in the van,' said Gillard.

BIGGIN HILL AIRPORT (7.18 p.m.)

A bomb-disposal technician in a full bomb suit used a large pair of industrial bolt-cutters to separate the last of the chains. A policeman in a fluorescent jacket rushed the woman hostage out of the hangar.

A second technician removed the vest, carried it to a line of sandbags and placed it carefully with the eight vests that had already been removed. The Asian man's wrists were bound behind his back with plastic ties, then two SAS troopers hustled him outside and made him kneel on the ground with the rest of the men who had been taken off the coach. All nine stared silently at their captors. Those who had tried to speak had been slapped and told to keep their mouths shut.

The Bomb Squad leader walked out of the hangar, removed his helmet and waved at Hawkins to join him.

Hawkins jogged over, his MP5 at his side. 'They're fake,' said the bomb-disposal expert.

'You mean they can't be detonated using the triggers?' said Hawkins.

The man shook his head. 'Nothing can detonate them. They're fake. The explosive isn't real. It's Plasticine or something. And the wiring's all wrong.'

'I was told they could be detonated by phone.'

'Then you were told wrong,' said the technician. 'They look the part, but they're totally inert. There was never a chance of them blowing up. It's a con. A scam. We've all been wasting our bloody time.'

RAF BIGGIN HILL (7.22 p.m.)

Inspector Adams drove from the hangar to RAF Biggin Hill in less than two minutes, his heart racing. The base was on the western side of the airport, to the south of the passenger terminal. It was the headquarters of 2427 Squadron of the Air Training Corps and there was a brick-built chapel, with a remembrance garden, to commemorate all the airmen who had lost their lives flying out of Biggin Hill during the Battle of Britain. Two full-size replicas of a Hurricane and a Spitfire stood guard at the entrance to the base and Adams drove between them, turned left in front of the chapel and parked in front of a two-storey featureless administration block. The prison van was at the side of the building with half a dozen armed police officers standing around it. Off to the left were the police motorcyclists who had escorted the van from Belmarsh. High overhead a police helicopter hovered, ever watchful.

Adams walked over to an SCO19 sergeant. 'Everything okay?' he asked.

'All good,' said the sergeant. 'Any idea what's happening?'

'The bombers are in custody. No shots fired, no one hurt,' said Adams.

The sergeant looked almost disappointed. 'It's over?'

'Pretty much,' said Adams. 'But I have to check that your prisoners are all accounted for.'

'No question,' said the sergeant. 'The doors haven't been opened since we left Belmarsh.'

'I'm under orders to see for myself,' said Adams.

Adams went to the van. A prison officer in white shirt and black trousers climbed out of the front and Adams asked him to unlock the back door. The door opened into a small metal corridor with four doors on each side. The prison officer climbed up and took a bunch of keys hanging from a chain attached to his belt. He unlocked the first door on the right and pulled it open so that Adams could look inside. It was a small cubicle, all white metal, with a small bench seat on which sat a bearded Asian man. He scowled up at Adams. 'Am I to be freed?' he asked.

'Not on my watch,' growled Adams, and nodded for the prison officer to relock the door.

The officer opened another five doors. Each cubicle was occupied.

'Satisfied, sir?' asked the sergeant, as Adams climbed out of the back of the van.

'Satisfied, but as confused as hell.'

LAMBETH CENTRAL COMMUNICATIONS COMMAND CENTRE (7.25 p.m.)

Kamran put down his mobile phone. He was sitting at a large table in a meeting room opposite the special operations room, which was normally used for press briefings, with lines of red chairs facing a raised podium. The Gold Command suite had been too small for the briefing that was now needed. Chief Superintendent Gillard was standing at the middle of the long desk on the podium, flanked by Kamran and Waterman on his left, Thatcher and Murray on his right. Facing them were more than a dozen Silver Commanders from the special operations room and representatives from most of the pods. Lisa Elphick was sitting in the front row, a notepad on her lap, Tony Drury next to her. Kamran looked up at Gillard. 'That was Silver Commander at Biggin Hill,' he said. 'All six of the prisoners are present and accounted for.'

'Well, that's a relief,' said Gillard.

'And the suicide vests are fake.'

Kamran's revelation was met by a stunned silence.

'I'm sorry, Mo, run that by us again,' said Gillard.

'The vests don't contain explosives. Or a detonation system. They're fake.'

'I'm confused. What the hell have we been dealing with all day? What has this all been about?'

'It was a scam, from the start,' said Kamran.

'But to what end?' said Gillard. 'The bombers have surrendered, the prisoners are still in custody, and we haven't heard from Shahid since, what, twenty to five? Almost three hours ago. He's been watching TV so he must know that the ISIS prisoners and his men are at the airport. Why hasn't he called?'

Tony Drury's mobile rang and he went to the far end of the room, talking into it with his hand over his mouth.

'Perhaps he realised it was a trap,' said Thatcher.

'In which case why did his men surrender so easily? There was no negotiation. No demands. No contact, even.'

Thatcher shrugged. 'Maybe the terrorists decided to take matters into their own hands once they realised they were trapped in the hangar.'

'But right from the start they said they would kill everyone if they didn't get what they wanted,' said Gillard. 'Okay, we now know that the vests weren't a real threat, but at the time we thought they were. At the very least, you would have thought Shahid would have tried to negotiate. It makes no sense that he'd just walk away.'

'Unless he already had what he wanted,' said Kamran.

Gillard turned to him. 'But what?' he asked. 'How is this in any way a victory for him?'

'It could have been a test,' said Waterman. 'Testing to see how we would react, how much leeway we would give them. Now they know that the government will bow to their demands, next time they will ask for even more. And next time the vests could be real.'

Murray nodded. 'We showed weakness,' he said. 'They'll take advantage of that.'

Drury finished his call and walked back to his seat. 'That was one of my guys,' he said. 'He confirms that the explosives weren't real, and neither were the detonators. The triggers looked like the real thing but they wouldn't have done anything if pressed. The vests were harmless. Totally harmless.'

Gillard was about to speak when the door opened. It was Sergeant Lumley. 'It's the prime minister, sir,' said the sergeant. 'On your direct line in the Gold Command suite so I can't transfer it.'

Gillard stood up. 'Mo, you'd better come with me.' He looked around the room. 'To be continued . . .' he said, and headed for the door with Kamran in tow.

BIGGIN HILL AIRPORT (7.26 p.m.)

Inspector Ian Adams stood next to the EOD technicians and watched as they worked. They had all nine vests on the ground and one was taking photographs with a digital camera. 'Have you ever seen anything like this before?' Adams asked the older of the two men.

'Fakes, you mean? Not outside the movies, no. But someone went to a lot of trouble to make them appear real. They'd fool me from a distance, no question.'

Adams walked out of the hangar.

'Sir! Are you the Silver Commander here?'

Adams turned to see who was shouting at him. SAS troopers with guns at the ready were guarding the nine men who had been wearing the vests. They were all kneeling facing the outside wall of the hangar, their wrists bound behind their backs. One of the men had twisted his head around to look at Adams. An SAS trooper stepped forward and shouted at the man to keep quiet.

'Yes, I am. Inspector Ian Adams.'

'My name is Kashif Talpur. I'm an undercover officer

with the National Crime Agency. My governor is Inspector Mark Biddulph. He was at Tavistock Square. He can vouch for me.'

'That's all right, I know who you are,' said Adams. He nodded at the SAS trooper standing behind Talpur. 'It's okay, he's one of ours.'

'I'm sorry, sir. My orders are to keep everyone here in this position.'

'He's a cop.'

'I'm sorry, sir.'

Adams opened his mouth to argue but could see from the look on the trooper's face that there would be no point. He glanced around for Sergeant Hawkins and saw him inside the hangar, standing by the coach. He went over and explained what had happened. Hawkins called over to the trooper, 'Let him go, Haggis. He's one of the good guys.'

Haggis used a knife to cut the plastic tie before helping Talpur to his feet.

Talpur hurried over to Adams. 'Thank you, sir,' he said. 'Any idea where my governor is?'

'I'm not sure,' said Adams. 'But I can find out. What the hell's going on? What were you doing with that vest on?'

'We were forced into it. They said if we didn't do as we were told, they'd set the bombs off.'

'The bombs were fake,' said Adams. 'You were never in any danger.'

'That can't be right. I saw one of them explode. It blew a guy to pieces.'

'Where was that?'

'I don't know. This morning some time. We were in a

warehouse. They blew a guy up and said the same would happen to us if we didn't follow instructions.'

'They? Who are they?'

'I only saw one of them. A guy calling himself Shahid. I never saw his face, had a ski mask on. Asian. Five ten, five eleven, maybe. London accent.' He sighed. 'I need a bath. And a meal.'

'No bath, not yet,' said Adams. 'We're going to need to take your clothes for Forensics. Then you'll have to be debriefed. But I'll see if I can get some food sorted.' He took out his phone. 'I'll call Gold.'

LAMBETH CENTRAL COMMUNICATIONS COMMAND CENTRE (7.27 p.m.)

Kamran followed Gillard into the Gold Command suite. The chief superintendent picked up the phone. He was expecting to be talking to an assistant but it was the prime minister himself. 'Well done, Chief Superintendent. A perfect resolution. It couldn't have gone better.'

'Thank you, sir,' said Gillard.

'Not a single shot fired, no one hurt, and the prisoners still in custody. Frankly, we're in awe of you. You'll have to come around when you're done and talk us through it.'

'Yes, sir,' said Gillard. 'I'll gladly do that.' He closed his eyes and exhaled, knowing that, as things stood, he had no idea how he would explain the events of the past ten hours, and certainly not the resolution.

'Please pass on my thanks to the whole team there. It really was a job well done.'

'I will, sir.'

'They gave up, is that what happened? They realised we weren't going to negotiate? Your strategy worked?'

'It was a complicated situation, sir. I'm still trying to get my head around it.'

'Well, I'll tell you this, Chief Superintendent. You deserve a medal, and if I have my way, you'll be getting one.'

'Thank you, sir,' said Gillard, but the line was already dead. He put down the phone. 'What the hell happened, Mo?' he said. 'I'll happily take the credit for a successful operation but we didn't do anything. Shahid just walked away.'

'Like Lynne said, it could have been a test.'

'They want something bigger than getting us to release six ISIS prisoners? And if it was a terrorist act, what could be worse than nine bombs going off across the city?'

Kamran's mobile rang and he took it out.

'Is it him? Is it Shahid?'

Kamran shook his head. 'Ian Adams, at the airport.' He put the phone to his ear. 'Yes, Ian.'

'Sorry to bother you, sir, but I need to run a few things by you.'

'No problem, Ian. Go ahead.'

'I'm here with Kashif Talpur, the NCA guy. He confirms that they were under duress. According to him, he saw a vest explode and kill the man wearing it.'

'Where was this?'

'He doesn't know. Sir, what do I do with him?'

'Get him to GT Ops as quickly as possible. His governor

can meet him here. Where are the men who were wearing the vests?'

'The SAS have them under guard at the hangar. But if they were acting under duress, I'm not sure if we can do that, right?'

'At the moment we're not sure of anything,' said Kamran. 'What have you done so far?'

'The ISIS prisoners are en route back to Belmarsh. I've removed everyone from the hangar, except for the Bomb Squad people and the men wearing the vests, though it's now definite that all the vests are inert. The hostages are being looked after at the main terminal. There was a chain and a padlock at the back of each vest so they had to be cut off. All the men wearing the vests are telling the same story – they were forced into it. They're claiming the vests could only be detonated by remote control and that they had been told if they didn't follow their instructions they'd be killed.'

'They all say that?' asked Kamran.

'All of them. The thing is, sir, do we arrest them? They claim that they were under duress. Can they be arrested? And what about the hostages? They're asking to go home. I don't see how we can continue to hold them against their will.'

'So far as the hostages go, tell them we want to make sure that they're physically and mentally well,' said Kamran. 'Take them to the nearest police station and get medics to give them the once-over. But keep them separate from each other. I don't want them comparing stories. While you're doing that, have them interviewed, but gently. Get them to tell us exactly what happened at each location. We're also going to need their shoes and clothing for Forensics. And have them photographed straight away. That goes for the men in the vests, too. We need to show the state they were in after the siege ended in case that becomes an issue down the line.'

'What if they insist on going home?'

'Just be tactful. Explain that we need their help, and ask them to give a full statement. And tell them we have a right to take their clothing as it's evidence. But if they absolutely insist and they have satisfactorily identified themselves, then, yes, take them home. But send officers with them and have the officers stay outside their houses. We'll send investigating officers later. Oh, and don't let them know that the vests were fake.'

Gillard was trying to catch Kamran's eye, so he asked Adams to wait.

'Everything okay?' asked Gillard.

'The undercover NCA guy confirms that they were all acting under duress,' said Kamran. 'I don't have the details, but it sounds as if Shahid forced them to carry out the attacks.'

'All of them? All nine?'

'That's what it sounds like. We should separate them and interview them individually, see if their stories match up.'

Gillard nodded. 'We need to talk to Talpur ourselves.'

'What about bringing all nine here to Lambeth? It'd make it easier to cross-reference their stories.'

'Go for it,' said Gillard.

'I'll get Sergeant Lumley to fix up the rooms. What about the interviews? Who's going to do them?'

'Let's you and I do the prelims. I'll draft in extra manpower from SO15.'

BIGGIN HILL AIRPORT (7.30 p.m.)

A uniformed constable walked over to Adams. 'Sorry, sir, but we have a problem with one of the hostages. Says he's an MP and he's refusing to stay.'

'Ah. The Right Honourable Roger Metcalfe,' said Adams.

'He's demanding to speak to whoever's in charge,' said the constable.

'That would be me,' said Adams. 'Come on, then.'

The constable took Adams to the main terminal where the hostages had been placed in the main arrivals area, seated apart from each other and accompanied by uniformed officers.

A uniformed sergeant came over. His name was Andy Peters, based at the Bromley station, and he was the Bronze Commander. 'I'm sorry, sir, but Mr Metcalfe is insisting that he talks to a senior officer.'

'Not a problem,' said Adams. 'How are you getting on?'

'We've got one forensic team here and there's another on the way,' said the sergeant. 'They'll do the photographs, too. We have a problem with one of the hostages. She's a Muslim and refuses to take off her clothes.'

'Let her be, then,' said Adam. 'Maybe suggest a female officer accompanies her home and collects the clothing there. And see about getting food for anyone who wants it. Let's try to keep everyone happy.'

Adams saw the MP was staring at them so he went over to introduce himself. 'I'm Inspector Ian Adams,' he said, 'Silver Commander here.'

'Which means you're the man in charge?' snapped the MP.

'That's correct.'

'Then you need to tell your men to stop preventing me from going home.'

'We just need you to help us with our enquiries for a little while longer, sir.'

'I'm not under arrest?'

'No, sir, you're not.'

'So I'm free to go. I can order a taxi and just go home?'

'As I said, sir, we'd prefer that you help us with our enquiries. We'll try to make it as quick and painless as possible. I'm sure you want us to catch whoever is responsible for this.'

'I'm not sure how holding me against my will achieves that objective,' said Metcalfe.

'You might have information that would assist us,' said Adams.

'I was taken hostage. My life was threatened. I was forced onto a coach and driven to the middle of nowhere. You have the man in custody and, as you like to say, he's bang to rights.'

Adams looked pained. 'That's not what we say, sir. That's more for television. We need to gather evidence and you are part of that process, I'm afraid.'

'Well, I've told you what happened, and now I would like to go home. Or are you holding me against my will?'

Adams shook his head. 'No one is holding you against your will, Mr Metcalfe.'

'Then I'd like to go.'

'Let me be frank with you, Mr Metcalfe. You're quite right, I cannot detain you against your will. But I can ask you to remove your shoes and clothing as they need to be examined forensically. I will be giving you a paper suit and paper shoe covers to wear. If you then want to call a taxi and go home, you are free to do so. But if you make your own travel arrangements there is nothing I can do to prevent the press getting pictures of you in that state and, trust me, those pictures won't be flattering.'

'Are you threatening me, Inspector?'

Adams smiled amiably. 'I'm just pointing out that if you make your own arrangements you'll be at the mercy of the press. If you let us do our job we can keep you away from the cameras. It's your call, sir.'

Metcalfe glared at the inspector for several seconds, then sighed. 'Fine. But do try to speed things up.'

'Absolutely,' said Adams. 'Believe me, no one wants this to drag on a moment longer than necessary.'

LAMBETH CENTRAL COMMUNICATIONS COMMAND CENTRE (7.32 p.m.)

Kamran and Gillard walked back into the briefing room and took their places on the podium. Kamran sat down but Gillard remained standing. 'Well, the prime minister wants to thank you all for a job well done. And you can add my thanks to his because this could have gone a lot worse. A lot worse. I still don't quite understand how or why it worked out the way it did, but we can all pat ourselves on the back for carrying out our duties as professionally as we did. Just to give you an update, the Bomb Squad has confirmed that all the devices were non-functioning.

There were no explosives, though it appears that the men wearing the vests believed that there were. It looks as if Shahid had somehow forced the men to do what they did.'

'But why?' asked Waterman. 'None of this makes any sense.'

'I'm as confused as you are, Lynne,' said Gillard. 'What we're going to do is split the nine bombers up and bring them here. We'll need nine interview rooms, which I know we don't have so we'll have to improvise. Mo and I will carry out preliminary interviews but I want two investigating officers assigned to each suspect and full statements taken. I also want DNA and fingerprints. At the moment we're not arresting them, we're asking them to help with our enquiries. If they insist on leaving, the only way to keep them is to arrest them and therein lies our problem. The NCA officer has already told Silver Commander at the scene that he was acting under duress. That being the case, we can hardly arrest him. But if we can't arrest him, it makes it very difficult for us to arrest any of the others. And if we arrest them, under PACE we can only hold them for twenty-four hours before charging them. But what do we charge them with?'

'Under the 2006 Terrorism Act they can be held for fourteen days before being charged,' said Waterman. She smiled. 'Sorry, don't mean to be teaching anyone to suck eggs.'

'No, you're absolutely right. But if we know, as we do, that they were acting under duress, we can hardly claim later that we were planning to lay terrorism charges against them. And we run up against the same problem, namely that one of the men is a serving police officer. We can't be seen to be treating him any differently from the rest of the suspects.'

'So if they were under duress, there's no offence?' asked Murray.

'It would depend on the nature of the duress,' said Gillard. 'But basically, yes. So our prime concern at the moment is to interview all nine. At this stage I think we do it without them being under caution. We interview them as witnesses rather than suspects. Hopefully, they'll give DNA and finger-prints to assist us with our enquiries.'

'What if they ask for a lawyer?' said Kamran.

'We explain that they're only helping us with our enquiries and they're not facing charges.'

'But if we charge them later we'll have problems,' said Kamran. 'If there is any possibility that they'll be facing charges, they have to be cautioned.'

Gillard nodded. 'My gut feeling is that they were all coerced and that they won't face charges, but let's not put the cart before the horse.' He looked at his watch. 'They should be here within the hour so let's see what we can do about getting interview rooms prepared and see what we have in the way of detectives available.' He nodded at Kamran. 'Mo, you and I will have first go at Kashif Talpur. Hopefully he'll have the answers we need.'

BIGGIN HILL AIRPORT (7.40 p.m.)

Inspector Adams walked into the hangar and went over to Sergeant Hawkins. 'The nine men who were wearing the vests are to be transferred to Lambeth Central Com-munications Command,' said the inspector.

Hawkins nodded. 'So I gathered,' he said. 'I'm to offer you any assistance you need.'

'First of all we need to split up all nine. Make that eight. I'll take care of Kashif Talpur. The other eight need to be separated and taken to Lambeth. The police can handle that. It does appear that they were acting under duress, which means they're not regarded as a direct threat. So it looks as if your job is done. Thanks. Much appreciated.'

Hawkins faked a salute. 'Happy to be of service.'

Adams went over to Talpur, who was sitting on the floor with his back to a stack of sandbags, drinking from a plastic bottle of water. 'Inspector Biddulph is on his way,' said Adams. 'He can take you to Lambeth.'

'Lambeth?'

'The Central Communications Command. SO15 is using that as a base for the time being.'

'Am I being treated as a suspect?'

'You're providing intel,' said Adams.

Two SOCO officers came over. One was holding a plastic bag containing a paper suit and another with paper shoes. 'I'm going to need your clothes,' he said.

Talpur sighed and got to his feet. 'It sure as hell feels like I'm being treated as a suspect,' he said.

LAMBETH CENTRAL COMMUNICATIONS
COMMAND CENTRE (8.30 p.m.)

Chief Superintendent Gillard walked into the interview room holding a cup of coffee in one hand and a cheese sandwich from the canteen in the other. Kashif Talpur was sitting at the table and Inspector Mark Biddulph was next to him. 'Apologies for me having to eat on the hoof,' said Gillard, sitting opposite them. 'I'm starving.'

'You and me both,' said Talpur. He was wearing a white paper forensic suit and had white paper slippers on his feet.

'Haven't they given you anything?' asked Gillard. He pushed the sandwich over the table. 'You have this. I'll get some more sent in.'

'We're having something brought down from the canteen,' said Biddulph. 'It's all been a bit frantic, obviously.'

On cue the door opened and a uniformed constable brought in a tray with two coffees and a selection of sandwiches and biscuits. He put the tray down on the table and left. Talpur had already started on Gillard's sandwich so the chief superintendent reached for another. It was tuna salad but he didn't care what it was: he just needed the calories. He took a bite, swallowed, and washed it down with coffee. 'So, Kashif, how are you?' he asked.

'Still a bit shaken up, sir,' said Talpur. 'And everyone calls me Kash.'

'Okay, Kash, I need you to tell us exactly what happened this morning.'

'It started last night,' said Talpur. 'I was getting home and a couple of guys approached me. One pushed something over my face and I passed out.'

'This was where? Your home?'

Talpur shook his head. 'I'm in a small flat in Brentford,' he said. 'Part of my cover. The gang I've infiltrated have been bringing in heroin from overseas through Heathrow.

Some of them are working as baggage handlers and they have a guy in Customs. He's the one I've been after.'

'So you've been undercover for how long?' asked Gillard.

'Three months. Almost four.'

'And you're in deep cover?'

Talpur nodded. 'I haven't been home in two months. I work part-time in a kebab shop owned by one of the targets.'

'Okay, so they knocked you out. What then?'

'I woke up in a warehouse. I was tied to a chair and there was a bag over my head. I don't know how long I was out or how long I stayed tied to the chair. Hours. All night for sure. When they took the bag off my head there was light coming through the roof skylights. It was eight o'clock, maybe.'

'You say "they". How many were they?'

'In the warehouse? Just one. Called himself Shahid. I never saw his face. He wore a ski mask. We all had ski masks on, under the hoods.'

'So they took the hood off you. What then?'

'Shahid told us what we had to do. We all had on suicide vests. He said we would each be given our instructions and that if we didn't do as we were told the vest would detonate. There were triggers that we had to keep in our hands, but the triggers wouldn't work. The vests could only be detonated by mobile phone. He said we were being watched and that if we didn't do as we were told we would be blown up. There was a pack around our waists containing our instructions and a phone. The phone couldn't be used to call out but he could call us.'

'And your instructions were to board a bus?'

Talpur nodded. 'They put us in a van and dropped us

off one by one. We had to wear the hoods in the van and he took them off when we got to where we were going.'

'Shahid took off the hood?'

'Yes.'

'So who was driving the van?'

'I don't know,' said Talpur. He frowned. 'No, I think it was Shahid who was driving. He drove, and when he had parked he climbed into the back.'

'So he was working alone?'

'I think so. Yes.'

Gillard took another bite of his sandwich and chewed thoughtfully.

'Is something wrong, sir?' asked Talpur.

'I just find it hard to believe that one man could have such complete control over all nine of you,' he said.

'We were scared,' said Talpur. 'Terrified. He could have killed any of us with just one phone call.'

'There were no explosives,' said Gillard. 'They were all fake. You were never in any danger. No one was.'

Talpur shook his head fiercely. 'I saw one of them explode. There was blood and shit everywhere. It was real, no question.'

'Tell me exactly what happened,' said Gillard.

'One of the guys started screaming that he wouldn't have anything to do with it. Shahid told him to be quiet. He wouldn't listen. He was hysterical. Shahid took him to the other end of the warehouse and used a phone to set off the vest. Fucking thing blew him into a thousand pieces.' He grimaced. 'Sorry. Didn't mean to swear, sir. But it was intense. I was sure I was going to die.'

'And you saw this man blown apart?'

Talpur nodded. 'No question.'

'But what about shrapnel? Why were none of you hurt? An explosion like that in a confined space . . .'

'There was this metal screen hanging from the roof. Shahid pulled the guy behind it before he set off the vest.'

'So you didn't actually see the explosion?'

'No, we saw it. And we heard it. There was a blast and blood and there was a leg.'

'A leg?'

'Part of a leg. A foot. In a trainer. Blood and bone and . . .' He shuddered. 'It scared the shit out of me. Out of all of us.'

Gillard wrinkled his nose. 'I think that was the intention,' he said.

Talpur frowned. 'I don't understand what you're getting at, sir.'

'Shock and awe, Kash,' said the chief superintendent. 'He wanted you to follow instructions and for that he needed you terrified.'

'We were, no question. Like I said, I was sure we were going to be killed.'

Kamran was watching the interview through a one-way mirror with Chris Thatcher. 'What do you think?' asked Kamran.

'He's nervous, but that's understandable,' said Thatcher. 'But all his body language and micro-expressions suggest he's telling the truth. He feared for his life, there's no question of that. He really believed Shahid would detonate the vest he was wearing.'

Kamran nodded thoughtfully. 'Let's see what the rest of them have to say for themselves.'

Gillard left the interview room and a few seconds later joined Kamran and Thatcher. 'What d'you think?' he asked Kamran.

'He seems to be telling the truth. And it makes sense. They thought they were going to die.'

'Shahid killed one of them, I get that,' said Gillard. 'Blew him to bits in front of them. But why the fake explosives in the vests? If he had access to the real thing, why send the rest of them out with dummies?'

Kamran shrugged. 'It doesn't make sense, does it?'

'We need to check that Talpur is telling us the whole story,' said Gillard. 'And we need to do that quickly. I suggest you and I lead the initial interviews. I'll take Bhashir, Ahmed, Malik and Masood. You take Pasha, Hussain, Chaudhry and Osman. We need to find out if they're all singing from the same hymn sheet.'

INTERVIEW WITH RABEEL BHASHIR (8.40 p.m.)

Rabeel Bhashir was sitting at a desk wearing a paper forensic suit and with paper shoe covers on his feet. He had been given a cup of tea and a chocolate muffin but didn't seem to have touched either. Chief Superintendent Gillard introduced himself and the detective sergeant who had accompanied him, Kevin Barlow, an SO15 detective, who was one of the anti-terrorism unit's best interrogators. Gillard stood with his back to the wall as Barlow sat down opposite Bhashir. Barlow had an A4 notepad. He placed it on the desk and took out a cheap biro. 'So you're an ISIS warrior, are you?' asked Barlow. 'You must be the first real adult ISIS member I've come across. They're usually kids who don't know any better. But you're, what, fifty?'

'I'm forty-five,' said Bhashir. 'And I'm not a terrorist.'

'The suicide vest you were wearing tells a different story,' said Barlow.

'They forced me to wear it,' said Bhashir.

Barlow smiled and sat back in his chair. He slowly tapped his pen on the notepad. 'Do you seriously expect me to believe that, Mr Bhashir?'

'It's the truth,' said Bhashir. 'Check the vest for yourself. The trigger didn't work. It could only be detonated by remote control.'

'By your boss, is that what you're saying?'

Bhashir shook his head. 'Not my boss. I don't know him. He said his name was Shahid. He said if I didn't do as he said, he'd kill me.'

'But he didn't, did he? You're still alive.'

'Maybe because I did as he wanted. I don't know.' Bhashir slumped in the chair.

'Why did you let him put the vest on you?' asked Barlow. 'Why didn't you resist?'

'It happened while I was unconscious,' said Bhashir.

'And how did that happen?' said Barlow, his face suggesting that he was sure Bhashir was lying.

'I left the mosque last night after the Isha'a prayers. I walked by a van. Someone called my name, I turned around and something was pressed over my face. When I woke up I was tied to a chair and I was wearing the vest.'

'You were tied to a chair all night?'

'I don't know. I think so. I don't know how long I was unconscious for.'

'You have to admit, Mr Bhashir, it sounds very unlikely.'

'That's easy for you to say,' said Bhashir. 'Your life wasn't on the line. You didn't see a man blown to pieces in front of you, like I did.'

Barlow leant forward and lowered his voice, for the first time sounding sympathetic. 'Tell me what happened.'

'We were all tied to chairs and had the vests on. One man kept arguing and Shahid told him to shut up but he wouldn't so Shahid used his mobile phone to detonate the man's vest.' He shuddered. 'It blew him to pieces. He said the same would happen to anyone else who disobeyed him. Do you think you would have done any differently?' He shook his head vehemently. 'No, you would have done as you were told. No one wants to die, not like that.'

'And what happened then?'

'Shahid put the hoods back on our heads and we were put in a van. Then he dropped us off one by one. When I left the van he removed the hood and told me to read the instructions in my waistpack. That's what I did.'

'What I don't understand is why your wife didn't report you missing,' said Barlow. 'You said you were taken after prayers. That means you didn't go home last night.'

'I work nights,' said Bhashir. 'I am a cleaner. Sometimes I go straight to work from the mosque.'

'And the man who was giving you your orders. This Shahid. What can you tell me about him?'

'He always wore a mask.'

'But you could tell if he was young or old?'

'Not young. Not old. Thirty, maybe. Or forty. He looked like he exercised. Like he went to the gym.'

'And his accent?'

'He spoke English well. But all accents sound the same to me. Except Scottish. I can never understand Scottish.'

'But did he sound like he was born here? Or from another country?'

'Born here, I suppose. Now, please, can I go home? I want to see my wife.'

'We are arranging transport for you, Mr Bhashir. In the meantime, I'd like to ask you about your daughters. They are in Syria, correct?'

Bhashir nodded but didn't reply.

'They both married ISIS soldiers?'

'They decided that was what they wanted to do. There was nothing I could do to stop them.'

'Jaleela was only fifteen. Still a child.'

'Do you have children?'

'Yes, I do,' Barlow said. 'And as a father I would not have allowed them to travel abroad on their own at fifteen.'

'They left without my knowledge.'

'Did they?'

Bhashir frowned. 'You think I sent my children to Syria?'

Barlow ignored the question. 'What are your feelings about ISIS?'

'I have no feelings.'

'Do you agree with their aims?'

'They fight for their religion,' said Bhashir. 'Who cannot agree with that?'

'And do you agree that people of other religions should be killed?'

Bhashir said nothing.

'You have called for Jews to be killed, haven't you?' said Barlow. 'There is a video of you saying just that outside the Israeli embassy.'

'I am a British citizen and I have the right to express an opinion,' said Bhashir, folding his arms. 'I have the right of free speech.'

'Yes, you do, Mr Bhashir.'

'And I also have the right to a lawyer, don't I?'

'You have not been arrested or charged, Mr Bhashir,' said Gillard. 'There's no need for a lawyer.'

'If I have not been arrested, I would like to go home,' said Bhashir. 'I have said all that I have to say.'

INTERVIEW WITH ALI PASHA (8.50 p.m.)

Kamran tapped the plastic bag containing the printed instructions that had been taken from Pasha's waistpack. 'You were told to handcuff yourself to Mr Metcalfe?'

Pasha nodded. He was wearing a paper forensic suit that rustled each time he moved. Kamran was sitting opposite Pasha while Sergeant Lumley sat next to him, taking notes.

'Did you know who he was?' asked Kamran. 'Did you know that he was an MP, for instance?'

'I knew only what is on the note,' said Pasha.

'You followed the instructions to the letter?'

'Shahid said that if I didn't he would kill me.'

'And how would he do that?'

'He said he would detonate the vest by remote control.'

'And you believed him?'

'I saw what happened to the guy who didn't do as he was told,' said Pasha.

'Tell me about that.'

'What's to tell? One of the guys was mouthing off and wouldn't shut up. Shahid warned him but he wouldn't let up. Eventually Shahid used his mobile to detonate the vest. Blew the guy to bits.' Pasha shuddered. 'Blood and shit everywhere, there was.'

'You saw it?'

Pasha nodded.

'You saw it with your own eyes?'

'I had no choice, I was tied to a bloody chair.' He shuddered again.

'The thing is, if it went off, how come you weren't hurt in the blast?'

'Because Shahid dragged him behind this metal screen that was hanging from the rafters. But we saw it. Blood and bits of body everywhere and a noise that made my ears ring.' He grimaced. 'Horrible way to die.'

'Would you say that you are a good Muslim, Mr Pasha?'

'I try. That's all one can do, try.'

'You pray five times a day?'

'I pray when I can.'

'But you have been in trouble with the police before?'

'Speeding tickets. That's all.'

'Now, that's not true, is it? You were involved in an underage grooming ring in Tower Hamlets, weren't you?'

'The case was dropped,' said Pasha.

'So I understand. But having sex with underage girls isn't the behaviour of a good Muslim, is it?'

'What part of "the case was dropped" don't you understand?'

'Just because the case was dropped doesn't mean you didn't do it,' said Kamran. 'Cases are dropped for many reasons.'

'I'm the victim here,' said Pasha. 'You're making it sound like I was the criminal. I was drugged, dragged off the street and forced to be a suicide bomber. Have you any idea what I've been through today? I thought I was going to die. Since nine thirty this morning I thought that at any moment I could be blown to bits. Have you any idea what that's like?'

Kamran shook his head. 'No, Mr Pasha, I haven't.'

INTERVIEW WITH ZACH AHMED (9.00 p.m.)

Zach Ahmed's hand trembled as he put the plastic cup on the desk and tea slopped over his hand. 'I can't stop shaking,' he said to Chief Superintendent Gillard, who was standing by the door. Lynne Waterman was sitting in on the interviews and was standing next to him, her back against the wall.

'It's a natural reaction,' said Gillard. 'It'll pass.'

'I was sure I was going to die.' Ahmed shook his head. 'That was all I could think about, that one minute I'd be here and the next I'd be in a thousand pieces. I kept wondering if it would hurt or if it would be like a light switching off.' He shuddered. 'My heart's still racing.'

'Do you want to see a doctor?' asked the chief superintendent.

Ahmed forced a smile. 'I'll be okay,' he said. 'And I need to thank you for saving me. The police did an amazing job. No one was hurt, right?'

Gillard nodded. 'Everyone is safe.'

'Except for the guy they killed at the start,' said Ahmed. He shuddered again.

'We need you to tell us what happened,' said Sergeant Barlow. 'But this time from the moment you entered the coffee shop, and work backwards.'

'I don't understand,' said Ahmed.

'I need you to go through it again, but this time in reverse. Going backwards in time.'

'Why?'

'It helps us check the facts,' said Gillard. 'Sometimes thinking about things in reverse brings up details you'd forgotten because the brain has to work harder.' In fact retelling events in reverse order was the best way of catching someone out in a lie. It was an interrogation technique he'd used on many occasions. When someone was telling a lie it was much harder to remember the details when the time frame was changed.

'Just take it step by step, from the time you walked into the coffee shop,' said Barlow.

Ahmed grimaced. 'I had read my instructions. You have those, right? They were in the waistpack I was wearing.'

'We have it,' Barlow said.

'I was to go into the coffee shop and handcuff myself to someone close to the door. Then I was to reveal my vest and tell everyone to do as they were told, to start tweeting that the ISIS Six had to be released.'

'And before that?'

'I was in a van. A white one. I had a hood over my head. Shahid took off the hood and told me to walk away from the van and not look back. I did and he drove off. I was in Edgware Road, near Marble Arch, about fifty yards from the coffee shop.'

'And before that?'

'We were driving. We were sitting in the back of the van with hoods over our heads. We kept stopping and Shahid would open and close the doors as he let us out, one by one.'

Barlow smiled and gestured with his pen for Ahmed to continue.

'Before that we were in the warehouse where we had been kept. We were tied to chairs and we were hooded and put in the back of the van. Our hands were tied behind us. He only untied us when he dropped us off.'

'And before you were put in the van?'

'We were sitting in a circle. Hooded. The vests were already on us. One of the men was arguing with Shahid. He wouldn't stop. He kept shouting that he wasn't going to do what Shahid wanted. Eventually Shahid dragged him behind a metal screen and used his mobile phone to detonate his vest.' He shuddered and folded his arms. 'It was . . . horrible. I mean, there were bits of him everywhere. There was this trainer with a bit of his leg sticking out. Bits of brain and skull and blood . . . I really thought I was going to die the same way.'

Gillard nodded. None of the men had been told that the vests were fake, that they had never been in any danger of being blown up. The police needed to be sure that all the men had truly been coerced and so far there seemed no doubt that they had all been in fear for their lives.

'So you were taken yesterday?' asked Barlow.

'In the morning.'

'And held all day and night?'

'When I woke up I was on the floor with a hood over my head. They took it off and put on a blindfold and gave me a sandwich to eat and water.'

'They?'

'I'm sure there was more than one person,' said Ahmed. 'Maybe three or four.'

'Why do you say that?'

'I heard them moving. And talking, sometimes.'

'What did you hear them talking about?'

'Just voices. The hood muffled what they were saying.'

'And definitely more than two people?'

'I'm not sure. Maybe. It just felt as if there were more. They let me use a toilet once and there were definitely two men then.'

'And no one reported you missing?'

'My family's in Leicester,' he said.

'No girlfriend?'

Ahmed smiled. 'No one wants a man with no money these days,' he said. 'I'd really like to go home. I've got to work the early shift tomorrow.'

'What is it you do?'

'I'm a security guard.'

'Where do you work, Mr Ahmed?'

'It varies. They move us around to stop us being complacent. I'm in the East End tomorrow.'

'Wouldn't your employer have been worried that you didn't turn up for work yesterday?'

'Of course. But they would probably have assumed I was sick.' He looked at his watch. 'Really, I'd like to go now.'

'We'd like you to give us a DNA sample and your finger-prints before you go.'

'Why?'

'It's just procedure.'

'I'm not being arrested, am I?'

'No, there's no question of that.'

'Because I was forced into it. I had no choice.'

'We understand that,' said Barlow.

'How do you feel about ISIS, Mr Ahmed?' asked Gillard.

'They're a bunch of murderers who give Islam a bad name,' said Ahmed. 'They haven't been released, have they? The ISIS prisoners in Belmarsh?'

'No, they're all back behind bars.'

'That's something at least,' said Ahmed. He glanced at his watch. 'Now, please, I'd like to go home.'

'It might take us a while to arrange a car,' said Gillard. 'And we will need to keep your shoes and clothing, I'm afraid.'

'But I can get compensation, right? For my clothes?'

'I'll make sure you get the requisite forms,' said the chief superintendent.

'What about my wages?' asked Ahmed. 'Can I have a letter or something that explains what happened? I'm on a zero-hours contract and they'll use any excuse not to pay me.'

'I'm sure we'll be able to do something for you,' said the chief superintendent.

INTERVIEW WITH ISMAIL HUSSAIN (9.15 p.m.)

'When the vest exploded, I couldn't believe it,' said Ismail Hussain. 'The whole place shook and there was blood and bits of body. I've never seen anything like it outside of the movies.'

'You were frightened?' said Kamran. He sipped his coffee. Hussain was holding a bottle of water with both hands as if he feared it would be taken from him. Sergeant Lumley was sitting next to Kamran, taking notes.

'I was terrified,' said Hussain. 'He killed the man without even thinking about it. He picked up his phone, pressed a button and bang!'

'What did he say about the trigger you had in your hand?'

'He said it wouldn't work, He said the only way the bomb could be detonated was by phone. But we had to make people think we were going to kill them. That's what he said. And he said that if we got the six ISIS warriors freed, we would all be able to go home.'

'How do you feel about ISIS?' asked Kamran.

Hussain's eyes narrowed. 'Why does that matter?'

'You're a Muslim. They're fighting for Islam, so they say. Do you agree with what they're doing?'

'Do you?'

'With the greatest of respect, Mr Hussain, I wasn't the one caught wearing a suicide vest.'

'I was forced to wear it,' said Hussain. 'I told you that. They knocked me out and when I woke up I was tied to a chair and wearing the vest. I've told you that a dozen times. Why does it matter what I believe in? You're a Muslim too, right? Are you an ISIS fan?'

'I'm never a fan of people who go around committing murder, who rape women and throw gays off roofs,' said Kamran.

'And you think I am?'

'You're a member of a group called Muslims Against Crusades. You've burned poppies and demonstrated against our armed forces.'

'I'm allowed to express an opinion, aren't I? It's still a free country. I burnt a few paper flowers. I shouted at soldiers. Are you going to send me to prison for that?'

'No one is threatening to send you to prison, Mr Hussain.'

Hussain held up his arms. 'Then why are you forcing me to wear this? Are you sending me to Guantánamo Bay so the Americans can torture me?'

'Please, Mr Hussain, there's no need to get upset. We need our Forensics people to examine your clothing for evidence. I apologise for what you're wearing now but it's all we have. As soon as we're done with this interview, we'll get you home, I promise. But at the moment we're trying to work out why you were kidnapped.'

'And you think it was because I'm a Muslim?'

'We're fairly sure that's the case. But there are more than a million Muslims living in London and we'd like to know why you were chosen.'

'So why are you asking me about ISIS?'

'Because you might have come into contact with this man Shahid before. You might know him.'

Hussain shook his head. 'No. I didn't recognise his voice. Now, please, I want to go home. I am a British citizen. I have rights.'

INTERVIEW WITH MOHAMMED SAMI MALIK
(9.30 p.m.)

Sergeant Barlow smiled at Mohammed Sami Malik and asked him if he needed anything else to eat or drink. He had been given an apple and a banana and a glass of orange juice. 'I just want to go home,' said Malik.

'Home is Southall, right?' said Barlow. 'You live with your parents?'

Malik nodded. 'They'll be worried shitless.'

'We've already informed them that you're safe and well and they're coming to collect you.'

Malik groaned. 'Shit.'

'What's the problem, Sami?' asked Gillard. He was standing by the door, his arms folded. 'What's the problem with your parents coming?'

'My mum's gonna be frantic, that's what. Especially when she sees me like this.' He gestured at the paper suit he was wearing. 'She'll go mental. She'll be sure I've done something wrong.'

'We've told them you're helping us with our enquiries, Sami,' said Barlow. 'No one's going to think you did anything wrong. From what you've told us, you were forced into it. You were in fear for your life?'

'Like I keep telling you, Shahid was running the show. He was the only one who could detonate the vests, using his mobile. He said if we didn't do exactly as he said, he'd blow us up.'

'And you believed him?'

'Fuck, yeah.'

'Because?'

'Because he killed a guy, blew him to fucking smithereens.'

'Where was this?'

'Some factory or something. The place where we were being held.'

'Tell me about that place.'

'I didn't see much,' said Malik. 'Most of the time I had a hood on.'

'But when the hood was off, what did you see?'

'It was an old place, concrete floors and metal girders overhead. There were pigeons in the roof. They scattered when the bomb went off.'

'Could you hear anything outside? Traffic? Trains? Planes overhead?'

Malik shook his head. 'He only took the hood off that one time to tell us what we had to do. I don't remember much about the place. After he'd killed the guy he put the hood back on and put us in the van.' He sipped his juice and grimaced. 'This tastes like shit.'

'We'll get you something else,' said Barlow. 'What would you like? Tea? Coffee? A Coke?'

'I'd like to go home,' said Malik.

'Just a few more questions, please,' said Barlow. 'What time were you taken?'

'About midnight. I'd been out with the lads and was on my way home. Someone shouted my name and when I turned something hit my head.'

'Did they shout Mohammed or Sami?'

'Sami. Like I said, no one calls me Mohammed.'

'So whoever it was, they must have known you?'

'I suppose so.'

'And you didn't recognise them?'

'I didn't see them. I just heard my name, turned, and bang.' He reached up and rubbed the back of his head. 'They could have killed me.'

'And when you woke up?'

'I was in a van with a hood over my head. They drove me to the warehouse and I spent most of my time lying on the floor before they tied me to the chair. Then I passed out, and when I woke up again I was wearing that fucking waistcoat.'

'Your parents didn't report you missing,' said Barlow.

'They probably didn't realise I hadn't come home. I usually get in late and leave for work before they're up.' He sat back in his chair and sighed. 'It's fucked up, isn't it? Why me? Why the fuck did they pick on me?'

'That's what we're trying to work out,' said Chief Superintendent Gillard.

'Wrong place, wrong time?' suggested Malik.

'No, they chose you,' said Gillard. 'They knew your name so it was you they wanted. You were all chosen, but the question is why.'

'Yeah, well, when you finally do find this Shahid, give me a few moments alone with him, will you? I'd like to give him a good kicking for what he put me through.'

INTERVIEW WITH FAISAL CHAUDHRY (9.45 p.m.)

'What time did they take you?' Kamran asked Faisal Chaudhry. 'You said it was after prayers at the mosque, but what time was that exactly?'

Chaudhry took a sip from his water bottle. 'I was at the mosque for sunrise prayers,' he said. 'I was walking home at about six thirty. A man asked me for the time. As I looked at my watch, another man grabbed me from behind and put something over my mouth.'

'The man who spoke to you, what did he look like?'

Chaudhry shrugged. 'Asian, bearded . . . He had a woven skullcap and he was wearing a grey Pashtun, the long tunic and pants. But I didn't get a good look at him.'

'How old was he?'

'I don't know. I didn't really see him. He had his head down when he spoke.'

'Do you think it was Shahid?'

Chaudhry frowned. 'Maybe.'

'And what happened then?'

'The next thing I remember is waking up tied to a chair with a hood over my head. Then he told us all what we had to do and that's when he killed the guy who was arguing.'

'But you didn't argue? Or put up a fight?'

Chaudhry tilted his head to one side, frowning. 'What do you mean?'

'You didn't resist?'

'Are you fucking serious, man? I'd just seen a man blown into a million fucking pieces. We were all in shock. He killed the guy without a second thought.'

Kamran nodded. 'I understand. But walking into a pub and holding dozens of people hostage, that's a ballsy thing to do.'

'Ballsy?'

'It's not easy, is what I meant. You had to control a lot

of people. You had to get them to do what you wanted them to do.'

'Hey, now, let's get this clear,' said Chaudhry. 'This wasn't my fucking idea. I was following Shahid's orders and he said I was being watched and that if I didn't follow his instructions he'd detonate the vest. I'd have been dead. Do you get that?'

'I get it,' said Kamran. 'And the people you were holding hostage, they were scared?'

'Of course they were scared. They knew what was happening. And then that YouTube video started playing. That was heavy stuff. So, yeah, everyone was scared.'

'What's your opinion of ISIS, Mr Chaudhry?'

'Idiots,' he said.

'Really?'

'They're fucking nutters, seriously. You've seen what they do, right?'

'But you're sympathetic to Al-Qaeda, aren't you?'

Chaudhry's eyes narrowed. 'Why do you say that?'

'It's a feeling I get,' said Kamran. There was nothing to be gained from letting Chaudhry know that MI5 were aware he had been in an Al-Qaeda training camp.

Chaudhry leant forward, his face so close that Kamran could smell the man's stale breath. 'You're a Muslim, right?'

'I am.'

'Then are you telling me you didn't feel any pride when the Sheikh struck back at the Americans?'

'By flying planes full of innocent people into office blocks? Why would I take pride in that?'

'Because finally Muslims were fighting back. For years

America helped Israel destroy the Palestinians and the world stood by. But when the Sheikh launched his attacks, the world took notice.'

'So what happened today, you're happy with it, are you? You're happy with what Shahid was trying to achieve?'

'No fucking way. I was scared shitless. And, like I said, ISIS are nutters. They kill people for the fun of it. You've seen what they do to gays? That's just fucked up. I've got gay mates. You don't go around killing people just because they're gay. But that doesn't mean we shouldn't fight for our religion.'

'We don't have to fight for Islam, not in England,' said Kamran. 'Here you can be whatever you want to be. Here people aren't persecuted for their religion.'

'The fight is a worldwide fight,' said Chaudhry. 'We have to support our brothers and sisters no matter where they are.'

'And what about those countries where women have to cover their faces and are not allowed to drive, where gays are stoned to death and a woman can be beaten for wearing the wrong clothes? You have to support those regimes, do you?'

Chaudhry gripped the plastic bottle so hard that it burst and water spilt over the desk, but he was glaring so intently at Kamran that he didn't seem to notice. He opened his mouth to speak, then visibly relaxed and sat back in his chair. 'I want a solicitor,' he said.

'You don't need a solicitor, Mr Chaudhry,' said Kamran. 'You haven't been charged with anything.'

Chaudhry stood up. 'Then I want to go home. Now.'

INTERVIEW WITH TARIQ MASOOD (10.00 p.m.)

Gillard sipped his coffee as he watched Sergeant Barlow interview Tariq Masood. He really wanted a cigarette but it was vital to get all the preliminary interviews conducted as quickly as possible, so his nicotine fix would have to wait.

'Tell me again how you came to be abducted,' said Barlow.

'I've told you three times already,' complained Masood.

'I just want to make sure you haven't forgotten something,' said Barlow. 'Sometimes the more you tell something, the more details you remember.'

'There's nothing to remember,' said Masood. 'I was in bed. I thought I heard something. I sat up, went to the bedroom door and someone grabbed me and put something over my face. I passed out and when I woke up I was tied to a chair with a hood over my face.'

'Did they say anything to you?'

'In my house? No. I don't even know how many of them there were.'

'And this Shahid, the man that threatened you, did you recognise him?'

'He had a ski mask on. I told you that.'

'What about his voice? Did you recognise his voice?'

Masood shook his head.

'Did he sound foreign? Or British?'

'British, for sure. Bit of a London accent, maybe.'

'London, are you sure?'

'I don't know. Maybe. I'm not good with accents.'

Barlow made a note on his pad. 'Young? Old?'

'Thirty, maybe. Looked like he worked out, you know?

He was wearing overalls but I could see he was fit. He spends time in the gym, I'm sure of that.' He consulted his watch. 'I want to go home,' he said. 'I need to get a shower.'

'Just a few more questions and then we'll take you wherever you want to go,' said Barlow.

INTERVIEW WITH MOHAMED OSMAN (10.20 p.m.)

'When that poor man was blown up, I was so sure I was going to die,' said Mohamed Osman. 'Shahid killed him without a second thought, as if he was no more than an animal.' He shuddered. 'May Allah rest his soul in peace.'

'And why was this man killed?' asked Kamran.

'He said he wouldn't do what Shahid wanted, sir. Shahid said we had to obey him, and that if we didn't, we would die too.'

'What about the trigger you were holding?'

'Shahid said the trigger would not work, sir. He said the only way the bomb could be detonated was by the phone he carried. Sir, check the bomb for yourself, you will see that I am telling the truth.'

'Which mosque do you attend, Mohamed?'

'I do not go to the mosque to pray, sir. I sometimes pray with my family at home.'

'Why do you not go to the mosque?'

'It is not our way, sir. And the mosques near us are not for Somalians.'

'The mosques are for all Muslims,' said Kamran.

Osman forced a smile. 'That is what they say, sir. But the Pakistanis at our local mosques do not make us welcome.'

'And how do you feel about ISIS?'

Osman frowned. 'How do I feel, sir? What do you mean?'

'Are you sympathetic to their aims?'

Osman shook his head. 'Oh, no, sir. I lived in Somalia before I moved to England. I have seen that violence solves nothing.' He reached up to touch the wicked scar that ran across his left cheek. 'When I was a child, robbers came to our house. They did this to me to force my father to hand over everything we had. My family came here to escape violence. That is the wonderful thing about England. Here we all live together in peace.' He grimaced. 'That is what I thought, anyway. Until today. I did not think that something like this would ever happen to me. Not in England.' He shuddered again. 'Do you think you will catch this man, sir? Do you think you will make this Shahid pay for his crimes?'

'I certainly hope so, Mr Osman.'

Osman nodded enthusiastically. 'I hope so too, sir. That is one of the great things about this country. There is justice for all.'

LAMBETH CENTRAL COMMUNICATIONS
COMMAND CENTRE (10.45 p.m.)

'Well, that's it, then,' said Gillard, blowing smoke towards the Houses of Parliament. He was standing with Kamran on the terrace outside the canteen. 'They were all in fear for their lives.'

'The timeline fits, too,' said Kamran. 'Starting with Zach Ahmed and ending with Faisal Chaudhry, they were abducted, fitted with the vests and terrorised. They all tell the same story, pretty much.'

'Plus they all have the same throwaway mobile phones and typewritten instructions. We're getting them checked for DNA and prints but I'm guessing that Shahid won't have left any traces.' He blew a tight plume of smoke towards the Shard. 'We need to find out where they were taken to,' he continued. 'They all give the same description of the factory or warehouse where they were held. I'm guessing somewhere in south London because that's where the first drop-offs were. It shouldn't be too hard to find.'

'And we have a murder enquiry now,' said Kamran. 'How do you want to handle that?'

'We'll keep it within SO15 at the moment,' said Gillard. 'We'll need to run a check on all Asian men who went missing over the past forty-eight hours, obviously.' He took a long drag on his cigarette and blew more smoke towards the Thames. 'I'm knackered, Mo.'

'It's been a long day.'

'Yeah, we should call it a night. Start fresh in the morning.'

'What about the men we're holding?'

'We have to let them go home,' said the chief superintendent.

'It might be helpful to keep them here overnight.'

'In a perfect world, sure. But we know they were forced to wear those vests. They're victims in this, and if we start to make it look as if they were anything but victims we run the risk of being seen as heavy-handed. We don't want anyone alleging that we're keeping them in custody because they're Asian men with beards. A couple of them have already tried to play the race card.' He took another drag on his cigarette. 'No, we let them go home. But we keep them under observation, for the time being at least. Our main aim now is to find the location of that warehouse, to identify the victim and, of course, to track down Shahid. I don't understand why he never got back to you.'

'Maybe something happened that we're not aware of,' said Kamran.

Gillard smiled tightly. 'Wouldn't it be ironic if he got hit by a bus?'

'There has to be some reason he hasn't called,' said Kamran. 'He'd won. He'd got what he wanted. The prisoners were at the airport. So far as he knew, there was a plane there ready to fly them out. Why didn't he follow through?'

'Maybe he realised we were calling his bluff,' said Gillard. 'He knew we were about to send in the SAS and that would mean game over. The vests were fake so once we called his bluff he was out of options.'

'But why didn't he use real explosives?' asked Kamran. 'He obviously had the real thing because he killed the guy in the warehouse. How come that vest was real and the rest weren't? None of this makes any sense.'

'Go home and sleep on it,' said Gillard. 'I'll tie things up here and see you first thing. And make sure you keep your mobile with you, just in case Shahid does call back.' He patted Kamran on the shoulder. 'You did bloody good work today, Mo. You should be proud.'

Kamran smiled at the compliment, but he wasn't sure

it was merited. He felt that somehow he'd been out-manoeuvred, that Shahid had got exactly what he wanted. The problem was, for the life of him Kamran couldn't work out what that was.

BAYSWATER (11.35 p.m.)

'There you go, Mr Ahmed,' said the female constable in the passenger seat in front of him. 'I'm sorry about the clothes. You'll get them back eventually.'

'That's okay. I'm just glad to be home,' said Ahmed. He climbed out of the car. He was holding a small plastic bag containing his wallet, mobile phone, spare change and keys. A woman with several carrier bags stared at him as she walked by, frowning. He knew how strange he looked in the paper suit and paper shoes, but the police had explained they needed all his clothing as evidence.

He let himself into the building and went up the stairs to his second-floor studio flat. Once inside he made himself a mug of tea, then spent the next hour carefully wiping down every surface in the flat, taking particular care to clean every knob, handle and switch he had touched. He used disposable cloths and placed the used ones in a black rubbish bag. When he was satisfied, he stripped off his paper suit, put it with the disposable shoes into the rubbish bag, and went into the cramped bathroom.

He stood in front of the mirror and stared at his reflection for several seconds. He had hated the beard from the start, but it had been necessary. He used a pair of scissors to hack away most of the facial hair then took a can of shaving foam and a Gillette razor and shaved off the rest.

He showered and changed into brand new clothes he'd bought a week earlier. Then he placed all of his old clothes in the black rubbish bags. Also into the bags went anything that identified him as Zach Ahmed. That wasn't his real name: it was an identity he'd carefully cultivated over the past two years. His real name was Daniel Khan.

He peered out of the window and saw the police car parked across the road. The two officers had bought coffees from one of the all-night cafés and were sipping them as they chatted.

He had a large nylon kitbag under his bed and pushed the rubbish bags into it, then zipped it up. He went around the flat one last time, checking he hadn't forgotten anything, then headed downstairs. One of the reasons Daniel had rented the flat in Bayswater was that it had a way out through a small backyard where the rubbish bins were stored. He locked the flat and went downstairs, out of the back door to the yard and through a wooden gate into the alley that ran behind the terrace.

He caught a black cab in Queensway and had the driver drop him at Victoria station. He caught a second cab to south London and got out in Peckham. He walked for a good ten minutes with the kitbag, doubling back several times to reassure himself that he wasn't being followed.

The warehouse had a for-sale sign over its door. It had been on the market for more than two years but planning restrictions meant it was proving difficult to sell. There was a chain-link fence running around it and the surrounding yard. The gate was unlocked and he walked through and around to the rear of the building where there was a delivery bay and a metal shutter that had been raised. He went inside.

The nine chairs were still standing in a circle. Shahid had taken off his ski mask and overalls and was wearing a pink polo shirt and faded blue jeans. He was taking the SIM card out of a phone as Daniel walked in. He grinned. 'Hello, bruv.'

Daniel dropped his bag and hugged his brother. Adam Khan was three years older than Daniel but they were often mistaken for twins. 'Did you get the money?' asked Daniel, as he stepped back.

'Of course. All five million.'

Daniel punched the air. 'Fucking ace.'

'I had it collected and put into the banking system. I'll move it around a bit but it's pretty much untraceable already. And you got the recording?'

Daniel pulled his mobile phone out of his back pocket. 'The quality's great. You can hear every word.'

'And the cops didn't examine it?'

'They took the other phone but I told them this was my personal one and they let me keep it.'

'How did the interrogation go?'

'Piece of cake. But there's something you need to know. The guy you sent to Tavistock Square? He was a cop.'

Adam's jaw dropped. 'No fucking way.'

'Undercover with the NCA. We thought he was a paedo but he was undercover.'

'Fuck me, he looked the part.'

Daniel grinned. 'Any Asian with a beard is a paedo or a jihadist? That's racial profiling, bruv. But once he told them what had happened here, they had to believe him. And us.'

Adam shook his head. 'Shit, that's not good. We went to a lot of trouble making sure they were bad. If not potential jihadists, at least they were criminals.'

'He was good at his job, that's for sure,' said Daniel. 'He looked as if he was part of that gang.'

'We were lucky he wasn't hurt,' said Adam.

'The plan was never for anyone to get hurt,' said Daniel. 'The only way he'd have got hurt is if the cops had over-reacted. But, yeah, we were lucky.'

The two men embraced again. 'Time to move,' said Adam. 'I cleaned up the body.'

Daniel laughed and went to look behind the screen. 'It worked a fucking treat, didn't it? They shat themselves.'

'It looked real, all right,' said Adam. 'That bit of leg sticking out of the trainer was the clincher.'

'Bog-standard special effects,' said Daniel. 'Shows you my degree wasn't a total waste of money.' He nodded at the kitbag. 'The stuff in there needs burning.'

'Put it in the car with the rest of the rubbish.' He took a deep breath and exhaled slowly. 'I'm looking forward to getting back to the real world.'

'Me too,' said Daniel.

SCOTLAND YARD, VICTORIA EMBANKMENT
(the next day)

Kamran's secretary put a mug of coffee on his desk, with a folder containing mail to be signed. He thanked her, picked up his pen and signed the letters one after another. When he'd finished he looked at the whiteboard on the wall to his right. He had fixed eighteen photographs to it. The top row were the surveillance photographs of the nine men wearing the suicide vests. Below them were the nine hostages. All had now been released and were back home with their families. The hunt for Shahid had been passed onto MI5 and GCHQ as there was virtually nothing that the police could do. They had no description or intel of any sort. All they had was his voice. So far GCHQ hadn't been able to come up with a match, and neither had their American counterparts, the National Security Agency. It was a mystery, and so far as Kamran could see, it was destined to remain that way.

He picked up his mug of coffee and stood up, his back aching from the two hours he'd spent at his desk. He walked over to the whiteboard and sipped his coffee as he studied the top row of photographs. All nine had told the same story, pretty much. Abducted, masked and hooded, a suicide vest put on them, covered with a raincoat. A waistpack with a phone and written instructions as to what they were to do. The men had seemingly been chosen at random, other than that they were all Muslims. Eight of Pakistani origin, one Somalian. Cleanskins, more or less. Not one considered a threat to the state. The picture of Zach Ahmed was the only one not taken as a close-up. Ahmed had refused to co-operate: he hadn't wanted to be photographed and had refused to give his fingerprints or a DNA sample. The picture on the whiteboard was the one that had been taken by the bomb-disposal officer through the window of the coffee shop.

He lowered his gaze and looked at the hostages. Another

nine people, again seemingly chosen at random. Wrong place, wrong time. Except for Roger Metcalfe, the MP. He'd obviously been chosen because of who he was. He peered at the photograph of Mohammed Al-Khalifa, the man taken hostage at the coffee bar in Marble Arch. He frowned as he stared at the photograph. Something wasn't right but he couldn't quite place it. He scratched the side of his face as he stared at the photograph, then back at the one of Zach Ahmed. His frown deepened. He called through to his secretary in the outer office. 'Amy, see if you can track down Kashif Talpur with the National Crime Agency. Ask him to come in as a matter of urgency.'

Two hours later, Amy showed Talpur into Kamran's office. At first Kamran didn't recognise the man: he'd shaved off his beard, cut his hair short and was wearing a dark pinstripe suit and a red-and-black-striped tie. 'You've certainly changed your appearance since we last met,' said Kamran, waving Talpur to a chair.

'What happened blew my cover on the drugs operation, obviously,' said Talpur. 'In fact, it's pretty much blown me for undercover work ever again. They're deciding where to use me next as we speak.' He shrugged. 'Probably for the best. Undercover work takes it out of you and plays havoc with your private life.'

'Do you want a coffee, water, anything?'

'I'm fine, sir. Just a little confused.' He gestured at the whiteboard. 'I thought MI5 were handling the case now.'

'They are. But SO15 is still involved and I had a thought or two that I wanted to run by you before I talk to Chief Superintendent Gillard. The day it all happened. Your instructions were to take a hostage, correct?'

Talpur nodded.

'Any hostage? Or a particular one?'

'Shahid said that as soon as I got on the bus I was to grab the nearest person. He said the driver was behind a screen so I should ignore him and just get the closest passenger. I grabbed a woman. With hindsight I should maybe have gone for a male but I wasn't thinking too clearly at the time.'

'And was there a key? For the handcuffs?'

Talpur shook his head.

'We didn't find one in the waistpack he gave you to wear, but I wondered if you had had a key and it was lost or thrown away.'

Talpur shook his head again. 'There was no key.'

'So if you'd had a change of heart at the time and wanted to swap the woman hostage for a man, you couldn't have done?'

'I'm confused, sir.'

'I'm sorry, just humour me for a little while longer. You couldn't have changed your hostage, once you'd made your choice?'

'That's right, sir.'

Talpur frowned as the superintendent walked over to the whiteboard and pulled off two photographs. He sat down again and pushed one of the photographs across the desk. It was of the hostage-taking at the coffee shop in Marble Arch, the shot taken by the bomb-disposal officer through the newspaper-covered window. The bearded Asian man in the vest could be seen close up, and behind him was half the face of his hostage. 'This was the bomber in Marble Arch,' said Kamran. He smiled ruefully. 'I suppose I shouldn't be calling him a bomber, should I? His name was Zach Ahmed.' He pushed the second photograph across the desk. 'This is a photograph of the hostage, taken after you were all off the coach. His name is Mohammed Al-Khalifa, an asylum-seeker from Sudan.'

Talpur stared at the two photographs. He nodded but had absolutely no idea what the superintendent was getting at.

'If you look at the photograph of Mr Ahmed, standing just behind him is his hostage. And if you look carefully, you'll see that it is most definitely not Mr Al-Khalifa.'

Talpur picked up the two pictures and looked at them in turn. The superintendent was right. The man in the picture taken through the window was in his early twenties. The head-and-shoulders shot taken afterwards was of a man in his forties. 'He switched hostages,' said Talpur.

'Yes, he did,' said Kamran. 'But how could he have done that unless he had a key? And why did he have a key and you didn't? In fact, keys weren't discovered on any of the bombers.' He grimaced. 'There I go again. I really must stop doing that. But you hear what I'm saying. There were no keys. But clearly Mr Ahmed had access to one.'

Talpur put down the photographs. 'Why would he change hostages? Like I said, I could imagine swapping a man for a woman, but why swap a younger man for an older one?'

'How about we go and ask him ourselves?' said Kamran. 'Are you free?'

Talpur nodded enthusiastically. 'Hell, yeah.' He grinned. 'Sir,' he added.

BAYSWATER

According to the statement taken by Chief Superintendent
Gillard, Zach Ahmed was a security guard. He had worked
for a north London firm for the past year. Prior to that
he'd worked as a security guard in Leicester. He was British
born of Pakistani parents. He'd never been in trouble with
the police, never even had a speeding or parking ticket. He
lived in a block of flats in a road close to Bayswater Tube
station in a four-storey terraced house that in the distant
past had been home to a single wealthy family and their
staff but, decades ago, had been converted into more than
a dozen studio flats.

Kamran's driver dropped them outside the building
and went off in search of a place to park. There was an
intercom to the left of black doors with fourteen buttons,
each with a handwritten number on it. Kamran rang
Zach Ahmed's bell several times but there was no answer.
On one of the buttons was the word 'CARETAKER'.
Kamran pressed it and eventually a man growled, 'Who
is it?'

'Police,' said Kamran. 'Can you come to the door, please?'

A minute or so later a black man with greying hair and
thick-lensed spectacles was standing in front of them. He
was short and squinted up at the two policemen. 'Is there
a problem?' he asked.

Kamran and Talpur showed him their warrant cards. 'Do
you know the tenant in number six? Zach Ahmed?'

The caretaker shook his head. 'People come and go. I
don't know all their names.'

'I'm not getting any answer from his bell.'

'Maybe he's not in,' said the caretaker. Kamran wasn't sure if the man was being sarcastic or matter-of-fact.

'When did you last see him?'

The caretaker screwed up his face. 'I'm not even sure what he looked like, to be honest.'

Kamran took out a photograph of Zach Ahmed and showed it to the caretaker. The man nodded. 'Ah, Mr Taliban.'

'Mr Taliban?'

The caretaker handed the photograph back. 'You know, with that beard. He looks like a terrorist. No offence.'

Kamran frowned. 'What do you mean?'

'Well, he's Asian, right? I didn't mean to say that all Asians are Al-Qaeda.'

'Just the ones with beards, right?' said Talpur.

The caretaker put up his hands. 'I said, no offence.'

'None taken,' said Kamran, putting the photograph back in his jacket. 'Do you have a spare key?'

The caretaker nodded.

'So how about you let us have a quick look at Mr Ahmed's room?'

The caretaker opened the door wide, suddenly eager to please. He took them up to the second floor and pulled a set of keys from a retractable chain on his belt. He unlocked the door and stepped aside.

It took Kamran less than a minute to realise that Ahmed had gone, and that he'd cleaned up before he'd left. 'The bird has flown.' He sighed. 'Fancy a coffee, Kash?'

'I'd love one, sir.'

They walked to Queensway and Talpur grabbed a table at the rear of a Costa Coffee while the superintendent ordered and paid. As Kamran stirred two sugars into his, he shook his head. 'I doubt we'll be seeing Mr Ahmed again. In fact, I doubt that's his real name.'

'He might just have moved to escape the press,' said Talpur. 'The newspapers and TV people have been all over the hostages and the guys forced to wear the vests. I'm hard to find but a lot of them have had press packs camped outside their houses.'

Kamran sipped his coffee. 'Let me ask you something, Kash. When they took the hood off your head in the ware-house, what did you see?'

'Guys like me wearing ski masks and tied to chairs. All with suicide vests on.'

'Did you see Ahmed, do you think?'

'Difficult to say. We all had ski masks on. And we were all pretty much the same height and build.'

Kamran nodded thoughtfully. 'And when they took the hood off, how many of you were sitting there?'

'Nine,' said Talpur.

'Including yourself?'

Talpur nodded. 'Eight plus me. Nine.'

Kamran sipped his coffee again. 'You're absolutely sure, Kash? Think carefully.'

'I remember counting them. There was no way of telling them apart because they were all wearing masks, but yes, there were eight.'

'Eight plus you? So nine in total?'

'Yes. Nine.'

Kamran smiled over the top of his mug. 'Don't you see it, Kash? Don't you see what happened?'

'What?' asked Talpur. 'What's going on?'

'There were nine of you tied to the chairs and wearing masks. Shahid took one of the nine and killed him. That left eight. But there were nine incidents. Nine hostages taken. Nine jihadists on the coach.'

'I'm sorry, sir,' said Talpur. 'You've lost me.'

'One of them was working with Shahid,' said Kamran. 'It was all a set-up. They faked the explosion, put the hood back over your head, then the dead jihadist came back to life. That dead jihadist was the man who called himself Zach Ahmed. Which is why I'm sure he's gone for good.'

'But why?' asked Talpur. 'They didn't get what they wanted. The prisoners weren't released. The whole thing was a waste of time.'

'Maybe not,' said Kamran, adding more sugar to his coffee. 'Maybe Shahid got exactly what he wanted.'

SCOTLAND YARD, VICTORIA EMBANKMENT

Kamran had only just got back to his office when his mobile phone rang. He looked at the screen. The caller was withholding his number. He wondered if someone was trying to sell him something he didn't want or need. He considered letting it go through to voicemail but then he had a prickling sensation at the back of his neck and pressed the green button to take the call.

'Superintendent Kamran, how are you this glorious day?'

Kamran recognised the voice immediately. Shahid. 'You're

the last person I expected to call,' he said. He considered attempting to trace the call but decided immediately that he would be wasting his time.

'Did you get my parcel?'

'Parcel?'

'A padded envelope. With a thumbdrive inside. Addressed to you and marked private and confidential.'

'I don't see it on my desk,' said Kamran. 'Give me a minute.' He got up and went over to his door. 'Amy, is there a parcel for me, private and confidential?'

His secretary rummaged through his in-basket and pulled out a small padded envelope. She hurried over to him and he took it. He opened it as he went back to his desk. 'I've got it,' he said. He tipped the envelope up and a small grey thumbdrive dropped onto his desk.

'You'll be interested to hear what's on the drive,' said Shahid. 'It's a confession, of sorts.'

'Yours?'

Shahid chuckled. 'No, Superintendent. You'll never be getting that from me. It's the confession of Imad El-Sayed. He runs a bureau de change on the Edgware Road, near Marble Arch. El-Sayed confesses to funding Al-Qaeda and ISIS. He sends funds raised here to wherever in the world the money is needed. He pays for British jihadists to go to Syria to fight for ISIS. He funded the bombs on the London Tube in 2005.'

'And how did you get this confession?'

'Does it matter?'

'Of course it matters,' said Kamran. 'This was a recording made during the siege, wasn't it?'

'You'll know that as soon as you listen to it,' said Shahid.

'Zach Ahmed, or whatever his name is, was wearing a wire?'

'And I recorded the calls at my end,' said Shahid. 'El-Sayed is an evil man. Responsible for a lot of deaths. A true terrorist.'

'But you're not, are you? It was never about terrorism, was it? What you and Zach did? Those nine people. The fake vests. This was all about bringing El-Sayed to justice.'

'Someone had to, Mo. He never seemed to be on your radar. You need to share that recording with the Americans. I'm happy for you to take the credit but if you don't I'll send a thumbdrive to the US Embassy. I have to say I was surprised not to see you on TV after it was all over.'

'I was busy, obviously.'

'But that chief superintendent – what was his name?'

'Gillard.'

'Yes, Chief Superintendent Gillard. From the number of interviews he gave, you'd have thought it was all his operation from start to finish.'

'He was Gold Commander.'

'I think you earned some credit, though, don't you? Anyway, the thumbdrive should go some way to addressing that.'

'You're not trying to buy me off, are you, Shahid?'

'What do you mean?'

'I mean that this doesn't change anything. I'll have to hunt you down. You and Zach broke the law. You put innocent lives at risk and you'll be punished for that.'

'No one died, Mo. No one got hurt. And the men I used, they weren't innocents.'

'One was,' said Kamran. 'The man you used on the bus at Tavistock Square. He was an undercover cop. One of ours. A good man.'

'So I gather, but I didn't know that. His cover was good. We thought he was a drug dealer. And he was part of a gang abusing young girls.'

'No. He was an undercover cop penetrating the gang.'

'As I said, I know that now. But by all means give him my apologies. It was a long time in the planning, but mistakes happen. And it was for the greater good, you have to admit that. El-Sayed deserves what's coming to him. So let's just say that all's well that ends well, shall we? And look for me all you want, Mo. Where I'm hiding, you'll never find me. And don't even bother tracing this call. I'm using Skype through half a dozen proxy servers.'

The line went dead.

TOWER HAMLETS

'Did he get it?' asked Daniel, as his brother closed the laptop and stood up. Daniel was sprawled on a sofa, watching a football match on a big-screen TV above the fireplace.

'He got it,' said Adam, dropping onto the sofa next to him.

'And you don't think we should leave the country?'

'This is our home, did you forget? Where do you want to go? Pakistan? Fuck me, bruv, the food's crap and it's too bloody hot most of the year.'

Daniel laughed. 'But Tower Hamlets? You really want to stay here?'

'Bruv, there are more than one and a quarter million Pakistanis in the UK, twenty per cent of them live in London and Khan is one of the most common surnames. We can hide in plain sight. No one knows what I look like anyway, and you're completely different now.'

'I won't miss that bloody beard, that's for sure,' said Daniel, rubbing his chin. 'What now?'

'We restart our lives. You start working in the movies again. I go back to being a doctor.'

'And how do we explain what we've been doing for the last two years?'

'Travelling the world, bruv. Finding ourselves.' He grinned. 'Probably best not to say that we took a sabbatical to get revenge on the bastard who killed our sister.' The smile vanished as quickly as it had flashed across his face. 'It took longer than I thought it would, but it was worth it. That bastard was responsible for the death of Sarah and everyone else who died on that day. I don't know why the cops didn't work it out for themselves. But they know now.' He sighed. 'We've got time, bruv. There's no rush. Five million quid minus expenses will last us years.'

'I hope Mo doesn't drop the ball. El-Sayed needs to go down for what he did.'

'It'll happen, don't worry,' said Adam. 'And once they start looking, the Yanks will want their pound of flesh. El-Sayed will spend the rest of his life locked inside a metal box. Don't worry.'

'We should have just killed him.'

'No, this way is better. Plus we got his money. We can do a lot of good with that.'

'Do you think Sarah knows what we did for her?'

Adam smiled. 'If there's a heaven, she knows.'

KING'S CROSS (7 July 2005, 8.40 a.m.)

Sarah Khan looked at her watch. 'You've plenty of time,' said Adam. 'Your interview isn't until ten.' They were standing on the main concourse at King's Cross station, close to the entrance to the Underground.

'Do you want us to come with you?' asked Daniel.

She smiled. 'I'm fine.'

'It's no big deal.'

She laughed. 'My big brothers, always looking after me.'

'Someone has to,' said Adam.

'Mum and Dad would have been so proud of you both,' she said.

'And they'd have been proud of you, too,' said Adam. 'Smart, pretty, a first in law from Oxford, going to work for the CPS.'

'If you're planning an arranged marriage for me, I'll kill you, you know that.'

'No guy is getting near you, not without getting past us,' said Daniel.

Sarah giggled. 'You guys are terrible,' she said. 'Anyway, it's only a first interview.'

'They'd be crazy not to hire you,' said Daniel.

She looked at her watch again. 'I should go.'

Both men hugged her tightly.

'Be careful,' said Daniel.

Sarah frowned. 'What do you mean?'

Daniel forced a smile. 'I don't know. I just . . .' He shrugged. 'Go on, off you go. And don't come back without a job offer.'

The two brothers stood and watched as Sarah walked to the escalators. She raised her right hand and waved without looking back as she disappeared from sight.

'Don't go,' whispered Daniel.

Adam turned to him. 'Why did you say that?'

'I don't know. I just had a bad feeling.'

'She's a big girl now. She can take care of herself.'

'She's our little sister. And since Mum and Dad died, she's our responsibility.'

'She got a first at Oxford,' said Adam. 'You got a two:two in special effects from Bolton.'

'Fuck you, bruv.'

'Fuck you too,' said Adam, ruffling his hair.

'We can't all be doctors,' said Daniel. 'I've got to run. We're on location.'

'Yeah? What's the movie?'

'A low-budget sci-fi thing they're filming up at Pinewood. I've got to make three heads explode on a budget of two grand.'

'I bet Spielberg never had these problems.'

'Everyone has to start somewhere.'

Adam put an arm around his younger brother's shoulders. 'I was joking, bruv. You'll make it big one day. This family's destined for greatness, I can feel it.' He took a last look at the entrance to the Underground, then headed outside with his brother.

PICCADILLY LINE (7 July 2005, 8.50 a.m.)

Sarah sat down in the last free seat in the carriage and took a deep breath. As the train pulled away from the platform she looked over at the young Asian man standing by the door with a backpack slung over one shoulder. He was staring at her with deep-set eyes. The train picked up speed. Now the man was staring at a woman with a young daughter. The child was three or four years old, holding a small Paddington Bear. She smiled at Sarah and Sarah smiled back.

The man straightened his back and raised his right hand. He was holding something in his hand, something metallic. He took a deep breath, threw back his head and screamed at the top of his voice, '*Allahu Akbar!*'

There was a blinding flash and then everything went dark.